WHAT A GODLY PRIVILEGE TO BE BORN A MAN

TABITHA BIEL LUAK

What a Godly Privilege to be Born a Man
Copyright © 2021 by Tabitha Biel Luak

All rights reserved. No part of this publication may be reproduced, distributed, or transmitted in any form or by any means, including photocopying, recording, or other electronic or mechanical methods, without the prior written permission of the author, except in the case of brief quotations embodied in critical reviews and certain other non-commercial uses permitted by copyright law.

tellwell

Tellwell Talent
www.tellwell.ca

ISBN
978-0-2288-5186-8 (Hardcover)
978-0-2288-5185-1 (Paperback)
978-0-2288-5187-5 (eBook)

AUTHOR'S NOTE

There is a famous saying among the Nuer people which goes a little like this: "Every family has its way of talking and eating." I don't know what thoughts may pop into your mind upon hearing this saying. Personally? I see it as a universal family description—or perhaps the nature of these two things, "talking and eating," are indeed that which differentiate us, the human race, universally.

Of course, there are other differences amongst people. And although one of the obvious differences is the colour of skin, there are also things formed with conscious intentions for the purpose of them becoming our ways of life. In most cases, although this can't really be said about skin colour, there are persuasive goals set prior to forming a way to live. For instance, we teach children how to do well behaviourally so *tomorrow* is a bit clearer for them. However, within a formation, a tendency is developed. Sometimes, these tendencies come in the form of beliefs, which influence what and how we teach them..

Take this belief from the place I call home. Where I come from, in South Sudan, it is overwhelmingly believed that there is a difference between a male child and a female child. Of course, there *is* a difference. And so this difference is often exhausted and exploited to identify potential inequalities between the two. Unfortunately, the further this persists, the more limits we place on what we consider males and females to be capable of.

Nevertheless, humans are known to loathe dwelling in a valley of non-competitive spirit. Therefore, the only way forward is still to lean strongly toward one side and confidently unwrap the other side as if someone was there when she was all assembled.

It has always been the belief here at home, exhaustedly theorized and relentlessly practised, that one thing must be different from another. Often, to roll out one thing is enough but the other is not. In a remote way, this perception unconsciously brings us to inherently believe one is the product while the other is the producer.

In other families, this way of reasoning may look a bit different; nonetheless, the derivation of the tendentious tendency in this family walks its way persistently from a claimed, precise understanding of fullness that can only be explained in four ways.

These involve precise understanding of the structural beauty of appearance, the strength of the structural body, the enormity of the group to which one belongs, and the sophistication or smoothness of the tongue.

As a result, every response, every act and every performance revolves around these four things. Therefore, how each family teaches the two is different, for each family believes the two exist for different, unbalanced reasons. And that, unlike other families, this family eats and talks differently.

The stories you are about to read, with the exception of names and certain places, are real people's stories, which, to this day, are still happening. As you flip through the pages, I urge you to ask yourself the following questions: What, then, is human? Who is human? And what does it mean to be one?

DEDICATION

This book is dedicated to my mother, Elizabeth Chuol Lam. Of everyone I know, it is her story I'm not able to process. But I'm certain that the time will come when all wounds will be healed and the toughest stories will serve to teach us about a past no one wants to relive.

To the women at the shelters, both those who seek help and those who provide it. You have heard the painful stories of what it still means to be a woman. Seek help, provide help. You never know how far it will go.

To the women at the intercultural daycares who have issued me and thousands of other women, both single and married, the freedom of mind which is only possible when a woman understands another woman's story in this merciless world.

To all the women along the way who have extended their hands to pull me up—even if most of them don't know the half of what I live with.

To all the beautiful sisters who had to be sold to Murle because you have no value.

This book is for you.

Thank you for wanting to read this book. As you read though, there are a few words I would like you to get a handle on. These are places, slang terms, terms and names you will come across throughout the book. There are also definitions of names of the characters, but those are defined as each character is revealed. Some spellings are as they are in Nuer, but other words are spelled in English.

Places:

Malakal: Capital city of Upper Nile State

Khartoum: Capital city of North Sudan.

Bipor: Capital city of Greater Pibor Administrative Area (GPAA)

Bieh state: A combination of three counties predominantly inhabited by Lou Nuer.

Pibor: Pibor River

Gezira: state in Sudan

Pulrieli: a currently abandoned town situated in Bieh state

Slang terms:

Nyada: A sneering name-calling, spoken as a warning (among women).

Nyade: My girl

Nyame: This girl

Mah: Mother

Maah: Used when requesting, advising or asking for favour. Used only by young men around the same age (please)

Gari: A demanding request to be given something or when something has to be done (used mostly by a husband)

Waa-wut: An interactive nicknaming between man and his son. Wut means man.

Wuri: It means 'man' and it is used by men of the same age when opposing each other.

Terms:

Pei: a cow that produces less milk.

Baba: father

Mama: mother

Guan: father of

Maan: mother of

Noong: escorts

Cou-nyade: sons in-law

Kaah: a name given to a divorced woman. The connotation is to say she is no longer valuable. Or as she becomes single again, she loses the value to be considered a girl or woman. A mere virtual female. No longer real or true of what makes a woman valuable.

Guandong: grandfather

Maan-dholi: mother of boys

Maan-wuni: mother of men

Balang: a name designated to man's popularity in social contact

Lawe: a thin traditional piece of clothing that goes over a woman's dress

Yat: a half-slip skirt that goes beneath a woman's clothing

Foul: bean

Names:

Kuoth: God

Murle: tribe

Nuer: tribe

Dinka: tribe

Shilluk: tribe

Bor: sub-tribe (Dinka)

Interjections:

Waah: a denial response when shocked by a sudden act or statement

Waaw: a way a girl responds when her attention is called to something (smooth and gentle).

Aah: a way a boy responds when his attention is called to something (rough and ungentle).

PROLOGUE

And here, getting older while still young—they are right, who am I? What is my purpose in life? It was the third time that a young lady had come to sit on a fallen tree between the house of her uncle—her father's brother—and a neighbouring church. In this suburban area, afternoons tended to be the least travelled times of the day. She would come here often, but not many would see her.

She was a mother of three children but at the time she was not allowed to see them. She was in her early twenties but in a stranger's eyes, no one would argue she was thirty-five.

In her community, she was someone whose life story has reached many. And in addition to her living shame, she had recently lost a battle she was mentally not ready to take on. The laws and the customs of this area had finally given the children to the man who bought them before they were born. So outside of the church she gave her leftover strength to the hope that God might hear the cry of the desperate. But at the same time, she couldn't drop the thought that He may not hear her since between God and woman there seemingly stands man, the deliverer.

Among the three children was a one-year-old child. On the day her ex collected his things, he insisted on taking this little one. But the assisted community jumped in, saying, "Why would you take a child who has so much growing left to do? Leave him and come back when he is a person." To finalize that she and her ex would no longer be together, the cows that he paid had come back to him. But this was complicated by the fact that the two had three children, which came with some subtractions. Out of the twenty-five cows he initially paid the girl's parents, eight came back to him. It was ruled that each of the two children would cost five cows because they were still under ten years of age, but the last child cost seven cows because he was a boy.

The man left with the rest, leaving the infant behind for the birth nanny to nurture, after weighing the number of cows he paid against the priceless energy it would take to raise his son up till he came back for him.

This is one of the greatest places the Nuer people have ever inhabited: call it beautiful, and green would immediately be an inherent characteristic of beauty. Green from the toes of her feet to the natural hair of her head. In this land, seasons have abandoned their natures and she is perpetually lush and verdant. She has all the good things to look for in a developed, caring mum though she may lack a good partner. Around her are the growing sisters but she and her reputation are the one attracting the brightest star! The fields are full of green grass. Cattle enjoy the gift of love from Above each morning. Green as her love is her name. She lacks a partner, though.

She is only 1.89 miles away from the city, the other sister. And in her, it was every Saturday's activity that the young, married, never impregnated, never divorced women gathered together and went to the church to practise songs for the next day. Today, like any other Saturday, the gathering began again. This young lady was part of the group until a month ago when the focus of the whole practice began to be about her twisted and messy life.

Her name was publicly withdrawn from the group as she no longer met the criteria for eligibility. As she sat on her fallen tree, she saw the group pouring into the church and as they walked in, laughing, she was triggered to call to mind some of the horrible, demeaning remarks she heard them say to her.

Some of the exact words of the demon-hearted women were as follows: "Why are you leaving your husband? Don't you know we all live the same life?" To which she responded, "Why shouldn't I leave? I don't see the things that happened in my marriage happening in yours."

"No. NO, no," the women would argue. "We just don't like going around and talking," they would say.

However, even if the young lady had mistaken this indirect blame for some advice, the intentional deceit often revealed itself. And so, as they would speak this way, they would act another way.

She had noticed some fake reunions among women whom she knew were rivals. While she still socialized with them, the women would laugh with each other and make her feel excluded for being the only one having made a universally considered sinful choice.

To the women, she was a "stand-out being" separated from them by a dirty status. And as she would wear the theme of her life around her neck like a silver chain, these sisters of hers had already made up their minds that she was more of a sinner than she was even aware of.

This way of thinking is the general view of most people in this society.

And almost every man has fallen in love with this attitude. To men, a struggling woman—one put to terror by her husband yet never refusing the suffering—is a woman worth a thousand praises. However, a woman who had found a man who strays from the only known way of men, deceives herself, thinking she has worked for it.

But overall, there is one reason for this: It's about finding one's purpose, secretively and recklessly overthrowing the world while simultaneously being madly loved back by the same world.

Nonetheless, the young lady was truly aware of what she had lived, and she was by no doubt convicted by what she saw.

"What could I have done differently?" said the young lady to herself as the group of women kept dripping into the church. "When you are supposed to love your virtual enemy husband, yet dare to keep the irrelevant title the same?"

"Not going to church this afternoon?" A voice startled her. She turned around and it was an old lady she knew from the community.

"No," she said. She then faked a smile on her face and suddenly turned her head in the direction of the church. She then began breathing heavily by blowing the air out through her mouth.

"I see you don't even give a care to the fact that there could be Murle behind these green shrubs around here!" the old lady said. The Murle are one of sixty-four tribes in South Sudan and a common fighter of the Nuer, living alongside the Pibor River with this part of the Nuer clan.

The young lady moved her shoulder to indicate she did not care. "Let them shoot me, I'm tired of living anyway."

The old lady stared at her for a moment then spoke. "You know what? You've got to stop doing that to yourself. Look around you. What is really going on? Do you think the world has an interest in anything still maintaining its validation? Or would you suppose it fears that it could destroy it?"

"Look around you," repeated the old lady. "It's not only you, alone. But anyone who examines and separates what is wrong and what isn't is questioned. Take Pastor Peter as an example," continued the old lady. "Look at the stones that get thrown at him by his brothers for a very simple conscious decision he made. Now that he has made this decision, some are even becoming concerned about why he still serves in the church."

The young lady still kept her head turned away. "You know Pastor Peter, huh?" asked the old lady.

"Yeah, I do," admitted the young lady. "And we all know how he has been living his life until now. Because now, when he finalized who he wanted to be with, he decided on a woman who was once married, for he doesn't think this godly-claimed 'perfection' of men depends on the purification of their consumptions. Consumptions! Ha ha! I always put it that way, but I have never been allowed to explain what I mean by it. Perfect women," the young lady mumbled to herself.

"But look at his brothers," the old lady went on. "Peter is the one righteous man who has ever been witnessed bending the will of God in the eye of men. He violated the fifth chapter, verse thirty-two of the New Testament's first book, making himself a sinner out of a woman's adulterous act."

"I don't know, Mama. I never met a man who was once a virgin angel and has now become a sinner. I don't know how we would relate," said the young lady.

"That is exactly my point, dear. If men aren't sinners, how do women become sinners on their own? Get up," said the old lady. "See that compound over there?" The young lady nodded her head. "In that compound, there's an eleven-year-old whose engagement ceremony will be happening at the end of this coming month."

"What about her?" asked the young lady impatiently as if she has never heard of her or the story itself.

"Eight months ago, the man she will be getting married to came back from Khartoum. The man has lived half and quarter of his life there. You know the ones that go and begin having trouble returning home?" she said this in a funny way as she wished to cheer up the young lady.

"Well, now he is back. And now he is ready to marry. Now he is finally ready to destroy a child that could have been his." The old lady continued, "The little girl has been projecting her voice. But who has a heart with functional normalcy around here? Here, where what matters is that anything having the likeness of man has to get married. She gained herself a name. She is now a disrespectful child to her parents for saying no. 'He is an old man,' she said, and her father asked her if she ever witnessed an old man producing an old child. That tells you something about the profit motive, doesn't it?"

"Hmm," the young lady mumbled as she kept her eyes fixed on the church.

"And I tell you this: the man is not only that old, but a drunkard and a smoker. He found himself in the firepan of alcohol as Shumal became his second home. He was constantly spotted in bars drinking anything that has a liquidy look with a group of other drinkers. That was his nighttime meal. When the end of the day came, he would come home to another Nuer man's family, demanding that this man's wife cook him Kob, the traditional food he loved. He would eat it, and nobody would know where he disappeared to again until the next day.

"Every woman knew him. He was the king of borrowing alcohol and would decline to pay it back. He would come to this man asking for money. The man would give him some so he could clear balances he owed people. Thanking the man for rescuing him, he would go and only buy alcohol for other drinkers who had bought it for the group yesterday. His daytime job was walking around the marketplace, begging anyone he saw enjoying a cigar to let him have it. Some people would refuse him the share of theirs and whether they liked it or not, he would find a way to pull it out of someone's mouth and pretend he didn't do anything. His greatest source of this smoke he craved came from the littered butts of cigars that had been thrown by other smokers. He would get into fights only to realize he has been wounded many times.

"A girl his family married for him was sent his way. She came as a surprise to him. Nevertheless, he accepted the surprise. And, like always, the man who had the home accommodated both of them. However, nothing about the wife was a motivation for him to let go of his habits. He continued everything he was doing. And to his surprise, he found that all that he had once had had been reduced to nothing . . . except, no one can really say it like that.

"The source of his problems had to be the wife. Like a man, he had told her one day the problem they both faced was due to her early years of playing with men. 'You have been with many, and all that which can accommodate a child has been destroyed," he said to his wife. The accusation led to brutal fights and one day, he beat her within an inch of her life, leaving them just one more day with her and then she was gone. After the incident, his family here informed the girl's family that they could just keep the cows as opposed to giving them back—as if she had just run away with another man. Without a rebuttal, her family kept the cows and that was the end of the story.

"It was then that the man with whom he was staying had become worried about the aging man's health. He didn't want to be informing his family when his time came. So, he saved money for his return. And that was the only way he was able to come home. The pending death had kind of stayed in the air. He is now a healthy person, and all that is left is a wife whom he is now marrying. He lost mostly everything that makes people look twice at a person. If you saw him, you would know he doesn't look like anybody. But like Nueri would say, 'Teeth are just bones; they serve no purpose.'

"You see, the moral of the story is that when you are a man, it doesn't matter—even a believable animal can take a girl," said the old lady.

"Hmm, how nice to be a male. How lucky to be a man. Let men consume," said the young lady quietly.

"Exactly," said the old lady. "Who will ever constrain this overflowing stream of desire of men? Let them eat till aging prevents them perhaps."

For a moment, the two keep quiet. "Look my child," said the old lady. "If I had the means to help you, I would wipe off your suffering at this very moment. But I don't. All I have is to tell you to be strong. Or else weep with you, like we have always been doing. Remaining where we lay our eggs, hoping this unreasonable price will only fall on us. But what does happen? This mistreating only gets passed along through generations. However, we can't stand against it; otherwise, we would risk losing our seeds.

"Seeds, with which we form such a closeness, even when they are just being put together." Her voice began to crack. The young lady put her hand on the old lady's shoulder; she looked up and the two looked into each other's eyes and were quiet for a moment.

When the young lady removed her hand, she said, "You mean their children?"

"No, they don't consider them their children unless they know their presence benefits them. Otherwise why would your ex leave the little one behind?" asked the old lady.

"Good point, but I still don't see how this girl and I would relate. She has a father. If at any moment the husband starts becoming her enemy, her father will step up. But not me. I'm an open place that wind crosses at its convenience," said the young lady grievously.

While she was still talking, a woman appeared suddenly in front of them, accompanied by a girl of approximately eight years. The girl had a big water container on her head. The woman was walking behind the child with a stick in her hand but carrying nothing else.

The young lady and the old lady knew who this woman was and that the child in front of her was her stepchild. It all began three years ago when the mother of that child was murdered by her husband. The mother, after giving birth to their three children, thought her marriage was draining her, and she couldn't do it anymore.

This resulted in her leaving, which the husband thought no woman was entitled to do. After the wife successfully left him, he came to conclude that no man should live with the shame of being left by the person he had bought. He went on as he desired, got rid of her and had been living happily after. Now the girl and her dear siblings had been living the life which was once their mother's.

The girl and the woman passed the two seated women without greeting each other. The young lady turned her head toward the stepmother, watching her walk away. Then she turned her head back and dropped it down in an emotional motion. And her tears began to drip.

"If I were you, I wouldn't cry. You know the unproved illogical ninety-nine percent belief that claims the only contribution women ever make is providing sacs for already made and fully developed people," said the old lady.

The young lady lifted her head and said, "The fact that I don't see them doesn't mean they aren't being enslaved." She turned her head back to the stepmother, who was now even further away. She held her breath and said, "What a godly privilege to be born a man."

"You really think so?" interrupted the old lady.

She nodded her head.

"I don't think so," the old lady said and shook her head.

"Well, who is a woman then?"

There was a long silence, then the young lady said, "I have witnessed on several occasions what she does everyday with these children. Everyday, she has her three stepchildren, plus her own two children, surrounding a one-dish meal. She pours the stew on it and asks the three siblings to hold up their spoons until her own two children carefully pick out each piece of meat, then she asks them to join. She often hides some food for her children and gives it to them in front of her stepchildren to eat after they all have eaten. Sometimes when the meal is small, she denies her stepchildren the meal and gives it to her children instead.

"This little girl right here is her maid. She does all the work. Many times, she will go for days without eating. She can't say no to anything or everything becomes about how her dead mother genetically transferred her laziness to her, which the woman always uses as the reason her mother was killed. And she does all of that right in front of him and he doesn't say a thing. How are these children theirs?" the young lady said unhappily.

The old woman gave her a look of disagreement. And she said, "You may think you are here for no reason, but there are some who believe there is a purpose to their existence."

"Who?" asked the young lady.

"Those women coming out of the church."

The two began to stare at them. Then the stepmother, who at this point was passing by the church, saw the women, as well. In the middle of the road, she asked the child to wait for a minute. The child tried to put down the water container as the mother detoured to the church. The mother yelled back, "Don't! I'm coming."

There at the churchyard where the group was gathered, they started laughing and engaged in what appeared to be deep conversations. In the distance, the young lady and the old lady kept watching. "They can't even ask the child to put down the container," said the young lady.

"I tell you, my child, you may stumble at the notion of enjoying life. But the first thing you get out of it is what it actually gets out of you," said the old lady.

"And what would that be?"

"A sense of awareness, and they all suffer from that."

"I can't look. I'm leaving, Mama," the young lady said and got up.

"Sure, but don't you come here again," the old lady advised her.

"It helps me. Nature helps me. Out here, I'm able to detach myself from my world. Of course, when it is really windy, it helps clear my mind."

"I understand that but try to put your time into something else." The two smiled at each other and went their separate ways.

The next day arrived. This was a day when the community freely left its many tasks for later and went to worship. From the youngest children to those having difficulties with walking due to aging, Sunday left no one out.

Like always, the worshippers poured themselves into the neighbour's church that was arranged according to the genders of the congregation. If you looked inside, you would find the chairs on the right belonged to men and those on the left side belonged to women and their crying children.

Around eight-thirty a.m., the old lady rushed to avoid missing a service which began thirty minutes ago. A baptism was being done for one of the families in the community at today's service. Baptism had been a thought in the mind of the mother of this family as a way to turn her worldly family to Christ. But it had hardly been possible. The father knew none of this free salvation and had no interest whatsoever. He had run his affairs through witchcraft. In fact, he had his third wife walked back to him this way. A girl who expressed her loathing for him by running away with another man surrendered herself to him after he said she would never have children until she came back to him. He could not have managed to have her all to himself if it wasn't something else the bridge of the song called "marriage." But he succeeded since his ability controlled the underlying gain of this union and destabilized the other man's claimed love. Here, no child equals no marriage. Luckily, this year he passed away. And the older wife among his wives couldn't wait to bring this dirty world for a free cleaning.

The old lady wanted to witness this life-changing event. She rushed out, hoping to catch the rest of the service, and to her surprise she stumbled upon the young lady sitting in the same spot as yesterday.

"Not going to church this morning?" asked the old lady in her untiring, motherly voice.

"Not when you have to eat the same food from the same plate, at the same time every Sunday. I mean, is the whole entire Bible written out for me alone?" asked the young lady.

"No, not really," said the old lady. "But from the perspectives of the interpreters, yes." In fact, the instructional underlying purposes of the words of God in the minds of these individuals these days has become about teaching women to become better at serving men. However, there is one thing you shouldn't let glide over your ears. And that is this. Life comes down to two things: you are either a learner or a consumer. And the understanding of either one comes with each situation and depends on what kind we find ourselves in; we pass it on, along with its danger."

The old lady looked around absurdly and asked, "What time did you come out here?" The young lady said nothing. "You shouldn't be coming out as early as this. You know what the Murle did last week."

"I wish they had taken me, as well," the young lady mumbled to herself. The old lady managed to hear it. Last week, the Murle came and took a large proportion of livestock from the Nuer people. And along with the animals, the attack left fifteen wounded. Seven died and thirty-five were abducted, mainly children and women. There is nothing too foreign about them killing and taking. That's the usual behaviour." The old lady glared at the glittery risen sun. She shook her head, remembering a time when the Murle waged a massive, senseless attack on Nuer people. It is these days referred to as "Khor Pulrieli" (The Pulrieli War). There were attacks prior and after the year 1977, but nothing comes close to the damage the Murle inflicted in just one night. Different sub-clans suffered from the attack as they were taking their livestock from the hayfields mostly situated in the eastern parts of the county. The Pulrieli War claims to be one of the few times when men were seen crying openly as they watched their fellow warriors, their wives, their children and their parents fall dead around them.

The old lady came back now. The flashback became too real as she relived seeing her father among the dead being thrown into one big grave. She shook her head again and said, "It should never be forgotten."

The young lady remained quiet. "Ready to go in now?" asked the old lady again.

"No, I have had enough of hearing 'Women, submit yourselves to your husbands. Women, submit yourselves to your husbands' every single day! I mean, I can speak for myself."

She raised her voice and clapped her hands in frustration. "I'm not going to church today." She went quiet again. "Plus—plus, those women," she said again.

"You worry about what they think of you?" asked the old lady.

"Not really, but I'm tired of being blamed for faults that were never mine," said the young lady.

"Oh, the service is over," remarked the old lady. Outside the church, the congregation exchanged peace with one another. In a moment, some women withdrew themselves from the crowd and stood aside.

"They are going to one of the ladies' houses," said the old lady.

"How do you know?"

"Just come with me, perhaps this will help you."

The women headed down the street. Not far from the church, one of the women tripped and accidentally knocked a poster beside the road. The poster read, "We know how to turn things around." Beneath the phrase was an amount in South Sudanese currency. "Thirty pounds a session," it said. The poster had tilted over. The woman who tripped over it quietly returned it to how it was. And they all bypassed it.

The two followed the women. As they approached the house the women had gone to, they saw five women circling a coffee table inside. As the two entered the house, two identical folding chairs were given to them. The energy changed the moment the young lady sat down. She had been expressing a difference in opinion toward the way most see things around here.

You have to be married only ONE time here to see the Kingdom of Heaven, but you cannot accept hell like that. Let some man sleep with you now that you got out—of course, that is always the reason you left or were left by your husband. It gives some of your sisters peace of mind. But, although they are sure about your particular sins, it does not stop a married man from lusting after you. As long as he is not marrying you, he loses no value for just sleeping with you. That worried some of these very women right here. However, as soon as they sat down, the mother of the house got up and put water on fire. She ran back with coffee cups and started distributing them. But the young lady refused to hold one. She dashed back to the kitchen and returned with boiled water.

xx

Prior to the arrival of the two, the women were discussing a serious topic. They were talking about age differences among them. The topic continued when they filled up their first cups of coffee. However, they now changed the direction of the conversation. They started talking about the age differences among the absent women. As they argued about the absent ones, they categorized them into the ones they liked and the ones they didn't. Those they disliked tended to be older and did not align with beauty standards, and so were married late.

The first cups of coffee ran out and some were already having their second cups. While they were still fixated on the age-gap topic, the old lady unexpectedly interrupted them with a new topic. "You know, back in our day, coffee was not allowed to be taken by groups of women such as this."

"Why?" the women cried and they put their cups down on the table and stared at the old lady.

"Well," said the old lady, "our husbands used to think when women got together like this, they would drink more than just coffee. And in one of my friends' cases, her husband would explicitly say that during those sittings she was meeting other men."

"Whoa!" Some women groaned and burned with anger. "Oh no! I could not live like that," they said.

The old lady giggled and slightly turned her head away. "I think she could have actually lived with it if that was the only thing she had to put up with. I mean, he was a man," she said.

The women relaxed their cheeks and demonstrated great eagerness to learn more about the suffering of this unknown woman. "What else did she have to put up with?" one of them asked.

"She never was proud of talking about it in front of others. However, everyone in the neighbourhood knew what was happening. The man was something else," continued the old lady. "Every night there was something new to fight about. And when morning came, he would find it reasonable to insult the girl's entire family. But what was very disturbing in my own eye was the fact that he would both insult and beat up his wife and his mother-in-law, who had come for the purpose of babysitting his young children. That part was too much for me to swallow. Though this beating of wives' mothers is not condemned in any way as wrong, it was hard seeing her go to her grave with a heart that had been hardened by her son in-law's unreasonable anger," said the old lady. Then there was a great silence.

"And every time his wife got pregnant, he would argue the child wasn't his. And the demand to know the child's father would become another unending fight. He would never accept female children as his, for that matter. Painful! Especially the births of his two first daughters. He said that in his family, female births were not a thing. And when the baby was a girl, he was a thousand percent sure she was not his."

"Wait. Wait, wait! And she had to stay with that guy for long?"

"Yes."

"Was he a drunkard?"

"No," said the old lady.

"No, no, I could not stay with such a person. Even if I knew he produces a hundred children a night. Ugh, I could not!" the same woman exclaimed. At this point, some of the other women started to laugh mockingly.

"I'm grateful I'm not her. God knows I couldn't stand someone like that," a woman at the corner of the coffee table said. She then crossed her legs and moved her body arrogantly. She and the old lady glanced at each other.

Or maybe because we have got some dark forces working on our behalf, the old lady thought to herself. She and this woman knew each other, too. The woman had been known to have won over the deepest, darkest portion of her man's heart. There was something a little odd about this woman. She'd had her man to herself since she stepped into the family as the fifth wife. The first, second, third and the fourth wife were all gone like that the moment she showed up. What happened?

The old lady knew about this, but she just smiled and said, "True. You are all able to say these things. And I get that. Because the only time we humans realize lives as harsh as these exist is when we live them ourselves. Isn't that true?"

"No, no, no, Mama. A woman who gets treated like this must lack something. Let's be honest. A man can't think he has the right to beat up my own mother and expect me to believe we can be together anymore," the woman said.

As this woman finished what she was saying, the rest burst into laughter again.

"Listen, my children. We cannot blame the victims here. It is not that people cannot get up the courage to stand up for themselves. It's because of people like you and me.

"Come to think of it. Don't we all play roles in each other's lives? Think of what our surroundings do: our parents, siblings, cousins, relatives, neighbours, community, and our society.

"All these people have the same capacity as we do, in that they can pretty much live our lives for us as far as this culture is concerned. And you can only imagine the depth of one's suffering if the interest of these individuals is fixated on the dark side of one's life.

"And there is a reason for this. Since the putting of the first two people on this earth, we have been campaigning for God's chair, haven't we? And in our own little families, the fight is about who could potentially be eligible to sit there. However, our judges' eyes do not see far since the distinction is to be between the skies and the earth," said the old lady.

"Today your men are somewhat better," said the old lady. "God knows I'm not easy to live with. He knows me, and a man like that cannot be cooked from the same firepan."

"We cannot be ready," interrupted another woman.

"Sure! And it is fascinating how God gives one according to her attitude and leads the non-classic ones into the hands of pain. I have a hard time understanding that part," said the old lady. Then she got up.

"Ready?" she asked the young lady. She gave her her hand, and they were on their way. And until the two disappeared out of their sight, none of the other five women realized the entire story of the unnamed friend was the story of the young lady they were all familiar with.

"They cannot understand even the faintest glimmer of what you've been through," said the old lady. The young lady nodded her head. "Because they haven't lived it themselves."

"What can I say? They have all cooked for God, haven't they?" said the young lady.

"Or it could be because of this. You see, a behaviour that's due to cultural practice is like the creativity of an artist. The beauty of creativity does not rely on the quality of sameness, but rather on the individuality of one's creativity. Likewise, the notion of being rough, ungentle, unfair is by far allowed in this way of life. And so, it's up to individuals to appropriate their behaviours according to their heart's desires. Unfortunately, this more creative individual chose you," said the old lady.

"But why don't they know that?" the young lady asked.

"Because their worth, like yours, is never outside of their social status. And while maintaining their distance, they cannot fight without ending up fighting alongside a woman's husband. It is inevitable," she added.

The two kept walking. "These rough roads! Rough, dry, unsmoothed muddy roads," the young lady said suddenly after stumbling over a few muddy ruts in the road.

"You be careful. The question is not why you feel hurt when you step on something ungentle. No, just know as far as having no proper roadmaps, the bruises are inevitable," the old lady said.

All of a sudden, they were struck by the sound of loud music. The noise was coming from a beautiful, posh, well-designed compound which belonged to a wealthy old man by the name of Malual, which is translated as "red," the colour of a cow or in this case, a red giant serpent god.

Mr. Malual was a man not only blessed by unspeakable wealth, but plenty of children. He had around one hundred and eighty cows, some of which were with other people for accommodation. He was a brother to three other siblings. Unlike his three other siblings, he alone, in this little community, owned half of the population. Owning fourteen wives alone, the production of his strength amounted to thirty-six children. At this time, most of the children had moved on and were parents of their own children. Out of the thirty-six, he killed two. Or, like the society would say, it was actually the mothers who had their children murdered.

Men are not called names here or the sun would die and you wouldn't know how he went about his day.

Inside the beautiful compound, though, Mr. Malual was still parenting three of his children. Of the three children, two were siblings resulting from his most recent marriage. Unfortunately, their mother passed away at the age of twenty-nine, leaving her eleven-year-old daughter, Rebecca, and her seven-year-old son, Gatwech (Son of the Land), behind.

From his second-most recent marriage was born a man by the name of Chuol (a name which was a reflection of the fatal incident intentionally brought upon the sibling he directly followed). Chuol means "repayment, given by God." This man, whose age was believed to be the same as that of his last stepmother, was the second last child Mr. Malual and his second-last wife had in their marriage. Chuol just returned home over two years ago from Khartoum, where he had spent over six years studying. He graduated from the University of Khartoum with two majors in business. Apart from his passion for business, his ambition was to one day become a ruler in this place. He returned and just as he had lived this life for the last twenty years, he dove back into all his old familiar behaviours. Except, Chuol hadn't really been himself since his return coincided with the passing of his younger brother by the name of Khor (War)

The two women ventured closer to catch a glimpse of what was going on. Outside the compound, they saw young and old. Children and women were dancing with great joy. At the gate, Mr. Malual saw the two staring, but he couldn't come forward for there were many elders arriving and he had to show them around.

The old lady at the gate knew what was going on but was not sure the day was today. And through what she could recall, the event was a result of an incident which took place seventeen years ago. Exactly seventeen years ago, when Chuol's elder brother was entering manhood, Mr. Malual thought it was his duty to order his son to find a wife for himself while still young and fresh.

At the time, the young man paired up with several girlfriends. When his father reached out to him, this ended with two pretty girls being impregnated by him at the same time. Like any other young man, Chuol's elder brother had the right to choose who between the two women would be the wife of his heart.

He did what he was rightly supposed to do and the rejected girl was sent away with her unborn child. She returned to her only family member, her brother. And at the end of her pregnancy, she didn't just give birth to a child, but to twin boys.

Since the father of the twins denied responsibility, the girl's brother took over the responsibility for a very profound reason.

After the birth of the twins, a hungry-for-marriage man was interested in the girl. And to no one's surprise, the man asked the girl's brother to marry both the girl and her twins.

The twins' uncle rejected this notion, although this kind of arrangement was considered normal. He told those gathered, "I'm raising these children because they are going to be my brothers."

Ever since the girl was taken by the new man, the uncle struggled bringing up his brothers with no help from anyone.

Time passed and, sure enough after sixteen years, the twins became persons. The biological father saw this and didn't sit by quietly. The father called the twins' uncle before the law about what he thought should belong to him.

This, according to this law, was his undeniable right. In the hearings, people from the uncle's side brought up the fact that he didn't specify that he just didn't like the girl, but that he would want the child when she gave birth.

To this he would respond by asking the law whether it was true that a man could rightfully produce children for another man. Here, it is not nurture that matters but the biological piece that forms a life, and the father knew this. While fighting with the father, the twins grew bored with the disappointment their uncle seemed to dwell in. With no permission from their uncle, the twins would privately visit their father. He would take them everywhere and to see everyone. Every time they visited, their desire to live with their father grew. It was a male thing to desire to be known among his sub-clan's men, and the twins were no strangers to this conceptual belief. For there is nothing which grants a man the same dignity and respect as knowing who and where his father is.

After their uncle's side had exhausted every argument, the year ended with the loss of the battle. The twins were given to their real father. The uncle was offered cows in replacement of the removal of the boys, but he refused the offer. "Who doesn't like yang (cow)?" Mr. Malual exclaimed. "These are men—they were going to come with me, anyway. Too bad you had to cling to the notion they would forever be yours. No, no. What belongs to somebody else only belongs to him." He went on, proving to those who were hearing the case that the uncle's behaviour was outrageous.

Today was the official welcoming party, the twins' official introduction to their community.

"Oh, come in, come in," said Mr. Malual. He managed to squeeze himself out of the crowd.

"So, finally, your son is being given his children?" said the old lady.

"Finally," said Mr. Malual joyfully. "Come in, please." The two shook hands. The old lady looked back at the young lady. The young lady shook her head, conveying that she would not go in.

The old lady followed Mr. Malual inside. In the middle of the compound, she threw her eyes around, gazing at the familiar dancers. It did not take long before the twins showned up in front of her. And behind them was the father, Chuol, and two other siblings. They were six siblings in number. All from one mother. Unfortunately, one of the three female siblings lived a tribe away by choice. Gatwech stood behind them as the siblings shared a moment of laughter. The twins' father looked behind him and saw Gatwech watching his cultural brother but biological father with the twins he shared his likeness with. Though there was a great amount of distance between them, one could not miss the fact that the three boys shared a closer biological centre other than the great man. And that was true. Long ago, things went terribly south with the great man. He tried his very best in moving the walls of the new and the young for a period of two years; however, he failed in that and the twins' father actually had to help in making these two children.

Unfortunately, the mother left for heaven before the two could give a third child to the elderly man.

"Oh, come. Meet them." Mr. Malual excitedly pulled the old lady toward the twins.

The old lady hugged them individually and spit saliva on each one's head as a traditional way of blessing them. "You are now men," she said with a great smile on her face.

The twins smiled back and passed her. The crowd bled after them and walked them out, showing them the rest of the land. Behind the crowd were Mr. Malual and another good friend of his by the name of Tut Gai Gatluak. ("Tut" means male). The two had much in common. They were both wealthy. Both had many wives. Both divorced their wives but for different reasons. Tut's wife didn't want to get pregnant so he returned her to her parents. Malual's wife bore him a disabled child. But no one in his family tree ever had a disability of any kind. So, he sent her back where she came from with the thing she had birthed. Both men had many children, but Tut had more daughters than his friend did.

As the crowd passed the gate, the little girl in the house pulled on her shoes and began to run after the crowd. Her seven-year-old brother, Gatwech, who was in the crowd already, realized she was joining them. "Where do you think you are going?" he asked after he stopped walking.

"Coming with you," Rebecca replied.

"Go back now! Who told you that you could walk with men? Go back!" Gatwech repeated. The sister returned to the compound. The young lady watched her as she walked by.

The old lady returned to the young lady at the gate. And before she reached her, she thought of something she wanted to share with the young lady, but instead, the young lady said to her, "What a life! Look at them. So proud to have a father, and the absence of the birth-giver gives no trouble, huh?"

"Don't think like that," argued the old lady. And she forgot what she was going to tell her.

"Why not? Who is a woman? A thing whose worth is dependent on the unknown richness of her womb?" she said while rolling her eyes.

The old lady shook her head. She came closer and wrapped her arm around the young lady's shoulder.

"I want you to take it easy on yourself," she said while still holding on to her shoulder.

"I am, but the pain isn't leaving me."

"It has to," said the old lady. The two walked a distance away from the compound then they stopped and continued talking.

"I see this in your heart. The trying of doing the right thing only to labour in vain isn't making sense right now to you." While the old lady was still talking, a man the two women knew passed by. The old lady greeted him. The man refused to greet the old lady back. He side-glanced at both of them with judging eyes and bypassed them.

"He cannot even respond because of me," said the young lady.

"And you don't have to fret about that either," the old lady replied. "You have to remember when you hurt one man, you have hurt every other walking man in this planet. And believe me or not, he could not greet me back now that I'm with you. There is an old saying that goes like this, 'Birds of a kind flock together.' I'm just as sinful as you are in his eyes. They judged the righteous Judge for that, didn't they?" she added.

The young lady became emotional suddenly. The old lady looked at her. "What is wrong?" she asked her.

"How do you avoid the wrong ones for a chance to escape becoming 'old' while still in the presence of your youth?"

"That will only be possible once the teaching has been refined. But for that to happen, we are in need of a miracle," said the old lady. She looked at the young lady, whose face was a mask of emotions. "Those thoughts will make your next breath laboured. Just swallow them if you can.

"Like I was saying, know that although this pains your heart, it has nothing to do with the view our society has of you. And there is nothing you can do about it. There are three scars which deplete the worth of a female: age, birth, and divorce. Each one of these is tied to some sort of deep meaning that no one can really explain, but those who believe a female is less of a human stand by this. Each one of these things applies to you. You see, when they price us, it is for a reason.

"Take a car, for example. A Qashqai two-door Nissan at £166,809 pounds was loaned out in the year prior to its release by a young family man. The man brought it back after a year with an interest in going with a newer model. An older man, who was the manager of the car dealership, inspected it inside and out. 'I had a minor collision five months ago,' said the man. 'Oh, yeah?' the manager said, while looking at some minor marks around the bumper area. 'You are one of those reckless drivers, aren't you? Thanks for telling us. We definitely need to look at it further in case there is some internal damage,' he said. He then glanced at the mileage. 'Oh, boy. It sure has passed many roads, hasn't it?' he said, laughing. He accepted the car and immediately marked it down at a reduced price and placed a sign on it that read 'Used.'"

"Wait, why couldn't he tell the guy to keep his used car and if he wanted, he could buy an additional one?" the young lady asked.

"Uh, where would he find a mouth to say that? You have to know that today's sellers are tomorrow's buyers," replied the old lady. "Anyway, the manager placed the sign. He asked him some silly questions as he tried to make some jokes around the depleting value of the car. But no, how could they be silly? While the recklessness of the driving should supposedly tell the manager something about the man's driving, it's the car that carries the record of that minor collision. The next buyer will learn how long this car has been around, as well as its current mileage and past behavioural description from the previous owner before they agree to pay the reduced price. It all comes together nice and clean when you look at it in the end. If ever we were what we are—human, priceless, beautiful souls—the time will never be called to mind, and neither a number popping up every now and then as the car passes a kilometre, nor the record of what happened some time back will ever bring us back to that place. But it is all relevant to the car's return. It is a business, and we ought to learn not so much about the speed at which a car's worth declines but about the policy. Because it is in this policy that our designated fate comes in the form of debt to which the past and present and future us physically, psychologically, mentally, emotionally and spiritually pays," said the old lady.

"You are a woman, and you know what that means. There was nothing designed with you in mind. Now that you are officially divorced, that he finally released his cows off your back, this society sees an open wound that has been left unprotected. My point is, move on. Get a husband! I know marriage is a gift from man to himself."

She hesitated a little after saying that. "I mean, here," she amended. "But certainly, thinking about what other women think of you will do you no good. And here is why: they cannot possibly feel your pain as long as they experience life differently.

"They, themselves, will come to want to know what they don't know. You see, a mind is a very simple living thing. As we age, we have to remind it to come along with us. Or else it remains young for the rest of time."

"Hey, you two still here?" shouted Mr. Malual.

"Yes," said the old lady. "Feeling at home already?" she asked the twins, who had appeared beside Mr. Malual.

"Yeah, this is their home." He raised his hands and opened them wide. "This is their home. They have finally come home." He repeated it as he walked the twins back into the compound.

"All this nonsense comes down to one thing," continued the old lady. "They say the lion rules over other animals. Where he is, he is surrounded by other animals. Where he inclines to go, he is followed. However, the difficulty is when there are many lions—and especially when the focal point is to be the most powerful one, the struggle is continuous," she concluded.

The young lady stared at the old lady as they were both silent for a moment. "I don't understand why," said the young lady suddenly.

"What don't you understand?"

"I don't understand why your life has been this painful. You don't deserve it."

"You mean then or now?"

"I mean then," said the young lady.

"It's okay. You know, one of the things that apparently surprises you but doesn't surprise me anymore, is what matters to our made-up ways of life is not about how, but when. Because with 'when' come shortcuts. And it really doesn't matter what those shortcuts may be as long as one reaches the expected finished line," said the old lady. There was another lingering silence between the two.

"I've heard all about it, but of course part of the story is altered to fit this society's view. Still, I have to admit, sometimes I place my feet on yours and sink down a little bit. And at the end of my thinking time, this question comes to my mind. 'Why didn't she remarry?'"

"Hahaha! See, one of the things which is wrong about our society is —is—" She stuttered a little and let go of what she was wanting to say.

"Here is the thing. When you can't even decide on who to marry, why to marry and when to marry, how much control do you think a woman has over whether she wants to remarry or not? After giving birth to my second son who was severely disabled, the father felt let down by me and, hence, refused to be part of the two of us. He took the perfect child, though, our older son. Three years later, the situation was badly worsened. My mum became really sick and just like that, followed my father. I did not remarry because nobody came to me. And for my son, he stayed alive until I ran out of all my womanhood."

The old lady looked very emotional after touching on her past. She appeared to be fighting back tears. "I guess when you are not lucky . . ." Her voice trailed off as she dabbed her tears with her shirt.

This was not her first marriage that had ended in painful agony. Her first marriage was between her and a man she had never laid eyes on by the name of Koang Pour (wine). Koang was in Khartoum at the time when his family married her to him. Everything was done in his absence and she was given to her in-laws only to find out that the man would not come back. Letter upon letter was sent out and his return was highly requested, even if it meant he would come for one day just so that he could give this poor girl a child, then be allowed to return afterward. He never came. One year turned into three years of being a wife without a husband.

At first, when letters were sent out to him, it was his response to the letters that kept hope in the hearts of his parents. He would often write back and say he should be expected in the next month or so. But three years after the completion of his marriage, he ghosted his parents. The bride was advised by others to forget about the husband and be married to someone else. She refused, thinking year four would be her lucky year. But like the previous ones, there was no sign of him.

In that year, her father-in-law pressured her to reproduce with someone else and she was forced out into the dating world where every inch of her mattered. Unlike she knew it when she was really a girl, it was now a world in doubt of her worth. It happened overnight; it all changed the moment the magical transitional cloth was pulled down on her waist. She could no longer go back to her original worth, no matter how much she still together. Her name then became "Koang's wife": the traditional identity for owned women. It is a title constructed using the man's name followed by an apostrophe and the word "wife." Women suddenly become recognized citizens once they are someone's. Their birth names are kept off the curve, and regardless of how many marriages they fail along the way, they are only known by the name of their previous husband. She had her new name, "Koang's wife," tattooed on her body and since then she was never known by her real name. "Who is she? Oh, she is the girl who was married to Koang Pour."

"Oh, Koang's wife" was how local bachelors learned about her and that was a destructive disqualification. She was no longer a girl (girl means "never married"), but a Kaah (not real, but a virtual form of a female now). "How would I explain to my country's men that I married a Kaah?" the bachelors would say. But they wanted her to be easy. Just be easy to compromise and allow herself to be taken down before any promise of marriage—what else could she still be pretending about? Once the magical cloth slid down her waist, the rest of her was labelled. No matter that she never shared a bed with the man, she was no longer worthy. Women only used to be "girls." But, eventually, she found a place for herself between a local man and his three wives, although he was not her choice.

The old lady looked away from the young lady, and then said, "After that, what use was I there for, providing that here marriage is not about companionship. Here, where injustice leads. Where intelligence, disability and sometimes being born alone like yourself suffers. I wish sometimes that the unhappiness of a heart matter in that it would delay conception." When she said this, she shook her head disappointedly. "And I wonder sometimes whether death is a genetic part of those that have been denied by the Above." She mumbled this to herself and then she redirected herself to face the sun. It was shining extra bright. She quickly turned back and said, "And so, here I am."

The two glanced at each other. They could overhear Mr. Malual speaking excitedly to his grandchildren. "Go home," said the old lady, "but take this with you. Life is both beautiful and ugly but a lot of it is a choice. It takes birth for death to succeed, but it's a choice to express your frustration in insult at the same place where your joyous love for the other caused you tears. I know the moment birth is granted, we are looking at meeting death someday. My problem with it is that you can be driven to take it upon yourself to end your suffering—and sometimes far too soon. What men are best at is guiding you intensely and carefully into your own pit. At the cliff overlooking the pit, they leave you, making sure anything that happens after that is between you and your Creator. 'There, now you may take your final step.' Or they hold you by the hand and say, 'Death, here.' Because they do not lack anything. They fit in with every generation. They may have been your mother's agemate, but they become the bachelors of your generation and the generation of your daughters and the generation of your granddaughters.

"I said, find yourself a husband, and I'm also saying don't show this burning fire in you when you do find someone. As I have looked at this my whole life, the real enemy to manhood is a woman who shows courage. See, if you chose to prostitute yourself today, you would be labelled a fool because, as it goes, the wisest of women know how to just be with one man while the foolhardiest of women are susceptible to sexual manipulation, and that is the most foolish a woman can be. But never would the phrase 'She thinks she is a man' be uttered other than when a woman has accused a man of being wrong. It will take the next generations through suffering before they can name the real enemy.

"So, in short, it's better to be without your children when the owners divide them among themselves, but alive. If you are still alive, you may see them again someday," said the old lady.

She looked directly at the beautiful compound behind them where the wealthiest man was still talking with his voice full of joy. "Oh, yeah, I remember what I wanted to tell you earlier," said the old lady. "Over ten years ago there used to be a girl in this compound, but she is no longer here."

"She passed away?" asked the young lady urgently.

"No, she made a huge mistake. She was impregnated by a man she dearly loved. Of course, she should not have done that. Her father's wrath shot through the roof and just like that she got her life's punishment. She was sold to the Murle along with her unborn child for having disappointed her family and this society and advantageously more cows were made. You should have heard Mr. Malual's insult to the young man. He kept calling him a 'nobody person' and would not stop insulting him until he sealed a deal with the men of the Murle. The girl was tall, with thick, shiny hair—a very beautiful piece of art. I believe she was so much extra to the Murlen people, since they usually give birth to things of their own nature. Oh, they gave abundantly. I guess Murlen men are not usually bothered by not having been the first man. But that was not it.

"Since she was a little girl, her father used to wish she was born a boy rather than a girl. She was sharper than some of the boys in his household. Out of all his children, she was the one who resembled him inside-out the most. Because of who she was, she didn't leave with tears in her eyes showering the rest of her face. No. Instead she said this, 'This is the last time you and I will ever set eyes on each other's physical forms. If for any reason we see them again, it will be at the expense of the ones we both value. I hope to stay away from here, so don't ever question the record of your legacy.'

"Mr. Malual is a man who has befriended nature and through all the generations he outlives, he enjoys that relationship specifically within the mirror of his inner bowl."

"Hmm, what a mistake!" the young lady said.

"Mistake? No man makes mistakes."

"He thinks that?"

"No, he knows that," the old lady said. "Anyway, one of his older daughters was married and the guy paid seventy-eight cows for her. And from that time on, his need for all the beautiful daughters he ever produced to follow the same step has continued."

The two went silent again. The old lady broke the silence a few minutes later. And she said, "Know this, they are brothers but not yours. Go," she said.

"I will think about what you told me," said the young lady.

CHAPTER ONE

"One, Nyakhor Biel. Two, Nyabiel Tut. Three, Sarah Mabiel. Four, Mary Gatwech. Five, Nyayang Jock." (Nya plus the letter "l" becomes Nyal, which means girl. The "l" gets replaced by the first later of the name, for example, Nyadet.)

"No, wait . . . she is your girlfriend, too?"

"Yeah, what do you think? She is mine," Chuol says to a group of young men sitting on a square table under a blossoming neem tree that has colourful bead-like fruits hanging to her neck and down to her shoulders. It is a cloudy afternoon outside his father's beautiful, well-put-together compound. They don't always do this, but it is the desire of most young men to gauge how far behind they are compared to other young men, in terms of how many girlfriends each has. It is a game. It is called, "Mo e jin wutdo, Tii Ke Luom-dii?" (If you are a man, how many girlfriends do you have?) And here is how it is played:

Each man takes a number of sticks and places them on his hand, and when prompted to reveal, he counts his girlfriends by placing each stick back on the table, and with each placement, he reveals the name of the girl it represents. At the end of each turn, the one who has the most is the "Balang," a name that is designated to a man's popularity within the social context.

The word "Balang" has a slightly different meaning for both genders. A man is a Balang on the basis of how many girlfriends he has or if he is a song-composer. But for women, it merely takes into consideration a beautiful physical appearance; if she is strong, vocally, in making her voice heard in response to the control of other girls; and if she is a singer. Those first two make her a lead and therefore a "Balang Nyal."

"Okay, my turn," says the man next to Chuol.

"No, I didn't finish," says Chuol.

"You are just going to go on forever!"

"No, I'm not!"

"Hey, guys," Chuol suddenly says to his nephews, the twins who join the young men at the table. "You have girls?" he asks as he makes a space for them to sit between him and the next guy.

One of the twins takes a seat and nods his head. The other one remains standing with a mouthful of neem fruit that he has plucked from the closest branches. He takes a seat afterward. They both look at Chuol and start laughing.

"Go on," Chuol says to the guy next to the twins.

"No, you go on," says the guy.

"Okay, if you have nothing to say because you have depleted your list of impregnations, let me go on," Chuol says while giggling at the guy. All the other young men laugh, too.

"When are you going to make someone a mother, you two?" the guy next to the twins asks them.

"I don't want to marry yet," says one of the twins.

"To impregnate a girl does not mean you have to marry her. But how are you a man if you don't stretch your arms within the space given to you?" he says.

"He is the expert; you should listen to him. He only said yes to one of the five girlfriends he impregnated and here he is aiming to be this year's Balang," Chuol says, while patting the back of the young man. The sun is going down quickly, and they realize it.

"We'll leave it and some time next week we shall get to the bottom of this. See who has more," Chuol says to the rest of them.

A week passes by. Chuol's big brother welcomes his boys to their mothers. It begins to rain, but the rain is not fulfilling the expectation of the farmers. During the spring season, those of Mr. Malual get really busy. The seventy-eight-year-old gets up before the appearance of the first star. But there is more about this old man that makes men look up to him.

He inherited the greatest dignity a man could possibly get. He was a trusted chief in this community for over ten years. After that many years of holding the chair, he voluntarily stepped down and passed the legacy to his elder son, following the way his father passed it to him. He is a man who practises traditions in his daily life. He is known for his communication style with his family, especially with his wives. It has been noted with his wives, Mr. Malual speaks to them through the children. He selects one child from each wife and communicates all that needs to be done by that wife through the child. He says women are the shallowest things God ever wasted His time on making. Furthermore, with every encounter he makes with inexperienced males, he tells them he believes men are made for bigger reasons, not limited to their distinctive physical appearance, but valued for their philosophical insights. He used to use his position in the community when he was the chief in charge of decisions. He still gets to influence how things go around here, since the chair has only moved from him to his older son.

It's early morning. As usual, Mr. Malual gets up and walks to the garden. Upon arriving at the gate, he unexpectedly sees his son, Chuol, coming from an overnight meeting with one of his girlfriends. "So, you are just coming back?" asks Mr. Malual. Chuol nods his head and expresses his overwhelming worry about something he and his father discussed a month ago.

It started with this ambiguous question that his father asked him: "What does your ideal wife look like?"

Chuol hesitated at first, but he eventually gave him the answer: "A light-skinned girl. Tall, but not taller than me. She has to have hair. I can't stand those bare-headed girls. No. Good teeth. White, and lined up properly. And definitely not those ones with big bodies. No, I don't like them."

Chuol's father then responded, "You kind of sound like me when I was a young man." But in term of the old man's discussion with him, nothing really went as he wanted. Chuol suddenly wanted to leave.

With no further hesitation, Mr. Malual cancels his work so that they can continue the unfinished discussion. It's been a year now since Chuol opened a small business in the city, and for the most part, he invests most of his time selling and advertising products. There are ships coming everyday. Ships, mostly from Malakal, come every day, bringing items of clothes, shoes, and home products. The tradesmen are busy. From the shore to their shops, they will spend hundreds of pounds to pay someone who can help them. Young men such as Chuol use their youthful strength to take the products out of the ship to the shore and from the shore to the shop.

"I know you know this," Mr. Malual begins. "People here have now turned the focus of these inter-sub-clan conflicts on those who are now coming back from the neighbouring countries, simply because they may have a higher education and they do see that as a threat. If they know you are from a particular sub-clan with which they may have an unsettled conflict and you have an education, they are looking for you."

"Do not worry, God is there," says Chuol. The two go quiet for a little.

"Have you thought about what we discussed?" asks Mr. Malual as the two still stand. But Chuol, who is reluctant to discuss this mindboggling matter again, decides to remain quiet.

Mr. Malual gently puts his hand on his son's shoulder and leads him to the "daddy room."

Inside the room, the two sit down opposite each other. "Chuol," his father says, "I'm getting old and your mother is, too. You see, my son, all of these come to pass: fame, girls, all of it. But when a man passes and leaves a family behind, there is a legacy. If I pass away today, I wouldn't worry because I would know I have you. But what if you were to die today, what would you leave?" The tension in the room can be felt.

"I want you to find the woman of your dreams. But I have one thing to say on that matter." Chuol glances at his father sharply. "You are walking to the girl's parents in the daytime and telling them 'I'm marrying your daughter,'" says his father.

"What?" Chuol jumps to the sky. "Baba, you know I can't do that, I'm a young man. That is for old people."

"I don't care," his father rebukes him. "What makes you think you have to steal at night?"

"It's not stealing." Chuol raises his manly voice and is almost at the point of leaving the room.

"Chuol, you know I'm a very respected man in this community. And I have enough to give in return to the girl's parents you choose. Don't try to make me feel small among men." His father slams the arm of the chair he sits on as he pushes the discussion onto the little man's throat.

Chuol looks at his father for a moment and remains quiet. "So, are we agreeing on this?" his father demands. His son throws his head aside, for he doesn't want to acknowledge the way this discussion is going against his will. *I'm not going to do this,* he thinks to himself while frowning.

To him, life's freedom is about making decisions on one's own. Especially when you are this young. Having had ten most sought-after girls as his girlfriends, Chuol cannot not picture himself arriving in front of one girl and explaining in detail that he is marrying her in the daytime. He just cannot not wrap his head around it.

"I'm not ready," exclaims Chuol. But unfortunately, this beautiful notion is not negotiable. It's a father's obligation to be involved in finalizing the legacy of his son.

The father drops his head upon hearing his son deceitfully grabbing at a worn-out branch.

The two go quiet for a minute. "So, when are you going to be ready?" asks Mr. Malual. Chuol still makes it his business to be quiet. "Okay, then. Let's open up a different chapter." Chuol brings back his head after hearing his father say this.

"So, if I'm not banned from asking questions. What kind of women do you prefer? Or attributes, I should say."

"Baba, I told you I'm not ready. I will let you know what I'm looking for in a woman once I'm ready," he responds to his father in an irritable voice.

"I think this discussion isn't all that interesting to you, huh? Okay, we can certainly close that curtain if that is what you want. But I want to tell you this." He begins to pinch his son's cheek.

"What?" asks Chuol with zero patience.

"I'm not entirely surprised by your response. You know, when my father sat me down for this very conversation, I responded the same way," continues his father.

"But when I actually had my family, I couldn't stop thanking him for several reasons.

"For one thing," he says, sitting upright on his rocky chair and giving his son a direct look, "when every girl you talk to seems to be madly in love with you, you know, you kind of abhor the idea of anything putting that feeling to an end. For us, this is what strongly confirms who we are." He says this while beating his chest. "No one would want to walk away from such a feeling.

"However, when my father finally extracted me out, man, I realized that I was never going to be ready. The other component of our discussion was actually an eye-opener for me. You know, at the time I talked to all kinds of girls. But I never paid heed to anything like the things my father told me. He told me how different personal behaviours and body features can have a huge impact on one's marriage."

Mr. Malual continues enthusiastically, "While you are conversing with girls in general, I advise you to pay special attention to these types of girls. My father told me and I'm telling you, there is this indiscreet, red-eyed-looking girl, the one whose eyes always look as if someone poured blood in them. This type is horribly fruitless. You see, the redness in her eyes isn't a random thing." He points at his eyes to verify his point. "But it occurs because of the weightlessness of her heart. This had been confirmed with any girl with this issue. She runs from one man to the next, and that is the number one problem.

"She always says yes and never no, even when the deception puts on the natural yellow colour. You see, that type can't be man's wife. So, watch out. If you spot one, never rest in the shade of her presence.

"There is also this other one. The talkative type. This is the one who, when you begin a discussion as a man, before it's her chance to talk, she tries to take over so that she can straighten the mistakes she thinks you are making. This is the manipulative type. And she cannot be a man's wife, either. No, no one would pass by your house," he says while shaking his head.

"Why?" asks Chuol sarcastically.

"Because everybody will know she is in full control of you and that she talks your talk."

"Wow! I never thought about any of these things," Chuol says.

"Well, you really don't get to think about any of them until you are on your way to finding some," his father answers and giggles afterward.

"So, what do you consider a good woman?" asks Chuol.

Mr. Malual looks at his son for a second. Then he moves to the edge of his rocking chair. "A good woman is one who has been raised to respect men. Because only when she has been raised to respect you, will she listen to your voice respectfully.

"An affable one. For only when she is affable will she agreeably submit herself to you. A faithful one, because only when a woman is faithful will you intuitively and respectfully appear superior among others."

"Ha ha!" Chuol laughs out loud.

"You are laughing?"

"Yes, I am. A girl with all these positive attributes isn't easy to find these days," says Chuol.

"What do you mean? None of the girlfriends you have is anything like this?"

"No, they are. A couple of them actually fit into these categories."

"So, what do you like about them?" asks his father impatiently.

"Well, they are not much alike, actually. But I think they could pretty much make good wives. One talks but not very much. And the other one is just the opposite of the first one. You know the girl who was here the other day?" Chuol asks his father.

"Oh, yeah. Oh, no, wait, you mean the one who came recently?"

"Yeah, that's the one."

"Okay, I remember that one. She said her name is Sarah."

"Yeah. I like that girl," says Chuol.

"I could see that. She seems to be a delightful young lady."

"The quiet one is another one that I like," Chuol continues. The previously unengaged mind of Chuol is now fully enticed by this "a man wants this; a man doesn't want that conversation." And there is no going back without him sharing his preferences now.

"Her name is Nyayang Jock. She is very amusing, very courteous. Her amiableness takes my breath away whenever I'm close," he says, smiling fondly at the thought of the girl. He suddenly wants to play with words. What he really loves about her the most is her quiet nature. Quietness denotes a permissive nature. Men love this character type a whole lot.

"Okay, okay. You sound like you are in something deep with this girl."

Chuol looks at his father and smiles. "She is also the youngest one among my girlfriends, and—" He almost says something else he really loves about this girl when his father cuts him off with words of agreement.

"I'm happy, son. I'm very happy. Take it, take the chance. These types of chances do not come around very often. When you are lucky enough to get one, you'd better wait no more. Nyayang must have been raised by a woman who respects her husband," says Mr. Malual excitedly.

But what else did Chuol really love about her? She was the youngest one in age compared to his other nine girlfriends. And that put her in a good place. She had also demonstrated that she was able to stand her ground without giving in. And, she was among the few women he had not been intimate with. That and the fact that she was the youngest made her the winner in Chuol's eyes.

She could not have been considered for this position of honour had beauty and usefulness not been associated with being young. Sarah came second for a good reason. She was older than Nyayang, but she was among the virgin girlfriends. But it was the size of her family that secured second place for her. She came from a big family and big families married from big families. But between family size and youth, he had to pick youth.

"You think she is good?"

"Good? Chuol, she is perfect! However, do not forget what I have told you. I don't care if she is your girlfriend or not, you must go through the barn's door," commands his father. "What religion is she by the way?"

"She is Catholic."

"Oh, okay. She'll come to us, anyway," Mr. Malual says after a moment's silence.

"But quick, before I let you go, does she have brothers?" asks his father.

"No, it's just her and her little sister." His father goes quiet after hearing this.

"Why did you ask?" asks Chuol.

"You know, sometimes it is better to avoid the ones whose backs are open. But anyhow, it's not a big deal," he says, seemingly disappointed. Then he dismisses his son.

Chuol leaves and enters his room. Mr. Malual gets ready to leave the compound. "Rebecca, Rebecca!" Chuol's mother is calling Rebecca from the kitchen.

"Aah!" says Rebecca.

"You don't say 'aah,' you say 'Waaw!' Like a girl. Not like a boy!" The mother disapproves of how she voices her responses when she gets a call like this.

"How should I respond?" Rebecca seems not to have the time for the lessons that seem to be a regular thing now. She is failing to see that this is the age at which the best behaved girls get picked by potential husbands before they reach puberty. She walks to the corner. She seems tired with these rites. Nothing she does go without being corrected or some small insulting words being added. She sits on a bench, legs open wide.

"Look at how you sit! How many times have I told you to close your legs like a girl!" says her stepmother. She walks over to her, and like she always does, she demonstrates how a girl should sit by grabbing her right leg violently and placing it on top of the other. "This is how girls sit," she says. Then she pinches her on the cheek and walks away.

Mr. Malual watches from the gate. "Who is going to marry her, looking like that?" he says, after exchanging a look with his wife. It disappoints him that she does not pick up the teachings quickly. She is physically all a man would want, but when beauty is paired with knowing how to service a man, the only thing that can get in her way is another woman.

There are a few men who have forwarded their proposals to the great man already. That she seems behind other girls worries him, though. Some men just need to have the rest of the land know they married someone whose father has a reputable social status, nothing else. They figure the rest can be straightened by the tongue or the all-time teaching tool, the belt.

Rebecca moves to the kitchen after overhearing her father. Mr. Malual exits the compound. He goes out into the open area, at the front of the barn where some of his many cows are leashed with animal-skin leashes onto individually curved wooden posts. He walks toward one of the new mothers. He grabs dirt from the ground and sprinkles it over her back. Then he comes closer and spreads it evenly over her back and starts scrubbing it with the sandy dirt. The cow seems to like it. Mr. Malual starts smiling and mumbling at the cows. The relationship between the old man and his cows seems to be a good one. He does not easily smile at anything. He starts singing some romantic song before he makes the move to another female cow. He reaches this female cow but seems to fix his attention to another female cow placed alone in front of the opened area. This cow is all leashed onto a wooden post that is above the cow's knees with a short animal-skinned leash. There is a male cow, big in appearance approaching the cow. The cow moves madly and tries to free herself. But the leash is very short. The more she pulls herself away, the more she brushes her chin and jaw painfully against the wooden post. Mr. Malual smiles as he sees the male cow coming. But that is not the only male cow around. There are others grazing while wandering freely around.

A week later, Chuol visits Nyayang. Chuol has given the notion some thought and now tries to move on with it. Under a gigantic hairy

Koat (tamarind tree), which is situated between Nyayang's parents' two separated rooms, Chuol and his girlfriend sit down to a romantic evening under the full moon.

The Koat, whose shade has coloured the connection of the two, has the look of an umbrella. Old, he looks, but he has a genetic resilience. He cannot be turned, altered or redefined in any way. There is no easy way to get to his top. He has many branches, nourished throughout the seasons, it seems; however, among the branches is another stand-out branch that had grown downward. The residents take shelter under the shade he provides. During the day, young and old bring about their different conversations under his shade. The boys use a rope to tighten the downwardly growing branch to get to the top of him. Girls are discouraged from trying to climb using the rope. It is believed that when a girl tries to climb using the rope, she ends up kicking her legs around and her underpants can be seen by those around.

In comparison to his tree family around him, he also births the sourest fruits. The boys snack from the top and when satisfied, they throw the rest to the ground for whomever is around. And although the leaves of the branches make the shade of this tree cool and different, this downwardly branch has barely any hair on his trunk. It is naked, yet it continues to grow bigger and stronger.

As is their habitual custom, when these two lovers are wrapping up their happy, overnight discussions, they will rise from their chairs and come and stand below the branch. Chuol will grasp the highest point of the branch and Nyayang will take its peak. Then the two will have their last words of the night.

For the two-and-a-half years this relationship has been active, the two have often sat under this thought-shaping shade of life from ten in the evening to five in the morning. But things are awkwardly different today. This visitation is surprisingly short. Chuol is supposed to announce the unbelievable news; however, his overthinking of how he still wants to do it and how his father wants it still weighs on his heart.

"I want to leave now," says Chuol tiredly.

"At this time? It's only twelve," says Nyayang with her delightful smile on her face, hoping it can distract Chuol from whatever the matter is.

"I need to go," insists Chuol. For about three minutes, the friends go on arguing. But then Chuol walks away with victory.

The next morning comes through. Mr. Malual, as always, wakes up and makes his way to the garden. Chuol, upon waking, follows his father to offer some help. However, he begins working on the opposite side of where his father is. Mr. Malual is with Mr. Tut Gai, discussing something about a trip Mr. Tut had previously taken to the city with three of his younger daughters. The trip was to the hospital. Mr. Tut has many traditions he keeps after having stayed in the deep freeze of Shariah laws. He believes that some of females' future mistakes can be controlled by employing some of these protocols. So, he went to have his three daughters circumcised. Thanks to the medical improvement that is taking place in the area, Mr. Tut went to the hospital this time around. Unlike this time, last time he went straight to a home-based circumciser who cuts females whatever way he feels is the right way to fight a woman's sinful feelings with his cut-wash blade. Six girls who had undergone this home-based procedure, including one of Mr. Tut's daughters, had been experiencing some abnormalities since the surgery, ranging from difficulty urinating to later on experiencing having their wombs refuse children.

The men appear very animated from where Chuol stands. Whatever their discussion is about, it is surely something the two old men wholeheartedly believe in. Another man joins them. Chuol notices the third man approach, but he cannot hear the conversation. The man leaves shortly.

"As if a cow is a nyal and you just say, 'Hey, here it is,' to someone who wants it. I asked him to have his wife come once in a while and take some milk for them. But no, he wants me to give him a cow," says Mr. Malual to Mr. Tut about the man who just left them.

"Ha ha! Ha ha ha!" Mr. Tut laughs.

Mr. Malual and Mr. Tut are two of the biggest guys this community has got. The two are somewhat close, united by the material things they possess. They both also come from the same sub-clan within this clan. They usually agree with each other's decisions. Mr. Tut leaves and Mr. Malual continues plowing.

In the distance, Mr. Tut shouts back at Mr. Malual, "Tomorrow, we need to be the first ones to arrive there. We are the fathers of the child, you know!"

"Oh, yes," says Mr. Malual. He slams his head with his hand as though he had forgotten about the event happening tomorrow.

Tomorrow is the day that Mr. Tut's elder son by the name of Gatwech Tut will be inaugurated into a recent role of leadership he finally claimed for himself from the other people he was racing against. Mr. Gatwech, for a good chunk of six months, had been campaigning for a chance to lead this part of the county. As expected, he got the role. Tomorrow would be a day of encouragement, laughter, good food, and, of course, true aspiration.

The sun comes up and brings with it some aggressively harsh heat, which leads Mr. Malual and Chuol to take a rest. Covered as they are in mud, the two walk to the nearby river where they stumble upon an elderly tradesman and his son. With the tradesman and his son, is a pregnant donkey. The back of the animal is loaded with all kinds of items ready for buyers.

At the riverbank, Chuol and his father kneel down to wash off the mud and so do the other two. The animal straightens her neck and readies to drink. By the time she has her mouth in the water, the other two are done.

"Get up, go. Move, move!" the son yells at the animal while slapping her thigh. The animal roars and groans. She turns her back to the river and then backs up slightly in the water. In a gesture of refusal, she then lowers her waist down. When her tail touches the water, she stops still, in a strange demonstration of reluctance. The son inhumanely pokes her below her belly. The animal moves forward. She shakes herself off forcefully, which leads the items on her back to fall to the ground.

This reckless move only ignites the feeling of hurry the son has, turning it into flaming hate. "You are a man, go on. Push it!" the reckless father thoughtlessly encourages his mindless son out loud.

The son moves on, pushing the animal even harder. This does not work. The animal appears to be in a stalemate. In his third attempt, the son picks up a fatty stick from the ground and starts beating the animal with it.

"What is this animal doing?" asks the father silently. He knows that just some kilometers away, all these items could be sold. He is coming with fresh fish. It's morning and women are buying fish to be prepared for lunches. He worries that by not arriving on time, buyers may end up buying yesterday's leftover fish, which would have been marked to half the price it was yesterday. But why would they, when he was coming with some fresh fish right from the water? Why would anyone take a gradually decaying thing when fresh was within reach?

The animal refuses to move. The two do not appreciate the challenge. But even weirder, with all the humiliation going on, Chuol and his father think to themselves that they see an encouraging example while watching the animal refuse her fate. Looking from a distance, they admire the size and the age of the animal.

"I will buy one for sure," says Chuol.

"It will make things easier. And if she gets pregnant, I can nurture the child and sell it later on," says his father.

"Hey, we have a problem here. Can you give us a hand?" yells the tradesman.

"Of course." The two flow like feathers. With eight hands, the items are quickly returned to the back of the animal.

"Move, fast. Fast, move! What do you think your responsibility is? I could easily bring you back to where you came from." The donkey startles after hearing the son says this. In a desperate motion, she moves. It is depressing to think, if it feels this hard in the presence of the one who first owned her, what would be the level of blame assigned to the one who nurtured her?

So, she continues making a concerted effort to carry the weight, since she is aware that tears and bleeding don't necessarily mean one is hurt.

In the midst of her pain, she thinks of what it would be like if she actually went back to her first fostering caregiver. How would another buyer evaluate her? "Oh, your donkey is now second-hand. I can't pay the full amount." She thinks of how it would be an older buyer who would claim her. Because the young, busy businessmen would not consider her young and fresh, but old, out of style, and of course getting hollower due to her previous offspring.

I have to accept this life, she tells herself. *All I have is to empty the richness of my unrecognized soul.* At this point, she is over the cliff of the river and ready to move faster. "Let's go!" She receives another painful slash. *And I'm pregnant, what else do I need to understand?* She swallows her tears. Chuol and his father watch until the three vanish out of sight. Then they return home while not talking to each other.

Inside the compound, the two find a few things have not been done. The elderly mother has not been able to bring water and so there is no lunch waiting for them. Tired after their physical labour, the son and the father decide to take an afternoon nap, each in his own room.

Close to sunset, the half-energized elderly mother tries everything she can do to feed the sleeping tigers. But it is when the two go for their nap that it becomes cloudy and eventually manages to squeeze a few drops down. And it is this small amount of water which makes the roads as smooth as a vein.

From the river, the elderly mother toughens herself to fight the slipperiness of the road she uses. But not when she arrives at the wooden gate of her compound. With one hand up on the water pot, a sneaky little branch at the highly sophisticated gate turns itself into an enemy of the night. At first, she strives to keep her composure in the moment. However, with the help of her uncooperative dress which seemingly favours nothing more than to see the whole family sleep in hands, stillness becomes not an option.

As she alternates her feet, she moves her right foot forth and when moving the other afterward, the long tail of her dress spreads its wings and decides to sit on the unseen branch instead.

With no one to warn her, the old-looking mother is held back by her dress, which leads to the water pot falling from her head. She carries on unstably, hoping she can still steady herself. Unfortunately, she falls on her side, brutally slamming her elbow down on the hard ground.

"Waah!" she cries. Upon hearing the pain in her voice, the men startlingly jump out of their beds and arrive at the scene of the broken water pot and painful, hurting elbow.

"You see!" Mr. Malual aims his hot eye at his son.

"What?" Chuol responds defensively. "You think this is my fault, too? Why don't you just get married instead?" asks Chuol, exhibiting his frustration.

"You know I had one. If only the sky hadn't taken her, this woman would not have hurt herself this badly." The men turn to each other.

"Waah! Can anyone lift me up?" the hurting mother sends out her voice again. The two hold her on either side of her arms and carry her to her room.

"What we need is for all of us to arrive on time. It does not look good when we arrive last. That never looks good." Mr. Tut starts hurrying up everybody as soon as the time hits seven in the morning. Gatwech and all his wives live in the city. That part, at least, lessens the distance for them. The celebration begins at noon. There are circles of elders, the gangs of young men, the groups of growing boys and the ever-serving women. Everybody sits according to their age and gender. Everyone who is a woman is serving except some of the older women: Mr. Tut's first woman, and Gatwech's first wife. Gatwech's mother is beyond thrilled after a long, unsteady race.

"Congratulations!" she cries. Gatwech beat the odds. He is the right person for the job, after all. His qualifications brings the sword to his hand. It is about the big things, it seems. Things like where you come from, how much you have, and of course, whether the sub-clan to which you belong is the next in line from which the leader would traditionally be selected—although that is not always as effective as the first two.

She is very happy; she starts singing the proper songs in Nuer. With one exception, though. The woman on her son's side is perhaps the wrong one. She always wished he would get a Shilluk one instead, some girl from the same tribe as her. The wife knows this internal conflict her mother in-law has, but she has narrowed her attention on the overwhelming number of wives her husband called to himself long ago. A moment like this would have meant so much to any of the wives, particularly wife number seven. She is among the most recent arrivals and Gatwech is getting lost between her two wings. She is by far the most beautiful one. Gatwech's first wife often wonders if the passing of years will fade this woman's beauty. She is rising to a scary position. She is becoming a Bok (The Goddess) and she seems to know what her beauty can do for her. But on days like this, she has to sit in the second row. These are the moments only available for first wives.

Sitting adjacent to her husband is one of the benefits of being the first wife a man marries. The elders, on the other hand, dominate the talks. It is one after the other. But that is about right, though. It is the elders who have attained the wisdom, after all. Sitting not far away from their son, Gatwech's parents all of a sudden have some negative thoughts run through their heads. Mr. Tut looks at his son and looks at this woman and finds something to stress about. The Shilluk girl tries to fix her mind on the talking, but it may as well mean she is finally okay with something else she has been refusing.

"This is your problem. You, Nueri. This is your stupid tradition. I'm not from Nuer. I don't want your stupid women controlling rules on me. I'm not your girl. I'm from the Shilluk tribe. The dying of my children had nothing to do with your brother," she had said. She spoke loudly and used some words considered insults, especially from the mouth of a female.

"Maybe in the Shilluk culture, it may not have anything to do with him but in Nuer culture, you have to be his to stop this death," the family would tell her. They wondered why she was disagreeing that much. Being Shilluk could be one of the reasons. Or perhaps she had not been informed about this when she and Mr. Tut met in Shumal. She had not been informed that she would be coming all the way from Shilluk land to be some dead person's wife, nor did Mr. Tut intend to bring some girl from afar to marry his deceased brother. But when the third, the fourth and the fifth child passed away in the same season, a traditional man made it clear to the family that the reason for the children's death was due to the fact that Mr. Tut's older brother was not happy, all the way from the grave.

Traditionally, men marry according to their birth number. Beginning with the first one, everyone awaits their turn. Death in this culture does not prevent one from marrying, either, and whether they are the next in line to marry doesn't change. Mr. Tut's brother's name was Lul (cry). He died at the age of twenty. Mr. Tut left for Shumal shortly after that.

According to the traditional man, all Lul wanted was to shift the ownership and socially title her his wife. He wanted to change the name of the children and put his as their last name. "You are still my wife. This doesn't change a thing," Mr. Tut said.

But no, it changed a thing. Perhaps two things, or even more. She could well be asked to live on her own as a result of this. But this, for Mr. Tut, came as the last resort, if she only knew it. He did something after returning from Shumal. He married a wife for his deceased brother, in refusal of giving up this Shilluk girl to his brother upon his return. However, the family had to let go of Lul's wife after two years. She was not working. Before she was finally let go, Mr. Tut secretly tried to delay her final release. But for how long? The brother wanted a family under his name, not a barren womb. And sadly, he, too, had to let go the strength of his hands as a result.

Through a series of conversations with the foreign elders, she learned that the wrath of the deceased would return to Mr. Tut. She lived through hurdles and trials. It appeared the change in her title also brought forth some physical changes, as she was often reminded by the other women, "You are not really his wife. You are Lul's." Mr. Tut lost his relationships. Even his love for the children changed. He treated them as his brother's children.

There was no comparison to the confusion she found herself in, however, as she had never been able to accept how it was all made possible. There were days she wished love was not blind. There were days when the only solution appeared to be to escape, but if she ran away, she wanted to escape with her two sons. And that was when she was placed under extra watch. It would not be a loss for her if she escaped to her foreign land with her boys in tow, but they would never let that happen. After all, all that the man from the grave wanted was children to guarantee that he was once a man on earth. Somehow through it all, she began to believe her suffering was due to the death of her husband whom she had never even laid eyes on.

She glances at Mr. Tut now and smiles. Her son is a commissioner now—What can she not do? Mr. Tut knows exactly what she has in mind. She finally wants to pull Lul's family out of Mr. Tut's so they can stand on their own—once Gatwech is on board, of course. But Mr. Tut has the opposite idea. He feels biologically attached to the children. Though she is looking at doing something now, Mr. Tut should really relax. Men don't take ideas from women and act on them. However much she wants this to happen, it will probably never come to fruition. After all, the dead are in the grave; the living make the changes.

Every speech praises the announced commissioner. At the end, his sons come forward. The beautiful celebration ends with him showing the number of men he has behind him. Everybody has always known him as the son of one of the wealthiest men in the area, but it is quite a point of pride that he now has male children of his own. People respect people with people behind them. People fear these people and hand over power to them.

Chuol and Gatwech's younger brother are among the young men in attendance. Their take at the end of the celebration? A man must have many males (children) should he consider a role in leadership. The outpouring of encouragement for the newly appointed leader is something else that these young men witness. To them the whole point of leadership is to prove that one is superior to other men. It is far from serving. It is far from giving. It is far from sympathy. If anything, you might be rewarded on failing promises on the very day you speak them to the community's blind eye and deaf ear.

Chuol and the rest could not be more thankful for being there. After the big man's boys are walked off from the centre of the stage, one elder who had a chance to speak earlier demands that he be given another chance to speak. This time, he keeps it short. He gives the big man a gift of a person, his daughter, with one caveat: She will remain with him for one more year and hopefully by this time next year, she will be ready. This gifting wraps up the event nicely. Gatwech now has his community's undivided support.

On the next morning, Chuol remains on the bed for several hours. His father becomes worried and knocks at his door. Chuol refuses to respond. A few minutes later, he emerges in his best clothes.

His father takes note of this sudden dressing up. "We have a journey?" asks the father sarcastically.

"Yes, I have a short journey," responds Chuol while pulling back the sleeves of his shirt. He then slips out of the compound.

On his way, he stops several times under the shade of a tree. He then asks himself whether this "seemingly abnormal notion" is finally slipping out of his heart today. He arrives, and on a clear, hot day, he walks straight to the shade of the beautiful tree he has known for years.

He stands tall with no fear of anyone who could potentially be angry at his ignorance. For it has been written on stone that a boyfriend is not a girl's daytime visitor.

He looks straight into the open compound that contains three individual rooms. And there, the two lovers' eyes meet.

Nyayang recognizes her boyfriend and immediately reacts in shock. *What is he doing here? What if someone notices his presence?* She tries to find a way to go to him or else he could be in danger. In a flash, she dashes to the beautiful tree.

"What is your problem?" asks Nyayang as she frequently glances over her shoulder.

"I'm here to talk to you about something extremely profound. Just bring some chairs we could sit on," Chuol replies softly.

"But we can't sit here during the day. My father and all my relatives are at home. You have to leave," Nyayang argues with her boyfriend.

"Why is everyone home?"

"Because they are going to my father's in-laws," she says tiredly.

"When are they leaving?" Chuol insists.

"Soon, and please leave if you are not trying to get us in trouble."

"Okay, okay, just know I'm coming back," he says as he walks backward, leaving the big, beautiful tree.

Meanwhile, in the room where Nyayang's father and all the relatives are, the "no solution" discussion is bearing down on these exhausted men. If they manage to leave for his in-laws' today, it will mark the third time they have this conversation with the in-laws.

"I have an idea," announces Nyayang's father's brother. "When we go today, here is what we may also say. Let us tell them that Nyayang is now mature and that she could get married at any time. Perhaps they will listen to us and give us their daughter," he says desperately.

On this idea, all the men agree except Mr. Jock, who seems to have not wanted to begin his marriage by deceiving his new in-laws. "I don't think that's a good idea," he says. "What if she is not going to be married? What if she is taken by those player boys? Because to be honest with you, I don't know what this girl thinks. I mean, this marriage has been going on since last year and she has known all along that a lack of cows has been the issue," he continues. There is some bizarreness in his way of talking lately. He has had many negative thoughts running through his mind since his in-laws asked for more cows in return.

One negative thing that has followed him since his youth is that society has known him as a nobody. He was the last and only child of his parents. There were five children who passed away before he was born. When he was born, his parents named him Jock (last)), which referred to the death that had taken their other children and to now say, this child will outlive and not die. His uncle, who turned out to be very productive, refused him his share of his daughters' cows since he didn't have a sister whose cows people could share. But although he was aware of this social labelling, he also believed that his social status would one day be washed away.

The way to become a somebody here mainly depends on whom a man marries. Ironically, the way for a nobody to become a somebody is through the woman he marries giving birth to lot of children for him. And then he marries more women, and from there, goes on to marry more. But most importantly, the more women he marries, the more children he has the opportunity to sire. That will erase this social stigma ten times faster. He has done what he could to shed this label, but it hasn't been without struggle. The girl he married was from a good-sized family. He was refused twice before he was officially accepted. Of course, only the girl and her mother knew about the two rejections from the father. They just kept pushing the father that he accept him before they lost hope and let him know about it. Luckily, the father changed his mind, but then charged him a bit more. The large sum of cows he paid led the two to naming their first child Nyayang.

"That's still okay, Jock. Whatever number we get from whoever she is going to end up with, we will promise your in-laws we will give them to them," one of the others says to Mr. Jock.

In the evening, the men prepare themselves to leave for Mr. Jock's in-laws. "They are leaving, Nyame, hurry up!" says Nyayang's mother to Nyayang. Nyayang just finished cooking. The men want to leave.

"How are you doing it? Is this how you are going to do it when you are married? The biggest portion of the food goes into the men's bowls. Here is how you do it," her mother says and demonstrates to Nyayang. All of the food in the cooking pot is emptied into one bowl. The men's bowl.

"What about us, Mama?" Nyayang asks.

"Never, never put a thing in your mouth till you know he is full."

Nyayang looks at her mother in disagreement. "Nyame, take the food to the men," says her mother. Nyayang takes the food. They eat it very quickly and leave.

Under the beautiful tree, Chuol coughs and claps his hands to notify his girl about his presence. On this great moonlit evening, Nyayang notices his presence and comes as though wind flows through her.

"I came here in the afternoon and I realize I made you very nervous," Chuol begins. "I came to tell you something I would rather discuss with you during daylight, but now is just fine."

Nyayang drops her jaw and suddenly feels a chill in her soul.

"I come to tell you about a decision I made. I come to tell you I'm marrying you," he says proudly, with the utmost confidence.

"Me?" Nyayang asks after a good two minutes of silence. She instantly feels a mixture of confusion and excitement. "Is this a joke?" she asks.

"No. If I usually joke about things with you, then this is not one of those times," Chuol reassures Nyayang who seems to be trying to hide her excitement.

"But how do I know this is not all a joke? Where are your brothers and friends?" Nyayang keeps digging for more reassurances.

"Really! I'm not someone new, Nyayang. I don't need anyone to come with so I can tell you this," Chuol exclaims.

"Okay then, if this is not all a joke, let me hear it from your brothers and friends, just like the way marriages usually get started," says Nyayang with part of her heart believing him now.

"Is this because you really don't believe me?" Chuol asks and gives the girl a long glance. Nyayang only stares at her love across from her. "Well then, if that is so, I will give you a week, then I will be back with the confirmers." He giggles as he says this. Nyayang smiles while looking at him. Chuol leaves with no answer to his question, but in his dear heart, doubt is absent.

Two days after the conversation, Nyayang is called in ambiguously by her father. "I just want to let you know my in-laws refused my offer again. They are asking for thirty-five cows and they want them in full. But we only have twenty-three," he says and turns his head away from his daughter.

"Sorry, Baba," Nyayang says in a fearful voice. She goes quiet but remains standing there.

"You can go now," says her father.

Prior to Chuol's return, Nyayang managed to inform all her closest friends of the news.

"Aren't you even a little ashamed of yourself? Another girl your age is being married and here you are, carrying a child whose father has impregnated you and proudly refused you!" the mother of a neighbour girl starts railing at her daughter.

Impregnation is one sin whose scar never leaves the skin, especially when other girls are being married legally in the same area. "I'm sorry, Nyayang, I cannot go with you," the neighbour girl says to Nyayang. Nyayang goes to visit others whose parents still hold on to the hope that their daughters have not been impregnated yet.

In the early morning on the appointed date, Nyayang comes outside to do her morning duties. And before her eyes is a home full of black crows: Some sit in the middle of the compound, some sit on the fence, others sit in the backyard.

Nyayang, upon seeing them, is stunned. She tries to chase them away. "Shoo, shoo, go away!" she says.

Her mother hears her. "What are all these doing here?" she asks as she rushes to help.

"I don't know. And they won't leave," says Nyayang. The daughter and the mother go on chasing them, but the evil black birds just turn around and come to sit on the opposite end.

Then the father hears the noise. He comes out of his dwelling; however, when he sees what is going on, he stands still and appears happy. "Can you help?" his wife yells at him.

"Help for what? Just leave them. They will leave on their own," he exclaims with no sign of worry.

He tries to go back to his room. He sees some boys, ages ten to fifteen, roaming loudly outside of his compound. He feels uneasy about them passing his home while making so much noise. He comes out and he sees some of them have come past the gate. While others are simply running back and forth, just being boys around the old man's property, these particular boys are carrying garden tools. Some have pruners, others carry axes and chainsaws. They are coming from a football field which they have been working on to make it more even and smooth. As they return to their homes, they seem to be refusing to keep the tools to themselves and are insisting on cutting other things around them.

One boy goes to stand under the beautiful tree and starts banging on it with an axe. Mr. Jock sees him. "Hey, what are you doing?" he says while running toward the boys. They start running in different directions. Mr. Jock runs toward the boy who tried to wound the beautiful tree. Mr. Jock follows him, but when he realizes he has been outrun, he passes by the tree to see if any harm has been done. He looks around. He checks the rope that the same boys use to climb the tree. The tree seems to be fine.

"Thank you," he says. It wasn't going to be an easy fix had anything been done to it. It takes him and a few others some time to look for the rope, and then they retwist it properly and tighten it so that they can continue to climb up and enjoy the tree's fruits. Mr. Jock then proceeds to the boy's compound and asks to speak to him upon his arrival. The father of the little boy thinks the boy has done Mr. Jock wrong. He gives him to him. Mr. Jock corners the young boy and gives him a few slaps and then takes off. He comes back and sees his daughter and her mother still fighting their fight. He bypasses them and enters into his dwelling.

About half an hour later, Nyayang and her mother have still not successfully chased away any of the crows. But all of a sudden, the birds start flying at once, all of them. Nyayang and her mother follow them, hoping they will go far away. However, the birds land on the vast beautiful tree between the two parents' rooms.

"Okay, okay, now it is much better. We can now go back," says Nyayang's mother. The two return to the compound.

At noon, the girls start coming one by one. They begin to prepare themselves, looking at each other's dresses, making sure they look their best before the men in the girls' room.

Meanwhile, Nyayang's mother is working outdoors. Suddenly, she realizes that under the big, beautiful tree there are about five fine men. She rushes to the girls' room and whispers what she saw at the door. "I believe you have some visitors."

"Uh, they are here already?" The girls rush up. At the door, one of the girls asks Nyayang, "Are you sure you don't know why Chuol is here in the daylight?"

"No!" she denies. "Let's go and find out," she says and pushes the girls out of the room.

Under the beautiful tree, the girls happily welcome the men and sit opposite them. "How is everybody?" The young people begin talking about topics irrelevant to the visitation. Some are already discussing their future relationships by now.

Quickly, the leader from the men's side realizes the arbitrary talk has almost eaten up all of the scheduled time. "Okay, sisters. The earth will soon go dark and we have not shared with you why we are here," he says.

"We all have become close friends because of Nyayang and Chuol's relationship. This relationship is unique and special to our dear friend, Chuol. And I'm sure it is the same for our sister, Nyayang. Today, we have come to tell you this boyfriend and girlfriend thing is breaking down into a marriage. Yes, we chose Nyayang for Chuol among all other girls. And like you may have already known, we are doing it the old way because we wanted to do it the old way," he says and returns to his seat.

The girls instantly feel shock, and finding what to say immediately becomes a thing.

"Well, we are glad this relationship is turning into something as beautiful as this. However, we have nothing to tell you now. We'd rather have you come back some other time. Then, we will be able to tell you what we think of the request," explains the leader from the girl's side.

"And how much time would you like to have?" asks the leader from the men's side.

"Two weeks is good."

"And the date?"

"Oh, take the sixteenth of May." As soon as the date is decided, the men say that they will leave.

According to tradition, when a man comes forward for marriage, a girl doesn't accept him without the official approval of her parents. So, the next day, the same girls gather again and discuss how they will present the news to Nyayang's father.

"We will say he has come for marriage, and if he asks who, we will tell him exactly who Chuol is," suggests one of the girls.

"I'm very nervous. This is terrifying," says Nyayang frantically.

"Why?"

"Because if we tell him who Chuol is, he may think Chuol and I are covering something up," says Nyayang.

"Don't believe that. This is extraordinarily beautiful." The girls try to encourage her. "Let's go."

The leader leads the girls to Nyayang's father and explains in detail who they are presenting. And to their surprise, they don't get the response that Nyayang anticipated they would.

"When are they coming back?" asks Mr. Jock.

"On the sixteenth of May," the girls reply.

"I know the family. He is from a good family," adds the father. Soon enough, the girls leave.

Left alone, Mr. Jock sits against the wall. And in the blink of an eye, he comes to the realization that dreams really do come true. And that this dream of his could be a gift at any given moment now. Unlike when he tried with a friend's wife, he finally can further himself with someone he married now.

The thought of this brings joy to his almost broken heart. Without knowing how he got there, he finds himself outside of his dwelling. He then remembers what he went outside for. He grabs some garden tools and goes on cutting the overgrown grass in the compound.

Looking from a distance and noticing the help he is freely offering, Nyayang's mother finds her eyes doubting what is before them. "It sure looks as though our sins have been forgiven, but when did it happen?" she asks herself.

Although Mr. Jock notices his sudden behaviour surprises his wife, he goes even further, calling the same woman who failed to give him a son, "Maan-Nyayang, gari, I want water. Maan-Nyayang, gari, I want to take a shower now."

Mr. Jock, as his wife puts it, may have been secretly visited by angels today.

CHAPTER TWO

On the appointed date, the men return. The girls accept the request and the first in a series of steps in the ritual of marriage is complete.

Before this gathering dissolves, the leaders from both sides arrange another date and time. At this time, the men return to hear another face-to-face, official acceptance from the fathers of Nyayang. Being accepted, even by the girls alone, gives these men an official name. Tonight, they are no longer just men, they are Cou-nyade (sons-in-law).

But as profound as this second acceptance from the fathers is, it traditionally starts with a sleepover. Traditionally, Cou-nyade come the night before they meet the fathers; however, with one obstacle in the way: they don't get to see the fathers till they pay their way in. The girls ask for money or anything they can later on divide among themselves before they let them go to the fathers. The Cuo-nyade try to negotiate on the amount requested. As there were leaders on the previous conversations, there are three totally different leaders to negotiate this exchange, namely, The Deaf and The Crow from the girls' side and a leader from the men side. During the negotiation, The Deaf is to remain silent until they get what they asked for. The Crow, on the other hand, leads the entire conversation along with the lead from the men's side. Other people remain relatively silent but can jump in any time they feel the need to talk. The likelihood of getting what the girls ask for exclusively rests on the shoulders of The Deaf and The Crow. But mostly The Deaf. The Deaf's silence is crucial for the amount asked. As The Crow negotiates with the leader from the men's side, the job of the remaining men is to cause The Deaf to laugh, get angry or just smile. The moment she can't retain her deafness, the amount asked becomes zero. But the men have already been accepted. They will proceed to the fathers regardless. And so, she tries her very best. The amount asked at the start was two-thousand South Sudanese pounds. As the night progresses, the negotiation leads to a reduction in the amount asked. Around five in the morning, the girls walk out with £1,500 pounds as the final amount.

The Cou-yade meet the fathers during the hours that follow. They discuss the possibility of blood relations between the two families. And from the look of it, the two are pretty distant. At the gathering, the ecstatic young men demonstrate how quick they want the process to be. And who could stand in the way at a time like this? These optimistic fathers hold nothing back but show willingness to officiate the next event date.

But there is another proposal the Cou-nyade die to explain to the fathers. In a typical marriage ritual, there are three official events that take place in the girl's parents' home and one last ceremony that takes place in the man's parents' home.

"This year, the season delays its usual activities, yet it doesn't mean it couldn't start any moment now," the lead begins. "So, our request is whether it's possible the two events could be combined into one big ceremony," he says and elaborates on the why.

The fathers give it a minute. "Let's go outside for a moment," says the leader from the fathers' side. When they return, the leader graciously lowers it into the gentlemen's ears and says, "We will let you go ahead with both ceremonies being combined. However, we ask that we have a month for the preparation."

Before they leave, the leader from the men's side calls the leader from the girls'. "It looks we are meeting again soon." He stares at her sideways. "Here." He hands her a golden Citizen watch for their wife-to-be, Nyayang, as a sign that shows she is now taken.

"Thank you," says the leader from the girls' side.

After they leave, Mr. Jock calls the family members together and distributes the inevitable responsibilities. To inform everyone, the mother goes door-to-door performing a traditional dance notification. Nyayang goes to notify the girls her age and the young mothers.

On Chuol's side, this door-to-door dance notification goes on as well, except they don't prepare anything since the ceremony takes place in Nyayang's parents' home. While the ceremony is in days, there are some rumours circulating that the two could be related. But the speculation never makes its way to Nyayang's family due to the fact that everything is condensed, and the ceremony is happening so soon. The hope remains that they will shine a light on this potential problem before further moves are made on the day of the ceremony.

Prior to the day of the ceremony, all the relatives from the girl's side make their way home with the wine and food items prepared for the people.

On the evening before the ceremony, Chuol arrives along with the fathers, brothers, his mother and all his sub-clan men, the Cou-nyade.

The morning of the ceremony arrives. To begin the detailed, ritualistic, long marriage discussion, both sides go into the prepared room where the fathers will specify the number of cows they are looking for in return. The in-laws go first with their request, carrying sticks in their hand.

In the circle designed with this cultural practice in mind, the room is divided into two sides, and on each side, the males sit in the first row. In the second row are the two mothers along with other close female relatives and some distant relatives. There, the traditional discussion begins with greetings among the elders.

Moving on, the talk splits into two important parts. Before the number is revealed, the chance that the two may be related by blood comes up.

As the empirical topic arrives on the tips of their tongues, the elders considered the wisest and more knowledgeable specifically zoom their crystal conscience into four roads.

On the first road, they look at Mr. Malual and the generations before him. They thoroughly investigate all the individuals who are the part of the main stream, as well as their connection to the outside.

This, they also do to Mr. Jock, and they look at every dimensional aspect that made up the generations before him. Fortunately, the elders find no blood. Next, they turn their focus on the generations before the two mothers. And again, they look at everyone whose blood has made these two. This time the elders think they find a bloodline, which strangely is not between the two mothers but between Mr. Malual and Nyayang's mother.

Immediately, the counting begins as they are urgently eager to track down the risk that could possibly befall the couple-to-be. Looking at both sides that have unequal numbers, the wise elders close their unhealthy eyes tight and dive curiously into each root, handling each bloodline with great care. Then they compile the number of the people from each side.

They begin peeling each branch off the main stream and examining it separately. What they find immediately chills the entire circle. And in just the blink of an eye, it freezes Chuol's thinking.

"What?" cries Chuol after many minutes in a long dark silence. "NO . . ." he says doubtfully. "It's not that close. It cannot be." Chuol continually questions the result. "Let's look at them again," he says, as though it's not their lives they are afraid to lose. "Let's. Let's look at each line again please." He stutters the words for he fears to lose this girl he likes so much.

"On my side, right? It's me, my father, his father, his grandfather. The great-grandfather, great-great-grandfather and the great-great-great-grandfather. This is long! How could this be even a big deal?" he asks as if he has never heard of the bad endings of these bloodline stories.

While he is still talking, the gathering tightens its mouth. Chuol becomes aware of this ghostly prolonged silence but does not know the reason for it. He leans back quickly and blends himself into the silence.

This bloodline issue is at the top of all deadly killers. And it owns the top position for a very ugly reason. You marry someone you are related to in blood, and either she dies or you die—instantly—as soon as you start living together. Having known a prior relationship exists between the two, the gathering can't stop thinking the two could potentially be pregnant.

"This conclusion is not right," repeats Chuol. "I want us to look at Nyayang's side."

"Go ahead," someone tells him.

"So, if I heard everything correctly, it's her, her mother, the mother of her mom. The mother of her grandmother, her great-great-grandmother and her great-great-great-grandmother. And it's her great-great-great-grandmother whose father was my father's great-great-great-grandfather's cousin, right?"

As he lowers his mouth, the knowledgeable elders intensely lean their eyes closer. After a short silence, each elder begins to look at, not who, or how many people there are on each line, but the sex of each person from each bloodline.

Thinking and rethinking, and this time doing so rationally, the elders realize one side of the blood line is harmlessly filled up with females' blood, which has been known to kill no one!

Instantly, the profound realization enlightens what was a dark, gloomy room a second ago. And now that it's declared there is no blood relation between the two families, the gathering moves on to the next portion of the discussion.

Traditionally, when no blood relation is declared, the fathers are asked to speak their minds. After the question, the fathers are up for forty-five cows. "We don't have that number," says the lead from Chuol's side. The fathers of the girl go outside. They return and say, "Our final number is forty. We will have it or we are going nowhere," they declare. Chuol's father glances at them a moment and quickly remembers the demand he had on his son a month ago. He winks at the lead with his eye. "We will give you that number," says the lead. He then presents the traditional sticks tied together with a white string, representing the number of cows available.

There are some cows which will have to come when they are available. These are the ones mostly contributed by Chuol's immediate family members. His uncle promised about three cows going toward his sister's son marriage. His best friend overzealously releases two cows. Upon hearing the voice of the lead, the non-vocal mothers boast in pride. The two stand up with their voices in the air, singing. Those outside hear the women singing, which usually indicates the marriage is proceeding. If the marriage was not proceeding, it would have been Chuol himself singing. The mothers and the elders proceed outside where everyone has started dancing upon hearing the voices.

The ceremonial dance continues into the evening. The elder in-laws leave but the Cou-nyande remain.

On the fourth day, the Cou-nyade sit down the fathers and discuss the possibility of performing the last ceremony of the marriage. And so, because the last ceremony takes place in the man's parents' home, the Cou-nyade want to have a yes to the question so the preparations can start.

"We don't have anything against your plan. Go ahead," say the fathers. Right after the Cou-nyade leave, Mr. Jock calls on everyone who is still around and announces that the day on which the Cou-nyade will return to take Noong (escorts) is in days. (Noong is a name given to the girls and young mothers who will go with the bride to her in-laws' home for the concluding part of the marriage ceremony.)

The Cou-nyade return in the evening on the appointed date to take Noong to Chuol's parents' home. Wine and food light up the mood as they wait for the time. Depending on how far the two families live, Noong are not taken till it is known they will be at the groom's parents' home roughly by five a.m. Around three, the Cou-nyade leave with the Noong. The distance is only about one hour and forty-five minutes by foot from Nyayang's parents' home to Chuol's parents' home. But Noong do become people of a different nature the moment they leave their regional territory. They begin to talk in a relatively insulting nature. Dancing becomes the way in which they move around each other. Some moves have rhythms to them, others don't. Singing odd songs whose lyrics consist of private parts becomes the next move. This behaviour extends the actual time of the journey to a two-hour period.

The last part of the marriage has an important meaning. This is because it is the last recognized celebration before the couple can officially be intimate. And so, this sexual behaviour shown by the Noong is relevant to this concluding piece of the marriage ceremony. The talking, the singing and the dancing are official preparations for the couple's imminent intimacy.

At Chuol's parents' home, Nyayang and her girlfriend go to a close-by home called the hiding place. But the Noong remain at home where singing songs and extreme insulting continues.

This improper behaviour goes on till evening arrives. At this time, the elders ask the Noong to sit and say the last prayer of the marriage. Nyayang and her girlfriend come from their hiding place.

At the sitting conducted by an elder from Chuol's side, people from both sides are given the chance to speak for the purposes of encouraging the newly couple to be pronounced man and wife. Once all the important advice has been spoken, one elder is given the floor to wrap everything up.

The man gets up. He clears his throat and says, "Marriage is a gift from God. A good wife is also a gift from Him." While the words are still sprouting out of his mouth, a woman walks toward the quiet crowd with a wrapped piece of cloth, carrying it with both of her hands like a ringbearer. She is one of Chuol's older brother's wives. She comes and stops beside the talking elder. The two periodically exchange eye contact and give the gift of a smile to each other. She opens the plastic bag. She pulls out the cloth and unfolds it.

It's a Yat in a purple *caput mortuum* colour: a half-slip skirt that goes beneath a woman's clothes in this culture. She walks toward Nyayang. She stops about two meters away from her. Slowly, she looks back at the elder, waiting for him to say something.

"Go ahead. Put it on," he says. The woman spreads it from its bottom. It has an elastic band at its top. Nyayang submissively tilts her head toward for the woman so she can put it on over her head and she pulls it all the way to her waist. There is a piece of cloth that hides her body from the crowd as the woman pulls down the Yat.

"Nyajock," the elder says, which translates as "daughter of Jock." "You are now a wife of this family. You have now permanently become Chuol's wife. And we cannot wait to see all the goodness that comes with you. And as for us, as far as God hears, the first fruit of your womb will be a boy in this family, and he shall be followed by his brother before any girl comes along," he says at last and walks back to his seat.

And as for the purpose of the Yat? Well, its job is to officially transition a girl to being a wife. It is like turning twenty-one. One can never go back to being twenty, no matter how much one may want to return. Unlike time, whose work can be seen on the surface, the Yat has an interesting design. It transcends the expected maturity onto the one who wears it, surpassingly even time. It is placed right on her waist so she must behave maturely, no matter how much she still feels like she is fifteen.

Yat separates the girl from the woman, and the two must no longer drink from the same well. The places a girl would go for her business are no longer visited by a woman with a Yat beneath her clothes. It has a very sentimental meaning. A psychological one, even. Once it passes by her waist—and again takes out only for the one known reason, divorce—she is no longer a hundred percent her worth. Instead, her value shrinks to a fraction of that percentage, even if the period she has been wearing it is as short as a minute. Now that it finally reaches her waist, it should never be removed for any reason. She can wash it, but only if she already has another one on. She has to have it on when her husband makes a child for himself. It's against this man's law for her to be doing anything without having it on. She can't cook a meal which her husband will eat without it. But that is not all. She must have it on when bringing that meal before him.

In about five minutes, the prayer is over. The Noong are freed again. The wife and her girlfriend return to the house they are kept in, leaving the awkwardness of the Noong at its peak.

By the next morning when a fat bull is killed for them, some of the Noong are using only their hands as a means to communicate, for they lost their voices. Yet the vigorous Noong behaviour continues for a week and half.

At the end of the established time, Nyayang returns home along with everybody.

"Well done, Chuol," Chuol's father extols him. "Now you have become a man," he says and moves his head. "With one thing remaining, of course."

"I know," says Chuol. "She has to come home."

His father nods his head. "But we are not going to do that now. That can wait until after the harvest."

CHAPTER THREE

The harvest is over. The in-laws bring the remaining cows which were mentioned but not given and that is when they ask for their wife, as well.

Mr. Jock calls on the blood relatives that he owes cows. This distribution took time for he refused to give anybody anything when the first promised number of cows made it in. He intended to finish his marriage ceremony instead. But as the tradition requires, the girl's extended family members have rights to be given cows, just as they have shares of cows to contribute when a man is getting married. To his brother, Mr. Jock gives five cows. He gives two to his brother-in-law, and to his sister and the sister of his wife, he gives a cow each.

Although Nyayang should have left home by now, her father's marriage is finally on the brink of its completion. And so, until it is completed, Nyayang has to remain at home.

At the end of this happy marriage, the family, including the relatives, is up for another exciting preparation.

Each and every relative gives Nyayang something new, and other cultural necessities that the family thinks would be delightfully impressive upon her arrival are prepared, as well.

Prior to the end of the month, the in-laws are informed about the date on which their wife shall be given to them.

To the in-laws, this approaching time is very important. So, across the land, Chuol's siblings gather together to welcome their wife home once and for all.

Every day, the appointed day approaches, and with so much to do, Nyayang's mother doesn't get a chance to chat with her daughter until the night before she is leaving.

Since the last official step is to give the girl to her husband, and since there are items to be taken along with the bride, the only people who will officially escort her are some girls of her age and some young mothers. Their age range is similar to that of the Noong, except not everyone is going this time.

After everyone who is escorting her has gone to bed, her mother inclines to have a silent moment with her child in her room.

Nyayang gently sits beside her mother. Her mother peacefully and gently massages her head as she used to do when she was a little girl.

"My blessings," says her mother. The two smile while exchanging eye contact. "Nyayang, I'm very proud of you. I know you have listened to my voice. However, there is something I want you to know.

"Where you are going is where every girl goes to at this age in life. Or, I should say, when she is given in marriage. Marriage is a place of expectations and less of giving. It is a place of many tests on many different subjects and not many lessons on these subjects beforehand. It is a place in which no mistakes are expected. A place of little human interaction. It takes me by surprise that this is all the life we live. Because, when we started living it, we lived a life of an alliance in a foreign land. Where, when foreigners lived among people who were poor at heart, the only thing considered wrong was when no one mistreated the alliance." She says this last part very gravely.

"I need you to be aware, and I need you to be ready." She holds her hands together. "You know, the life you are about to experience is like that of a soldier in a training camp. Where rigid orders are followed. Where when a fellow falls down as a result of the fact that he has been standing for hours on a hot, sunny day, it's because he is weak and never because of the severity of the rulers.

"If this conceptual misreading lingers, the fellow's colleagues consider dismissing him. For, to them, they see how he has failed them and not merely how those in charge asked more and more of him."

"Sometimes I see the reason a fellow may get kicked out of training camp," continues the mother. "Usually, soldiers train themselves to prepare for what may befall them later on. And if those in charge don't get the reassurance they need now, they probably won't believe the fellow would have their backs later on. However, what still stuns me is why is this our only life.

"At some point, what seems to have drowned other people, to you will lose its taste. Instead, you will become the one who was confusingly mistaken for goodness.

"When you refuse to be you anymore because a rat got stuck inside a water jug with the lid on, a consideration of another type will be considered.

"Sometimes you will work without eating. And before you start thinking about your empty belly, you will be expected to work more.

"When you give your empty stomach something, a voice will be whispering that you are taking too much and that you are wasting it. However, when you adjust how much you are taking, they will say you are eating in dark places.

"They will pay more heed to how you present yourself. You will not say anything using your outside voice or your name will be 'Quarreler.' Anything you believe needs your participation orally will be examined in great detail, and you will be seen as insulting the family members, or negatively questioning the upbringing of the family.

"At anytime you try to point out something seemingly wrong, you will be told you have brought your mother's head with you and that you are trying to control the man. Because refutation is their number one enemy.

"And always remember, nothing gets learned as a result of your meekness, your charming personal behaviour. If you are a pleasant, charming, lively, delightful individual who has a heart that doesn't question anything and forgives before one has to ask for forgiveness, well, that means life is still at home. Then they won't have to do anything in order to mold you into what they want.

"If you think you can be a sensitive, sassy, ridiculous wife, well, in that case, you may have to take your bad attitude and live elsewhere.

"And lastly, if at any moment they think they have had enough of you, before our eyes you will be brought back. Either explicitly, or they may want you to plan your own departure.

"But however severe your living conditions will be, I have a lot of confidence in you. For the last sixteen years I have known you, you have been a hardworking person. I know you will bear the heaviness of whatever will drop on your table. Regardless of what happens, show them your respect. All of them.

"Most importantly, distance yourself from feelings of anger. When you know what you do or say has no place of rest, it's easy to slip into the water-pudding. Have peace. And this is not about peace you should have with people, but within yourself. For when you have peace within you, you remain with strength even though you have none to draw from," she says emphatically at last.

Nyayang, having listened to her mother for almost an hour now, smiles back at her mother. But she is having trouble swallowing the reality of all of what her mother has said.

Her heart starts to sink into the flood of fear, and worry begins to rain into her troubled soul. "I'm going to be okay. Just like you were and still are," says Nyayang after her confidence overrides the shaking.

"Yes, you will," confirms her mother.

From there, she goes back to her room where all the girls are sleeping. She lights a candle and lies flat on her back. She then stares up at the invisible stars in heaven.

"Nyayang," says one of the elder cousins in the room. She gets up from her sleeping position. Nyayang gets up, too, and sits down facing the woman. "Home is something big," she says suddenly. "Very soon you will know about it. But I say, home is you as a woman. There are all kinds of things coming your way, but the moment you say 'This is my home,' you begin to conquer your way in and be home for that man.

"Here is how you win. Find what he likes first and do that to the best of your ability. There are many things, but the two main things that I know serve him are his bowl and that bed," she says, extending her hand to the left of her as if she sees the bed now.

Nyayang smiles and asks, "What else?"

"Love his family. Some of us believe we are there to be part of the family. No, we are not. You have been called to serve a purpose. You are there to create a sense of a home that then becomes part of his family. And what creates a home depends on each man and at what point.

"Me, for example, I do not have a child with my husband, but I'm a home to him because of other things, and his acceptance of my doings creates a sense of a home for me," she says.

"Shouldn't we say because he has other wives who are bearing children for him, that a woman like you should serve the other ones, since the top ability for creating a home has been made possible by other women? I mean, when did not having children become a requirement?" Nyayang says, and it seems as though she has accidentally revealed one of her concerns.

The woman is silent and says nothing for a moment. Then she says, "No woman wants to come out again."

"It is the cause of many deaths," Nyayang says.

"Finally, you are going to your husband."

"Finally, I'm reaching out for a reason of my own," Nyayang says. They both smile and go back to their original positions. Until the day overcomes the night, Nyayang's eyelids remain open.

The next morning, there is a sentimental, energetic happiness roaming in everyone's heart. And although she is the source of their jubilation, Nyayang excludes herself. She spends the entire morning thinking pensively about her inevitable life.

With so many hands in the house, everything that should have supposedly taken hours is done in minutes. This quick handling of things in the house becomes resentfully worrisome in Nyayang's unstable and unripe heart.

Not due to any particular issue, but over the deal the girls made the day before this big day. Yesterday, the girls agreed the quicker things got done, the sooner they would leave. So, how fast one could get things done, would bring them that much closer to leaving.

The day goes by like a cold blowing wind on a hot summer day, leaving Nyayang to wonder if the day even ever really existed in the first place.

However, what else is there left to do? This is it!

"Is everybody ready?" shouts her mother as the sun reaches his place.

"Almost," everyone replies.

Nyayang, meanwhile, is putting on her most ornate, most stylish dress—the kind you would want your in-laws to see you in the first time you step on their soil.

But she is moving at the pace she prefers inside the room. "Are you nervous?" asks her little sister behind her.

"Yeah, a little," Nyayang admits.

"I will come and take care of the child when you give birth."

"Sure, but I'm not pregnant yet."

"Yeah, I know. But I know you will be. Just like Mama Nyalock." Mama Nyalok is one of the girls in the area who recently was impregnated and rejected by her boyfriend. After the birth of her child, her parents named the child Nyalok, meaning refused.

"Stop it," says Nyayang. The two start laughing.

"Ready, Nyayang?" calls her mother from outside.

"Yes," she says. The two emerge.

"Call your father, we need to pray," her mother urges her little sister.

When their father comes, they hold hands together. Then their father leads them in prayer. In his prayer, he is grateful about the weather and then he blesses their journey. "Amen, amen," he ends the prayer.

Their mother opens her eyes, and she realizes something in the depth of her chest is troubling her. She prayed about it, just now, like she has been praying about it since after the last scheduled event of the marriage ceremony. Although she knows it's weird to bring it to the table and pray about it at the start of the marriage, she knows its absence can bring about poor and ugly judgment between the only two people on earth.

"You can go now," says the father.

"Go in peace," says the mother.

The girls leave with Nyayang. Nyayang's mother watches her daughter getting smaller and smaller until she can't see her anymore, and then she returns to the compound.

At Chuol's parents' home where most of the siblings are gathered, Nyayang and her sisters are received to humble adulation.

"Oh, wow!" Some of the women who were clearly not at the last marriage ceremony event which took place in this very place, express their awe at their impressions of the big, beautiful place Mr. Malual has built for his children. Like many compounds here, it's divided into three sections. The men's area, the women's area and the children's area. There are also the men's rooms and the women's rooms, the boys' rooms and the girls' rooms, all in this huge compound. A pleasant place has been neatly prepared for them. Upon their arrival, they are rushed into the room and then "the home females" follow for chats.

On the next day, this in-and-out continues. But today, it leaves no neighbours or brothers out. In fact, it includes the husband himself. The neighbours come by, and when they are done, they leave. The brothers, along with the husband, come as well. Nyayang, like she did with the neighbours, tries to avoid eye contact with everybody. But most noticeably with the husband.

This evasion has nothing to do with fear but is a great manifestation of respect. Another week goes by and the family considers showing their wife around, prior to her sisters leaving.

Traditionally, this showing around is a cerebration in itself. Mr. Malual's entire family shows up. Like many things in this in-law atmosphere, serving food has its own traditions, too. The guests are served according to their ages; Gatwech and his group are served separately, and the husband is served separately as well as Mr. Malual. Nyayang and Rebecca get to eat after everyone else has eaten; Chuol's mother waits on the leftover food from the big man's bowl. When Mr. Malual eats his meals, regardless of what time it is during the day, he intentionally leaves some food at the bottom of the bowl for his wife.

Whatever their meal is—it could be Walwal (a traditional food made with corn or sorghum flour) with milk, or Kob (couscous-like and made with corn or sorghum flour by hand) with dry fish in a slimy okra-powdered stew—the leftovers are what Mr. Malual's wife would have for her lunch or dinner that day. It has always been like this since she was married, except when her marriage was at the phase Nyayang's is at now. When new, there is a stage for getting to know people. This means eating out of people's sight, eating little and, like the big man, leaving something at the bottom of the bowl though nobody looks forward to it, so nobody is alarmed about your future eating. But that stage has passed for her. When there was more then one wife in the compound during Chuol's mother's glory days, their lunches and dinners would come from all kinds of leftovers. Most of them would rely on their children's leftovers after feeding them. Or the main bowl of the family.

Chuol's mother thinks that Nyayang should enjoy this stage since it only lasts for a short time. That is the eating way. There is very little talking between the men and the women, and every man has his own style when talking.

On this day, Nyayang takes over the preparation of everything. At the end of the celebration, she wipes the sweat off and it is just the beginning of her long duties.

Prior to her sisters' leaving, Nyayang begins to adjust to her ritualistic schedule. Before everyone lays eyes on the new day, she has already cooked the meal. She milks the cows before they are released into the nearby rangelands to graze during the day. While everyone is bending hands, she is on her way to the river to bring water. The greatest of all? Ah-hem! That is when Chuol wants to talk to her. He just does "ah-hem" in his throat.

As time goes by, she becomes the best at paying attention. With her mother's voice never too far away, she begins to appreciate how well being friendly plays in her favour. She juggles many things and does them in a short period of time, most of the time. The food. The water for showers. All on time! She leaves the compound only if she has a reason. If any woman wants to talk to her, she comes to Nyayang instead. If there are quarrels among groups of women and she happens to be there, she withdraws from the crowd quickly and comes home. That was one of the rules on the bucket list that Chuol shared with her the moment she was welcomed into his family.

One time she found herself unintentionally lingering around a small crowd of women who were watching a pregnant woman who was being shown the way by her brother-in-law. The woman had made everyone wait for their dinner. The brother in-law was furious and beat her until she bled. Nyayang did not mean to watch. She was just passing by. Some women laughed as they watched. Some said, "You deserve it. A woman is married so people can eat. Unless a man doesn't bring any food home, your job is to cook." They weren't really talking to her but among themselves as they watched her get beaten.

Nyayang hadn't run into not being able to cook food for her in-laws yet, and so in her attempt to show that she wasn't like that, she smiled just a bit.

A woman had tapped her on the shoulder. Nyayang turned around and they both locked eyes. "I know we are taught to laugh along when it's not one of us. But the difference here is that there will be a time where each one of us will find herself in the same shoes." Nyayang suddenly felt embarrassed. She left the scene quickly and went home.

At this point, she knows exactly what things need to get done and when she needs to do them. She knows what time the children take a shower, that her father-in-law is always the first to take a shower, and that Chuol is no longer going to the river to bathe.

Nyayang has received some warnings from a few family members telling her who to avoid. Chuol has talked to her about how he wants her to be. There is nothing desirable about a woman who gets easily wound up in a crowd of women, simply for being part of the same community. When Chuol's mother comes to her and speaks these scenarios in her ears again, it gets Nyayang thinking.

"These are bad women. They have no respect for their husbands. Whose wife could leave her house, come in between compounds and brazenly open her mouth and say things that only an elephant could swallow? These women are misleaders. They don't like seeing young women like you staying in their marriages, because in many ways, they are not really in one. They are just misleaders." She says this to her daughter-in-law in a way that it seems as if she is not really talking to her, but the fact that there is not any other wife in the compound narrows it down to Nyayang that she is speaking to her.

Nyayang looks around. She doesn't know anything about what she is talking about. Women get into fights all the time. Sometimes it is about their children, other times it is about their husbands. There is no connection, Nyayang thinks. But she is not supposed to say anything and so she says nothing. But the mother-in-law knows what she is talking about, she just came back from separating some women. She knows what she is talking about. But, even if she knows, is there any reason to talk about these lost souls who have often had the misfortune of being on the wrong side of other women? That is all they know. Blaming each other.

Nyayang walks back to her things. She knows if it had been her mother, she would have spoken up and said something contrary. She could not say anything to her mother-in-law, but she knows these are not bad women. They are women whom the society has labelled bad because they find themselves silently advocating for unpopular causes. They are the ones who still believe that at the age of thirty, they should not be asked to leave their husbands simply because their firstborns who were married at the age of seven are now mothers to their own firstborns at the age of fourteen, and it is presumed that because they are grandmothers, they don't need a man, or simply because he has other young women, they fall to the bottom of the pecking order.

But instead of agreeing that this is a problem, the underlying issue gets abandoned and they turn on themselves. Of course they talk, because if it were not for these spaces between compounds, where would they go and blame themselves? Who would they talk to in order to have their thinking reoriented? Women like Chuol's mother can't see beyond their own happy life. She has been married to the wealthiest man in the area, got there when he was late in age—what does she know about having a bad husband?

But Nyayang realizes the issue is not really hers. *Just worry about your own situation; don't worry about others,* she thinks to herself as if her problems have already started.

"Who are you? If you are the decent person you think you are, why did your husband marry another young girl while you are still this young?" one of the women says to another, making the reason men marry many wives the women's fault somehow.

"Oh, now that was my fault? What about when your husband impregnated another girl and paid her cows in full before you, when you were already in his house? You think we don't know that he doesn't love you and that you are forcing yourself to be his wife?" the other woman fires back.

Nyayang and her mother-in-law lower their ears in their location within the compound.

"I told them to stop," she says. Nyayang gives her a soft, direct look. Then she moves on to her tasks for the next day.

As months go by and as she devotes all her attention to her enormous tasks, Nyayang's surrounding finds something worth worrying..

This living together started before the harvest. And if they had to cut off that time, the last six months she has been with the family have been suffice enough for anything to begin. But no. Not at all. Nyayang is as quiet as the river at night. And tired already seeing months go to waste, her mother-in-law's disappointment in her is now over the roof. It is something she would be right about, if only she were blaming the right person.

Every twenty-eight days since Nyayang stepped inside her beautiful home, she gets to experience the "absence of the expected." And there is a very special way she gets to notice it. When Nyayang's special day returns, her choice of what to eat or drink must exclude milk. To avoid doing some damage to these culturally significant cows, females are denied milk in their diet during this time. For the duration of her period, the separation of utensils begins; all the utensils that have been in contact with milk are washed extra carefully before she can use them to eat. And no one else is aware of this but the girl's mother-in-law, since eating happens at separate locations. And now she complains.

The talking lingers for another entire month among family members. The siblings take it into great consideration. Toward the seventh month, this thing becomes something that can no longer be ignored, not only by the insiders, but outsiders as well.

In that period, Nyayang has had several encounters with women of her age, some of whom were married at the same time she was. On those occasions, Nyayang learned that the wind revealingly blew up her dress. However, being quiet and accepting what seems to be the norm has helped her mask her emotions. The confusion of not knowing what the problem really is with her has been weighing on her. And seeing the situation being handled by every mouth she comes in contact with, there is no opportunity to think it could be anyone's fault but her own.

However, it is true time doesn't stop and wait for those who cannot figure out things or let go as quickly as possible. Rather, it flows like the breeze of the dawn that dies with it, and better people dance along with exploitation resting in their hearts.

Her day begins with cooking and ends with showering all the family members. At this point, nobody cares whether she eats anything or not. She works and works and it's up to her to sit herself down to eat or not. And often she chooses not to. It is unlike the old days when she was new to the family, when she would prepare the meal but whether she, too, would eat from the same meal was up to the little girl in the house. After Nyayang would serve everybody else first, Rebecca would come and remind her to eat from the food she had prepared for the family.

However now, the small female who usually sat down with her is out of reach. She comes when she wants and leaves the compound unexpectedly. Neither the mother-in-law nor the father or even the husband himself dares to ask the little girl to come sit. Up to now, Chuol's parents have never taken this concern to the street or talked about it in front of non-family members, but talking between the two of them about how this young thing seems to be a piece of deception is out of question.

The star, Chuol, is a sun at night. He barely comes around during the daytime. And whenever he wants to make a sweet surprise appearance, he makes sure he is a commander from his workplace to his home. So, the only time Nyayang truly feels she sees her husband is during nighttime. Except that lately, he has begun to adopt his daytime nature at night, as well.

For some time now, Nyayang has thought that there must be a correlation between her husband's behaviour and that mind-destroying facial expression she sees around every corner of her surroundings.

But she soon comes to understand that it is strongly perceived in this living space that women talk a lot at night. So, those who wish to live life of a man must only give what they give and then quickly die for the rest of the night. That part she gets and sees it as a potential question no longer. But that is all she can mentally escape within the compound. Outside, the women cannot stop bragging about their flourishing successes, which isolates her from everybody. And in her isolation, she prays for Divine intervention. And sometimes she wishes others would place the blame where it belongs and join her. But no, they think a new thing should work. They know who to ask and how to ask, but what would have been the point of paying something if she would still need a praying help? Except inside here, outside, they pray for all kinds of needs. Even pregnancy, they pray for it. Yesterday evening ended with hope in the hearts of a couple in the neighbourhood whose inner wall has been dry for some time now.

"And this is the promise from the God we serve; He promises us that whatever we ask, it shall be given unto us in His name. Fellows, we gather today to do just that. Our brother and our sister have started this journey for a long time now, but like we have been instructed from Genesis, go and feel the earth; their part in doing that has been prohibited. But we know who to turn to when we can't answer the 'why' ourselves. We know who to ask. Let us pray, 'You know our why of reason, you know we know our place to turn to is You though we often turn elsewhere first. Man has learned and therefore has enjoyed the simpleness of the Giver, but no man has observed enough of the complexity of His nature. But You know the reasons, and You know our needs. We are here, not that we push because we know You know, but we are here because we know You give when we ask. To your servants, let there be forgiveness for them and grant them as they wish and as we pray on their behalf. Grant them, oh Lord! Grant them a child so they may enjoy the splendidness of this gift of reproduction. Amen, amen," Mr. Malual prayed for the couple. The hope was in their heart again.

"Oh, this girl! She has been waiting for so long. Let it be that God will hear our cries," said Mr. Malual's wife after returning from the prayer.

"He hears us when we ask. I know that," Mr. Malual said as he adjusted himself on his rocking chair.

"Please come. Please! They are killing her!"

A mother ran urgently into the compound directly toward Mr. Malual. She wanted him to come with her quick. "They are killing her!" she said.

"Who is being killed?" he asked.

"My daughter!" she screamed and threw herself at his feet.

"What? Why? Why are they killing her?"

"She is pregnant. She is pregnant. Please come. Maybe my sons will respect your voice. I know they will. I know they will."

"Why don't you talk to them?" Mr. Malual asked the woman..

"How? They almost beat me up along with her. They have accused me of knowing about her pregnancy as though we both agreed that she would go and be impregnated," she said while gasping for air.

"And don't you?" Mr. Malual asked cynically as he searched for ways to refuse to help.

"Please. Come with me."

"You know what? I'm not coming with you. Your daughter deserves to be beat up."

"You are not coming?" she asked, shock in her voice.

"No. Go and take care of the situation yourself," he said.

The woman returned back to her home..

Once the woman had left, he said, "They let their daughters walk their lower parts to men and then they go, 'Oh waah, help me' as if I was there when the two agreed. Go!" He gestured with his hand to the woman who had passed the gate already.

There is a distinguishable response to every incident, it seems to Nyayang. But the thing is, it is possible to pretend to know there is a person in charge of things and yet take matters into hands in another. It is her problem; new things should work.

CHAPTER FOUR

The year ends, yet Nyayang has still not conceived. "Maah! What is going on? We have been waiting, thinking one day you are going to walk up to us and surprise us, but instead we just run out of saliva over the Koat's unripened fruits. What is going on?" Chuol's father frustratingly asks Chuol this question one afternoon.

Chuol shakes his head but remains quiet for a few minutes. And then he says, "I don't know." He turns his head away from his father as a way to hide his frustration, as well.

"Did you ever ask her why?" asks Mr. Malual.

"Yeah, we went over it a few times and . . . " Then he stops.

"Then what?" Mr. Malual follows impatiently.

"She said it's because God hasn't yet offered one for us. I'm leaving," he responds and informs his father that he is leaving for downtown.

There is some truth to this. There was one time when she brought up the name of the One she thinks controls the flow of things. But since Chuol found himself in the state of this lingering disappointment, everything that he has spoken to his wife about has had something to do with who she shouldn't talk to and walk with, as if that is where the problem lies.

One woman in particular comes up often. Out of all the women in the entire area, it is this young lady whose spirit he dislikes the most. And quite the opposite of what you'd think, it is for the other reason. The knowing reason. The young lady and the man she finally calls a home have decided to reside within the area. Chuol finds her very man-like. There is something about this woman that throws most of the men of this area off. After she and her man got together, people showed some sense of loathing for the union, predicting she was going to divorce the man once he refused to let her take on the man's role. There is something about the way she talks that is distinctly unfeminine.

Chuol found her one day speaking to a group of young women whose game had become about who death hits the least, got the last laugh, figuratively. He stopped and waited until she finished what she was saying.

"None of us need to go through what she had gone through to understand the pain she had been living with." She was speaking about a young woman who, in the early stages of her marriage, dealt with Death by taking the first two fruits of her womb. The cause of their departure was believed to be the mother.

"You are the one who brought death over our family. We never buried a child until you showed up to the door of our deathless home," her in-laws said. In this culture, death and Death's coming are two things that always have to be somebody's doing. No man who has used his cows is down with the notion that death comes on its own accord. It always has to be the wife's fault.

"Like the good spirit, ready to convict us, knowing is looking right at us, waiting for our inner space to surrender ourselves to the need of it," the young lady said. "Knowing things outside of the things we are allowed to live is possible. We just need to be aware about the possibility of 'What if?' It is that simple. But if we judge others based on the fact that what happened to them hasn't happened to us, we allow ourselves to know only one thing. And that is to not know anything. And then our state of consciousness is only aware of one thing.

"And that is the life we live. We go about our ways with eyes that bypass the hurt that underlies the physical tears others walk with, yet we still feel the need to mention the absence of our tears to prove their sinful manner of living. Our minds become the ears and the eyes with which we judge what we should know differently. This is according to our rationalized state of consciousness. We simply overlook the suffering of others because we ourselves suffer as well from the lack of knowing it. That part I get it. When your sister buries her dear child, please mourn from the heart. You don't have to bury someone to know death is painful. In fact, he should never be anyone's eye, let alone you.

"How many times have we seen sisters losing homes they have been called into simply because men feel they have been failed in some way? But of course, we can understand that. Men are not our people. But we are. We are our own people. So, when life hits hard, we should be able to find our common ground," she said and gazed at the women. She wanted them to say something back, to agree with her, but instead, she got this: "You always talk like you are better than anybody here." A statement that was rather vague, but it didn't surprise her. Though many times she chose to talk, she knew her relationship with these women had always been challenging. It was not that "you did me wrong and now let us talk" kind of problem. She had snatched a man who was supposed to be for their daughters. This was unforgiveable.

But if they could only believe her, this young lady. They knew she was right. They were there when she was denied the free accommodation she had been provided by the only family member she had.

"Year after year, I have to be the provider for you and your child. Not anymore. Not when you are refusing men intentionally," said her uncle. "I don't want that, I don't want this. You have to know that you are not growing down, you are growing up," he added. He really wanted to shovel her off onto somebody and be done. It was much harder now that she had become husbandless. There was not much for him to play with.

With girls, you could play with the market a little bit if it was believed their virginity was still intact. But there wasn't a lot of negotiating with this one.

"If you want to keep refusing the men I find for you, you can go, get out of my home." Those were the last words she and her uncle exchanged.

While she was out and just wandering around, a lazy-spirited woman took her and her child in. But she was soon ordered to let her go, not by the uncle this time but her ex-husband. And because she was a woman, the ex-husband expressed his issues with seeing his ex-wife in their home with her husband. But he, too, had a lazy spirit as a man.

"She will take shelter in this home as long as she needs it," the man said.

"Then you leave me no choice," the ex declared. The two made it physical. In the end, not only did he leave the man with a broken leg but the whole community lined up behind him, condemning this man who had interfered in someone else's family affairs, and after that, there was not a heck of a lot the couple could do to keep the young lady and her child. The women knew this, too.

Chuol took off immediately after he saw some women leaving the scene. At that point, Chuol's dislike for this young lady intensified and his mission became about how Nyayang would not be around her.

"Yeah, that is what she says," Chuol repeats.

"No. Not God. No, for a whole year? How could that possibly be because of God?" Chuol's father raises his voice. Chuol begins to leave, leaving his father mumbling.

A few minutes later, Chuol's mother arrives home from a walk she took earlier. The husband and the wife begin conversing on various topics, when all of a sudden they hear the voice of a laughing child from a neighbour's compound.

This laughing, with no conscious intention, triggers the two to wistfully slide into how on earth would the womb of a healthy woman refuse to conceive a child?

"There has got to be something wrong with this woman!" complains Chuol's mother. "There has got to be!" she repeats.

"What are you going to do about it?" asks her husband.

"I don't know," says his wife. "It's very painful." The two avoid eye contact for a moment. "Look at all the cows we just spent on her, and she is only telling us now that she has a problem?" his wife says.

They speak poorly of her, gossiping. For something that cost so many animals, this complaint seems reasonable.

What is life gonna do? The cows' owners do not like the confidence that comes with the pre-confirmed girls; however, expecting that she has to work perfectly the moment she is opened . . . What is life gonna do?

"Yep, Nyayang is a dry, empty, woody nest that not even the bird which builds it can tear apart," says Mr. Malual with the volume of his voice lowered, as though he is giving up something he really, really loves.

Mr. Malual has some provisional advice for Chuol, who shows up the next day in the afternoon.

When he returns, the father thinks of rushing the notion to his son's mind. "You know what?" says Mr. Malual. "I have been thinking that we shouldn't be waiting, putting our hands on our laps while not quite comprehending the complexity of this young woman's problem." He walks closer. "I don't think we are ever going to measure the depth of what this woman walks with," he adds.

"Clearly, I don't know, Father," Chuol responds while holding his head away. "I guess whatever will further our lives from this hold-up must certainly be done. I mean she is clearly the first, but apparently not the last."

Another month passes by. Chuol's mother calls her son one morning. "Why, why? It's been nearly a year and a half now, yet there is nothing. What is the problem?" she asks him. But strangely, Chuol says nothing. He starts talking to her as if he is uncomfortable being around her.

"Well," says his mother, "I clearly see you don't want to talk to me about anything. But I must tell you this. If you are not going to wake up from this draining sleeping, this girl will finish your stomach." Chuol begins walking back as she finishes her advice.

"Wow! This is new. This is very new. I never experienced this. With all my other sons, everybody comes today and boom! there is a baby the next day. Where must he have gotten this from?" Chuol's mother continues mumbling after Chuol leaves.

Though Nyayang at this time still focuses on her duties through internalizing the pain, she sure becomes disturbed, knowing that she can never fix what she is being told to fix. The feeling pushes her to the edge.

A couple of months later, the formerly beautiful Nyayang is now as thin as air. Her cheekbones can be spotted from ten miles away.

The family jots down this profound changes in her and according to her mother-in-law's definition, Nyayang has a "fear to work" issue.

On more than three occasions now, when she has gone to the river, the palms of her hands have been looked at by women. It seems that everyone has noticed the skeleton she is becoming. The good thing is, her weight loss has been open to many interpretations. Some think she is losing weight for she is no longer able to face her duties. Others take a shot at the notion that the problem she has may just be exhibiting itself in the form of a sick-looking body.

Among the women who makes a guess is the young lady. She looks at it differently. She makes arguments out of the other women's assumptions of Nyayang's situation in Nyayang's absence. This becomes one of the many things women don't like about her. Although Nyayang should know there is a person who has her back when no one else stands up for her, there has always been a wall between her and the young lady. One of the things on Chuol's bucket list is that Nyayang stays away from those who have chosen to shift from one husband to the next and who see no sins in doing so. Such behaviour is one of the many taboos men abhor. It is not just that there is speculation that she may mislead the new woman by being the only woman on her second marriage in the entire area, but she is also considered a second-hand being with resiliency. Hadn't she been misplaced to live in this space? *Stubborn, arrogant, picky, not worthy of the prize,* are just some of the words women choose to describe her when they have something to say about her in her absence. But in her presence, they choose to call her a prostitute. A term that is used to describe any woman who had been intimate with more than one man, or in her case, any divorced woman. They also call her an evil person. If they are correct, someone was dismissed from the earth and the other one walks with lame. All because of her.

Before she accepted her current man, this young lady was seen turning down some individuals after scrutinizing their moral character. But here, the rules get a little simpler once she has been divorced. Once she has been confirmed divorced, she should no longer care what a man is like; any man who is willing to take her under his mosquito net should qualify. In other words, she should take anyone who comes along instead of giving men a headache about their character.

And so she has no friends. Even Nyayang is not her friend. However, during these times at the river, the two periodically meet. Sometimes the two exchange their personal experiences. And each finds some similarities in the other one's story. Like there are no shades of blue in the absence of pregnancy and in the sin of once having been in another man's house and yet still believing you have self-worth, the two are held under the same 'she failed' commitment and therefore loathed by other strong women. But now that the young lady is being given a second chance, it is not merely blamed on her, as such, but on the weak young man who refused to go the extra mile and bring home a real girl—one with a lid that is still on.

"You see these dark lines inside your palm?"

"Yeah," says Nyayang. Nyayang has the one with an A.R. figure.

"It means when you become pregnant, there is a high chance your child will be a girl," explains the young lady.

Nyayang shows a little worry. After having her husband wait so long, the only way she can make it up to him is by giving him a male child. The young lady notices her concern. She looks at her palms again. However, that is not actually the initial reason as to why she looked in the first place. Nyayng's palms appear more white then normal palms.

This is a great indication of a change in a woman's body, the culture believes. And though the young lady notices it, she thinks the sign is too invisible to talk about.

Another time, the two are at the riverside, bathing. The young lady comes to notice two other signs. She notices the size of her breasts is much larger then she has previously known it to be. She also notices the bones around her neck are more visible than usual.

The two come out of the water and the young lady stops Nyayang. But she immediately pushes her away, as some boys begin giving the women a hard time.

"When you are out here at the riverside, don't just take off your clothes and throw yourself in the water in the presence of strangers," says the young lady.

"Why?" asks Nyayang.

"Well, just lower yourself in the water with your clothes on if you really need to take a bath."

"But why, though?" insists Nyayang.

"Well . . ." She hesitates to say why. "Okay, here is why. I believe I know your story. And to tell you why, I'm literally telling you what the rumour is going to be once everyone realizes this."

"What? What do you mean?"

"I think you are pregnant. And I want to be the one to tell you first so you know how to clothe yourself."

"You think I'm pregnant?"

"Yeah, I do," she says. Nyayang looks confused. A boy comes and kicks the young lady's open water container.

"Hey, why did you do that?" the young lady asks the boy.

The boy says nothing. Instead, he kicks the water container again but this time, he says, "I don't care!"

"Come back here!" says the young lady.

"Don't call me. I don't talk to women."

"I'm going to call somebody right now," says the young lady. The boy laughs and runs off. The young lady takes the water container and fills it up again. "Come, let's go." The young lady holds Nyayang's hand and pulls her on. The two leave the riverside.

Toward the evening, Nyayang cuts onions in the kitchen to begin supper. She suddenly feels nauseous. She runs outside, but nothing comes out. She turns around, and as she walks back into the kitchen, her mother-in-law, who was watching her from afar, appears behind her suddenly.

"All is okay here?" she asks.

"Yeah everything is okay." She keeps her head away.

"You know you can talk to me about anything," says her mother-in-law as though she sympathizes with any pain she may feel.

"I know," says Nyayang.

Inside the kitchen, Nyayang can't believe the voice of the young lady echoing inside her ears. In her blurred mind, she can't sew together exactly the last time she received her monthly special. That tells she has been swimming alternately between the water bodies of the river and the lake. "Really?" she says to herself. She then realizes she mumbled out loud.

On the kitchen floor, she sits down, trying to believe some being is finally growing inside her long-dry womb. She gets up quickly and can't deny her heart wants to experience the excitement.

She comes out with it, and as though she had told her mother-in-law a month ago, she walks in with a surprised, happy smile, side by side with the clouds of heaven.

Two days later, Chuol returns from his usual business trip. Before he can rest, he receives the good news. His parents talk to him about what exactly they think Nyayang is becoming.

The three share their jubilation, but Chuol pulls away to satisfy himself from the main bowl. "So I guess He has finally given us something, huh?" Chuol asks.

Nyayang begins talking with an "I've got nothing to reveal" attitude and ends up giving him no firm assurance.

"Well, I guess in one more month we shall have more accurate details." Chuol leaves the bowl alone.

Angry morning sickness shows up. Morning becomes Nyayang's enemy time of the day. But things are done by women here. Some food she can't stand. Some people she just seems to have issues with. But she reveals neither to anyone. But her mother-in-law, who was once pregnant before, seems to know exactly what's going on. She calls her daughter-in-law a temptation to her family. "She hates me" and "She wants my son dead" becomes her morning song.

Feeling as usual, Nyayang starts her morning with disturbing feelings. She tells her mother in-law, who just shrugs her off. "They are coming, you know that?" asks her mother-in-law.

Who? she thinks to herself. Nyayang didn't know there were some family members coming today.

She goes on to prepare some food for the people who are coming, and it turns out they are family members and they show up before she finishes the meal. They are Mr. Malual's brother and younger brother's son, along with his mother. A few minutes later, the younger brother's newest wife's parents show up with their daughter, as well.

"Food is ready?" Chuol asks his wife.

"It should be ready in a few minutes," she replies. The food is almost ready. Nyayang worries. Impatiently, the people wait.

"You have taken too long," Chuol says roughly after he comes out of the room where they are waiting.

"I'm coming with it," she says.

"People are waiting, what are you still doing?" says her mother-in-law suddenly from behind her. Nyayang swallows it. She picks up a silver bowl and a green plastic bowl. She pours the soup in the silver bowl and places the food in the plastic one. Her mother-in-law passes her by. She places both bowls on a square baking sheet. She gets up and grabs the sheet by its sides then starts walking, but suddenly she places it on the ground. Her mother-in-law now stands at the gate for no specified reason. She sees her sudden move. Of all the reasons she could have chosen to put the full bowls on the ground, she mumbles, "Lazy good-for-nothing," snapping her lips and shaking her head at the same time.

Looking around, Nyayang's eyes fail her. All around her is blurry and she can't see a thing. It all happens so quick. She remains where she stands. All of a sudden, there is another confusing thing she is feeling: a sudden gush of blood. She runs, directing herself to her room. Her mother-in-law notices. She comes to the door and, at this time, Nyayang takes her dress and Yat off. She searches for another Yat. She can't find it easily. She takes another dress with a hollow, empty inner part and buries her head down again to search for the Yat.

"They are asking if food is still coming," says Rebecca at the door.

"It is," she says and tries to get out of the room quickly. She stops at the door. She turns around and gives Rebecca a look of "help me."

"Could you please give them the food for me?" Nyayang asks Rebecca. Rebecca grabs the silver tray with the food on it. She arrives and quickly places the food on the table before them. Chuol can't believe his eyes.

"How come you have to bring the food when Nyayang is around?" Chuol asks Rebecca angrily. Rebecca remains silent. She should have refused, she thinks to herself. It is not her duty and she knows this. This home has someone who has been married into it.

"Come, come. Come take it back and let Nyayang bring it herself," Chuol says to Rebecca. She comes back and picks up the tray from the table. She goes away and places the food back where she found it. Nyayang is still looking for the Yat and can't remember where she placed it.

"Chuol asked me to bring back the food. He is not happy I took the food to them."

Nyayang turns around and gives her a look of "thank you." Rebecca exits the room. Nyayang comes out of the room, as well. She grabs the tray and walks over to the other room.

Her mother-in-law looks at her in disbelief as Nyayang takes the food in. She rushes into the room crying, "DON'T EAT THAT FOOD, CHUOL! I know this woman will find a way to kill you. WAAAAAAY!" She places both of her hands on her head as though she is mourning for a loved one. She stamps her feet on the ground repeatedly. Luckily, Chuol hasn't touched anything yet.

"What did she do?" Mr. Malual asks his wife.

"In front of me, right in front of me, she just walked to her room, took her Yat out and came back and gave my son food!" She explains what she witnessed in tears. Everybody at this point stops eating. But they can carry on now; this issue doesn't really concern everybody.

The lunch is done, and Mr. Malual calls everybody in except Nyayang. He groans as he begins to talk. He shocks and coughs constantly as some memories are triggered in his mind. At last, he says, "I miss my brother." The silence settles in and everybody now begins taking some weird, loud breaths.

"It's hard, you know," he says. It was about eight months ago when this family was notified of some horrific news. Mr. Malual's younger brother had made his final trip to heaven.

The news brought more than just deep sorrow for their loss. This went so much beyond the shock of his departure. The painful hurt instantly robbed the family of its normal joy and became their permanent place of dwelling.

There had been no sickness, no sign of it. His death had come as a thief in the night. "How could God do that?" People were disappointed in God for taking His person. But in all honesty, the crying was not so much over the one they had lost, but for the one who had been left behind: his wife.

The brother left behind his new wife. Yesterday would have marked their two-year anniversary, if only hadn't Death been a little impatient. Exactly two years ago, his brother called it an end to something which almost took him a decade: his marriage. At age forty-five, he felt his heart liking a girl. However, she was only eight, which suggested she was not riped yet.

By the time she was fourteen, the parents rashly surrendered her into his old hands. Last year, the couple had their son. Then this selfish death stole her husband, leaving her with the unthinkable anguish.

However, now that this had truly happened, there was nothing that could be compared with the painful dilemma fast approaching. It was time to officially pass her on to one of her in-law's family members. Culturally, a woman is a family belonging. Whenever something unfortunate happens to her husband, she goes nowhere. If the husband has other sons from the other wives, one of his sons takes his stepmother, and usually it's the elder son. If no son is old enough, his brother takes his wife if he has one. Fortunately, in this case he has brothers.

"No, I don't want him," she says, refusing the husband's older brother. She then indicates her desire that she would rather go with her stepson, who is only twenty-one and has not yet married a wife of his own.

But he refuses her.

"He hasn't married yet. He is too young to begin a family with his father's wife" his mother convinces him. The girl is stuck!

Usually there is a quick solution to this dilemma. When you choose someone you can never have in refusal of the one who should have you, women do have a choice. Some choose to stay with zero men in their lives. But that is for the older women. Here, it is different. She only has one child and that is not a world.

The discussion which took the two families two days finally ends at the big brother's house. The husband's brother wins. And because the girl has her father with her, she now can't shake her head. She is lucky, she should know. In some families, the choice to be taken within the family doesn't exist. Instead, when your husband dies, they bury you alongside him, claiming your life is over as well.

At the end of the spoken month, it's proven Nyayang indeed finally said yes to pregnancy. But this doesn't mean the thick chain between her husband and the outside is coming off any time soon. In fact, what was a desperate search for a child-bearing womb has now just turned into a second search.

And, sure enough, the pregnancy brings little peace, though it's a temporal celebration for the in-laws never let her forget she is just the new inmate.

Nyayang continues her duties as usual, pulling this and pushing that and no one feels the need to reduce the load. There should be a reason to do so, because toward the sixth month, this child almost comes out. But other than the pain she feels, there are no other voices advocating for her rest. In fact, heavy chores are explicitly planned for her each sunrise. Like when Chuol took her yesterday to help with the arrival of his shop's items that came with yesterday's ship. He didn't want to pay anyone to help unload the items. But on her way home from downtown, her child almost made it out. Five trips from the shore to the main marketplace, carrying heavy items, and Nyayang's body failed her. On her way home, she stopped under the shade of many trees and took long rests. She bled. It stopped. She continued. But on behalf of her mother, the pain claimed and she bled its tears.

"Gaari, how come there is no food today?" Gatwech asks and speaks his concern through the air, trusting the echo to send it to the cook who hasn't been able to get off the bed since morning.

"I'm not feeling well," Nyayang remarks. Her voice seems faraway, suggesting she is not well, indeed. But those who have made the whole payment at once can't chance some undeclared illness.

Gatwech turns around, mumbling, "What kind of a wife is this? How can people go without eating since morning and yet she sees no wrong?"

He comes back around noon. Nyayang has come out of the room by then.

"Here, I need them washed right now." Gatwech throws some of his dirty clothes at Nyayang and demands she wash them right away. She gets up and limps over to the place where she washes people's clothes. She washes them slowly.

"Gaari, what is taking this woman years to do? This is what's taking you so long to do?" He comes and pulls a piece of clothing out of the bucket and holds it up to her face. "This is what's taking you forever to do?" he asks again, angrily.

Nyayang says nothing. Her mother-in-law watches from a distance. She knows Gatwech's plan, but what she is ready to document is whether Nyayang will respond defensively. Nyayang keeps her head down, washing his clothes. He steps out the compound and she wrings them with clean water. She limps again over the drying rack. She stretches to hang the last piece and trips dizzily, falling on her side.

In the distance, her husband's mother refuses to come to her aid. Instead, she says, "And she looks at you as if she wants to kill you when you mention what a poor job her mother did with her."

Nyayang struggles to standing up. She limps to her room afterward. She enters, and before she sits, her mother-in-law calls her to the door. "Nyajock, Gatwech and his group are asking if there is food and I can't tell them there is no food. You come out and tell them yourself," she says and leaves the door quickly.

Nyayang painfully limps out of the room a few minutes after. There are other young people with Gatwech. She stands, looking into Gatwech's room. She considers how she is going to tell him there is no food. There are other ways anyone who is not a family member can take this "there is no food" announcement. When there is a wife at home, there should be food when it is requested. Gatwech knows the cook has not done her job today; however, for the sake of exercising his ownership, he demands Nyayang has to come to explain why. She limps over again, and when he sees her coming, he tells those with him to leave. They exit the compound before she can explain.

The limp progressively becomes worse toward the evening. Whatever caused it hit close to the baby. On a day like this, people should help with some of the chores in the house—especially the growing little girl, Rebecca. But this would mean the cows were given in vain. It would be as though they had just given them away.

"Gaari, let my water go to the shower room," Chuol demands after his return from the shop. In Nyayang's regular body, she could have run out as quickly as she could and proceeded as directed. But not in this body.

"Gaari, is Nyajock listening to me?" he says for the second time. This avoidance on Nyayang's part could cause some tears to fall. There are no excuses for not responding to him the first time, let alone the second time.

She appears from her room. Chuol looks at her from the perspective of "Why am I being ignored?" She pulls the water to the shower room and she says, "It is ready." Then she walks back, and this time she has both of her hands on her sides and a walk that is rather funny. It should be easy to see that she is struggling and not just being purposely defiant.

"Nyajock, come back here," he calls his wife angrily. "Where on earth is this disrespect coming from?"

"I have been just…"

"No, no. Don't talk back to me," he says. Nyayang stops. He looks at her. She looks at the ground. "Go, get out of my face." Nyayang limps away. She goes straight to her room and lies on her back. A sound emerges from Nyayang's room suddenly.

"There is something wrong with the baby," she says.

"Are you giving birth already?" says the mother of the man who made the baby.

"At six months?" How am I going to give birth?" says Nyayang.

"What else is this pain then? Chuol, come. She is going to die now in our hands," her mother-in-law says, quickly cutting Nyayang off when she tries to explain how it may have started.

Chuol hears his mother but he has a girlfriend visiting tonight and he leaves before she can summon him again. Gatwech enters. He walks into the compound with some fat sticks in his hands. He appears mad.

"Nyajock, Nyajock," he calls his brother's wife who is currently either dying or miscarrying their child.

"Gatwech, come and help me. She is going to die in our hands now," finally acting as the active voice for the suffering wife, Chuol's mother demands. She goes out and calls for help from the available men in the compound. Nyayang is bleeding the baby out. Her breathing becomes laboured. She sweats excessively. She sounds as if she is going to burst in the next moment. She is suffering but there is no one shedding tears on her behalf.

Gatwech comes into the room. Nyayang is lying on the bed. He places the sticks beneath the pillow she uses. "Sit upright," he says. Nyayang tries her best.

"I really can't," she says. He comes over and picks her up from her head, supporting her as she rises from the bed. He and Chuol's mother slowly push her out the door and begin the long journey to the hospital.

"Either the mother or the baby is at some potential risk," the doctor announces right after they arrive. The bleeding continues throughout the night. Toward the morning, she catches her breath and the bleeding stops.

"The good news is the baby is okay, too," says the doctor. Toward the evening, she is allowed to go home. She comes and is thrown right back into the kitchen. The little girl ended up cooking last night. They can't wait for Nyayang to do her job again. But how healed is she? No one gives it a thought. She is here to work.

"I'm going. Come quickly," says Chuol to Nyayang. A ship has just arrived. There are products onboard Chuol wants to take to the shop. But Mr. Malual wakes up with something to complain about today. He says that he wants Walwal for dinner.. Chuol goes away in a hurry. Nyayang promises Chuol she won't be far behind him. That promise falls short. There is one thing after another that Mr. Malual can't deny himself. Chuol manages to push all of his items from the ship to the shore by himself. Thirty minutes turn into an hour. He pays someone to oversee the shipment while he is away and then comes home.

He enters and finds Nyayang trying to eat something out of what she was cooking for the elderly man. It has been noticed that Nyayang, as the result of this pregnancy, unreasonably craves Walwal, too. In fact, she has been spotted cooking Walwal for herself.

"Come. Come over here."

Nyayang puts the plate down and follows Chuol to his room. He closes the door quietly. "I asked that you come and help me take the items to the shop. What happened?" he asks. Nyayang learned long ago that answering a question is just another form of talking back. So she remains quiet, which just ignites his anger.

His mother comes to the door when she hears Nyayang crying. Chuol refuses to open the door. She runs back to Mr. Malual, who is busy singing war songs. "You have to talk to your son, he is going to kill her in our hands," says Chuol's mother to her husband.

"Isn't she his anyway?" Mr. Malual says. She looks at him. The phrase sounds like a question. But like she knows herself, a question is not for a woman to answer. Not even a no or yes. A few minutes after his wife leaves him, Mr. Malual gets up. At the door, he calls Chuol to come at once. Chuol opens the door and he pushes Nyayang out. She rolls like a ball on an even surface. She stops and dizziness prevents her from getting up quickly.

Mr. Malual walks back to the sitting area. "Get up now," Chuol demands. He then kicks Nyayang in her side. She moves her body. "Lazy. Did I bring you here just so you can eat my food? Get up," he says again. Nyayang gets up. "Now, that is the road." He points at the gate. "Go. Someone is waiting for you at the shore. I want everything at the shop when I go there today," he says and, as always, his voice sounds disappointed.

Nyayang pushes herself up and walks all the way to the shore. And although it takes her a bit longer, she knows she would rather do this than be beaten up, which would pose more of a risk to the unborn baby. She feels the heaviness of the things she is carrying and the heaviness of an eight-month-old baby on her never-resting body. This is one of the reasons she wants to leave for her parents' home. She is at her eight-month period and as tradition requires, a girl who is pregnant the first time must go back to her parents and give birth there. According to this rule, Nyayang should have gone back the moment they discovered she was pregnant.

However, there has been no one else to take care of her elderly in-laws. And so, it was decided that she would leave in the very last month of her pregnancy.

As the time gets closer, Nyayang unfortunately learns a severe illness has struck her mother. Within a short period of time, the illness has gotten worse, and now there is nothing left to pray for but the alleviation of the symptoms. There is a slim chance that she will have the joy of holding her grandchild in her hands.

Every week, as everyone keeps their knees on the ground, the stubborn sickness continues to produce more and more life-threating symptoms, from severe back pain to losing the ability to walk, leaving everybody feeling hopeless.

"Nyayang, we can't let you go," says her mother-in-law.

"Why?" she asks, with sadness on her face. She has been looking forward to her leaving day.

"Because your mama is sick, there is no one who will take care of you. You know your stepmother is as little as you are. She wouldn't know what to do," explains her mother-in-law.

Nyayang becomes even more sad.

"My child, I know you are supposed to be with your mom for the birth of your firstborn but I'm afraid we can't let you go as we thought you would," continues the mother-in-law.

"So, I guess visiting wouldn't be allowed either?" says the sad girl.

"Oh, no. No. if you want to visit her, I will go with you," says the mother-in-law.

On the next day, the two visit Nyayang's sick mother and return the same day. Yet Nyayang still has her unhappy face on. And she doesn't dare disclose the underlying reason for it.

Sometime after she finishes doing her chores, she sits by herself, meditating and thinking about the complexities of her life. Sometimes she imagines how much easier it would be if she was with her mother. However, there is something else below the surface of her fear.

Having known how mothers-in-law respond when their sons' wive giving birth does not spare a moment of relaxation for the new mother to be.

Terrified it will be the same for her, Nyayang keeps implicitly asking her husband, who for the most part is not there to listen, that she really needs to go home. In fact, the two have become quite distant since Chuol accomplished his mission of impregnating her. Chuol did a massive talking reduction which is unsurprisingly the same as always except he looks pissed off more now.

When Chuol can't be located, she goes to her mother-in-law. "Nyayang, we are just being cautious about what may end up happening, dear," responds her mother-in-law.

Her expected month arrives like a thief. This makes her more frantic. The siblings keep their ears open from a distance. The father-to-be can't wait to see his son. Unfortunately, Nyayang passes her due month without even a day of pain.

At the very end of the month, the two in-laws sit down. From their previous experiences, a girl married into the family hasn't gone beyond the typical nine months. What could this mean? they ask themselves. In this culture, there can only be one of two explanations for this. One possibility is that the girl has been married to a sub-clan whose wives typically carry for twelve months. But Mr. Malual does not come from such a sub-clan so there is no way his son's wife would go beyond the nine-month period.

The other possibility is that Nyayang lied to people about the month in which she claimed to have conceived the child. And if this was true, there was a greater chance the child could have a different father.

This ugly consideration makes the man furiously unhappy. He keeps his mouth shut and wants nothing to do with a woman who might have had her child by another man.

Another two weeks pass by. And yet Nyayang stands still like night water. And the more and more days pass, the more and more people talk. "Wasn't she supposed to sleep last month?" At the end of the month people reach out to the family members. Chuol thinks at first that not talking to her is the best medication for his anger. But surely he has to answer the questions of others. "She was," he answers, while feeling ashamed.

This unpleasant talk continues to the point that the in-laws finally decide to send her back to her parents. However, the final decision rests with her husband. Chuol explains to his parents how uncomfortable he feels having to answer everyone's questions.

On the next day, he comes home from his business around noon. He is fired up and ready to tell her that she can now go to her parents. But Nyayang is not at home. She went to the river a while ago. He walks around and when he can't wait any longer, he slips out of the compound. Things are not going Chuol's way at home but it is not the same in his social life. Recently, Commissioner Gatwech has had some militant, relational issues to deal with, involving people from the rest of the country. There have been a mixture of Nuer, Dinka and a few other peoples from around the country in the city, and the commissioner called Chuol to supervise a few things for him. Looking to the future, Chuol knows his involvement now will help him to learn how things are done.

In the evening, Nyayang's mother-in-law leaves the house. There is something extraordinary happening at Mr. Tut Gai's house nearby this evening. One of Tut's good daughters has been engaged to one of the local bachelors for quite some time now. The engagement has gone on for longer than usual because there were a whole two months of rest during the time. This was not according to the plan. The groom had all he had to give handy, and all he wanted in return was a girl who reciprocated his feelings. He is a young man in his late thirties, but he has curse behind his back. This has been going on since, early in his youth, he impregnated a girl but rejected her, saying, "I didn't mean it." He said this while he was with another girl he said he truly loved. This girl was without child, though. He stole her heart and the two ran away without anyone's knowledge. The rejection didn't stop there. The pregnant girl's parents brutally beat their daughter to death.

Early on in his relationship with this girl he did not like, the two were advised by elders about some possibility of blood relation between them. But they didn't listen. They decided the one-sided, incomplete love between the two was worth the risk. Knowing this fuelled her family's anger. They said she had embarrassed them. And they were right. It would be better in the long run if the girl could predict she would be turned down before being lured into the relationship and then having to go back and undo everything. She ran away and the pregnancy was not easy on her. Toward the end of it, her mother was asked to join her daughter because she was worried about her daughter's situation. Unfortunately, the girl passed away during childbirth. No one was surprised when the child came out. It was a boy and suddenly his mother's death was relevant. Blood kills! However, if things had been left at the meet-and-miss point, blood's power would have been at its vulnerable state. Or the blood would have been less aggressively bitter had the child not been a boy. But no. None of the above. The two passed each other at the gate of coming into and leaving life.

But life was very generous. She spared a few minutes for the one who was to leave. And those were the minutes she used to clear a few things up. To her absent, once-deceitful lover, she said a few things. But first, she said this to her mother: "The day you let my father give my child to his father will be the day he leaves this earth." And about her lover, she said: "Every girl who will take shelter in this man's trust will test death at the exact time death found me." There are many records of similar situations which followed through. And the reality of her words unfolded, taking the beloved girl the moment she and this gentleman welcomed their first child into the world.

He had been trying his luck ever since: five attempts so far. Two girls followed the first two girls early on. The other three ran away, either before the marriage was concluded or before they conceived any children. There was a time when he refrained from the search. In that year, he called the law to give him the son whose mother he had refused. The grandmother who knew what was said strongly condemned the giving of the child to his father. But she could keep saying that something would happen as much as she wanted and nothing would change the mind of the leading voice, the grandfather who had already moved fast some long-ago curses. He gave the son to his father after he poured cows into the grandfather's hands in order to take his child, and that was the last time the grandparents saw their grandchild.

Everybody knew that when he married, the girl would just go to waste, and so for those who were not trying to reduce the amount of females in their households or trying to punish some uninterested individual within their family, or both, he was a resounding NO. But not Mr. Tut. The man was wise. He first sought Mr. Tut's approval. And the father knew who to pick. Just like any average man here, there was little to no love remaining for the children of a wife you had lost interest in. So, the man came to him, and despite the girl's mother's refusal, he asked her to keep her lips shut and stay far away, adding, "This is not your child."

The mother of this child and Mr. Tut have a long history. Among his many wives, she is one of the least important. There have been a few things that have led to the instability of their relationship. According to the man, she is the one responsible for the births of the overwhelming number of females in his family. If it wasn't for the importance of "how many wives a man owns," he would have let her go long ago. He did something simpler, though. He refused to produce children through her anymore at a young age.

The marriage is finally concluded and per tradition, the man follows the feet of his bride quickly after the last ceremony. But this first time of meeting the bride means something else to the girl's family. One way to tell a girl has not been playing is discovered on a day like this. Women, including Chuol's mother, gather prior to the arrival of the groom. He arrives and the bride's small sisters lead him to the all-white room previously set up for the evening and the rest of that night for the newly wedded couple.

The bedding arrangement goes a little like this: the white fitted sheet and the white top sheet go first. A white duvet cover follows. The top and duvet sheets get folded back together. And to spice it up, both the white throw pillows and the head-resting pillows are rested nicely against the headboard. This is finished with a white throw blanket resting patiently at their feet. All this is done by the bride's brothers' wives. The room given to the couple is within the compound. The bride joins her husband shortly after. But whatever has to happen has to happen now, because the mothers-in-law are waiting at the doorstep for the part that includes them. They are singing traditional songs that have something to do with praising virgins.

The two inside finally get it right while the mothers-in-law are holding their ears against the closed door. There are moments when she screams, the volume of their voices rises and they clap their hands harder. What are they waiting for? Or what are they trying to hear? At this point, the bride is in a bit of pain. Things go a bit quiet for a moment and that is the indication that it is time to do the viewing. The groom swings the door open and the mothers-in-law back up to the middle of the compound and begin dancing. The bride's older brother's wife goes in the room. She asks the bride to get off the bed. Nicely, she folds the all-white bed set. She runs out with it while screaming at the top of her lungs with joy. All the women come at once. They spread the bedding out piece by piece. And yes, each piece has some bloodstains on it. And the discovery of each stain seems to prolong this joyous dance.

Chuol's mother, along with the other mothers, cannot wait for when this kind of viewing is going to happen in their house. She has some bright hope, for her own daughter has had her first menstrual cycle. A girl's period is the key that keep this business flowing. Without it, there is nothing. Her daughter's came at the right time. There was no confusion about its coming. There were no women making ill assumptions about it. It was perfect timing. Chuol's mother looks very happy; she could be holding this kind of gathering soon in her home.

It is around eight-thirty p.m. now. Nyayang puts water to the fire for her father-in-law to shower. "Do you want it hot or just warm?" asks Nyayang.

"No, not now. It seems a bit cold now. I will shower later on," he responds.

Nyayang remains silent after he has said no. "Did you hear me?" he tries to confirm. Still no response. Mr. Malual adjusts himself on his rocking chair, perches his glasses on the temple of his nose and sews off his mouth.

Nyayang finally manages to answer him, after an unfamiliar pain left her unable to speak, let alone move. The whole time her father-in-law was talking, she was leaning against the wall trying to ease her pain.

"Yes, I heard you. Let me know when you want it," she finally responds. In her eyes is clear exhaustion, which appears normal in the eyes of the old man.

She moves slowly to her room and once there, she is hit hard by the pain again. A moment passes and then she hears her father-in-law calling her. "Actually, I think I want to take that shower now," he commands.

From the depth of her room, she swallows the call.

"Am I here with anybody in this compound?" he asks again. Nyayang clenches her teeth and runs out like a storm in a dusty desert. She returns the water to the fire and dances back straight to the room without answering him. He registers her presence but chooses to ignore her.

After a few minutes, she flows back, and puts both the hot water and the cold water in the bathroom. And when she informs him, she dashes away quickly. This time, Mr. Malual wonders about her a bit. But it's a minor concern for a man like him to risk his guard and say a word to a woman.

The ground goes dark, yet neither Nyayang's mother-in-law nor her husband make it back. After she showers the individuals, she pushes herself to bed, thinking sleep will ease the pain. But she doesn't realize the starting point is always the least amount of pain.

Throughout the night, she struggles with the pain and yet keeps her lips together. While in her room, the missing family members return home and each goes to his or her room. And, when the King changes the night to day, this unbelievable young woman thinks she still has the pain under her control; however, she is shortly proven wrong.

Chuol wakes up and starts wandering around, hoping the usual morning things are happening. But eventually he slips away. Mr. Malual wakes up and leaves the house, as well. Nyayang stays in her room until eight in the morning. Then she pushes her door open and it appears she cannot resist the exhaustion anymore. Her eyes appear wearyingly tired. Yet, she still attempts to do her chores. Several times, she is stopped unexpectedly and she freezes. At the time this is occurring, her mother-in-law, who is picking grass in the compound, realizes something is unusual about Nyayang's movements.

"Are you okay?" She relocates closer to the girl and holds her hand.

"No," she says. She pulls her mother-in-law's hand away and puts both of hers around her waist. Then she walks away and stands at a distance in an unbalanced way.

"Are you giving birth?" Nyayang remains quiet. Instead of answering her, she enters her room. Her mother-in-law runs after her. "Why didn't you tell me?" she asks. Without responding to her, Nyayang exits the room again. Her mother-in-law follows her. In the middle of the compound, the two find it easier to look at each other. "I'm calling somebody," says her mother-in-law and exits the compound hurriedly. In a minute, she dashes back with a middle-aged woman who identifies herself as a midwife.

The woman immediately begins asking her about the exact approximation of when the contractions began. "Since the dawn." Nyayang forces the phrase out of her tired mouth. The midwife keeps looking for signs of the child.

"The child is still very far," declares the midwife. And this response gives Nyayang no relief, for the pain is drastically surging.

"Walk around the compound," the two women advise her. She begins to walk around but her legs can cover only short distances at a time.

The two follow and stop behind her whenever she makes a sudden stop. After circling the entire compound, she returns to her room with the two women after her. The sun comes up high and the severity of the pain is tripled. Inside the room, she remains standing.

"My daughter, is this all? Don't you have something you would like to talk to us about?" asks the midwife. A dark silence follows. Nyayang, after hearing the midwife, turns to her mother-in-law. The two exchange eye contact. The moment lasts less than a second, but

Nyayang tries to impart a question, which unfortunately hits the ground unread by the mother-in-law. Instead, during their eye contact, she nods her head, exhibiting that she thinks the same way as the midwife does.

"I mean this is absolutely not normal. A normal birth could not last this long. That is not how I know this situation," repeats the midwife. Nyayang gives her a glance over her shoulder but says nothing. She bites her lip and just keeps staring. At this moment there is no strength left to even think about the approaching concern.

The midwife stops herself and says, "Let me leave that between you and your mother-in-law." She then backs up and lowers her back against the wall. She quickly gets up again as though she felt uncomfortable siting in that spot.

"Because I don't know you, I don't have a right to question you," she adds after finding a suitable spot to sit.

"Nyayang." Her mother-in-law steps forward.

"Hmm," she groans when her mother-in-law pinches her chin. She keeps quiet.

"I don't know if you and your mother every discussed this issue," says her mother-in-law. "There is this very complicated problem which usually occurs during child birth when there are many potential fathers.

"I believe, Nyayang, you slept with more than one man during the time of conception."

Upon hearing her voice, Nyayang cannot believe her ears. She turns around and gives her a long stare.

"Yeah, you look surprised," says her mother-in-law. "Well, let me tell you what this issue comes down to in case you have never been told.

"When a woman mixes men, she has a very complicated delivery. And here are the things which happen. First, contractions are prolonged, which is what we are seeing right now.

"And your child will not come into this world until you name all the men you have slept with. And until your child hears his father's name, you will not see him," explains her mother-in-law, with profound disappointment flashing on her face.

"Are you done?" asks Nyayang. "The answer is no. I have never done anything like that." Nyayang, with softness in her voice, tries to profess her innocence. She turns her head away. At this point, she is extremely exhausted. Her lips are dry and no longer have saliva moisturizing them.

"Then what would you call this?" her mother-in-law points at her huge belly.

"Let me tell you this, Nyajock." The midwife gets up. "I see you acting like you are unaware about this issue's implications. Having this much of a prolonged delivery can be a threat to your life," she says and walks toward Nyayang. "Turn around. No, the other way. Let me see." She goes on scrutinizing her anxiously. "No," says the midwife.

"Yeig!" cries her mother-in-law suddenly. She stamps her feet on the rocky ground and distances herself for a moment. "Nyayang, Nyayang! Nyaame!" She comes back. "Why are you doing this? Do you even have a clue where this could take you? Do you know?"

She glances at her mother-in-law over her shoulder. Nyayang lifts up her hands but declines to physically react. The pain is now devastating.

"Nyayang, Nyade, say names! Mention whoever you think might have been involved in this." Her mother-in-law has become frantic. "Maybe that first name you mention will be the name of your child's father. Please, I'm begging you!"

"Chuol is the father." Nyayang forces the statement out after she begins breathing normally again.

"But Nyayang, nature doesn't recognize that. Otherwise we would have been chatting with your son by now."

Meanwhile, Mr. Malual is approaching the house. And behind him in the distance is Chuol. But neither of them knew they are following each other. Mr. Malual arrives first and upon his arrival, he overhears voices coming from Nyayang's room. With one foot on the ground at a time and one ear intensely open, he comes closer. "What is going on?" he shouts while waiting outside.

"Chuol's wife is giving birth." His wife rushes out and narrates the severity of the situation.

"And did she mention a name?"

"No, that's what we have been pushing her to do, but so far she has said nothing," says the wife.

"How can she not names any names when clearly the child is refusing to come out?" Mr. Malual is disappointed.

"What child?" asks Chuol who emerges from behind his parents. The three stare at each other's eye with no words to proceed with. Then Mr. Malual pulls his son away, leaving the mother alone

"Your wife is giving birth and there seems to be a problem," Mr. Malual says. He begins talking to his son in his inside voice. "Your mother and the midwife believe something is going on. We know what the likely cause is, but she is not cooperating at all. She is not saying any names."

"She is refusing to say who else she has been sleeping with?" Chuol turns his head in the direction of his wife's room.

"Chuol, wait. Chuol listen to me." His father calls him, but he is already in the room where Nyayang is pleading with pain.

"Say the names of all the men you have been having affairs with. All of them," Chuol demands.

But Nyayang remains quiet. She gets a contraction and she bends strangely over on her knees and unstably supports herself with her hands.

Chuol goes slightly closer to her and stands there, shaking.

"Chuol, Chuol, Chu, Chu! Don't you dare touch her!" His mother screams and jumps in between them.

Chuol attempts to leave the room; however, with so much anger swallowed up in his chest, he returns. He stands between his mother and his wife and continues demanding that she names names. Nyayang backs up from where she was standing and begins to circle the inner room. The six angry eyes follow her.

She keeps roaming the room and this time, she comes within closer range of Chuol. Then she gets struck by a contraction while standing side by side with him. She presses her head against the wall. And when the pain will not let her hear a thing, she unleashes her hands from her waist and irrationally tries to push the wall.

The contraction lasts longer than usual and she feels helplessly weak. Chuol, as he stares at her, feels the need to extend his hand. He touches her shoulder. Nyayang lifts up her head and releases her hands from the wall. She leans slightly over him. With her eyes closed tight, she manages to get a hold of his collar.

Chuol feels her body weighing over him. "Sit, sit. Sit down on your knees," he asks. Nyayang lowers herself with Chuol helping her, holding her right hand. Halfway to the ground, Chuol tries to come in front of her. But she suddenly starts falling, and he immediately senses she needs an urgent recue.

Without giving it any rational thought, he places one hand firmly below her huge belly and the other hand on her arm. The two come down slowly together. He puts her down gently on her knees. Before he can withdraw his hands, Nyayang loudly sends her voice out. "The baby!" She clenches her teeth and yells again. She calls her mother-in-law. Chuol, upon hearing her, takes his hands off her immediately, as though he has been burned.

As the two women rush to receive the baby, Chuol then exits the room and vanishes before he can see the child. A beautiful girl sends her voice out into the world the moment she lands in their hands.

"What is it? What is it?" shouts the grandfather, who has been protecting his manly values outside this entire time.

"A girl!" his wife shouts back.

"A girl?" he asks.

"Yes, the baby is a girl," his wife repeats.

"Okay," he says and walks away and enters his dwelling.

Chuol returns home at the end of the day and finds everybody has gone to bed. He dashes to his room. He places a large shopping bag beside his bed. He takes a smaller plastic bag from inside the big bag and throws it over to the bed. He takes his clothes off and tiredly throws himself on the bed. He gets up quickly after his back is poked by something in the plastic bag. He sits up and begins taking out what is in the plastic bag.

He brings out a black toy truck, which he begins to polish as though he has picked it up from the dusty ground. He puts it back inside the plastic bag and puts it away. He does not seem excited about the truck like he was when he first ordered it to be shipped with his shop items. He seems neither happy nor sad as he flips the toy truck over a million times in his hands, but he sure looks a little disappointed. It is not about the truck it seems. Will the truck be the perfect gift for his child? he wonders. And what if it is not? Millions of questions crowd his mind. It is not fair, he thinks to himself. Life is not. There are some men who are now counting down the arrival of their third births and have no stress about whether the child is theirs or not. Finally, he goes to bed.

The next morning, he delays waking up. When he finally gets up, he reaches for the plastic bag. He intends to enter his wife's room, but the door is still closed.

"Hey, what time did you come back last night?" Chuol's father asks him.

"When you all went to bed," responds Chuol.

"Well, then you need to meet your daughter," Mr. Malual says with a mouthful of Colgate paste in his mouth.

"My what?"

"My daughter?"

"The baby is a girl?" he asks. He drops the plastic bag on the ground and the toy drops out.

"Uh, what is it?"

"A toy car."

"For who?" his father asks him. Chuol remains silent. He lingers for few seconds and then walks back to his room. Mr. Malual walks over to the toy and picks it up. He then takes it with him.

Chuol manages to get over the disappointing outcome a week later. Nyayang brings the child out. "Aren't you happy now? You got what you wanted," Chuol says while tickling the tiny feet of the undesired angel.

I wish I knew how to make them, because I would have rather made a boy, Nyayang thinks to herself. However, saying so out loud would presumably sound harsh to the man's ears. So, she just smiles after his indirect, blaming remark.

Chuol looks at the clothes, which were washed yesterday and are now stashed in the corner, and says, "They are not ironed properly. Take them away."

Nyayang holds all the clothes on her arm and heads to the place she does the ironing after calling her mother-in-law to look after the child.

"Those clothes need to be rewashed before they are ironed again. Wash them first," Chuol says as Nyayang tries to re-iron the clothes, when in fact, she should wash them first to soften the wrinkles and then straighten with the iron.

"For sure," says Nyayang.

"I have the food prepared,. You should sit first before you leave, says Nyayang.

"I don't feel like eating," he says while rolling up his sleeves.

"Please at least try," Nyayang begs her husband. Little does she know it is because of her that he is refusing the food. Mr. Malual laughed at him last week about refusing the food made by the hands of a new mother.

"And now I just don't care. All I care about is whether there is something sitting at the bottom of my belly at the end of the day."

"Oh, really? What happened?"

Chuol was surprised. It used to be that both of them had the same loathing for the same issue. "What happened? 'No choice' happened!" The two laugh out loud.

After that, he comes near his wife's room and at the door, he says, "I'm leaving. The clothes I have been wearing are on my bed and they need to be washed." Then he walks away.

That is the nicest way he has ever asked me to do my duties, she thinks. *It must be because of the of the child or otherwise it would had been, "Why haven't my clothes been washed?"*

CHAPTER FIVE

A week and some days after the birth go by, and per tradition, Chuol calls on his friends, cousins and his siblings for the proposes of naming his daughter.

In this tradition, names are chosen for specific reasons. It is not about how nice a name sounds or how common a name is, but about how the letters form the perfect seasonal meaning.

At the circle, they table their suggestions. Some say "We can name her Nyagoa, meaning beautiful." But this name is somewhat shallow since its meaning focuses on the physical connection between the parents.

Others suggest she should be named Nyahok, implying that her father has spent a great number of cows on her mother. However, the two have been in a 'long wait' for a child and they'd rather honor that than anything.

"Oh, I think I have a name or two!" shouts Chuol's best friend.

"Go ahead, let's hear it," says Chuol.

"We could name her Nyadhiel, which means perseverance, or we could name her Nyamuch, meaning gift."

"Well, I believe any of these names would be perfect for her," Chuol says. "All I want at the end of this is for her to have a meaningful name. A name that underscores our previous childless situation. So, I want to omit the first two names we came up with.

"I want us to focus on the last two names," Chuol continues. "The name Nyadhiel is sure full of vigorous character and so is the name Nyamuch.

"But like I had said earlier, what I ultimately want in the end is for her to have a name which references the time her mom and I spent without a child. But now that God has finally turned His face favourably on us, I am so thankful." He shakes his head as he keeps talking. "So, without further ado, I choose to name her Nyamuch!

"Hereby, I pronounce her, Nyamuch Chuol Malual." The people clap their hands and joyfully laugh together.

About three minutes later, the women start separating the people. Children in one section, men and women on their own.

The serving women begin taking the lids off the cooking pots to serve the men, who have already start talking and arguing about the pros and cons of the current government. The women move to the children next, and at last they serve the other women who are presently speaking ill of some of the women who are absent today. One woman's name in particular circles their mouths.

"I'm not entirely okay with how we normalize it here," says an older-looking woman. She speaks with a minimal accent that indicates she may only have learned to speak the language as an adult. But she speaks well. "I'm not okay with the children of this area getting sick simply because a nursing mom goes back to bed with her husband," she repeats.

In this culture, it's entirely forbidden to be nursing a young baby while sharing a room with one's husband. It is believed to make other children sick. The other women laugh.

"You should watch out. When your child gets sick, know that it is her fault," a young woman warns Nyayang.

The men finish eating. The serving women push their plates off their laps to remove the plates from the men's tables. The older-looking woman announces she is leaving. In her absence, one of the serving women says, "She seems very concerned with what this woman does. What is she doing that is any different? She is still sharing her bed with her man when her firstborn is a mother already. Why doesn't she let the younger women have him? Foreign girls are prostitutes," she says with a disrespectful attitude toward the old-looking woman. The women laugh and shake their heads. Even Nyayang laughs.

"Didn't she help her daughter abort her fetus, too?" another woman takes her shot.

"Hahaha, she did," yet another woman answers. They fall into a silence for a while.

"We mock her based on the choices she makes and link those choices to the fact that she is a foreigner, but we refuse to acknowledge that it is her understanding of our culture on which she bases the choices she makes. What is not a disadvantage to a female? While aborting a child is never right, she at least made the choice and now her daughter has a husband to call home. Some of our daughters who have made these inevitable mistakes are still waiting at the shore of 'I can be your slave if you call me wife' because there were children who passed through their uteruses outside of unions. What is still not clear while on your watch, the wolves are unleashed to hunt the corralled sheep!

"Women, when will we be our own people? You must know that whatever is done against one of us, is done against all of us. It always starts with one woman, I know, but it always goes to the next one. This is why you should not laugh or speak poorly about one another." The speaker comes and places her hand on one of the other women's shoulders. The women stare at her disgustedly. She is the young lady who thinks she knows more than the rest. But who is she? A leftover of some man! Ha! And maybe that is to her advantage? But as always, what really matters is not just having a husband but being a woman who has never shifted a man.

One by one, the women leave the naming party, leaving Nyayang alone with the young lady.

There is no substitute for being a parent of a child but, surely, God could have done better than this. Every day this bothers the rhythm of Chuol's thinking. It seems that he got the opposite of what he was looking for. Traditionally, females do not do a good job of securing one's future leadership opportunities. But males do, which is why men want to start having them early, so they can accumulate them beginning with their first child. But things have to move on now. Chuol looks forward to the next one.

Every day, Chuol comes home with visitors, mainly males. He is starting to side-campaign now for his future leadership. He makes his friends walk from downtown to this compound to show them that he is the future. He brings them home at lunchtime as well as for supper, and he expects the food they are served should taste good.

It turns out this is not something Nyayang seems to be doing to her husband's standards. Food sometimes comes late and other times the taste is not what he expected. To show these men that he is the future, it must be backed up by the quality of services he offers the public now. But in addition to Nyayang's husband's expectations is a child who seems to be needing more and more attention.

It is nine months later when an unknown problem arises. Nyamuch, who by now should have known crawling, seems to have a problem pointing her knees to the ground.

Sometimes she tries pushing herself but merely falls flat. Although this problem has been observed by the family members, something else is concerning the entire family. And to some extent, it is the most troublesome and more worrisome to the family. It is the child's physical appearance.

Nyamuch, from the hair of her head to the feet with which she walks the earth, looks nothing like anybody but her mother.

People who visit the family always remark on the resemblance between the child and her mother, and the total absence of any resemblance to anyone on Chuol's side of the family. The family members have taken this into considerable account and hope for a clear clarification. While everyone is taking the side of Chuol, Nyayang worries about something else: What if she will never walk like a normal person?

Children are born to one day have reproductive lives of their own. However, from now to then, that takes perfection on a person's part, especially if they are the one with the womb. Women have one job. They are here to deliver children men make. But to be chosen for this job, she has to be practically perfect. And that worries Nyayang a lot.

"I don't get it. How could you entirely look nothing like this family?" the child's grandma talks to the child as if she is going to give her the answer herself. The more time passes, the more distance lies between Nyayang and her in-laws, it seems.

It has been a year and half now. And although Nyamuch is now able to walk on her own, there is another alarming concern. The child has a speech impairment. She barely says "Mama." This speech delay is accompanied by constant fever and diarrhea, which the mother often deals with alone as she fights to keep food in the mouths of the colourful individuals within the compound.

"Look at her. Look at her ears, her mouth. Look at her whole body." Chuol gets mad at Nyayang one morning.

"And what is wrong with it?" Nyayang, for some reason forgets this is taken very seriously, and she asks her master as if both of them lived in a heavenly place where doing wrong deeds was distanced from intention.

Chuol looks at his wife with a shocked expression on his unfriendly face. Nyayang instantly becomes worried, as though she has just been informed she has one hour to live.

In a matter of a second or two, she wishes she could take back the deplorable way she spoke back to him. But too late is not a thing to be overshadowed by personal impulsiveness. Especially in a moment like this where fear, respect and accuracy come hand in hand, she quickly realizes.

"What kind of question is that? 'And what is wrong with it?'" he mimics his wife in an unkind and mocking way, the way a child would mock another child he despises.

"You don't know what is wrong with this?" Chuol asks harshly.

"I don't think it means that something is wrong just because our child looks like me." Nyayang, untraditionally, tries exchanging words with the man.

"Really!" he says with surprise in his voice, and then there is a long pause. "Is this how you were taught? Whose head are you bringing into this house?" continues the husband.

Nyayang goes quiet after recalling the voice of her mother. Then she lingers around him, trying to prevent another sinful act from happening.

"Nyayang, are you trying to hide something?"

"What something?" Nyayang decides on talking again, knowing that neither talking nor silence is symbolic of the peace she yearns for.

"Okay then, tell me what it means that our child looks only like you?" Nyayang swallows that and decides on silence this time. Children belong to men; Nyayang seems to be behind the news about this. Something that is derived exclusively from him should look like him. But her confusion seizes up a bit the moment more reasons are required from her.

"Tell me why I should believe this child is even mine?" Chuol asks again, angrily. Looking like one's father prevents wars stemming from the "I'm not the father issue." Women like Nyayang would rather avoid this inevitable mental suffering if the key to avoiding this catastrophic chaos was truly as simple as staying faithful to just one man.

Oh, wait, isn't it true that the only reason a child wouldn't look like his father is because he has been cheated on? "Tell me." Chuol continues nagging her.

"Hey, are you ready?" Someone has shown up at the gate. Chuol looks at the man over his shoulder.

"Yes," he says. He starts walking toward the man while utilizing his eye language to impart his disappointment to his disrespectful wife. He and this man at the gate are going to a court hearing happening between Chuol's father's best friend's son and a girl of his youth. The case for the hearing today has been a long time coming for Mr. Tut's family and the girl whose son he denies having fathered.

After sobering up from the bitter attack on her character, Nyayang soon recalls to mind what was on her to-do list for this afternoon.

Nearly two months ago, Chuol bought some land in the city closer to his shop. This property is in the core of the city, not far away from the main marketplace. Everything is within reach. The school and the main hospital are both some metres away. The neighbourhood is known as one of the prestigious areas in town. The current commissioner's home is within this neighbourhood. He lives with all of his thirteen wives in the same compound. Chuol placed everything just like everyone else in the neighborhood. There is a compound to every home. There is only one exit to every compound except every man norths, souths, easts or wests his own exit desirably.

So far, Chuol has finished putting together the compound's base and the two individual rooms inside it.

At noontime, Nyayang leaves for downtown to sand-paint the rooms. At the new location, she sand-paints one and moves on to the other, but forgets to keep her eye on the time, as well. When she realizes what time it is, she rushes home, where she worries that her husband will have returned before her.

"Where has she gone?" Chuol asks his mother upon his return.

"Wah, my son. Your wife who routinely walks out of the compound for nothing, how would I know where she has gone this time?" says his mother. She knows where Nyayang had gone, but she denies it because she wants her daughter-in-law to be in trouble.

"Where were you?" Chuol asks Nyayang harshly when she finally arrives.

"I went to sand-paint the rooms at the new house."

"What kind of sand-painting takes that long? Why don't you just tell me you were with one of your other husbands?" Chuol loses it.

Nyayang tries to disengage by distancing herself. But the more steps back she takes, the angrier and more annoyed he becomes.

"Maah, I'm ready, let's go." The same man who came in the morning returns.

"Let me tell you this," Chuol says after moving closer to her. "From now on, you are never going to leave this compound without me knowing where you are going, what you are going to do, and how much time you are going to spend. I hope we are very clear on this!" He stares at her a little longer before he says the next thing he has in mind. "Many times I see you going to that woman's house, and I see you cannot tell I'm against it."

Clearly, Chuol and the young lady do not like each other. After the hearing today, Chuol's hate for this woman gets even thicker as does that of so many other men, including her husband. It is in the way she talks. She does not leave the big words for men, it seems. The young lady had to be among the crowd today, unfortunately, for she was part of the other waring party. The girl who was being denied was a relative of the young lady.

It all began when Mr. Tut's first woman travelled to her home city. She came back with a girl from her native tribe for her son to marry. But there was another person in the picture: the local girl. Nonetheless, finding a wife from the Shilluk tribe had been her wish come true. True, her son could have easily wound up with both women, but that would have ruined the secretive part of his mother's plan, which was and still is to have this son marry wives exclusively from the Shilluk tribe. A series of conversations followed right after she brought the wife home, and it was decided that the local girl with the child had to be let go, but how? By this point, the Shilluk girl had become pregnant, as well.

"I'm not the father," he told the local girl.

"No, you are the father."

"Tell me the month, the place, and the time we met if I'm the father?" he said to her. The girl, as though she knew this day would come, provided the answers and even the hour in which it all happened. The man denied it all, claiming a different time, place and even the hour.

"I'm not the father," he insisted. "Find the father of your child elsewhere."

"I'm not the father" is a denial trick that tends to work all the time. Men marry for children; once a child is not his, he has no other business with the womb it came from.

In the hearing today, he claimed that the father of her child must be among the newly arrived soldiers. He said he is very sure that the father is one of the Bor men among the soldiers.

"How do you know?" she asked him just as she has asked him before.

"I know, I know. He is one of them," he said.

"I know" is the men's line for leaving women to bear all the guilt when there is no evidence to prove otherwise. When a man says he knows, that is all the evidence he needs and the whole world does not deny itself the chance to be on his side. Mr. Tut's woman was also among the crowd and she wanted things to be over with quickly. She joined her son in he war of insults, saying anything they could come up with so they could soon be left alone.

"I know you, you deceived yourself that I don't know you, but I do. You are the girl who always sleeps with men for money. Now you think you can just bring some Dinka's child into our home because you have realized there will be no future with the soldier. Prostitutes!" Mr. Tut's son said..

"I have brought a good girl from home. A girl who wouldn't let herself be shared by men for money," his mother exclaimed.

The girl and her family felt defeated. The young lady, who was watching all of this, felt her emotions rise within her like combined salt and baking power in the need of malleablizing a molded flour. On her watch, the word *Nuer* and the word *pure* have never competed for the same meaning, and she suddenly found herself unable to stop herself from speaking up.

"You are a liar! You know this girl could have never done this. It is okay to admit you, too, have been aware of this plan of your mother's to detoxify the blood of the Nuer, instead of shaming this family for something this girl didn't do."

"You say that I'm a liar? I know you look down on your husband. I know you talk his talk. I know you have firmly knotted the Yat on your husband's waist so that you look at him as your wife instead. But let me tell you this." Mr. Tut's son got up. "I am not him to whom you walk on like a shallow canal. There is no way I will be asked to accept a child whose father I'm not. There is no way!" He leaped forward to slap the young lady whose eyes now met Chuol's. They both stared at each other for a few seconds.

"No, leave her," his father said.

"Just so that you know, I'm not the same as some men who end up raising other men's children, regardless of the fact that they are not Nuer children. Prostitutes! Like she is anything of value!" the son said as he returned to where he was sitting.

The young lady looked directly at him. She knew his reason for denying paternity was not because of what he was saying. And that was the reason his whole family tried to hide.

"Just that it's clear, how Nuer is a child whose mother is of Shilluk blood anyway?" While she was saying this, she looked back and forth between Mr. Tut and his son. Women do not do this. Looking directly into a man's eyes is the equivalent of saying "I'm a man, but you are not."

While everyone else was talking, Mr. Tut got even quieter. The crowd's noise dissolved the moment he said, "I heard about you. I have been told you have zero respect for men." He then looked in the young lady's husband's eyes. He said this while looking at the husband, "Is that a woman or a man?"

"Let's get out of here!" The husband became furious and forced his wife to leave as if she would have resisted. He chased the young lady out and right there, the two had a good fight.

"I see you want to be like her, but remember this, I'm not like her husband," Chuol says to Nyayang then storms off.

Nyayang looks surprised. Every time she gets a warning such as this, she looks surprised as if she is hearing him for the first time. However, if there is anyone to be blamed it is herself. Especially in the case of talking to this particular woman. If there is anything he has said he explicitly abhors, it is her associating with second-married women. And he was not speaking in vain at that time, nor is he now.

The young lady had lived in the area prior to Nyayang's arrival; however, the mixing of second-married women and first-time married women has been linked to negative influences, especially on the first-time married women. But the truth is, she does not talk to her often. Only sometimes, when the two cross each other's paths. Since she is strongly encouraged not to associate with anyone around her, the young lady lives with the same predicament. Except some of the young lady's pain is deliberately produced by the women she shares her man with.

What makes one woman so powerful that she can control whether other woman will or will not share some nights with their husbands? If she is a person of few friends and a scarring divorce record on her evaluable worth, she qualifies for the harshest treatment. And especially when all of that is paired with her tendency to say the most emboldened things that only men are known to say, there is no one to come to her aid.

"It is time to let all of it go. My two sons are enough," the young lady said to Nyayang before she made it to her compound from downtown. Instead of complaining about her wounds, she opened a different chapter with Nyayang. As if knowing how to say enough is enough is not another form of strength a woman should never know how to practice, the young lady defiantly thinks that remaining a wife in title alone should reduce the fights she has with the women she shares the man with. But unless the man himself says so, the way in which he would view the nature of this refusal would have a lot to do with the state of flipped balance the young lady seems to live in.

"That is giving up, don't you think?" said Nyayang.

"But how much control do I have here? He has decided that I'm not of any use anymore," the young lady said.

"No, no, that is not him saying it."

"Yes, it isn't, and we all know that because apparently one of his other wives has claimed the responsibility for the decisions our husband makes. She says until she says so, he and I will not have another child together."

"That is why you should fight," Nyayang said.

"Fight?"

"Yes, fight! Show him that you are a good person."

"Oh, that is what I thought I needed to be and that has been who I have been, a good person. But you know what I learned; you can never be enough for them, especially in the presence of their thriving kingship. I was just enough at the time when the plan was still beneath the earth. Like Nueri say, 'No one knows the ruler's mother.' I honestly bore this man some males was I not divorced once. But not anymore, and he knows that. And he wants to mold it to his desired shape and size so that when he presents it, it is what makes a man a man. And I get that. And I get it because I know, growing up, there was never 'her,' and so I could never bring myself to ask 'What about me?' because there is never 'me' in this."

Nyayang looked worried.

"No, no no, there is no need to fear. Now know this: I am letting it all go so I can maintain the health of the most important part of my life, and that is my mind. Because it matters. And it matters because I'm deciding to stay so they don't get to stepmother my sons." She gestures her hands to the right, pointing at some women. "Do you get that? In short, cleverly he wants me to decide by refusing the suffering he is putting me through. Cleverly I'm letting him go so I still have my mind and I'm able to stay with my sons," she said.

Still, Nyayang looked puzzled.

"There is nothing to fear once you identify the issue," she repeated. Nyayang nodded her head.

"So how are you going to do this?"

"I'm going to happily announce to him that I won't be bothered anymore for I'm now too old for sharing a bed with him."

"And he will get it?"

"He will. He will think I am just being thoughtful and surrendering a spot for his future wife. That will actually spark his creativity and allow him to think about adding another wife. And as for the other two, they will be over the moon. It will look like they finally won and I lost." Nyayang still had a confused look on her face.

"Come in with me. He is not in yet," said Nyayang. "It is okay."

"It never was him alone that saw me as a threat. Many do." The young lady saw Mr. Malual earlier raking the dead leaves in the backyard. But he did not see her; he was busy piling up the leaves and setting them on fire.

"Go in," said the young lady. Nyayang dashed inside the compound.

"I wanted everything to be gone before the arrival of April," Chuol tells his wife and stresses how badly he wants to leave and wants to leave now. So much is in the hands of the wife, it appears. But even though downtown is where the new home is, as well as the business, Chuol gets up and only stresses how important it is that everything arrives on time, but he does not take so much as a thing with him as he commutes to his business each morning. "These are not going. Those ones are not going; they are used. They need to be taken back to the marketplace where they can be sold as used clothing. I'm sure somebody will want to buy them." Chuol says to his wife in his rather harsh tone, throwing the clothes at her so she could be the one to take them to the marketplace to the used clothing buyers there.

Chuol sits down his parents to talk about their moving. "Nyayang will be coming and doing everything as usual." Chuol explains how everything will be the same after their move.

Nyayang loves that she can now leave this part of the land. For the most part, life here has been nothing but hard. The constant blame is just one of the hardships. And she has never been able to get a grip on how to handle it. If it is her mother's fault for ending up with two female children, then definitely she has something to do with her child's condition. Too many times, she has heard from women of her age that she made her child the way she turned out, apart from simply making her a girl in the first place. But most importantly, Nyayang sees the two of them moving as a chance for her to prove to him that she is a good wife. She knows there are many good layers of her that are just being overshadowed by the small voice she has here.

Chuol, on the other hand, is happy about leaving his father's home for different reasons. For one, to be finally in a home under his name, and for the other, he can now be closer to the city he could one day rule.

Moving day arrives. The couple along with their child move into their new location, which happens to be in the middle between Nyayang's parents' home and her in-laws. Knowing this, she feels liberated, though she is still expected to work for her elderly in-laws. It is a new place and everything in it is new to Nyayang. The people and the directions to things are different, too. It should be easy, Nyayang believes.

"Hi, my name is Nyayang Jock. We are new in the neighbourhood," Nyayang introduces herself to the nearest neighbour, a woman who is not very far from her in age.

"Oh, you are the new neighbours! And you are whose wife?"

"I'm Chuol Malual's wife."

"Very good. I am Gatwech's wife. The commissioner."

"Oh, I've heard a lot about him. But I've never met him in person."

"Well, I hope you will get to meet him soon. I have to go," she announces after hearing her name being called by a seemingly older woman. She re-enters the compound and Nyayang sees enough to know there are more then a dozen women inside their compound. It is a big one. There are about five individual rooms. Most of the women share together. Busy, they seem. Like twins, they all wear the same colour Lawe (a thin traditional piece of clothing that women wear over a dress or whatever else they are wearing). It didn't use to be like this in the earliest days. But Gatwech's rules even on how his wives should dress got rigid when the chair landed in his hands. They now wear an orange Lawe. It was the colour he picked out for them when he first wanted them to dress uniformly. He likes the colour because when they wear it, it will make a statement and therefore they will be known for whom they belong to.

Nyayang looks inside a bit longer. They are different women. Most of them come from different generations. They have different roles it seems. Some look old enough to have no use but to manage the younger ones for the man. There are many children inside the compound. Some are big, others are small. Some are males, others are females. And as she lingers needlessly at the corner of the gate, she can see that only the children are laughing. Clearly, some of the women have been having a dispute. They speak in an autocratic tone to one another. She backs away. There are children playing around the neighbourhood. There are children returning from the nearby school. For a moment, she thinks about her daughter. There are not a lot of girls in the classrooms, let alone those that have delayed development. These new longings are suspected to have led girls astray. Since these buildings with labelled rooms have been introduced into the society, girls leave children on the road on any given day.

Nyayang returns to her compound. "Ahem." Chuol clears his throat. Nyayang reports to him immediately. "Who do you already know here that you had to leave the child alone with me while you went off?" Chuol asks his wife.

"Nobody. I just went to introduce myself to our neighbour, that is all. And Nyamuch was sleeping at the time," she adds.

"So what if she was asleep! Is this how you are going to be?" Nyayang swallows. He keeps staring. She looks down on her feet. Chuol loves it when he speaks boldly, as the adult husband correcting her, the child wife. And true enough, Nyayang still believes otherwise.

"I will be taking Nyamuch to my mother for a warm water massage," Nyayang announces to Chuol.

"No, you will do no such thing. I don't want that," he responds.

With so much flexibility in her schedule, Nyayang tries to reason that one day a week or two visitations a week would not bend the man's rules.

But Chuol is not happy about this. He thinks there is a hidden agenda behind this plan. For the protection of his manly interests, a woman who leaves her house is after another man. Chuol and the culture believes this. And this, of course, does not only question the assuredness of the man's ownership of the woman but shames him among his countrymen.

The truth is, he has never considered laying it straight out on the table. And it is for good reason. In this culture, men are only to use their eyes, tone and hands to communicate their dislikes or refusals. But Nyayang has not really been picking up on these cues.

"Now that we live in the middle, I am in the perfect position to visit both our parents." Nyayang kneels before her husband one evening.

"Is that one of the reasons we relocated here?"

"No," she admits.

"Then no visitations." He follows that with, "And no unnecessary neighbourhood walk-arounds. I do not want any women to come into this compound for stupid women's talks," he says.

"But Guan Nyamuch, I believe this is a great chance, too, for the child to get to know both our parents." Nyayang presses on, undaunted, which in the face of a man, ironically represents disrespect.

As is his habitual response, he begins staring at who is supposed to be his dear wife with no words to process what he is hearing.

Nyayang quickly remembers that, as a wife, she has to look down at her feet since exchanging eye contact with a tiger means a fight.

As the man keeps thinking deeply on what he usually blames on her upbringing, the wife, with sunken wings, keeps her eyes on the ground.

"Is this how things normally get handled at home?" asks the husband implying whether this is how her mother talks to her father.

But Nyayang keeps quiet still, which ends when the man walks over to her to discuss the matter at a close distance.

"What things?" she asks softly, thinking a soothing, soft, gentle response will dissolve his simmering anger. Nyayang does not realize the pleasant tone she uses in her response is not enough. There is no hammer heavy enough that can properly reshape the sharp sword that has been honed perfectly for this moment.

Chuol has been firmly warning her not to eat the words out of his mouth, but repeated disrespect is all that Nyayang seems to have learned from her parents. Unfortunately, she will have to experience another beating this evening.

CHAPTER SIX

The light overcomes the darkness, and with no chance to complain about the severity of last night's beating, Nyayang's day begins and ends while between two worlds. Nyayang's duties have increased as of the last five weeks when the family learned the teenage Rebecca had to have her right leg amputated.

Sixteen-year-old Rebecca was at her grandmother's home for a visit when a day of fun turned into a nightmare. With a few of her other age mates, she was playing in an open area as the sun was going home. With no certainty of how it happened, she suddenly stumbled into a pit and cried immediately for help. She was rescued quickly, but with noticeable bruises on her foot. But that was not it.

She spent the two-minute-walking-distance between the open area and her grandmother's home on her rescuers' shoulders. The next stop was the hospital. Her foot was discovered to have further damage—damage which quickly led to the amputation of her leg. Mr. Malual was devastated. He called the event "a betrayal" from the Above.

"This is the age she should be doing something for the family," Mr. Malual said with flowing tears. And he would ambiguously be referring to a specific event. Now that she was adjusting to a wheelchair, the heart of the elderly man had moved from its place.

Since this tragic event, Nyayang has been between two worlds. "Nyamuch, hurry up, we need to go," she says.

Nyamuch pulls on her falling-apart shoes. Her mother bends over, offering her help. The two leave the compound; however, on reaching a block away, one of her shoes quits on her, and the little girl bravely carries on the rest of the walking periodically on her one bare foot and on her mother's back.

"Nyayang, wait!" Nyayang's new friend calls behind her. Nyayang stops and waits. "I don't know what to do," she says.

Nyayang gives her a sympathetic gaze. They both know what she is talking about. "I'm sorry but I can't think of a way to deal with this right now."

"Okay, I'll let you go," says the friend.

"Just take it easy," says Nyayang as she grabs her daughter's hand to go. The friend goes back to her compound.

Nyayang arrives at her in-laws' home around eleven in the morning. She hands over everything she comes with, food that is both raw and cooked. She goes on doing all that awaits her. And though she spends three hours working in the midst of them, none of them dare ask the obvious question of what happened to her.

She leaves the in-laws' home and immediately Chuol replaces her. "Hey, talking about girlfriends now, huh?" Chuol says to a group of young teens sitting around the very table he and other men used to sit at in years gone by.

"Welcome back!" says Gatwech. He goes back to the topic on which he was speaking. "I just threaten her if she doesn't talk to me."

"Does it work?" another boy asks.

"Yeah, it works. The good thing is she will never report you, or who will marry her? Hahaha!" Gatwech says to the group. In their midst, there are some who were not successful in the use of this threat.

"What about you?" Chuol asks one of the boys. The boy shakes his head. "Who do you go for?" he asks again. The boy stares at him. "You probably lack hunting skills." He comes and sits beside the boy. "Do you want sleep with a girl?" The boy nods his head. "At this age, don't go for the ones who are older than you. Go for the younger age. Or go for the . . ." He finishes by raising his hand away from the earth, measuring the age he is talking about. "All right, I will leave you alone, young men." He enters the compound. Chuol has come to visit. Since the couple started living on their own, Chuol never forgets to check on his elderly parents. In fact, he visits them about once every three days.

However today, he has come for a different reason. He has come to inform his fruitful-minded father about an inclusive decision he has been considering for some time. He is not merely seeking advice, but knows it is best if he doesn't hide anything from a man like his father.

"Where is Dad?" asks Chuol.

"Your father has gone to a federal hearing that's being held now," says his mother.

"Oh, no, who is it?"

"A woman."

"A woman?" Chuol asks. But his mother exits the compound quickly.

"A woman in the neighbourhood. You know her," she says when she returns.

"What happened?"

"She got killed."

"Okay." He then starts walking around, showing no further interest in what happened.

"She got killed last night," continues his mother. She looks around and sees Chuol at a distance, looking around at everything in the compound as if he left them a century ago.

However, the page she almost opens has all the neighbour women wondering who will possibly be the next, as many have just learned of the death this morning.

It was a fight between the young lady and the woman who currently is the mother of her children by the law. The young lady, on several occasions, had questioned how the stepmother was taking care of the children. Six months ago, the young lady heard something that led her to question her decision to run away from the father of her children. Her firstborn was now fifteen, and that time came with monthly bleeding. The stepmother noticed it. She said it was too soon for her to be having her period yet. "She is still too young for it to come," she said to a few other women. *Unless she has been sleeping with boys*, the stepmother thought and her group agreed. Somehow, she had drawn a line between the child and her biological mother, calling both of them prostitutes. In the eyes of the stepmother, she did not see what this child did or didn't do; her only association with an early period was one's love for boys. That it might not be her fault was never something that occurred to her.

There are all kinds of associations in this culture. Everything is linked to something else. Like redness in a girl's eye correlates to prostitution, early breast growth or the size of a girl's breasts, for that matter, suggests her chest has been massaged too many times. The young lady only lived here; her heart was where the children were.

"You don't ask me how I treat the children. You abandoned them yourself. They are now my children and I get to do what I want with them," the stepmother said. It was all the response the young lady would get.

Every time the two got caught up, the community sided with the stepmother. There was nothing she could do that would make the community switch sides. Not even when she arranged for the young lady's daughter to be married by an older relative of hers, simply because she wanted to defeat the ex-wife of her husband, the young lady. After the girl had only had her period a few times, the stepmother suggested to her husband that they would soon lose out if he let her sleep among the wolves for too long. The girl's father agreed. He also agreed that the old man was the suiter for his daughter.

The young lady knew the whole thing was a plan. She approached her ex-husband about it and only got severely beaten up. She returned home with wounds. Her husband heated up and again beat the hell out of her. It was as if the two men somehow motivated her creativity. She met her daughter one dark evening and asked her to run away somewhere she had known as home, her uncle's home. The child did as she was directed. When her father realized this, he knew who could show him where the child was.

"All I'm asking is you ask your wife about where my child is, and we won't have any issue," he said to his ex-wife's husband, broadening the scope of the problem. "Where have you hidden her?" The husband turned to the young lady.

"I do not know," she said in a tone that both showed her knowledge of where the child was and her readiness to deal with whatever came after. The two of them could tell. It was all written on her face. She couldn't hide it. It was all in her attitude, the way she said the words to her husband and looked at her ex.

"You will tell us." And that was the last thing her husband said, prior to taking the belt off his trousers. In what became an egotistically motivated beating, the husband turned into a killing machine, throwing sticks and punches, like always, anywhere. "You will show us where she is!" he would shout at her, periodically.

The enemy soon left the two and went back to his home where he found the daughter had been returned by a man who spoke his language: the young lady's family member, her uncle. He said, "I have never seen this before, and as a father, I feel a little ashamed of how she couldn't stop being involving in your decision-making. This child is yours and it doesn't matter whether you throw her out or into the sea. She is yours," he added as if he couldn't wait to have his share of the cows as soon as she was given to the old man.

On the day following the big fight, she saw her ex's wife. Like a protective mother eagle hovering over her unhatched egg, she hopped onto her back and would not have refused to kill her if that was the step that followed. The woman was soon rescued. It was found that it was the young lady's fault.

"The children are this woman's now. Whatever she and her husband decide to do with the children will be absolutely up to them," the elders of the community explained to the young lady they all seemed to have lost respect for now.

The marriage went ahead. On the day of the ceremony, all the women from the same area went to celebrate the marriage of the young lady's daughter. It was their final payback to her after she had long ago taken a potential suitor away from their young daughters. The child was given to the man, who paid a good number of cows. Soon, the husband successfully finished the last celebration of the marriage; he called his nephew, his sister's son, to produce his children, for he never had a male child and he was long gone during his time with the second last one.

Yesterday, the young lady saw one of her children being mistreated on the road by the stepmother, and as always, she did not like it. She approached the woman with her eyes closed and the two angry women got caught up in an endless, mostly unproductive argument.

From a distance, people felt drawn to have a look at the fight. The young lady's current husband saw the fight and opened his mouth. "Hey, hey. Get out of there!" he yelled. He started walking toward the scene while demanding her to get out before he reached the crowd. But no one heard him.

"You don't listen to me?" he asked angrily as he made his way through the crowd surrounding the two fighting women. "Hey!" repeated the husband. Still, the wife was too busy fighting for her child.

In the crowd was the ex-husband. And he made his work clear. Before and after the present husband arrived, he had gone on insulting his ex-wife of running away from her womanly life.

He continued even more, calling on his ex-wife's current husband to pull back his wife. The man jumped to a dirty conclusion, prematurely thinking the ex-husband was testing whether his wife would listen to him. The husband spread his thick wings wide open. He called her. Yet the two women were not listening to any degree of wind blowing by.

"Maah, talk to your wife! Why do you let a wife show you she doesn't have to listen to you in a crowd like this?" Another man brought the concern to the husband's hot mind.

Upon hearing the man, the husband began feeling small. He thought of all the things others had said about this woman. The warning advice, which others did not sit quiet about. He remembered ignoring others when they mentioned how unconventional it was in this culture for men of all ages to first see themselves through opened packages. He remembered when he heard his father saying, "Why don't you marry her daughter instead? What are you going to do with a grandma?" to which he said, "Can she still be pregnant?" pretending he did not believe that a woman's value was any different when she was still unmarried. He refused to hear his father's wise remark. The young lady's daughter was almost eleven at the time and of course, she was living with her father and stepmother at the time. But this man wanted something ready. Something that could give birth now without having to go through all the "give me cows first." He referred to her as his concubine openly.

The young lady couldn't care less. From the beginning of her conversation with him, she was interested in the possible benefits of him having stayed in two cities and how that may have framed his thinking now. But, after having her, he fell short of his words and he left for the real thing. He married his first wife and shortly after that, married the second one. Recently, he offered two cows and five goats to the young lady's uncle after she gave him a couple of boys. And that, magically, changed her title to officially being a wife. Yet, nobody left him alone. As long as people would see her fifteen-year-old daughter in the neighbourhood, they all still believed she was too old for him. Their togetherness was widely disapproved by almost everyone.

"It is going to cause a big problem between the two of us if you are not going to let go of this woman!" the young lady's ex-husband said to her current man.

"You want her back or what?" her current husband said.

"Even if she was the last woman on earth, I would rather go with the animal kind if all else was exhausted from man's kingdom. I will never take her back," the ex-husband declared.

"Then I have done you no wrong," her current man said.

His ignorant refusal to acknowledge his error ended up stealing a life a week later, when the ex-husband and his sub-clan's men waged war against the current man's sub-clan's men, claiming their wife was taken away. The issue was resulted through traditional means. The two sub-clans were rejoined, and the dispute was resolved by elders and chiefs in charge from both sides. The current husband was found at fault by the counsel. Somehow, this expression of wrath was expected from a man who at some point husbanded a woman. Somehow, once she was sold, she was always yours, even though you would rather go with the animal kind if all else was exhausted from the man's kingdom the second time.

This is not to say that no other man should produce children by a divorced woman. But it just cannot be a neighbour. In their minds, the death of the individual who died during the interclan dispute was caused by the young lady. This twisted accusation imprinted an image on the minds of those around her that she was the "devil," that someone's life was taken because of her. If only she had stayed far away from the citizens, no one would have been taken from earth before their time, or so every adult believed. The current husband remembered specifically last year when a man of his age refused to let him speak at a gathering and stirred him to anger and made him feel less of a man because he husbanded another man's leftovers when the man himself lived in the neighbourhood with him. And that incident had been among the few things which kept a frown on his face.

How he made some of his choices, especially being with this woman, had been blamed on the time he had spent in Gezira, eating Foul Khartoum. And that he had turned out this foolish was irrefutably seen when he naively denied that a woman who had given birth automatically became older than a man, even when the difference between them was as evident as ten years. All these things he remembered. He became disturbed and demonstrably bitter. He walked to his wife and pulled her by the hand. "Let go of me!" yelled the wife. "I'm not leaving my child," she added.

At this moment, she had a sudden flashback of the painful birth of this child that she was now fighting for, and it kept showing up in her mind every time she threw another retaliatory, insulting word back at her opponent.

"Your child? Hahaha! Do you even hear yourself? If you love them, why did you leave them?"

The ex-husband began questioning her out of her earshot, and when he was done, he held the child by the hand and started dragging him home.

At once, the crowd dissolved. Everyone started going back to where they came from. But things got a little intense when the young lady reached home. A man had his pride put in question when a stranger asked him not to let his wife go far.

In this culture, a man knows his pride is on the line when a stranger asks him why he lets a woman talk to him as though she is on the same level as he is. His allowing this to happen confirms that she has dug a hole beneath the man's dignity.

"Even when we are surrounded by men, you shamelessly continue demonstrating your lack of respect for me," the man said to the young lady, once they were at home.

"I didn't show you any respect," she said, as if she did not know what the man was talking about.

"Oh, really? What was that then, when I couldn't even hold your hand?" the husband said with frustration in his voice.

"I was supposed to listen to you? Even when my heart is being broken at the desperation of my children's suffering, I was supposed to listen to you?"

While the young lady still asked this and that, thinking this was just a typical argument between a man and his supposed rib, the husband fully made it his mission to get to the root of her impulsive nature.

"Is this how you were raised to talk to men?" he asked her. *Why didn't I know this before?* he thought to himself. *No wonder you were divorced in the first place.* He pushed her back hard. "I know, you grew up alone. Why would I blame you? But this has to be over between us today," he said. He followed her and pushed her farther. He then pulled her back and twisted her arm. He then pushed her back again. The young lady stumbled and tripped here and there and finally stabilized herself.

The husband followed her and when he lifted up his hand, he heard a voice from the gate. "Maah, don't kill the woman!"

"If she is your wife, then hold my hand. But if she is my wife, I will kill her!" responded the husband. He then became even more enraged. He went on throwing punches at his wife.

The neighbour who tried to help stood a distance away where some other men joined him. At that distance, they all seemed to have been convinced the husband was just punishing his rule-breaker wife for not listening to him.

But that was not all. The men who witnessed this knew that they would falsely end up being accused by the husband if they even thought of stopping him.

Suddenly, they heard the triumphant voice of the young lady: "Let's now see!"

They rushed in and found the man crawling on the ground. The husband realized the others had learned of his loss. Feeling ashamed and embarrassed, he got up quickly to show that between him and her, he was the man here.

The wife turned around and fearlessly returned the husband to the ground where she had first put him.

This time, the fact of who had won the fight was beyond a doubt. The women who had arrived at the scene were terrified and astonished. The young lady became aware of the people watching and withdrew herself. She confidently walked inside one of the rooms.

The women at the scene remained, roaming the compound with uneasy motion. And what terrified them the most? In this culture, if you are fighting with your husband in a crowd, you pretend he brutally beats you down at all levels. Because putting yourself in a man's place comes with an interesting fine.

Unfortunately, for this manly, strong woman, things quickly turned into the opposite direction.

It all came down to what the previous lives have lived. Historically, a man is not easily knocked down, especially not by a woman. But in the few rare cases where this occurs, enforcement is followed. You knock down your man, he won't get up until your parents pay a fine.

While the husband waited patiently on the ground, the young lady refused to run to her uncle and let him know about the incident. Soon enough, each woman who had had been loitering about returned to her own house. The young lady's co-wives secretly loved what was going on. They did not understand the young lady just like their husband. To them, sending this woman back to where she came from would not be the worst thing that could happen. The husband continued to lie on the bare ground; one could spot him miles away for a period of three to four hours. The young lady remained in her room.

This childish behaviour continued until the dark came to visit. Around this time, the husband decided to get up by himself, which came with a painful cause.

He walked to his room. Only the wind knew that he was at this time walking on the earth. He went to his personal space noiselessly, refusing to be heard by anyone.

And in the room that sheltered the woman of his youth, the last thing that loudly woke up the neighbour was the sound of his P.K.

The proud husband walked out of the same door he'd walked into, and on the doorstep, he sat down and waited for the curious to come.

Some moments passed. And sure enough, the beautiful sound of the man's life-claiming gun had permeated the air and startled the community.

"What is going?" asked the first arrivals. But he refused to talk, letting his facial expression communicate the unfortunate, real-man consequences he had unleashed on his wife. "What did you do?" asked an elderly woman. She then pushed him out of the way and made her way into the room. There, on the bed, was the body of the beautiful young lady, hated by all and taken too soon simply for being physically and mentally strong.

"You killed her?" said the elderly woman. She pushed him again as she was leaving the room. But she was immediately asked to leave the scene, along with other women.

Left alone, the men all went quiet. And none felt compelled to ask him why. They all seemed to understand the situation. Minute by minute, the non-female crowd increased. Some elders in the crowd eventually encouraged the murderer to go elsewhere and take rest. The rest called the uncle.

The body was covered, and the elders intended to bury the body.

"Hey, how did it go?" Chuol's mother asks her husband as she sees him coming in.

"Well, he killed her."

"But she was his wife."

"Hey, baba," Chuol says.

"Oh, you are here?"

"Yeah," says Chuol.

"I had to go to a painful meeting this morning," says Mr. Malual.

"Hmm, she got herself killed. You reap what you sow," says Chuol nonchalantly.

"Business is good?" asks the father after the two sit down.

"Everything is a waterfall," responds Chuol with a hopeful smile on his face.

"So how is life? Anything new?" Mr. Malual asks impatiently while tapping his son's back—the kind of tapping you do to someone your own age.

"Well, nothing at the moment, but if we want—" He smiles excitedly before he can finish his thought "—we can definitely come up with something.

"So, I came to share an idea with you," Chuol continues.

"Me? Wow!" His father taps his shoulder. "Let me hear it, son."

"I believe I have enough money now. I want to get myself another wife."

After hearing his son, Mr. Malual goes weirdly quiet.

"What? It's not a great idea?" Chuol wonders at his father's silence.

"Great idea? It's amazing!" Mr. Malual shouts after exchanging a firm glace that says he is proud of his son. "Wow! I think it's terrific, son. I am so proud of you. It is always a good idea to get married while you are young and then grow along with your children. Always! That has always been my philosophy."

"So where will she come from?" Mr. Malual asks urgently, referring to which sub-clan she belongs to.

"I can choose from many different places. Where will she come from? I do not know. I wouldn't know since looking is all I'm doing right now," Chuol responds with the purpose of limiting his father's knowledge of how he will get married this time around.

"Let me know the family. It's always good to know where they come from," says the father.

"Really? Tell me about it!" Chuol bursts into laughter and says, "But I don't think I'm going to care much about where this one comes from. I know you always want to know where they come from but that doesn't guarantee the things we value."

"What do you mean?" asks Mr. Malual.

"Well, look at the kind of woman Nyayang has become. Compare who she is now to why I married her."

"I feel you, son. Nyayang is someone else now," agrees his father.

"Exactly. She is so annoying and disrespectful to me, so irritatingly quarrelsome. A 'loves to leave her home' human being."

"Oh, no," says Mr. Malual before Chuol finishes. "Where does she go?"

"To her parents' home," says Chuol.

"Don't let her. You know what they say: if she is slipping out too much, she is up to something. Don't let her lie. What else is she still in need of from her parents?"

"So, you see," Chuol begins, "they always make sure they size themselves to empty spaces. And once they have occupied them, you would be surprised and shocked about the kinds of animals they really are." Chuol talks with nature of disappointment in the tune of his voice.

"That's very minor," says the father suddenly.

"Minor? Dad, you know how embarrassed I feel whenever she groans while I'm talking? Hello, aren't women supposed to be women? What is it she knows that she can teach me about?" says Chuol, annoyance in his voice.

"That is very minor," repeats the father.

"Really?" Chuol is surprised at what he thinks is a purely ignorant response from his dear father.

"Hear me well," says the father. "I know how frustrated this can make you." He then giggles a bit while utilizing his hands to explain his point. "You've heard me repeating the word 'minor' because there is a lesson in every situation. And in your case, this behavioural attitude is nothing. If you don't feel she is following the set of rules you want her to follow, teach her a lesson," his father says.

Chuol lowers his wings and dusts off his eyes. "What do you suppose is the lesson? I mean I fight her every day."

"You really worry. Hahaha. You want to know? You are already doing it." He taps his son's back as he finishes his ambiguous statement.

"Well, my time is up. I'm leaving." Chuol is on his feet.

"Sure, we will see you when you come back," says his father.

"Bye, Mum," he says to his mother.

"Chuol, Chuol, wait." His mother stops him. "Come in," she calls him inside her room. Chuol goes in. With the sweat of remorse and frustration dancing on her forehead, she says, "What is the problem?" after staring at her son for half a minute.

"I don't know. I guess it's the same problem we all know," says Chuol.

"I do not like this," she says and goes back to what she was doing. "I guess a pei yang (pei being a cow that produces very little milk) cannot satisfy a larger family like ours during days of famine, can it?" she says and walks back to her son. "What do you think?" she asks him while wrapping his arm.

"Well, I'm giving it some thought."

"Good!" she says.

"How are you doing in general, in town? The little business is growing?"

"Yeah, it is," he says as though it does not interest him anymore.

"You make sure you tell Nyayang to take that little angel to church every Sunday."

"Yes, I will. Actually, we all go to church. I even help the pastor sometimes. And sometimes we pray about people who are sick." He says this in a happy way. Serving is fun when you get to tell those who don't really care how you do it. He serves, but it is more like wanting to change things to what he wants to see. He desires to see these women be more like those in the northern part of the country, undoubtedly. Things such as wearing hair coverings more often, not just during church services, and cultural practices such as female mutilation, or sewing off some of the troubling parts of their bodies, are some of the dark thoughts he surrounds himself with. But the way of life has already been like that of the northern people in many ways. In fact, if it were not for the physical crosses on the tops of these buildings under the name of Christianity, there would be no distinction whatsoever between the North and South. But there is something else that should be added, according to Chuol. And yet that something else has been adapted and embedded into this way of life here, already.

Sometimes it feels as if the people here are the Northerners and the Northerners are the Southerners. Because anything the North practises is ten times more cherished and restrictively practised here than where it originated from. With his eyes on his future goal of becoming a leader, he finds his present self advocating for men's freedom. Things like maintaining a physical distance between women and men, which women seem to be violating these days.

"These are the reasons women don't respect men these days," he says to a man who has recently returned from Kenya. The man tells Chuol and some other folks about how men are losing their manhood everywhere.

"Even the architects are taking sides. You see, there you have to rent according to how many family members you have. For example if you have a family of one girl and one boy, your choice is two small rooms and one big room."

"Oh, wait, where is the man's room then?" Chuol seizes the moment.

"I know!" says the man. "They tell you you have to share it with the woman!"

"What? Me, share a room with a woman? What happens to the land? Can't they make more rooms? What if you have a big family with many wives?" Chuol asks.

"They don't care."

"I'm dying here," Chuol says.

Another time, he left the church and found one of his neighbours fighting with his wife. It was not like he did know anything about this fight, because it all began during the church service. This woman violently slapped her son who has some physical defects and is obviously disabled. He was crying uncontrollably. Earlier on, she said to her husband that she would rather stay home with him since his behaviour was so distracting. He refused. "What about the others? How are they going to get to church?" her husband said. She closed her lips, though she could have said, "What about you?"

She knew it's a woman's job to take the children to church. It is not that a man cannot take the children to church, as long as they are not females, pee independently, and aren't sick. But the two have two more children all under the age that only women take care of. At the church, she slapped her son for a reason only she herself can understand. She was likely at a point where her mental state was no longer a reliable source of strength for her. From time to time, she has been mocked in public by other women due to the disability of her child.

Disability and death are two things that when they go together, prove a woman may be a sinner. And those two happened to her. All that pointed to it being her fault, instantly coating her with blame. And because she held the one who proved her arguable sin in her arms, her hands overrode her motherly instincts and landed painfully on his head. The child instantly added a pitch to his cry. This upset the other churchgoers, but it was the husband who sat on the men's side who was the most upset. This sudden uproar between the mother and her child had served as a disruption. There was a great verse being poured into the stilled souls of the good people. Mathew 5:32 is once and for all the clearest explanation of what God doesn't like. They hear a piece of that verse almost every Sunday. It is used to drive any thoughts of 'I would like a divorce' from a woman's mind throughout the coming week and remind her that the chance to see the kingdom of God belongs to those who don't leave their husbands.

The mother whispered in her son's ear, "It wasn't you. It was the pain." Chuol stood beside the church's pastor. They both agreed the couple would have to leave the service immediately. Chuol escorted the couple out. And though he could easily draw the dotted line between the child's physical inability and that of the father, he walked the couple out with his internal voice seething at the mother.

Women should be blamed for failing men in many ways, Chuol believes. He also thinks sometimes the universe gives them credit for contributions they do not make. Like that false claim that says a child gets fifty percent of their genes from each parent. He made this his first focus when he began his studies at the University of Khartoum and then went into business.

He found the man hitting his wife after the service. "Maah, just let it go. She will not do it again, I am sure," Chuol said to the man at his gate. And passed on. Not far away, he mumbled to himself, "Prostitutes.

Why are you crying now when you had to turn this world upside down for your personal comfort?" He was right. What are their names? Prostitutes. He is right. Women should be blamed for everything that isn't right in the world. Except when it is indeed a man's fault, which goes unmentioned all the time.

It is as if man is in charge of production. And just like in factories, where the inventors pass on the creativity of their hands to be delivered to the people, women gas up their vehicles and they deliver the creations of man. Each of this woman's three children had their father's outside look, which was derived exclusively from him. This was a look that made him appear different from other people. If whatever brought about the look could be determined, it could be given a name here, locally, but since there is still so little known about life, it is common practice to blame all unknown problems on women. That is the health department. Education, on the other hand, does its part. Really, there is no chance for these female creatures to one day say, "Hey, look, it's not me," because intentional walls have been built and each generation increases their height and thickness. Like when a woman is mocked for having her eyes fixed on scientific lectures, especially when the lecturer is dissecting the body parts and the names of their functions.

How do you swallow the shame of being a female? Boys laugh at girls when body parts are mentioned, for by nature, women are not properly formed, they are told to believe. And because of that, girls should be ashamed. Elders, the society's upholders, believe when she is exposed to such lectures, it increases the chances of impregnation. And so, her chance to one day prove that all these genetic deformities were not from her side is buried, and layers of cement are piled on top.

Despite her knowing the odds, the woman once said to her family that she needed a divorce. And NO was the answer she got. She once was let go by a man who married her first due to infertility issues. If she indeed left this marriage, that would mark the second time she had wound up in another man's arms and that was not a shame her brothers were willing to take upon themselves. It is not that she desperately wanted to abandon her marriage—She just wished that people would see the physical deformity was not genetically from her side but from the father, whom the children resembled the most. Or even better, she wished that her husband would see that she did not magically alter what he thought he formed so perfectly, and that he would stop blaming her for providing him with men who were never going to the frontlines.

"I love the sound of that," Chuol's mother says suddenly. Chuol turns around with an ambiguous look on his face. His mother looks at him. "Oh, my God. Does she even cook for you?" Chuol, after hearing her, refuses to say anything. He gets up and begins roaming the inner room.

"I wish we ended up with that little sweet girl."

"Who?" asks Chuol immediately.

"Your other girlfriend. What is her name . . . What is her name?"

"Huh. Sarah, you mean."

"Yes, Sarah," confirms his mother. "Oh, what a good soul she has."

"Yep. If I had her instead, we would have gotten along pretty well."

"Then you should never forget that a man's intuition can never be overshadowed."

"Hmm," Chuol groans. "You know what bothers me about her is the fact that how she is, is the very least you can expect from a woman. She is lazy, careless, quarrelsome, and do not tell her one thing, there she is on my neck. What kind of wife is that?"

"I'm a young man." He points at himself. "A wife cannot show me disrespect or how am I going to walk among men? How are they going to respect me if they know I'm not respected at home?" Chuol continues complaining.

As the man throws himself to the edge, the mother stops working. "I know what you are thinking. But if I were you, I wouldn't limit myself," says his mother. "Wow, there are thousands of them out there."

Irritated, Chuol shouts, "I know, I know!"

"But do you know you can pretty much use the presence of another to bend the horns of the untaught one?" says the mother.

"I don't care now. This time I am going for someone who is open. An open-minded person who says something, not like those kinds of position-diggers."

"Oh wow, you need to be extra cautious here. One who is talkative while she is still a girl will rip off the many layers this earth has got once she finds herself a place," his mother advises him.

"No, she won't." He walks to the door and readies to leave. When he walks out and his mother follows behind him, Mr. Malual also comes out of his room. He wants to ask Chuol about something. But suddenly an uproarious noise stuns them. All are now looking at where the crying is coming from. Then a lady runs into the vast compound and desperately throws herself in front of Mr. Malual. She tries explaining what it is she is crying about, but she cannot make herself clear. Some people who were following her are now staring.

"What happened?" Mr. Malual asks the people. Some people move their shoulders, indicating they have no clue.

"She had a fight with her husband," says one person.

"And he has now killed my child!" cries the woman on the ground.

"Why?" says Mr. Malual.

Long before this moment, a disagreement between this woman and her master reached a disturbing point. The man is a man of a big family. He made it his goal long ago that every three to four years, he would marry himself a new, young girl, someone that nobody had ever touched before. But things changed a bit this year as he was going for his plan. Five years ago, this woman was blessed with twins, who were demanding her time and resources. She also has a little one who was competing for his mother's attention.

Their food store was getting smaller and she was starting to freak out. Not as a result of the food shortage but because she worried about what would happen when her husband married. When marrying a new wife, he would build a room over on the other side of the backyard for the current wife. And when he finally took his new wife, the current wife would move into the new place he built. He did this with all of his five wives. However, there was something different about this woman's situation. Unlike his other moved-out wives, her children were still small. And she was not sitting by quietly. The quarrel went on for months until the man decided to do something ugly about it.

He started to refuse the meals she made for him, which is a cultural signal that something fishy was about to be done by the husband. Two days ago, the littlest one became sick. And while the time was not a pleasant one for the whole family, this father refused to see his dear child. Hey, what better way to teach your wife than to cause the death of the children you claimed to have carefully created?

This morning, the child passed away. "Come, let me take you back," says Mr. Malual to the woman.

"No, don't take her back yet!" shouts Chuol's mother.

"No, you two cannot hold someone else's wife. Wasn't that his child he killed, anyway?" says Chuol as he exits the compound.

CHAPTER SEVEN

Back in the town, Chuol detours to Guadh-koka (The Place of Selling), as its sign reads above everyone's height. On the right side of the billboard is a waving flag in blue that has a picture of a white spiral-horned bull. This Guath-koke is a place with an arrangement pleasing all owners. The fishers have their own place, and those who sell all kinds of goods have their structural place within. There are also some small franchised food purveyors owned entirely by women. Anything that exists, a place is dedicated for it. Unlike the structural design of the owners' homes, this place is unfenced. You can come in, go in any direction and find your way to where you want to go.

As he intended to, Chuol spends the rest of the day's light in his shop.

"How much is this?" asks the first customer.

He looks up and says, "Which one?" The customer points at a dress and before Chuol can say how much the dress is worth, the customer comes closer and touches the dress. Chuol looks at the customer and waits. The customer touches the dress a third time now. Chuol still says nothing about how much the dress costs. Usually, this touching to determine the quality of goods is permitted. The seller knows where he will apply his strength. The customer lets go of the dress. Chuol looks at the customer and says the price of the dress.

"Is there a way you can come down?" says the customer and suggests an amount that is about half of its original price.

"This dress, as you can see, is not used. It is one of the new arrivals. Come, look. Touch this." Chuol hands the customer another dress. The customer runs a hand over it to feel its quality.

"Good quality, but it has been tried on a few times you know," Chuol says as he tries to persuade the customer to buy the new item in his shop.

"I will go with the new dress if you let me take it for this amount." The man shows him the money.

"Are you mad? Does it look used to you?" Chuol turns to words for help. "The dress looks beautiful!" The customer leaves the shop. "Go, you won't find it anywhere for that price!"

"I will go. I do not like its quality, either!" the customer yells back.

It is a busy day for many people, it appears. Commissioner Gatwech truly meant what he said. People can stand united if the right leader has been selected. Like he promised the elders and young men, he welcomed back their common enemy with open arms to work out some of their cow-stealing issues. It was a vision many bought into. Elders, in particular. There were other benefits for this tribe to come. Peace between the two tribes is wanted by both sides for two separate reasons. The Murle come for their animals' survival. The benefits on their end double when they leave. They take the chaff of the land, as these people free themselves of what is no longer deemed perfect by the recognized standards.

It feels kind of like when a seller puts all the clothes that have been worn out from several wears on clearance, sometimes at fifty percent off or even ninety percent off. The season ends and the Murlen men want to go back home. From the surrounding areas and within the city, elders have come to have these important negotiations with him at this section of the marketplace. Systemically, this section has been turned into an auction place.

"I have a beautiful girl. She is beautiful and strong!" an elderly Nuer man says to a middle-aged Murlen man.

The Murle man smiles and says, "How many do you want?"

The elderly Nuer man turns around and asks another Nuer man who acts as their translator, "Maah, come. Help me here. How much should I charge him? He is taking my daughter."

"A lot," says the translator. He turns back to the ones he was translating for before. There seems to be some disagreement about the number of cows requested in this case. The elder Nuer man follows him. He taps the translator on the shoulder. He turns around and says, "What do you think? He is taking her. You may never see her again. There is no such thing as small number of cows between us and the Murle. Charge him as though he is giving compensation. There is no blood between the Murle and the Nuer except cows and girls," he says.

The father turns around to face his daughter's potential murderer and begins folding and unfolding his palms five times. The Murlen man repeats the number after him.

"Yeah, fifty cows," the father confirms.

"Fifty?" the Murlen man reconfirms and this time he folds his palms once.

"Fifty." The father nods his head twice. The soon-be-son-in-law walks away and to another crowd of men consisting of the two tribes. He pulls away a Murlen man. The two go on in their native language. The father can see them talking but does not know what they may be discussing. He comes back and starts talking to the elderly Nuer man. The elderly Nuer man quickly reaches for the translator. The translator turns around and stares at the Murlen man. He says something about "tomorrow." The translator turns to the elderly Nuer man and says, "They are leaving tomorrow." Then he comes back to the Murlen man.

"Fifty, I have," the man says. "Tell him he says he can do fifty. Ask him if he wants them tonight."

He says, "Do you want them tonight?"

"Yes, can he bring them tonight?"

"Yeah, that is what he is asking you."

"Okay, tell him I want them tonight."

The translator turns to the Murlen man and says, "He will take them tonight."

"Okay, great!" says the Murlen man. He looks away quickly and at his fellows Murlen men who are conversing in different groups. "On that note, though, I would like to have my wife come to me tonight. We are leaving early in the morning tomorrow, so . . ." he lets his voice trail off, making his reason for wanting her tonight stronger.

"Oh, sure. There is no problem. Once we exchange our hands, she is yours," says the elderly Nuer man. "Maah, there is something I didn't tell him. I'm wondering if I should let him know," he adds.

"What didn't you say?"

"I didn't mention that my daughter has a baby boy with someone else."

"Does that someone want to marry her?"

"No, he doesn't. He doesn't even want the baby. He said he will never come back for him."

"Then I say you don't bring it up."

"What if he finds out?"

"How? How is he going to find out?"

"I'm not sure. But he may. Even if he sees the shape of her breasts, he may realize they belong to someone who is a woman and not a girl anymore."

"Okay, if you feel that it is something he needs to know, go ahead and tell him."

"You are going to translate that, right?"

"Yeah, I will."

The translator turns to the Murlen man. "He says, 'My son, there is one thing that I forgot to mention. But this is a marriage between you and I, so I cannot hide something I know is there. This daughter of mine you are about to take has a baby. She was impregnated and the boy who was just playing with her rejected her. But she is as new as she was before. She is ready to be married again. She is very hardworking. There is nothing missing. She is perfect."

The Murlen man just nods his head and shows no sign of changing his mind. When the translator finishes, the Murlen man asks, "Is the baby a boy or a girl and how old is the baby?"

"The baby is a boy," says the translator. "How old is the boy?" he then asks the elderly Nuer man.

"He is two-and-a-half years old."

"He is two-and-a-half years old."

"Okay," the Murlen man says and shakes his head. "I don't have any problem."

"He doesn't have any problem with that." The translator says to the elderly Nuer man.

"Please tell him, I want to take both of them. I can add more cows if he wants," says the Murlen man.

"He says he wants to take her and her son. He can add more cows if you want."

The elderly man looks around for second or so and says, "Yeah. I do not have any problem with that. Give me sixty."

"Great!" the Murlen man says and nods his head at the same time.

"So, he needs to know where my house is. Can he bring them to my house?"

"He wants you to bring the cows to his house and thereafter you can take your wife."

"Where is his house?"

"We will show you," says the translator.

"I need to call my son so he can show them my house tonight," the elderly Nuer man says and starts leaving the two.

"He is calling his son."

"Where is his son?"

"Somewhere here in this marketplace."

"I will be back very soon!" the elderly Nuer man says from a distance.

"He will be back soon."

"Sure."

Another Nuer man passes and greets the translator. "Everything is good here?"

"Yeah, he is taking his daughter and her son," he says, pointing at the elderly Nuer man in the distance and the Murlen man beside him.

"What? Why?" It appears the man knows the father of the son whom the grandfather is giving away. "No, no. I'm letting his father know."

"I cannot be held accountable for being the one who let you know about this," the translator says.

"No, you are safe. This is an open space. Everybody has access to the information," he says as he walks away from the two.

"If one day, the chair is opened to everybody, this will need to be changed," a common, wandering man says at the front of Chuol's shop as the elderly Nuer man grabs his son and another young man. Chuol gives him a quick look.

"It is never going to be open to the general public. It is about where you come from," Chuol says.

"I mean, it doesn't necessarily need to be me, but anyone can easily see what is wrong with what is happening here. Can you see it?" he askes Chuol.

Chuol buries his head behind his shop clothes. He reappears and says, "Women are stubborn. How else are they going to listen?"

"You understand these are not our people, right?"

"Neither are women our people!" Chuol says.

The man can hear the frustration in his tone. They both stare at the elderly Nuer man going back to the auction place straight ahead. "Do you know anything can happen once they are taken to Bipor or wherever else they take them to? If this is how we see them, they will also see them the same way," the man says.

Instead of carrying on the conversation with the man, Chuol tries to end it. He finds the topic uninteresting. A few customers enter the shop. They look at the sale section. There is nothing different about these clothes except the fact that he has just received the new ones.

"Once you buy it, there is no return or exchange," Chuol says to the customers. Customers are right always except on this policy of return.

"Why? How come?"

"The reduction in price is due to your own bias. That is neither the fault of the customers, nor is it the fault of the clothes, of course! I propose you charge the same amount for these clothes with the policy that they can bring them back if something goes wrong." Really wanting to talk to Chuol, the man keeps coming back and asking and suggesting things only a man of his ability can think about.

The elderly Nuer man hurries back with two young men. He introduces the first as his younger son and the second as his son's friend. "Tell him that these guys will help him bring the cows tonight."

"These are the gentlemen who will help you bring the cows over tonight."

"Please tell him to also come with someone who is a bit older. This is a marriage between us and I want to have a real conversation with his family."

"If you have anyone in your family who is older than you, please do bring him with you tonight."

"Thank you, I will," says the Murlen man. The elderly Nuer man parts ways, leaving the four gentlemen talking to each other. He really wants to go home and let his daughter know what is about to happen.

The sun is going home. This means deals have to be closed. "How tall is she?" another Murlen man nearby asks someone, seemingly the brother of the girl over whom the negotiation is being held.

"She is very tall," he says. He raises his hand above his head, suggesting she is taller than he is.

"She is taller than you?" the Murlen man ask, surprised.

"Yes, taller than me." The Murlen man smiles. "How far is home? I want to see her."

"Thirty to forty-five minutes away from here. But don't worry, I can bring her to your place tomorrow morning. When are you leaving for Bipor?"

"Tomorrow. Tomorrow morning. How many cows you want?"

"You have thirty-five? I can give her to you for thirsty-five cows." The negotiation between these two individuals runs smoothly. It seems they can understand each other without any translator coming in between them. The Murlen man seems to have some understanding of the language. Even though the two get as far as how many cows, the brother stops short of letting the Murlen man know any details about the girl's history. The fact that she first left her family for a man they later refused to approve of. They said to the man that they would never come to accept him as a son-in-law. But the girl was with a child already. A few years later, the two repeated the same behaviour. They ran away for a year. This brother searched for her until he found her when the two had a second child. He tried to give her away to another older gentleman he liked after separating the two, but he passed away before he could finish marrying her. He insisted the marriage proceed because the old man had a son. While the marriage progressed, the common enemy came and attacked. A few people were killed at the frontline, including the old man's son. There was no younger son for the dead old man. The brother did not have a choice as result. The cows were returned. This became the third window for the sister. She seized the chance with the man she loved and immediately added a third child to their denied union. But her brother promised her one thing. And that was, it didn't matter how many children they added after each run, he would come and find her and bring her back.

Now that this peace treaty between the Murle and this clan Nuer has been signed, the brother has decided to finally put the whole runaround to rest. But he is only giving her away. The children are not going; otherwise, this would be the perfect moment to bring up the children.

"What do we do? I say, either your sister or you come with me and see the bulls I have for you," he says smiling a lot now as the sister's husband.

"I'll come with you and see the bulls," says the brother. "I'll bring her tomorrow before you leave." It is a wise choice that he is not selling her with the children.

The mob dissolves and the people who have signed deals with the Murlen men continue. Some go to the controlled area where they keep their animals. The other successful ones go home to the women who have no idea that they have just been sold.

Soon enough the marketplace is empty. About six girls are leaving tomorrow for Bipor. Chuol walks home after a busy day. It has been a busy one but there were many customers buying things as well today. He comes and sits on his lovely chair where he has no interaction with his wife or his daughter.

Nyayang, after realizing her husband is home, brings his food and kneels before him before leaving him to have him his meal. And after the father of her child finishes, he calls her for two things, one of which is rather profound. Upon hearing the usual rough voice of her master, she tiptoes over to where he sits and, in front of him, she sits on the plain ground putting one leg on top of the other respectfully.

"Tomorrow, I have some visitors coming. They will be here by noon."

"Okay, sure," she says.

"Yeah, the bedsheets need to be washed and it's important the room is clean. That's all. Take your utensils," he says.

Nyayang leaves with no knowledge of who is coming or how many there are. Whether they are the type she should cook for or not. And she goes away without asking for a reason.

At this phase in their marriage, she has learned the ugliness of how whatever she means to say gets twisted. She completely understands asking questions is not part of their marriage agreement. She begins to experience happiness after leaving her husband. It is beginning to feel as though Chuol wants her now.

It is quiet in this part of the neighbourhood. Everyone is at ease. The elders are overjoyed; they made a lot of cows today. It could be a lasting peace. The man who made it all possible is probably not in bed yet or maybe has not yet come home at all. But at least his wives seem to be taking the evening off from fighting. Nyayang gets up and walks to the gate. Chuol sees this and says, "What business do you have at the gate at this time of the night?" Nyayang walks back to the compound quietly. Chuol rises from his chair. He goes to the gate and sticks out his head. Four men and a girl pass the gate. To someone else it might appear that the girl has been arrested, but the one who witnesses their passing knows something else is happening.

"I said you are going. You like it or not, you are going," is all Nyayang can hear from the inside.

"You will go whether you like it or not," says Chuol suddenly. He laughs mockingly afterward. "Prostitutes! Who told you to throw your lower half to men. Women!" he says and walks back inside. He walks straight to his room. "Hey, stop giving people headache for something whose base began by you," he says to the woman whose face he does not even see. Nyayang looks at him and quickly withdraws her head as soon as he turns around. He must be speaking to her indirectly. He stares at her and she goes in her room. He walks back to the gate. He can now see the girl being asked to walk in front of them. And after her are the two brothers. They move with her every time she attempts to veer off the road.

"Why don't you just kill me? I know I will never amount to anything. Why don't you just kill me yourself?" she says to one of the brothers. "If you are not going to go, I'm going to make you do it myself!" he says. She comes back to the road and stops to face her brother. She grabs his spear by its pointed tip and points it right at her chest. "Please kill me," she says softly.

A teardrop drifts down her cheek and dissolves as it reaches the earth. All of them stop. The two Murlen men behind her start speaking in their native language. The other brother holding a stick slashes her on her back. "Move." She turns around and moves. The one with spear pushes her from her back with the mouth of the spear. He pushes so forcefully that she moves suddenly and falls on her knees. "Get up. You did it to yourself," he says. She tries. She seems to have no strength left. In fact, she has been with no strength since early this evening when her father hurriedly came home from the marketplace and announced that he had sold her and her son for sixty cows.

"If there is anything you wish to take with you, put it in your bag right now," he said after finishing with her mother.

Her mother said, "After all this time, you refuse to put an end to her life yourself but instead are going to let the Murlen man finish it for you?"

"She is my daughter. She will go to Bipor tonight," he said. But the mother refused to be quiet. And so the husband made it physical. Soon enough, the two young men, along with the four Murlen men, arrived with the cows. The elderly Nuer man became the happiest man on the land.

After having made his daughter accept her fate, and having cornered the mother, he stood up, trying to see if he could count the animals with his naked eye. He couldn't do it. There were all kind of them. There were many young mothers with calves. Others looked very loose. They could give birth anytime. There were bulls and other generations in between. He couldn't count them all, but one thing became very clear although he never doubted it before. A child was indeed man's.

He turned around to finish up the evening with his family's new in-laws. A somewhat older man was among the four Murlen men as requested. The elderly Nuer man made the old Murlen man the centre of attention as he attempted to reconstruct a rough ceremonial circle. Unfortunately, they were soon joined by three officials.

"We are here to take the child. This child belongs to his father. He doesn't belong to your daughter," the officials said.

"This man said he will never come after this child. So, technically, this child belongs to me," said the elderly Nuer man.

"Where is it written that I can produce a child for you?" The father of the child was at the gate now. He walked into the compound and, in his face, he said, "If yours is for the Murlen man, mine is not."

"Hey, take your child." The officials gave the order.

"Maa-wut, come. Come to Daddy." The child refused to come. They hadn't seen each other since birth. The father came closer and grabbed him by the hand. The child started crying. He glued himself to his mother. The mother wrapped her hands around him tightly and refused to let go.

"Give the father his child," the officials ordered.

"Let my son go right now," said the father.

The Murlen men arose from their chairs. The elderly Nuer man walked to them. He started speaking to them, forgetting he first needed a translator. He motioned to them with his hands, asking them to remain seated. There was a chaotic sound from the outside. The animals were moving in different directions. The elderly Nuer man went to the gate. He was frightened by the voices made by the animals. He had the terrifying feeling their number may not be the same if he stayed inside any longer.

The hurting mother emerged from the room where she had been asked to remain. She had bloodstains all over her clothes. "Take your child," the officials told the father. The father snatched the child away from his mother's body. The child slipped out of his hands and fell down on his head. He started crying while looking straight into his grandmother's eyes.

"Please let him come to me before you take him," said the grandmother.

"You have come out of the room," said her husband by the gate. But the child and his grandmother were tightly embracing each other now. They closed their eyes and went on crying. The Murlen men arose again. They wanted to go, the elderly Nuer man sensed it. The officials separated the two. She began to let go slowly. She opened her eyes which were now full of tears. The officials placed the child in his father's arms and asked him to leave. The mother of the child ran after him.

"Now go this way," her father wrestled with her at the gate and pointed her in the direction where the Murlen man was standing. "You, go back to the room or else I'm coming where you are," he said to his wife.

"If she were mine, I would not be selling her. But she is not. Leave me here. I want to watch her leaving, though the pain will be more than the pain I went through when she was coming into this world for you, and for him." She pointed at him and the Murlen man, waiting. "I must be here if only for the fact that I was there when you were making her for you and apparently for him, too."

The officials stood at the gate listening to her nonsense. Then they moved out of the compound quickly while showing sympathy for the elderly Nuer man. The husband moved swiftly and grabbed his wife by the neck. He bent it forcefully. He pushed her back into the room then walked to the Murlen men. It took a few moments before he could start speaking with his fingers.

"Out of the six cows, ten will go back. No child." He gestured with his hands. The Murlen men appeared to have understood him. They just witnessed the father taking what belonged to him. The husband among them spoke a few words to the other. Two of the four parted ways. They went outside and they took ten animals and started going back the same way they came.

"Take everything you want to take. And hurry up," the elderly Nuer man said to his daughter.

"I have nothing to take with me." She walked to the gate and before she could exit the compound, her mother came out of the room and called her by her name.

She turned around and said, "Let her live to her meaning, Mama." Then she exited. The two brothers followed in case she tried to outrun them. One grabbed his stick and the other one his spear. The Murlen men followed. The elderly Nuer man followed, and quickly branched off to go to the animals.

The mother followed and, at the gate, she looked straight out at the road. That was when it hit her. She felt on her knees and said "Kuoth, (God) why?"

"Let's go," the brothers said. The mother could still hear them pushing her daughter. At the gate, she collapsed facing the road. They soon vanished into the neighbourhood.

"Let's see if you can't go now," Chuol says at the gate. They soon vanish. The cattle campground is only across the city. It is on the other side of the surrounding area. Chuol comes in and goes to his room. Nyayang lies flat on her back on the bed and rests uneasily like her previous self that was aware of all the activities of the night. She opens her ears as if she can still hear her desperate voice. But they are getting farther away from her gate. The farther they get, the calmer she seems. The girl is now walking willingly.

The Murlen husband steps to the front the moment they reach the cattle campground. It is an open field. Around the specific area they occupy, there are flags installed in the ground with a young man holding a spear on them. He gives everyone coming a confident glare. The Murlen husband says something to his people. A young woman who is naked from the waist up walks up to them. She has a Yat made of out an animal skin that falls from the waist down. She has beads threaded individually on top of her animal-skin Yat. She greets the people as she comes closer. She turns around and quickly grabs some fur sleeping mats. She spreads them on the ground some distance away. Then she comes and motions to the wife. The Murlen man leads his brothers-in-law to the place prepared for them.

Surrounded entirely by Murlen speaking people, it soon feels like they are natives in a foreign land. But that feeling will soon go away. When a seller sells, anyone else is a customer. The brothers-in-law soon announce that they will leave. They both walk to their sister and, while standing, one of them says, "You see, they are not animals. They are just like us."

She looks up at him and says, "No, not at all. They are very unlike us. But in the end, money is money no matter the kind of job you get paid for." The brothers leave immediately.

There are children, women and men both old and young around them. People are resting as she gazes around her; it will be a long day tomorrow. The young woman gets up and puts together the sleeping mat. She then threads the poles of a non see-through sleeping net and tucks in the edges of it. She comes back and offers the bride some milk to drink. The wife waves her hand to signify her refusal. The young woman shows her what will be her resting place for the night. The non see-through sleeping net. She leads her to it and return immediately. Soon everyone takes a place to rest, the husband following his bride.

Before the next day completely declares its ivory nature, Nyayang wraps herself in her dress and Lawe and finds herself in a small grocery shop with her child along her side. Before asking the prices of the items on her list, a man appears with a woman in front of him. They seem to be in disagreement with each other. He pushes her as she refuses to go farther. "Let us just go." He slaps her from the back with a bell. The head of the bell lands on the top of her shoulder, leaving a large imprint on her skin. She responds in shock. She wants to cry, it appears, but tears don't come. It feels unreal. She is leaving for Bipor all of a sudden. She had never been informed about this journey until this very morning. It may be that the process of giving her up to the Murle man wasn't wrapped up as needed yesterday, so her brother went to see the animals with the man to whom she was in her absence betrothed to. Nothing was mentioned to her during the night, otherwise she may have found a way to flee, leaving the family indebted to the Murlen tribe.

Nyamuch looks scared. She sees the woman struggling with the wound on her shoulder. She jumps behind her mother's back and hides.

Nyayang reaches out and grabs her by the hand. Nyamuch lands back at the front of her mother and immediately buries her eyes behind her hands as if she is peek-a-booing with another child. She starts crying as she leans over her mother's body heavily.

"You are good; he is not going to beat you," Nyayang says. The man is the brother of the woman. Unlike the elderly Nuer man who tried to erase all that was his daughter's, this man is leaving all the mistakes she made at home. They are all males, so the notion of giving the four of them away didn't come as easy as it did to the elderly Nuer man. Males are considered essential—it is wise thing that he left them behind.

"You can open your eyes now. He is gone," says Nyayang. Nyamuch frees her eyes, but still she continues to cling to her mother's loose clothes. She watches the man chasing his sister like a criminal through the store. She keeps looking. There are no words to describe the horror she feels.

Nyayang moves on to buying the freshest goat meat, for which she is the first customer. She buys vegetables along with all the herbs she knows will add flavour to the food she prepares. Like a bird returning to her unprotected eggs, Nyayang, in her hurried, married-woman manner, wheels back determinedly to her house. On her way in, Chuol exits the compound.

To place her out of the range of fire, she shields her dear child, who instantly seems to violate the cooperation her mother is looking for. Nevertheless, Nyayang thinks a sinful ignorant act would not harm her child, as long as this meal is going to put a smile on her dear owner's face.

Nyayang begins preparing the meal. Nyamuch starts to cry. She cries and cries and when she runs out of her previous tears, she feels asleep. Upon the time of the meal's completion, Chuol arrives home, walking heavily.

"They are here?" he asks.

"No," says his wife.

He retreats to his room. Nyayang goes to him and says, "Guan Nyamuch, can I give you something to eat?"

"Yes and hurry up," he says as though he has just finished arguing with his worst enemy.

At this time, it's already eleven forty-five. Chuol expects the visitors to arrive at any time now. Nyayang knew exactly what she had to do once her man finished. Interested in what the visitors will take with them as they head back, she rushes back into her man's room and cleans up the crumbs that have fallen on the ground.

She dashes out and clears away the scraps. However, on her way to put the plate back in the kitchen, she hears her not-so-cooperative child carrying on crying. She runs to the child instead. By this time, the visitors have arrived. In her mind, she thinks the visitors will notify their hosts of their arrival.

Chuol, on the other hand, anticipates Nyayang will monitor the arrival of the visitors and bring them into his room.

Inside her room, the child refuses to let her mother go. She suddenly shows a strong food craving which makes the mother feel even more guilty and leads her to forget entirely about the visitors.

"Hey Nyayang, I think you have visitors," a neighbourhood woman who has observed the arrival of the visitors shows up at the gate and informs her. Chuol, inside his room, notices Nyayang has been notified by someone else.

The wife immediately pushes the child off her lap and rushes outside. She arrives at the gate with wings of the wind, only to instantly think she is looking at the wrong visitors.

"I'm sorry. I didn't realize you had arrived." Nyayang starts apologizing to two girls, both of whom appear to be less then twenty years of age.

"Is this Chuol's home?" asks one of the girls.

"Yes, yes," she says, making sure her coming late is not mistaken for something else.

Chuol, who overheard his wife talking to the neighbour and now to the visitors, comes out of his cage. He then starts coughing strangely, which the wife immediately recognizes for what it represents.

"Come, come in," she says happily, welcoming the visitors, and directs them to the man's room. She sits beside them and goes on introducing herself. She asks them to do the same. In the few minutes they are together, she talks to them as though she knew them beforehand. She talks and asks them about different things, all except for the reason they are here.

In a moment, the husband makes his way in and that is when the wife excuses herself. One of the girls announces she is also leaving, leaving the other sister with the man. At this point, Nyayang realizes which one of the girls is her husband's girlfriend. Nyayang escorts the other girl out of the compound. Chuol closes the door after the two walk out of the room.

"I'm not sure of what I'm supposed to do now," says Nyayang's friend after Nyayang escorts the vistor out.

"What is she doing?" Nyayang asks, knowing what they both know.

"Last night was supposed to be my turn. But the moment he came home, she warmed some water and quickly took it to the bathroom for him. I was supposed to do that. It was supposed to be my turn."

"She is cutting you off from him. She will do what she needs to do to mess things up when it is your turn with him."

"Ah," she says, seeming a bit surprised when Nyayang cuts her off while she was talking.

"You are her biggest threat, you should know that."

"I know, but I sometimes think he should say something about it, especially when he is the one who ordered me to."

"Oh wow, how? Where will he get the care to do that?" Nyayang says. She also wants to leave the friend. Her husband and his girlfriend might declare they are done with each other soon, and not being in the compound at the time may not be the wisest thing.

"I didn't sleep the entire night last night," the friend says again.

"Were you waiting?"

"I was, but she ended being the one with him."

Nyayang looks concerned. She takes a deep breath and says, "I was awake, too, last night."

"Was he fighting with you?"

"No, no. I just had a lot on my mind," Nyayang says. She realizes they are both stalling. "Later?"

"Okay," says the friend.

Nyayang goes back inside and walks straight to her room. She sits down with a face that could only be described as disappointed. In a bit, she pulls herself closer to her sleeping child.

"Why didn't he tell me? Why didn't he tell me?" she repeats. "I ignored the suffering of my child for a meal no one will lay a hand on." There beside her child, she lies and takes a nap. Four hours later, Chuol comes out and, at the doorstep of his room, he stands still and proud with both of his hands in his pockets.

"Nyayang, Nyayang!" he begins calling on her with normalcy in his voice. "Nyayang!" he calls again, and this time, his voice picks up a little bit. Nyayang is not responding; however, for some reason she begins dreaming about her name being called. Nyayang understands clearly that when her man is done, she has to escort the girlfriend out.

She suddenly startles from her nap. She dashes outside.

"Yes?" she says while she hurries to put on her shoes.

"Come, escort this visitor," he says roughly, though he softens his voice, for he appears to not want to be poorly judged by the "visitor." He then turns his back on her.

Nyayang escorts her husband's girlfriend. On her way back, she becomes disturbed about what her husband might think about her service. When she gets home, though, Chuol ironically remains reactionless. Nyayang knows the red light she saw earlier couldn't just be a piece of ice melting on such a snowy day.

The next day comes, and the mother takes her child to her mother. Since the couple relocated, Nyayang has only taken her child twice to visit her mother, and this will mark the third time. And though she has never fully received permission to take her child to her mother, she sticks to the fight for her child happens to benefit from the visits.

Once they arrive at her parents' home, Nyayang's mother massages the child's legs, using warm water. In a short amount of time, the method has shown some undeniable progress. The little one has markedly improved her walking. And in her heart, Nyayang cannot help aiming for further improvement.

"This is what I was talking about, and people like you, Chuol, have the nerve to refuse the very fact that we all have witnessed over and over and over again."

"What do you think we should do, huh? These people don't listen to anybody. Let's face it," Chuol said.

"So, you are saying they deserve to be punished?"

"Hey, one thing we all know is that women are like children. They don't learn from hearing. They learn from seeing," he says to the annoying man.

"So we are better off picking up their bodies after the Murlen men are done with them?" The man irritates Chuol with questions which appear irrelevant to the topic at hand. Chuol believes that things have heated up on a topic that should not be of concern to them.

They started the argument the other day, when neither of them knew what the outcome would be for the young woman whom the Murlen man took home. He showed so much interest in the appearance of the woman. That was the one thing he assured the elderly Nuer man about. Whatever led to this sudden, mournful, tragic incident must had been precipitated by unplanned emotion. This man said before, "These are not our people," but what the hell was wrong with exchanging these perceived animals with Murlen animals?

"But if that is how we see them, they also will see them the same way!" the man had also said. And he was right. Normally, there is no distinction between a young Holstein cow and a light-skinned Nyawude with a full head of hair and white teeth. There is none. The two can be exchanged at the gate and none of the physical qualities would be weighed on a different scale. But this girl gave them a hard time from the moment they left yesterday. What exactly she had in mind was not clear to the husband until she vigorously grabbed his gun. She instantly pointed it at her chest. The Murlen husband yelled something in his own language while trying to snatch the gun out of her hands. She swung her arms, and as she released the trigger, the gun slipped out of her hand and the bullet shot a nearby cow. The husband grabbed the gun. The cow collapsed instantly. She glared at the husband, who all of a sudden showed the need to save the cow's life over hers.

In the midst of what was entirely a Murlen crowd, she stared at him and it evidently became a situation of them versus her. The gun was no longer at reach. There was no easy way for her to finish what she had started now. She took off. She ran, and when the husband realized she was getting away, he carefully seized his gun and finished her with just one bullet.

"Now it's equal," he whispered. He turned around to his people and gestured with his hand that they had to start going. He glared at the lifeless body of the Nuer woman. He looked at the dying body of the Murlen cow. He walked to the cow and touched her from the forehead down. He closed her eyes.

The woman's body was later discovered by some Nuer hurters. It was brought to a nearby home to be identified. Nobody was able to identify her body for it was rapidly changing. The news of the discovered body was circulated, and soon enough someone was able to identify who she was. The father was informed. The body was buried.

"How do we not know that this has to stop when it has happened a million times?" the man said again.

Chuol gave him a fierce glare and said, "Is this the reason you want to be commissioner?"

"Is there a reason I can't run for it?" They both stared at each other. Some people who were around came in between them and separated them.

"Why not my mother?" Chuol argues with his wife after they both return home.

"I know your mum knows this traditional body massage, but my mother is much closer to us," Nyayang counters.

However, Chuol still believes this constant leaving the compound is being used as an excuse. And to prove his point, it seems to happen in the morning after they have been arguing.

As Nyayang is on her way home from the small grocery shop, out of nowhere, a man appears asking for directions. "My uncle lives around here, not sure exactly where," the man says. Then he tells her the name of his uncle. Nyayang happens to know the uncle and exactly where he lives.

"He lives a couple of blocks away." Nyayang points in that direction. But for the man to reach there, he has to detour by two or more roads.

As the conversation goes on between Nyayang and the man, Chuol becomes aware of his wife standing with an unfamiliar man. It instantly becomes clear to him that the two are talking about something. He wants to walk over to the two, but he has two of his businessmen with him and he can't let them know what he sees.

In a few moments, Nyayang and the stranger disappear from Chuol's sight. Suddenly he thinks of telling his dear friends to leave, but this is the usual time that the three sit down and chat about men's topics since it's Sunday and all businesses are closed.

More time passes, and the discomfort the man feels is almost too much for him to bear. Fortunately, Nyamuch, who was left to sleep by her mother, suddenly starts to cry.

Seeing an excuse, Chuol dashes to her room as quickly as he can and begins doing what he has never done since the day this little girl was born.

He throws her over his manly shoulder and walks out while rubbing her back. Nyamuch quickly relaxes, enjoying her dad's care for the very first time.

"Chuol, what do you think? Should we go?" shouts one of the men from a distance.

"Umm, I'm afraid you may have to do that. I don't know when her mother is coming home," says Chuol with a hint of embarrassment in his voice, knowing that he has just revealed he is okay with his wife taking too much time away.

"Okay, then we will see you tomorrow. See you," the man says back.

About three minutes later, Nyayang enters the compound with her usual smile flashing on her face from miles away. "Oh, you're up already?" she asks her child. She walks toward the two. Chuol unleashes the child and suddenly storms off, walking with his hands up in the air.

Nyayang sees right away that her husband is not in a good mood. Chuol seems more pieced off. He sits down in his chair, brainstorming the many ways he could potentially change this deplorable way of life.

Another moment goes by. Nyayang seems more focused. She scurries from here to there, making sure her master gets his meal in a timely manner. "Nyamuch, Nyamuch!" Chuol begins to call the child. Nyayang hears her husband calling and passes this on to their child. Nyamuch runs to her father unstably.

The two start talking but are too far away for Nyayang to hear. In the midst of the discussion, Chuol slaps the child on the head.

Nyamuch sends her voice into the air. She tries to run away but her father holds her two hands and holds them firm. With all the strength he has, he pulls his dear child forcefully toward him and pushes her down in front of him.

Nyamuch, over her shoulder, looks pleadingly into her mother's eyes. Chuol notices the two have exchanged a glace. "So it's your mother who has told you not to obey me?" He pinches the child on the cheek. He speaks loudly as he intends to let her mother know about it. He then looks back at his wife to see whether she will say anything.

Nyayang knows this and so turns her head away before their eyes meet. And she holds it away, refusing the bitter moment when she must confront him to come any sooner. As he fixes his eyes on his servant, his dear innocent child finds a chance to pull her hands away, but then makes the mistake of running to her mother and nervously hiding behind her back, thinking she has found a good hiding place.

Chuol gets up and walks to the females. "Come, come. Come here," he demands of the child.

"Nyamuch, go back to daddy." Nyayang encourages the child to go back even while a portion of her soul hurts to say it. But Nyamuch just keeps running from one side of her mother to the other as her father tries to catch her.

"I think she understands her mistake. Maybe just leave her and get her some other time if she repeats it." Nyayang clenches her teeth and tries to stop Chuol.

"Oh, really? So it has been you who taught the child to disobey me?" Chuol stops moving and stares at her, his eyes overflowing with hate.

"Waah, guan Nyamuch! How would I even begin to tell the child not to listen to her father?" says his wife while avoiding eye contact.

"Okay, then why would you say I should leave the child, if you know I'm the father?" Chuol presses.

"Because she just keeps running and hiding behind me," says Nyayang, beginning to show her frustration.

"Which means I should just leave her alone whenever she runs to you and hides behind you, right?" Chuol keeps going.

"No no, no. That's not what I'm saying."

"Okay, then tell me what you are really saying." Nyayang, at this point, becomes aware of the man's boiling anger and that any more excuses from her will mean red bruises.

She turns her head away but quickly recalls that doing so represents that she thinks what he just said carries no weight. She turns around again and looks down at her feet.

"No, don't go quiet. Go on. You have always liked arguing with me. So, go on." Nyayang stills keeps quiet. But despite her resistance, Chuol needs to find out what it is he is looking for. "Are you saying the child is not mine and that I cannot make any corrections?"

"What? Who said that?" cries Nyayang.

"You are saying that. Like you don't think I know what is going on," Chuol bursts out.

"What is going on?" Nyayang becomes even more disrespectful, daring to question what the man thinks is correct.

"You are asking me? You stupid prostitute! You are asking me?" Chuol zooms his unfriendly eyes on the person who is supposed to be his dear wife. And with no time left to waste, he lays his fists on her. She falls easily. Nyamuch, watching what is happening in front of her, realizes the fight is now becoming her parents' fight. And she does the only one thing she is able to do: she flees the scene. But she doesn't close her lips. The child keeps crying. A cry that makes the neighbour wonder what is going on.

Inside the compound, the wife manages to get up. She holds firm the fat dried stick in her husband's hand and as they pull it back and forth, it breaks into two. About a minute or so later, two men approach the scene. One is ahead of the other. The first one passes the gate and rushes to help. At that point, the one in behind calls him back.

"Why are you helping?" he asks. "Look, it's like a rock colliding with another rock. Who are you offering your help to?" The man behind says while laughing. The first man stops and returns to the gate. Nyayang, out of character, demonstrates some surprising strength. She breaks all the objects her husband intends on using against her.

But behaving like this usually doesn't turn out well for the woman. Especially when it involves other men watching. Chuol's anger is fuelled even further. He bitterly approaches her with his bare hands fisted tightly, caring less that he could easily shorten her life.

The wrestling carries on. The two men adjust themselves to be able to capture its wonderful moments. The fight gets intense and Nyayang decides to use what she has been born with as a weapon. She unzips her beautiful lips and purposely bites her beautiful husband.

Chuol instantly realizes he now carries a wound, and he loses it even more. He becomes a fire-breathing being. However, with everyone arriving at the scene, he is allowed not to unleash his blind bitterness.

"Leave. Leave my house," Chuol demands of Nyayang. Nyayang hesitates to exit the compound.

"No, no, you have to leave," the women at the scene say. They push her out. "You have to leave or you are going to orphan your child." Chuol, in the midst of everyone, is just a flame you wouldn't dare touch.

Nyayang arrives at her parents' home and before she can catch her breath, her father asks her to go back. Mr. Jock is a man who speaks from his head. He looks for solid evidence but bloody bruises and a constant nosebleed won't easily get him to change his stance.

"How do I know that you are not spending too much time away, leaving the child with the man to take care of, huh?" he asks after she tries to explain to him how the whole thing got fuelled. He turns around and walks away, annoyed.

"Come, come. Sit here," says her mother. "Maybe when you go back tomorrow things will look different."

Nyayang returns to her house the next morning. However, this morning, she finds her father-in-law has come for a reason she wouldn't have learned otherwise. A month ago, Mr. Malual requested the presence of one of Chuol's girlfriends to check on them like he had done with all of his sons' previous girlfriends. Today is the day.

Chuol, upon seeing his enemy, rises up and readies for another fight. Mr. Malual gets in between them and refuses to let them resume the fight. Nevertheless, why she would ever bite her husband is something the old man still doesn't understand.

"Does it happen that when there is a fight, a wife bites her husband?" asks Mr. Malual. Nyayang remains silent, and Nyamuch unleashes herself.

"I think it would have been wise for you if you would have just withdrawn yourself instead of biting your husband like that," he adds, seemingly disappointed.

"No, untaught, disrespectful girls don't stop there. They keep going until they touch the untouchable," Chuol emerges through words. "Now leave my house," he angrily demands of his wife.

Nyayang keeps her lips together and remains still, hoping her father-in-law will refute his son. But no. Instead, Mr. Malual says this to the twins who have returned to the city early this morning, "Haven't you made somebody a mother yet?" The twins laugh simultaneously. "No? You obviously aren't descended from me!" says the grandfather.

This time Chuol laughs, too. He immediately stops laughing once he sees Nyayang still standing there. It's nearly the time for his visitor to arrive. "Get out before I throw you out myself," says Chuol.

Nyayang leaves with her child again.

She goes out of the compound and into the street with Nyamuch at her side, and out of nowhere, her neighbour's friend runs toward her with her child. "Hold him, hold him for me," she says while ungently throwing the child at Nyayang and quickly turning her back on her and running back into the compound.

Nyayang holds the child and follows her. She comes to and stop out of their view. It turns out the friend was running away from a fight with her enemy from among her husband's wives. She finally said something about the abuse she had been enduring, surprisingly not from the husband but from one of his wives. This woman had gone as far as finding girls to sleep with their husband whenever she knew it was going to be this wife's turn. And although men claim to be the strongest sex, her husband couldn't even ask about the one who was scheduled to be with him whenever the plan switched. But she had been fighting with the child mingling around her legs. She would disentangle him and push him away as hard as she could many times and he would come right back to her and would hold his mother as tight as he could. And now all Nyayang can hear her friend say is, "Have I stopped you from having many children?"

"I will show you," says the co-wife.

"Who are you? How do you even consider yourself a real wife when you were just given to him like food by your parents?" she continues.

This is an insult. In this culture, the way to respectfully marry someone involves paying something to the family, or the whole process of how the two found each other is thought to come back and haunt the woman. The child is crying, trying to go to his mother. Nyayang tries her best but she can only hold him down. She is unable to do anything about the crying.

Chuol hears her speaking with the child. He comes out, still very angry at her, but as soon as he steps outside, he sees his girlfriend coming. He stops, pretending he is waiting for her. While waiting, he asks Nyayang, while looking at his girlfriend, "So this is where you have been?"

Nyayang hears his voice but says nothing and doesn't look at him. Nyamuch turns around after hearing him, too, but looks at him. She keeps staring him as he greets his girlfriend. He walks her in quickly. The two women who were fighting get separated but the insults keep flying. The friend returns to Nyayang at the gate and the co-wife says, "Don't you know I know all your husbands? If you were a decent girl, why else would your parents give away their daughter like a cloth if it wasn't because your father knew you were a worthless being, shared often by anything that is male?"

Nyayang turns around when the co-wife says this. Nyayang holds her friend's hand up and says, "Don't, please."

The friend takes her child from Nyayang and as she takes him, she says to the co-wife, "It is not my fault. I didn't ask your barren womb to refuse a child. You spend every minute of the day with him. You even take my time for yourself, and each time you spend my time with him, you come out just as clean as you were going in."

The co-wife hears her and it begins to hurt as if this was the worst insult she's heard during today's fight. She storms off as swiftly as she can, and instead of punching her enemy, she grabs the child and throws him on the ground. The child passes out instantly. The mother throws herself at the co-wife. The two get separated immediately. An older co-wife runs toward the child, unconscious on the ground. She grabs him. She looks at Nyayang at the gate. Nyayang has the face of a guilty person. She runs back into a room. Nyayang walks back slowly. She comes back to the main street between the two compounds. Mr. Malual and his grandchildren are laughing. She stops in front of the gate. Nyamuch pulls on her hand trying to get her mother to go back inside the compound. She tugs on her quickly and says, "This way", leading both of them back to her parents' home.

Upon reaching her parents' home, she relates that her in-laws demanded she return. Her father is not surprised. But he knows there is something that usually gets done in this unfortunate situation.

Three days later, Mr. Jock calls on his daughter's in-laws. Chuol and his father arrive the next day, pretentiously curious to hear what they have been called for.

"Nyayang has related to me all that has taken place," the father begins. "I called you here to give you my apology. It is absolutely disgraceful that Nyayang has wronged you this much. I have ready for you what a father must do in this deplorable situation."

Mr. Jock pays the fine.

"Guan Nyayang, we are glad you called us. I was disappointed when I found out about all of this," Mr. Malual begins. "In my mind, I went like this, didn't anyone teach Nyayang what is expected of a wife?" continues Mr. Malual.

Mr. Jock begins feeling small. He thinks of shortening the length of the discussion, as Mr. Malual implicitly continues questioning whether he and his wife taught their daughter about the important things in life.

"Gat-Malual, I know how disappointing this can be," Mr. Jock interrupts.

"Yes. And I believe we all can be happy if nothing like this repeats itself again," says Mr. Malual and then the two leave.

In the evening of the same day, Mr. Jock calls in his wife before him. He wants his wife to give him a more reasonable explanation as to why Nyayang had bitten her husband.

"I—I cannot think of any other reason Nyayang did this other than the fact that she was protecting herself," explains the mother.

There is never a need for a wife to bite her husband if she doesn't mean to bring disgrace upon the family. He gets up and complains as he walks around. "Look," he says. "Look at the shame this act has brought on our family. I felt very insulted today in my own dwelling. Very insulted." He turns his head away from his wife for a moment.

"I don't want an insult destroying the reputation of this family simply because . . . " He stops. "Because somebody tries to be a rule-breaker," he adds. He throws his hand around and instantly his wife loses the colour in her face. "Tonight you must talk to your daughter. Tell your daughter that it's not right in the eye of the law for a woman to be loud in the presence of her husband.

"Tell her she must always—and I mean always—be considerate of the words coming out of her mouth when talking to her husband. And before I forget, tell Nyayang women don't just see the feet of a fight emerging and like feathers in the wind, fly away. They stay!" he says with a flame of frustration. "NO, they *stay* until the fight is calm."

Through the night, Nyayang and her dear mother go through all the behaviours which seem to have helped women remain in men's houses. At the end of their discussion, the mother tells her child, "You must remain humble, my child. Despite your suffering. Because it's the only way you can remain in that house and mother your child." Her voice begins to shake. Nyayang gets up and wipes off her mother's tears. The next morning, she returns to her house with her child intent on continuing to live out her marriage, despite knowing what she knows.

CHAPTER EIGHT

Chuol still has not come to a firm conclusion even after months of now being with Nyayang. Up to this point, he has seen ladies in relationships with him seemingly behave in the same meek way Nyayang presented herself prior to their relationship moving forward.

But with his parents expecting him to have more children, Chuol feels pressure. And every time nothing happens, he gets to prove his point, which his parents wouldn't disagree with. However, the parents know one important thing, and that's that a man is not rich until he has many soul mates, some of whom serve the purpose of serving.

"Just go and find the woman that will treat your heart," Chuol's parents encourage him. But one never knows what the Creator has planned for them. With no one knowing, the dry Loge grows a leaf again. The unexpected happens and the joy that comes from the news that a mother is pregnant again is breathtaking. Nyayang has finally made herself pregnant again. She has joyfully conceived her second child.

Except something is questionable in the eye of the one who claims to have known the time and date on which branches grow new leaves. The inevitable argument erupts when the pregnancy reaches its fourth month.

"It's true? This is all?" Chuol asks.

"How small do you think this could be?" asks Nyayang. "How small? You feel no shame asking me that question?"

"Okay, how should I have asked?" Nyayang, again, is showing him her disrespectful attitude. Chuol just goes numb.

"I know how much a four-month pregnancy should have grown," he exclaims irritably.

"Waah, guan Nyamuch!" cries the wife. "Don't accuse me of a deed I did not commit."

"Oh, really? So you think if I said you committed adultery I would be accusing you? Very impressive!" he says.

"Well," he goes on, "I know you have committed adultery. And I have to tell you this: I cannot share a wife with another man. Never! Not to mention the many cows I have spent on you," he mumbles to himself. He turns around as though he wants to leave her. Then he stops suddenly.

Nyayang, with her mind diving into a bowl of dark confusion, remains frozen in the same spot. All that she thinks make her who she is, now begins to untangle. She begins to feel her self-esteem, pride and her dignity sweat off her skin.

"No, that is not true. I didn't commit adultery and I will never commit it and you know that."

"Oh yeah? So then you are telling me I'm a liar?" Nyayang, torn between her husband and a mind that can't take any more suffering, bows her head down so the man can perhaps take a moment to reconsider the situation.

But no. He will not. "Well, let's see . . . " Chuol says with a triumphant air. With prepared deliberation, he goes on surprising his dear wife with supposed evidence to back up his statement. Besides the man who asked Nyayang for directions a year ago, none of the other "evidence" he brings up can be proven. Nonetheless, disapproving the other occurrences would just be adding "fuel to fire."

In a blind fury, Chuol walks over to his wife. Nyayang senses something very ungentle approaching. She flees, leaving her child behind. On her way to her parents' home, Nyayang realizes the response her dear father will have when she walks in. She also knows if she goes back, Chuol will be waiting for her, especially now that their child is with him. She spends the rest of the day with the neighbour.

"If I keep you here with me, first, the other women would not let me and they would accuse me that I have helped you to run away. And

I can't go and wander around with you as my absence from home has already been linked to having stayed with some men I don't know," Nyayang's neighbour friend says.

"You are?" asks Nyayang.

"I am." Nyayang looks concerned, forgetting about her problem for a moment. Nyayang does not know the trouble her friend has been going through since the two are mostly kept separate. She holds her hands.

"I don't know what to say," Nyayang says.

"Oh, it is nothing. What is the matter with you, if I may ask?" asks the friend.

Nyayang, like her friend says, "Oh, it is nothing." Denying the length to which they both have been oppressed by their accusers, the two decide not to talk about their concerns anymore. "You stay strong," Nyayang tells her friend as she hurriedly walks back to the compound. Nyayang remains still, not knowing which direction her mind can deal with now.

At last, she makes her mind up. She goes ahead to her parents' home so she can spend the night there. "Another fight?" asks her mother after she sits down. At this point Mr. Jock is taking a shower. About five minutes later, he makes his way out and the first thing he notices is his daughter's presence.

"What is wrong? Why are you here at night?" he asks.

"Chuol and I almost fought," says Nyayang.

"And then what happened?" asks her father impatiently as he keeps wrapping his body with a towel.

"I think, Guan Nyayang, you need to speak with your son-in-law. Because the things he is coming up with are kind of hard to swallow now," says her mother, cutting off her daughter after closing a chapter she was reading from the bible.

"Tell me what happened." He stops a short distance away from his daughter. Nyayang hesitates as this is the first time she and her father will speak about something outside of the typical father-daughter conversations. She mumbles right before letting the words leave her mouth.

"Chuol is saying the baby isn't his," she says. She looks at her father's face.

"Really!" Mr. Jock goes on examining what seems to be a perfect body. "I don't believe you," he says. "I think you have made that up. Because I realize what you and your stupid mother are doing. You are trying to make me a fool among the men of this place."

Nyayang, upon hearing her father's cynical response, shrinks to a smaller size.

"Making this whole deplorable thing up? How could you be so ignorant?" Nyayang's mother lets the words fly, forgetting the fact she has been warned to keep her hands off when it comes to matters between Nyayang and her in-laws.

"You again!" He points at his wife and uses the rest of the time to glare at her.

"And as for you, Nyayang, I don't believe you. Whose head are you wishing to cover? Mine? Huh? If your husband accused you of adultery, would you be walking free of bruises? Would you?" The two women feel their souls get even colder as he continues to tear them down.

"You are not spending the night here," he says. "You are making me look small and like a fool among other men." Nyayang gets up and begins to walk away.

"Where are you going? In the middle of the night?" her mother asks.

"I don't know. But what am I supposed to do?" She stamps her feet on the rocky ground in frustration.

"Come back here. Come, spend the night here. Perhaps when you return tomorrow, the situation will look a little bit lighter," her mother says.

Nyayang spends the night with the permission of her mother. And because her mother takes it upon herself, Nyayang shortens her stay by leaving before her father lays an eye on the new day. At home, she arrives and falls into her ritualistic morning tasks. She sweeps the compound. And with her hand, she fries up the most delicious dish, the type of breakfast she knows finishes her man's morning right.

"Hey, Mama." Nyamuch wakes up and runs to her mother. Chuol wakes up immediately after, surprised by the presence of his wife. About a half an hour later, the wife rushes the breakfast to her husband. She stops in between her husband's room and hers. It seems as if she is trying to remember something. She shakes her head as she tries to call it to mind. Chuol watches her from his room. Finally, she runs back. She quickly throws the bowl she carried away and starts cooking all over again. She almost committed a criminal act! She must have been in a rush. She knows she must not cook or go before her husband without a Yat. Good thing she caught herself. After returning from her family today, Nyayang quickly showered to wash off the sweat from the walk over but she completely forgot about putting on another Yat after she had washed the one she had on. It takes another half an hour to finish the new dish. She kneels to rest it on the table but Chuol says, "I need no food. Take it away."

With no discussion as to why, she takes the food back to the kitchen. She puts some into a second bowl for her child and the two walk to their room. But before the two can get comfortable, Nyayang hears the voice of her dear husband echoing from one end of the compound to the other. And instead of "Ahem!" the distinct way he calls his wife, he actually calls out his daughter's name.

"Nyamuch, Nyamuch!" The child hears her name. She pushes away the bowl but she hesitates before she exits the room. There is only one reason that her father would be calling her in her mind, and that is that she is going to get slapped on the head for reasons that are not discussed neither prior nor after. There is zero relationship between her father and her. Or, it is very ill and needs some work if there was ever a relationship there in the first place. She tries her part and anytime she gets any closer, he says, "Go, go, go over there." And she fears that if she persists, it may escalate to the point where she regrets it. "Nyamuch!" Her father calls for a third time. Nyamuch exits the room. She shows up in his room and she is immediately sent somewhere in the neighbourhood to play.

Immediately, Chuol rushes to his wife's room. "So," he begins, "where have you been?"

"I went to my parents' home," she says.

"You went there because they were the ones who asked you to commit adultery, right?"

"Guan Nyamuch, why are you accusing me of a deed you know I didn't commit?" Nyayang says. And with no wise intentions on her exhausted mind, she stands tall like a man in front of the real man. This unanticipated stance of course fuels and ignites the already flaming anger he has lidded off in his heart for far too long.

"I'm accusing you?" he asks and returns the pretend man back to the ground with a good punch. "You stupid prostitutes! You think I'm the type of man that accepts filthiness?"

Seeing her on the ground now, Chuol gladly takes off the belt that has been holding up his trousers.

Some time passes. Nyamuch, who was sent away a while ago, returns to the compound, breathing heavily for some reason. She looks for her father in his room and when she doesn't see him, she dashes to her mother's room. Standing in front of the locked door, the little girl hears a weird noise. Nyayang is not necessarily crying, but the intensity of the pain in her voice leaves her no choice either.

Nyamuch begins pushing the locked door, but she can't even crack the dry bark of the tree. With no obvious luck, she hopelessly throws herself on the ground with the word "Mom!" filling her mouth.

As she continues crying, her mother's voice echoes beyond the compound. Except it makes no one wonder beyond what the neighbour knows. Which are two things: There is a chance that it's either her, the child, being shown the way, or Chuol's other child being re-instructed.

A few moments pass and for some reason, Nyayang goes quiet. The child relocates closer and puts her ear against the door. And there is her father opening the door from the inside. The two pass each other at the door, saying no words to each other. Chuol goes out and quickly vanishes. Nyamuch, on the other hand, runs in and throws herself at the dying body of her mother.

Nyayang at this time can't even reassure her dear child of what will happen in the next moment. She bleeds through the nose and coughs out blood. And Nyamuch, not knowing what to do, sits beside her mother.

It is about half an hour later on that morning that a strange woman walks on the main road across from the gate. The woman feels thirty and thinks of getting some water to drink. When she sees the gate open, she decides to go inside the compound. She stops closer to the gate, then greets the people in the compound. When she comes closer, she says. "Is there anybody home?"

Nyamuch emerges all of a sudden and walks toward the woman with tears flowing down her cheeks silently. "Why are you crying?" asks the woman. Nyamuch keeps silent but, instead, walks even closer to the woman. The woman gently puts her hand on the child's head as a way to give her comfort so she can talk. Nyamuch, with a stutter, tries to communicate the situation. But nothing makes it out. "Where is your mother?" the woman insists. Nyamuch goes on again but none of what she says is understandable to the woman.

Then she runs back to the room, leaving the woman unaware of anything. The woman becomes curious and wants to know more about the strange moment the two just had. So she goes further into the compound.

She immediately feels uncomfortable, not knowing what may underlie this lingering silence. "Is there an adult in this compound? I would like to have some water, please," she says while standing still. Yet she receives no response.

At last she turns around and begins s walking away. But something at the back of her mind disturbs her.

In the room, the little girl is perplexed. She takes a quick look outside at the direction in which she left the strange woman standing. There she sees the woman has turned her back and is on her way, leaving the compound.

With everything she has, she runs after her and grabs her by the hand. The woman startles as a result, and the little girl holds down firmly on the woman's hand. With no further delay, the woman senses there must be something else beyond the little girl's tears.

The two run inside the room where Nyayang lies on the flour. There is a constant flow of blood from her nose. The woman grabs a piece of cloth quick and begins to compress the bleeding.

"Can you hear me?" asks the woman. And before she can expect an answer, she realizes the abnormality in Nyayang's breathing. Second by second, the breathing gets even more laboured.

The woman kneels and begins rubbing her back. Nyayang moves her legs. At this point, the situation becomes clear to the woman. She thinks that whoever did this to her and left is a real piece of work.

She stands up suddenly and is faced with a profound predicament. She knows Nyayang needs urgent recue, but she also doesn't want to overstep her bounds. Giving the moment a glance, she turns to the little girl and gives her a long look. At last, she asks her, "Where is your father?" without paying any heed to what may be underlying his absence in this dire moment. Nyamuch goes on stuttering, which doesn't help the woman at all. Frustrated, she turns back again to Nyayang on the ground.

If I leave now, I know I will be leaving someone who truly needs my help, the woman thinks to herself. There is a great dilemma on her mind: the woman cannot decide whether she should seek help for the suffering lady on the floor or go on her way.

I have to help this mother. What am I thinking? Wouldn't she have done the same if life took me down this path? The woman finally convinces herself after calling to mind a challenging time of her own. She turns around and, at the door, she looks confused. She knows not which neighbour's house she should go to for help. Or whether the reaction will be as she would like.

There. She slips out anyway and finds herself at the nearest neighbour's gate.

In the middle of the compound is a tree with few leaves under which two men play chess. "Mali," she greets them in a rather urgent voice. Upon hearing her unmannered voice, the seated men turn toward her at once without responding to the greeting. Instead, one of the men, being the owner of the compound, calls someone to respond to the visitor.

"Women, come, there is someone at the gate." But the woman needs to say why she is at the gate now. And so she continues saying what she needs to say.

"I come to tell you a mother in that home is in critical condition," she says nervously while pointing at Chuol's big compound, as the two unfriendly faces keep staring at her.

"Where do you come from and how do you know this?" asks one of the men.

"Maybe she is her relative," says the other man before the woman can reply.

"No, she said 'a mother in that home.' That means she doesn't know who the woman is," explains the first man.

"Actually, I was just trying to get some water to drink. That is how I found out about her."

"So what do you want?" the woman is asked.

"I'm saying she needs urgent medical attention. But she needs someone who can assist her, for she is lying on the floor in pain," explains the woman.

"Okay, we will see what we can do," say the men. They bow their heads and begin talking in low voices. To her shock, it appears the two are talking chess. In the game, the winning guarantor is the number of pieces to which a player adds on and the winner becomes the one with more on his side. The two make it seem as though it is physical. A game with physical characteristics. It grasps their souls. It is all they think of, it seems.

"I think you need to help her now," demands the woman.

"Oh, you still here?" asks one of the men.

"Is that how you speak to your husband?" a voice on her right asks her. The woman turns to her right and there is one of the women from the compound walking toward her. She is number seven of seventeen wives. She emerges from one of the many rooms contained in this compound. It appears that a number of women were in that one room. And as this women walks toward the strange woman, she first washes her hands as though they just finished eating. And given what time it is now, they were indeed eating.

This is the time when they would group themselves: young women around one bowl, older women around another bowl, after everyone else had eaten and after each one had finished her tasks for the morning part of the day. It could have been any one of the women. Nyayang's friend would have perhaps responded differently had she not still been at the bottom of the ranking order. Being at the top of the "good wives" list, this woman rose to the occasion.

"You don't sit down when speaking to your husband?" she asks the woman ambiguously as she walks even closer, with both of her hands around her sides while emphasizing how uncultured she appears to men when speaking while standing.

The woman instantly becomes confused. She knows nothing to say. "You just shout at the top of your lungs at men without showing respect? What kind of a woman are you? Huh? What is wrong with you?" she goes on speaking on behalf of her husband and his friend, who have already turned back to their game.

"Nothing is wrong with me. I just want her to get help," responds the woman.

"Well, then why didn't you sit down first?"

"Sit down first? Why should I sit down while someone is in pain?" the woman shoots back.

"Very disrespectful!" she says.

"Hey, don't you dare insult me," the woman reproaches.

"Well then, you should have asked your friend why she is constantly getting beat up like a detestable bird."

"Don't call her my friend. If there is anyone who could have been a friend, that would have been you. But clearly, you are not. I'm just trying to help here."

"You get out of my compound," she says while gesturing with her hand, and she starts walking back to her room. "They walk with rhino horns on their head and forget to show a little bit of respect," she mumbles as she distances herself from the woman. She passes the two men who have fixed their attention on nothing but their game.

The woman backs up and tries to return to Nyayang's house but then stops herself in the middle. *How about trying that house?* she says to herself. At the house, she finds a woman braiding a little girl's hair.

"Mali," she greets the two.

"Mali," responds the mother. The mother and her daughter get up and walk to the woman at the gate.

"A woman in that home is dying," says the woman while pointing at Nyayang's house.

"Nyayang?" The mother looks shocked. "No, no!" she cries. "Her husband always tries to kill her."

"Her husband did that and left?" asks the woman.

"Yes, he did."

Now the little girl is standing between the two women, and she sees her father coming behind them. He alternates his feet hoping to hear what the discussion between the two women is about.

As he gets closer, leaving no footprints on the ground, the little girl pinches the back of her mother's palm painfully so that she moves suddenly.

With a frown on her face, she gives her daughter a look and the daughter signals the meaning of her sudden act to her. The mother turns around and there is her husband.

"What is going on here?" he asks with a thick voice.

"Oh, she came to tell us Nyayang, our neighbour, is in a difficult situation," the wife says, preparing herself and immediately backing up to give her husband some room.

"How is she doing? Has she said anything yet?" she asks her husband as she starts to walk away about another situation this husband attended earlier.

"Yeah, she did," the husband responds. As the words came out of his mouth, his wife looks back at the other two. And in her eyes, the woman can read there is something else this wife and her husband were talking about, and there are two different conversations being held here.

But what is going on? the woman thinks to herself. As she tries to talk to the woman's husband, it appears there are children crying in another compound behind this compound.

"I think she really needs help. Maybe someone who can get her to the hospital," the woman tries telling him what she thinks.

Then there is a long silence. While the two avoid talking, another woman passes the gate. She mumbles things that are not clear to the woman standing at the gate except one thing she keeps repeating: "He did it. He is the one."

She seems very sad! She passes the gate but someone urgently calls her back. And all the woman at the gate can hear is, "She is now conscious. She said something." But what are they talking about?

Around eleven a.m. this morning, a man who went hunting with his dog stumbled upon a woman's body lying down at the river's bank. He recognized the woman. And to reduce the confusion he knew would come up, he brought her to her home, even though she was not fully conscious.

"What happened?" people asked the man.

"I just found her lying on the ground," the man said. Those who became aware of the situation came to her house. But there was someone who was not present.

The woman's brother-in-law. A child was sent to his house to get him. He declined to come. This man's brother passed away a year ago. As he remained in charge of his and his brother's family, he boldly expressed that he wanted to carry on reproducing children for his deceased brother. But she said no. And that led to a brutal argument between the two.

Early this morning, this man came to his brother's house and asked his late brother's wife to do him a favour. He said he needed help bringing some logs he'd gathered the day before back to his home. She agreed and nobody really knew what happened after that.

"I knew it. He did it, but who will talk about it?" says the woman who is called back. The woman at the gate watches her running back. She then turns to the man before her and waits for him to say something.

"Woman!" says the man. "You see, that woman you are talking about is someone's else wife. I'm afraid I cannot involve myself," explains the man.

He turns around as though he wants to leave. "You know, here it's not necessarily about what has been done, or how the harm had been delivered, but about who could legitimately be the one who started it," he says.

"This is my house," continues the man. "I run it the way I want. And as far as I know, Chuol is just doing the same thing."

The woman remains stunned after hearing the man tell her the very truth that has destroyed generations of these people.

"But how could he have left someone he killed like that?" she asks with her voice full of frustration.

With no answer to the question, the man gives her a long gaze. "Killed, huh? Where are you from?" The woman bows her head. "Is that how you speak in the presence of your husband?"

"I think I need to go," says the woman.

"Yes, you'd better be leaving," the man agrees.

At Nyayang's house, the woman finds Nyayang has come out of the room. "You are alive!" She claps her hands joyfully as she throws herself beside her. "I found no body. I thought I would, but no," says the woman.

"And that's okay," says Nyayang.

"Then I don't know how I'm going to help you," says the woman sadly.

"Don't fret. You have done your part," says Nyayang. "You see when a woman cries during childbirth, it's not necessarily the pain. Because pain is an inherent part of birth. But rather, it is what the pain does to a woman. This is my life. You cannot refuse who you are or the implications that come along with it."

"Don't talk like that," refutes the woman.

"Why? Why not? Is this not part of the reason God created me a woman?"

"Oh, no. Don't say that. God loves all that He creates," says the woman.

"No. I will give no ears to that. If He loves all, He would have created all of us men."

The woman wraps her arm around Nyayang's shoulders.

"Anyway, this is my life," continues Nyayang. "I'm already in this world. It's just sometimes . . . " She goes quiet. Tears begin to roll down her cheeks.

The woman lets go of her shoulders and says, "It's just what?"

"It's just that sometimes tears don't listen, because I would have held them back." She weeps the rest of her flowing tears.

"There is nothing to be worried about. I'm able to walk to my parents' home. You should go," Nyayang tells the woman.

With that, the woman leaves and Nyayang and her child go on their way.

CHAPTER NINE

At her parents' home, she drops her child off and her mother walks with her back to the downtown hospital where she is admitted immediately. Closer to sunset, her father comes as well. The pain becomes so unreal that it leads to heavy bleeding. The bleeding continues and eventually washes the unborn fetus out. Sadness overcomes Nyayang's mother. She weeps and weeps. As she cries, Nyayang's father looks to the right of his wife and sees a baby being rocked on the doctor on duty's arm. It is a baby boy. "Yours?" he asks.

"No, one of those dumped survivors left by, well, you know who," the doctor says while looking down at the baby.

"Oh, I know. One day God will make me see a woman dumping a baby. I will beat the hell out of her until she can't cry anymore. Prostitutes. They take men's blood and, just like that, dump them with no feeling of remorse or shame!"

Nyayang's mother turns around and says something to her husband, and instead of asking, "Why do you think they throw away men's blood?" she says, "Maybe the blood was refused by its owner. What can the carrier do?" She says it in a tone which suggests that she doesn't really want him to give an answer.

The husband swells up, anyway, and although it was clearly stated in a tone that required no answer, he says, "What could be a reason? They just want to go back and be treated as though they are still girls when clearly we know they are not. If you throw away a man's blood because you think you are successfully going to deceive us, no! We know! We see right through you. We know it when we see your breasts. We know who has given birth or not. We know."

Nyayang turns to her mother as her father continues speaking on behalf of men. And in response to her father's argument, she says, "Mom!"

Her mother looks at her. "They know."

"How are you feeling right now?" her doctor shows at that moment, and after seeing the unfortunate result, he prolongs her stay to three days. The three days go by, but people who have heard the "not-so-great news" pay their respects by visiting—except for the husband and his family.

"You are now good to go," the doctor announces and reassures the parents the rest of the pain will be well managed at home.

Before Nyayang and her doctor can say their goodbyes, a woman runs toward them and in a fearful voice says, "Doctor, doctor! She is going to die! Help my child, I'm begging you!" She throws herself at his feet and grabs his hands. Then she quickly gets up. "Please!" She starts pulling at him with tears in her eyes, staring at the man with the magical healing powers.

The two hurry to the other side of the building and, in one of the many wards, the doctor can't believe his eyes.

"Look. She is going die. My child will die." The woman pulls her child to her side.

"No, no, you are going to do some damage to the child in her womb," says the doctor. "Get over there," he says, as he makes his way to the child with a child in her womb. He comes and places his hand on her forehead. "How old is she?" the doctor asks. "She is fifteen," a woman with the child's mother says.

The doctor remains quiet. He pulls out his gloves and throws them into a nearby trash can. He grabs another set of gloves from a nurse who is with him. "One, two, three. Let's go." With the help of another doctor and the nurse, they place the pregnant child onto a moving bed. "Grab the head," he says to the other doctor.

"She is really going to die now," says the mother.

"Don't follow us with the word 'death' . . . " the doctor yells at her and lets go of the wheeling bed, leaving the other two to guide it.

"I don't know what will happen. All I know is that she is not going be able to give birth naturally. We have to do a C-section." He then storms off after the patient.

Meanwhile, Nyayang and her mother are overwhelmed, watching from a distance on the other side of the building which is separated by the nurses' stations.

"Come, let's go," says Nyayang's mother.

"I let go my own pain when I see them suffering this much," says Nyayang.

"Because they are suffering more than you are?" asks her mother.

"No. But there is a difference between knowing what is wrong though you may not have a way to refute it, and simply believing what you are taught to believe by society."

"Her mother's son now has a family, that's something good," says Nyayang's mother.

"You know the story?" Nyayang asks.

"It is not always as your father puts it. But yeah, there are stories of people to whom society is blind. Who cares about the truth behind them? The women are always the ones blamed in the end. And you know why? It's the blood," she says.

"It's good enough to risk her life, I suppose," says Nyayang. The two begin leaving. Nyayang's mother looks over her shoulder and in her spirit, she senses the need for hope in the eyes of another mother.

"Maybe we should pray with her before we leave," says her mother.

"Sure, let's pray."

She walks to the woman and tilts her head over her shoulder. "I just want to let you know that I just went through a similar situation with my daughter. Not entirely similar but somewhat. I was afraid, just like you are now," says Nyayang's mother. She starts wiping her tears and brushing them off with her clothing. "She will be fine." She tries offering her some words of hope."

"How do I know she is going to make it? How?" says the woman.

"She will, just have faith," says Nyayang's mother. "Just have faith," she says again.

"I don't know. I don't know my faith will make it. I have been without it the moment C-section was mentioned."

"They are doing a C-section, huh?"

"They said she wouldn't be able to deliver naturally. She is still young and is carrying twins.

"What am I going to do?" she says frantically. "I will blame it on my husband if anything ends up happening."

"No, no. Don't put that on your mind. Nothing will happen, okay?"

"I told him 'Don't.' Look, he is not even here," she says with her eyes looking around and her hands gesturing.

"You know men," says Nyayang's mother. "Come, let's sit down." She sits her down nicely and wipes her tears off one more time.

"I told my husband don't give your dear child to a man whose cows you are willing to put to use and expect him to be with her like his own daughter. I told him. But now look. And he said unless I declared I was the man, he was not going to listen."

"What happened?" Nyayang's mother asks with her good listening ears.

"She got married. Our son needs to marry but there were not enough cows for him to marry. So, when she got married at age ten, her father promised her husband that he would not be disappointed if he kept the girl for a couple of years. In the third year, we all feared, even myself, that she may betray us and go with somebody else." She cries while telling Nyayang's mother what happened.

"Take it easy. Remember you don't need to tell me about this if it brings tears to your eyes."

"The husband came back and said he feared his wife would be taken by the boys," the mother continues. "The two agreed, with him promising my husband he would not touch her till she turns fifteen. But now look. She just turned fifteen and she is now with twins. What have I done, God?" she says.

"No, you have done nothing. It's just this life," says Nyayang's mother. "Just have faith. She will be okay."

There is a moment of silence. Now the woman is thinking about other repercussions if she doesn't make it. She shakes her heads and sweats excessively. "What if she dies, what if . . . He will then take back his cows and my son will lose his wife. And then I'll be thrown back into having no head of my own. But I don't care about that."

"You are worrying a lot. But please have faith. Let's pray." The four heads bow and when they finish, Nyayang's mother announces they will proceed home. They leave. And unfortunately, the aging day takes the soul of the new mother.

"You are not here to stay," says Nyayang's father irritably after his child asks him if she can spend a month at her parent's house before she goes back. Two weeks have gone by and though Mr. Malual's family has heard the unfortunate news, they have not seen a reason to come visit.

And then this happens. On a bright, blessed day, Chuol unexpectedly arrives at his in-laws' home with a mission only another man like him could understand. His appearance surprises the females, who are blown away when the reason he has come reaches their ears, but not the man in the house.

As the conversation unfolds, Mr. Jock and his daughter's husband try to focus on the normalcy of the situation. And it's this cultural belief that allows for a better understanding between the two. For centuries now, it has had been strongly believed and commonly practised that the biological father of a woman's unborn child cannot cause any damage to his child if he ever decides on teaching a lesson to his pregnant wife. No matter how brutal or severely she gets hit or how many times she gets thrown on the ground, as long as he is the real father of the child in her womb, the child will be unharmed. At the end of the discussion, Chuol demands that his wife return home to him.

The evening arrives and Mr. Jock calls on the two females. "Your husband has come and is deeply sorry about what has happened," he starts to say.

"I don't believe it for a second." Nyayang turns away.

"What is it you don't believe?" her father questions.

"That he was sorry when he imposed this much hurt on me." Nyayang turns up the volume of her voice. "And he knew anything that could hurt me, could hurt the child as well," she continues angrily.

"How could he accuse me of a deed I didn't commit?" Her voice cracks this time. Then the tears flow.

"Oh, my child. Men are all like that. We don't trust woman until they die," says her father.

"Really? And what is that saying about them?" Nyayang turns back her angry face and faces her father. "Of course, they always sleep with the dust in the air, don't they? How could I have forgotten that," she corrects herself with sarcasm in the meaning.

She is silent for a moment, hoping her father will reflect deeply on what she meant. But clearly, he can't even grasp it on a surface level.

"He couldn't even show up at the hospital," mumbles Nyayang. "What kind of a person is he?"

"That is why he is here," Mr. Jock says. "He wants you and the child to go back. Very soon, if possible," he adds.

"No! You cannot do this to your daughter again, Jock!" yells Nyayang's mother, who has been holding her thoughts since the two were called in. "Nyayang is not going back. After all he has done to her? You have to have a serious talk with this man before you dump your child into his unsafe hands again." Her mother just vomits out the words.

Mr. Jock looks at his wife and instantly becomes angry. "You! You still haven't listened to my voice!" His voice is swimming with disappointment. "I warn you for the very last time." He begins to shake. "I warn you. And if Nyayang refuses to go back, I—I will know you have had a hand in her refusal."

"Really? Like I always close my eyes to the injustices I see?" says the mother and then slips out of the room.

"And to you, Nyayang." Her father turns to his daughter after her mother steps out of the room. "You and your child are leaving tomorrow. All families are the same!" he yells at her in his manly voice. Nyayang falls humbly silent before him.

"You can go all over the world, but you will never find a family in which you would spit butter out of your mouth. Never!" he adds. "Besides, your husband has done something no other husband has done before."

"What did he do?" Nyayang asks impatiently.

He looks at her and almost refuses to answer this stupid question. But he wants her to go back. "He apologized. Do you have any clue how hard it is for a man to admit he has done something wrong?" her father answers, and follows it with a question.

"No. But I know now. And I'm just wondering what that really says about a man," says Nyayang.

Mr. Jock stares disappointedly at his daughter. "You are leaving tomorrow." He ends the conversation.

In the night, Nyayang and her mother come up with a sneaky plan. The real goal is to have her father speaks to his daughter's husband.

"You go and stay there until I advise you otherwise," her mother advises her daughter. Nyayang leaves her parents' home during the night and hides at the house of one of her friends, less than four blocks away from her father. "You are not going back until he talks to Chuol," says her mother as she pushes her daughter out of the compound.

In the morning, the grounds are empty. Nyayang has disappeared. "Where is she?" demands her father.

"I don't know," denies the mother.

"You know! You told her to leave. I know you wholly. I know how dark you become when it comes to me. ."

"Tell me, do you want to divorce her?" continues Mr. Jock.

"Of course not. Why would I divorce my daughter?"

"Okay, then tell me. What are you doing?"

"Jock, I want you to talk to your child's husband."

"But I just talked to him. What do you want me to say to him?"

"Warn him. Tell him he can't play with your child," says his wife in her distraught voice.

"And then if he refuses the warning, I will divorce my child, right?"

"No!" cries his wife.

"And you claim you read. Really? How do you read the Book? And what does it say about anyone standing between two people?" he asks her again.

The wife begins walking away the moment the husband become so strong. At a distance, she stands.

"Infidel women. They shout in churches about things their evil hearts comprehend not."

"Evil, huh? Whose heart is really the evil one? Like you would know when your view of life reflects that of men in the desert. This world! Why does everyone have to come through His name? What is the matter? Why don't you just make an official declaration about one thing instead of diving among the rainy clouds, picking up decaying seeds and calling them your rules?

"Do you know how others move since you claimed to have met knowledge?" his wife rambles from the distance like a spring thunderstorm. The Husband and wife look at each other in deep anger.

"Go. Find Nyayang," he says after he stops staring. She hears him. She says nothing. Instead, she disappears from his sight.

"I'm leaving and when I return, I want to find her here," he announces, pointing at the ground with his finger. His wife hears him as he storms through the gate. Mr. Jock, early this morning, was informed about the burial of a body which was found in the river this morning.

This morning, unlike regular mornings, there is a cry in the mothers' hearts. It seems like, due to the nature of "this way of life," what just happened can just happen at any time to any girl. Tears floods from eyes as the morning lingers most painfully. The body was buried, and the thirst to know who could have done this and the motive behind it becomes the subject.

The search began yesterday evening when a sixteen-year-old girl disappeared after having attended a marital dance. She and her peers flocked together afterward. But it was time to go home and she was alone. A man greeted her shortly after, out of blue. This man had pursued her before, but she was not interested in him.

"What are you doing to me?" asked the girl after she realized there were three additional men alongside this man, who at once tried to encircle her in an attempt to do one of the things a man can do to marry the girl of his dream in the absence of her agreement.

"Now, what are you going to do?" asked the man.

"I may not escape what you are about to do to me, but I will tell you that I don't like you and I never will," she said as the hands of the four men enclosed her.

A moment after that, they lifted her up and toasted her above their heads. Then they lowered her down on her feet. Three men stood behind her and the man stood before her. "You can walk away if you want but know that I have toasted and lifted you up. I pulled a piece of your hair and swallowed it a long time ago. In case you choose to go, just know that there is no future for you. Whoever you will be married to, you won't be able to bear them children until you come back to me," said the man, intentionally cursing the girl.

She looked him in the eye and, disregarding the man's speech, she walked right past him. "I would rather bear no child than give a child to the likes of you." She walked away.

"No, you don't have that choice!" said the man. He immediately called his fellows. She tried really hard to run, but they ran her over. The four men stifled her voice and carried her away, heading to the man's parents' home. At the man's parents' home, they rushed her into the man's room. Two of the men held her feet. One man held her head down. And the man himself went on with his mission.

A few minutes later, he repeated himself and said, "You can go if you want, but in case you choose to, know that I have already slept with you," he said it deliberately to hurt her already crushed spirit. She stood up, firm and clear-eyed, and in her now broken body, she comforted her heart. Ironically, she felt stronger than she'd ever felt, in defiance of all this culture's beliefs about her—the fact that she was now worth half of what she was worth before this man destroyed her. She walked herself out and emerged into the now bustling street, with many people witnessing one of the disadvantages of being born a female.

Like wind coming and heading where no one really knew, she passed everybody who was there at the scene. The people kept their gaze on her, for never in a million years during which these kinds of atrocities were done unto women had a woman just gotten up and left. The reason for these kinds of atrocities? You may have been put together in an imperfect way by the Creator, one's heart would say! But hey, here, where men are overjoyed to have been born men, no male feature is a disadvantage.

He was a twin with a visibly deformed head. He was in not beautiful, in poor shape. But none of that really matters here; here, you just need to have been born with male organs and the rest is just there ready for your consumption.

She vanished from their sight. Alone, she kept walking. Her thoughts began to darken. Her inner person started refusing her. She immediately loathed the notion she was still feeling her physical body moving her spirit. Everything which was alive around her seemed to be laughing at her. She kept walking. She saw her chance, her window: the river. She headed there. And God only knew what happened after that.

People finished burying her body, but the question of who could have drowned her held everybody hostage. Could her death have been caused by someone her parents knew? Nobody really knew at the moment. The elders who performed the burial departed each to his home.

Mr. Jock returns and finds the compound as he left it three hours ago. "Where is she? Oh, you haven't gone anywhere," he answers himself.

"Jock, where do you expect me to go?" she asks him disrespectfully while standing with both of her hands around her waist like she is going to fly in the next few seconds.

Her husband relocates with his good-looking cane in his hand. When his wife sees he is coming closer, she says, "I don't know where she is."

"Oh, yes you do," he says and lets his fat walking cane land at her back. His wife falls on the ground as a result. At this point, Nyamuch, their grandchild, enters the room.

"Go away, Nyamuch!" shouts her grandmother from the ground. The child refuses to leave the scene. She remains in the same spot with her big eyes staring at her grandparents. She then strangely fixes her eyes on her grandfather, as he flits here and there like a bird that can't find a place to rest.

Strangely the grandfather pays no attention to what the girl's staring may imply. Nyayang's little sister arises from her room. She dashes to her father's hand. "Waah! Why are you killing Mum, Baba?" she cries. She tries to hold his hand, but he isn't finished getting out his anger yet.

"Mali," someone says at the gate and opens it gate at the same time. It's Mr. Jock's second wife. She walks really fast.

"Why?" she says, while holding her husband's hand. Jock lets go of the cane he beats up Nyayang's mother with and walks away. Mr. Jock's wife had been gone for a while now. She had their third child a few months ago and she came today because the girl in the house was getting married.

By the evening, the horrible news reaches Nyayang. The news moves her, and she immediately wants to see her mother. The following day, the two meet. "He will kill you. I have to go back," says Nyayang.

"Me? Let him kill me. He has already killed me." The two fall into silence for a while. "Will I feel alive if all I hear every day is that you are living miserably?" her mother finally asks.

"Well, I'm afraid it's the reality we have to deal with. I have to get back," says Nyayang. She gets up. "I cannot risk your life and the life of my child, so I can live as though I was meant to live to my fullest," she says while dusting off her dirty skirt which has almost lost all its flowery colours.

"Aaah, you are not going anywhere."

"Then dad will kill you. Nyamuch will be given to Chuol the moment Dad realizes I've disappeared for good. Then what kind of life am I going to live if I know all of this will take place?" Nyayang becomes uncomfortable and frustrated as she speaks.

She sits again beside her mother. "Mother, when God created me, He said, 'Out of this dust, I will form a female,' and this is what He meant," Nyayang with great hopelessness, tries again. She quickly grabs some dust from the ground. In the palm of her hand, she squeezes it and lets it flow back to the earth. She watches the dust as it leaves her open fingers in the form of unsettled clouds.

"Listen to your daughter," an older woman says to Nyayang's mother. Nyayang's mother looks at her.

"Let's go," says Nyayang after recalling something this old woman said last night.

"My daughter, as you know, there are only powerless people in this house. If your father is to come, I would be in much trouble with my husband," she said.

Nyayang's friend looked at her over her shoulder and winked at her to indicate she was not in agreement with the old woman. Nyayang smiled at the old woman. The house seemed safe to Nyayang. The man that the old woman was speaking about does not know where Nyayang was, at least for now. The husband she mentioned doesn't live at this house. The two young friends smiled at each other. Nyayang bowed her head. Her friend shook her head. The old woman was right, though, this is her house; her husband would have rejected the notion that Nyayang hides in it. However, unless someone calls him, he lives some distance away with the rest of his family.

He is the owner of eight wives. This old woman was his number one wife. But things went south when she only had girls—five girls to be exact. And because she lacked a son, she married for the boy she should have had, after she carefully turned over every last one of her gifts from farming and bought cows. She borrowed the blood so that he could produce children for her household. Her grandchild, her older daughter's son, accepted the call. But now she fears that any man could see the wrong of Nyayang hiding here, and he would be right, although this is her household and should be under her rule.

Nyayang's mother looks at her. She still cannot agree with her daughter. But she also sees the worry in the old woman's eyes.

Nyayang gets up and gives her mother a hand to pull her up. The mother and daughter walk home, where Nyayang leaves for her Chuol's house immediately.

"I told you, you will bring her back to me," says Mr. Jock after he sent Nyayang back to her husband. "'I want you to talk to your child's husband, I want you to talk to your child's husband.'" He starts mimicking her voice and what she advised him to do the day before.

"I know you want to divorce Nyayang," he says pointing his finger at her. Nyayang's mother keeps her lips together. "If you divorce her today, who do you think will marry her? Kaah! "Who will marry Kaah? I warn you, yet you don't listen.

"You go to church every day and come back not knowing what the Book says? Women! They talk about faith and what they think it means only when it's convenience to their immoral ways of life!" He begins circling around her. "They pay no heed to the words or how the words differ from the everyday activities they practise. Women!"

"Don't generalize all women. If you think I'm wrong for being right, then just stop right there," refutes the wife.

"Oh, you are talking! Good! Because I have a question for you."

"What is it?" asks his wife.

"As I'm sure you read every day, you know the Book forbids us from doing all these evil, corrupted things that you are doing. The Book says that whoever divorces the other, commits adultery. How does that verse speak to you as a mother?"

"Well, Jock, I'm glad you asked. Because if there is anything that bothers me more in this life, it is this guilt that follows women every step of the way. Yes, the Bible says that. Yes, I read it. But to answer your question, you will have to tell me this first, how does saying no to a miserable life become an act of adultery?" For the next few seconds, Mr. Jock refuses to answer. He lets the silence fill the air.

"When saying 'no' by the person who has been dehumanized becomes the big deal, what does the commission of adultery really become a commission of?" continues the wife.

"If I left you when you took your friend's wife, how would that have been a commitment of adultery? Really, how does one divorce the other by refusing to be mistreated?"

Mr. Jock looks around to see a way in which to argue. And when he can't get any closer to answering her, he says, "Yeah, where would you have gone if you left this house?"

The wife smiles for a second. This pathetic answer seems to have no impact on the woman who has pretty much lived it all. "I think you mean who else would have married me if I had left you."

"Yeah, however you want to interpret it," says the husband.

"Um, that's actually true," says his wife. "But the worst thing about this perception that you call awareness is that your refusal to understand any of this will haunt you for years to come."

"Hey, don't talk to me like that!" he yells at her when he realizes he has nothing to stand on.

"Well, Mr. Right, I will leave you alone. But, first, here is something you really need to know. I know you believe the way that God judges women depends on some sort of paper reports men send Him detailing what they do and how they do it. But that's not how it goes. And maybe I'm wrong since no one can prove whether this is true or not," continues his wife.

"But I tell you this. When you hide your blind desires behind the shadows of the words of God, you need to understand a word saves only the implementer; it is not the result of one's spouse's righteousness. This privilege is only available here. When you ask us to be faithful from the clothes we wear to the depth of our thought, so that you can smear the surface of your skin with faithful oil, again, we may do our part and that would be for us. But don't confuse fear with submission.

"Jock, I have a question. Why is that after what paints a woman, when she has really sweat with pain, after the longingness of her suffering, it is only then that you begin to speak like believers?"

Mr. Jock loses his rational mind. Not knowing when he approaches her, he jumps with the greedy desire to kill her. And the only time he knows a part of her is still alive is when she cries.

His wife remains on the ground for few minutes. And when she finally manages to get up, she brushes off her dress and says, "You may keep doing this, but, Jock, you cannot own something if you personally don't feel responsible for its creation or its existence." She walks away. Mr. Jock is furious and refuses to accept the consequences of what he has started.

CHAPTER TEN

Nyayang returns. Chuol, knowing exactly what he is going to do about the situation, shows no desire for her. This time, he says not a thing to his wife. When he wants to speak, he calls the child instead. He eats outside more and when a meal is presented before him, he complains he is sick. He reduces the number of male visitors he mingles with daily. He looks down at his wife as though she has lost her humanity, instead. That is Nyayang's interpretation. A man can refuse you a child and you don't have a mouth to complain about it. But when he refuses a meal you have cooked, it bothers you a whole lot.

She complains to her in-laws about him complaining of sickness when she brings a meal before him and she get this: "Maybe the food doesn't taste good," her mother-in-law says. Nyayang feels stuck. There is nothing more puzzling than dealing with people when you do not know what they want. One way or the other, nonetheless, she is dealing with made-up minds.

Chuol's behaviour gets worse since he now lacks an extra ear. It used to be like this: when it was one of his impulsive, selfish actions leading his kingdom, like beating her on a daily basis, his brother, the twins' father would step in and tells him that inconsistency sometimes works, too. The twins' father found him torturing her one evening about an issue that should not have been an issue between the two. Prior to that moment, a girl had run into the compound seemingly to hide herself.

"They are taking me," she said to Nyayang.

"Then come in really quick," Nyayang said, as if she knew the rest of her story.

An hour later, someone appeared at the gate, assuming the girl was hidden somewhere in the compound. Nyayang denied it. However, the person was not satisfied. Nyayang should have made it easy on herself and just said, "Here, she is," but she did not.

"You are whose wife?"

"My name is Nyayang Jock."

"NO, what is your husband's name," the man said.

"He is not at home."

"It is not whether he is at home that I'm asking. I want to know your involvement in my family's problem. So, what is your husband's name?"

Nyayang was stunned. She glared at the man. She knew giving Chuol's name was like giving him a criminal record: you pull out the name and the deed is identified. But maybe it was the payback she feared most. Chuol would act innocent as a lamb when this man confronted him about his wife's involvement, but she would pay the bigger price, soon or maybe now.

Chuol arrived home. He greeted the man. "Is this your wife?" the man asked as if he disapproved of Nyayang being Chuol's wife. Chuol gave him a head nod. "She has my daughter. Talk to your wife and let me have my daughter."

Chuol, as soon as he heard the man, went into a state of shock and anger. "YOU ARE HIDING HIS DAUGHTER?" he screamed.

As soon as Nyayang heard Chuol's question, she rushed into her room and, seemingly by force, grabbed the girl's hand and walked right back silently and said, "Your daughter." She stepped back. Chuol kept his eyes on her from the time she had gone to the room until now. Without even thanking the man who effectively gave him his daughter back, the man pushed his daughter in front of him and said something about tomorrow, the airport, and Bipore. That was all Nyayang was able to hear before she was paid back for the embarrassment she had caused to her husband.

"GO TO THE ROOM," Chuol said. Nyayang walked herself in. They both left Nyamuch looking helplessly confused in the compound. Nyamuch ran out of the compound as soon as she heard her mom's distinctive pain-enduring sounds. But thank God, someone walked by and didn't shy away from calling him out. It was the twins' father who walked into the compound. He called him out as soon as he heard the fight inside the room. "You want to kill her? Why don't you let her go instead," he said. Chuol silently bypassed him and vanished again.

But now that his extra ear (his brother) is gone, Chuol tends to lead poorly. The twins' father lost his life in a war over his leadership position not long ago. He held the position for over five years, right up to the day his life was no longer his, and yet he would rather risk his life than let anyone else have the chair although he was the third male in Malual's family to have it.

In this rural area, they still elected their leaders based not on qualifications or experiences or knowledge, instead routinely selecting people from among the closest sub-clans. The war was an inside war, and it was mainly fuelled by Mr. Malual and a few new acquaintances he had started spending time with. They were usually on the move, running their mouths about what was not done right by others, and their mouths were usually kept shut when it was their boys wronging others.

Mr. Malual and others knew this chair had to go to the other sub-clan, which had not had its turn for a long time now. But he had a lot of people on his team, and he relied on them. He knew that even if he was wronging someone else, the harm would always be so much more painful on the other end. By force, those supporters of Mr. Malual took the chair, which led to the fight. The fight left many people dead, including the twins' father. To add to the tragedy, the retaliation that occurred after the twins' father's death ended up taking the life of one of the best children's doctors, who was serving in the local hospital.

Chuol's strange behaviour continues, and closer to the end of the month, Chuol unexpectedly calls on his long forgotten wife one evening. Like always, he "ahems." Nyayang hears his typical throat calling and she walks over to where her master sits.

When she reaches him however, he silently points at the gate with his finger. Nyayang gladly walks to the gate. At the gate, she yield to her right. She yield to her left. But sees nothing. She walks a bit farther. Behind the angle of the compound is small tree. And she sees a lady standing there. She walks over and before she reaches her, Nyayang recognizes the lady. It is her long-ago competitor.

So this is the moon which I have been holding a place for, thinks the star as she gets closer. "Hello," she says in greeting.

"Hi," says the visitor. The two walks into the compound and, as she does with all of Chuol's girlfriends, Nyayang directs the visitor to the man's room. She quickly retreats for it is already bedtime. Inside her room, Nyayang becomes very disturbed about a question that does not stop niggling at her brain.

In her mind, she cannot figure out exactly why Chuol is hiding things that are this big of a deal from her. And she complains to the invisible Chuol for a good reason. In this culture sometimes, a man tells his wives or his wife that he is heading back to the field. For this is the only privilege a woman gains out of what soon becomes a shared husband. So the fact that this man could be up to something ugly still not clear to Nyayang.

The next morning, the man approaches his upset servant. "You knew this and yet you could not be bothered," says Chuol.

Nyayang looks confused, as if she needs more of an explanation. But Chuol has already done a lot. What does she not understand? The visitor came last night and now it is the next day. That is a sign that she is here to stay, at least for now. Nyayang must suspect, even if she is not completely sure, that she has just welcomed her first ever co-wife.

"I will do it," she says to her husband. Chuol walks back to the visitor. Nyayang walks into her room and she comes out with something red, bagged nicely in a small, transparent plastic bag. She walks to Chuol's room. Chuol excuses himself once Nyayang walks in.

"If you had come today and not last night, I would have had time to call your sisters-in-law to witness this moment with me. But we cannot wait any longer; you need to at least take water." She glances at the girl's face and can tell the visitor is with child. Sarah tilts her head toward Nyayang. Nyayang spreads the red Yat from the bottom. Once it reaches her neck, she leaves it for her to pull it down by herself. Once it reaches all the way to her waist, they both smile at each other. Nyayang leaves the room quickly. Chuol comes back to what is now official. The visitor is now a wife, and yes, she can now eat. Like a storm, Nyayang finishes cooking something for her. She comes back and askes Chuol to excuse them. She can now eat but not while Chuol is around. This time he leaves for a little longer.

Chuol comes home an hour later. He goes straight to Nyayang, who seems to have few things on the mind now. He begins as if he is advising her but just ends up briefly mentioning a predictable issue which arises when two females share a compound. "I believe you remember her. So I don't have to do an introduction," says Chuol impolitely. "But I want you to be respectful to her. Also she is expecting, so she showers at home."

Nyayang nods her head, then lifts up her eyes to her master and says, "But why didn't you tell me you were bringing somebody home?"

"Do I have to consult with you first if I want to do something?"

"No, of course not," she concedes.

Chuol walks away. Nyayang moves to the kitchen for her afternoon duties. But just before she can step on the kitchen floor, she stops and the thought of when the two actually reunited begins to linger in her froze mind.

Nyayang knew when she and her husband got married, that was when the lady refused to be seen by Chuol anymore. And up to this point, Chuol had only been bringing different faces to the house. This reunion is something Chuol has really been secretive about. Even his father has not known of this yet.

It happened over those moments Chuol shared with his fellows tradesmen. Usually, after the men closed their shops, they would walk to their preferred restaurant. There, they would chat for hours about the current government system and how things should be fixed.

This was how it came to Chuol's and his friends' attention that a new restaurant had opened in the area. Eager to see what the new place offered, the men decided to try it out.

Upon their arrival, they were pleasantly received and welcomed. The greeter took the gentlemen to a table in the corner of the room.

Being situated on the left side of the kitchen, the table was perfectly parallel with the kitchen door.

As the men waited around the table for their order to be taken, they noticed that in the middle of the room were two unfamiliar good-looking young ladies, roaming from one customer to the next.

"He still doesn't get it", one of the men said to the other two, intending to continue a conversation they were having on their way there about some nobody who wanted to change the failing system.

"Who is going to vote for him? He just wastes his time and his resources," Chuol agreed.

"Well, who can he blame for his shortcomings? His dear dead mama maybe?" The third of the three men put in. "It's not easy to earn people's trust when you have so much of your mom's uncultured record in your background." The man had been born out of matrimony. The father happened to be a soldier who was a Nuer man but not from this native clan.

"People will not elect him as their commissioner, no way," said Chuol. Chuol detested this gentleman from the moment he let it be known he thought there was something wrong with the Murlen man taking the Nuer girl. People here were recognized for their culturally acceptable behaviour and whether they were citizens of the sons of the sons of the land. The current favourite opponent of the unwanted candidate was good for the leadership. He was a son of the land whose mother was originally from Shilluk. Most important, he was a real man. He was loved because he kept the recognized order in check. He was very restrictive in terms of keeping the existing gap between men and women and, ironically, he scooped out his share of what the Creator molded out of the first man's rib in a good number. That made him make a lot of people. And it also meant he had a lot of support.

After only having been elected for a few years, he increased the number of his wives from ten to seventeen, two of whom were given to him free of charge. As a thank-you for his restrictive policies, two elders gave him free wives. And within a few months of being with the newly added wives, he accused one of them of adultery and took a frightening action. He ordered the girl to be taken to the hospital and have the baby aborted, claiming it would be seen out of character for him to raise a child that was never his, and after the success of his plan, he asked the girl to leave his house, saying, how would he explain to his fellow countrymen that he slept with a woman who slept with other men?

Recently, he ordered a wife of a recently returned soldier to be buried alive after the solder lost his mind after finding his woman with child, upon his return from Malakal's soldiers' camp. He divided the task between women and men. Women dug her grave; men buried her live body. Of course, he threw the first dust. That was normal.

"Well, we will find out soon enough. The election day is tomorrow," said the first man.

Another moment passed. One of the ladies came over to them. She asked what the men preferred to eat and began jotting down the orders with a smile on her pretty face. However, she was really only taking Chuol's order. The other two had menus in their hands and their minds on the waitress's full, round-cheeked face.

"I'm assuming the orders are the same, hmm?" asked the pretty girl.

"Oh, no. Ours are different." The two glanced at their menus but were clearly delaying placing their orders.

"So, you're new in the area?" asked one of the men.

"Yeah," she said while nodding her head at the same time.

"The food looks great," the other man said, hoping this might lead to further conversation.

"Anything visiting your eye for the first time always looks great," she said and smiled.

"Where are you from if I'm allowed to ask?" the first man carried on.

"Not far away from here," replied the girl. She finally took their orders and left for the kitchen.

"Wow! So unreal how the new ones have it all," one of the two men said.

"Yeah, if only it would last," exclaimed Chuol with most of his focus on the desserts at the bottom of the menu in his hands. The girl returned with the food. This time, she was accompanied by the girl she was with earlier.

At the table, the pretty girls put the men's meals down in front of them and told the gentlemen to enjoy the food. Chuol began to dig into his meal immediately, but the other two men were eager to continue on the unfinished small talk initiated earlier and wouldn't let the girls go. From the girls' names to from what time they normally worked, the two men couldn't hold back their desire to get to know the two strangers.

Chuol, on the other hand, only occasionally lifted up his head while the other four were talking. And, having no desire to join in, he concentrated on his meal. In a matter of five minutes, the persistence of these seemingly manipulative, hungry, early-thirties, married men to get to know these visionless young ladies began to bear fruit. More than they had all prepared for, in fact. The girls revealed what time they would be ending their shifts. They knew these strangers must have families, but like other blind girls raised in this society, they had the "once I have become his wife, I will take over" attitude: a cultural attitude that has made them each other's enemy.

"Umm, the food is really tasty," announced one of the two men, trying to praise the cook—in case it happened to be one of the girls.

"Were you the one who prepared this meal?" the same man pointed at his preferred girl.

"No," she said. "Our friend did."

"No, I think it was you," argued the man.

"No, it wasn't me," she repeated.

"Who was it then? What is her name, if it wasn't you?"

"Oh, her name? Her name is Sarah. She is the one who usually prepares the evening meals along with the other cooks. And we help, too, because we know how to cook. Or who would cook for our . . ." and before she could finish whatever she was saying, the other quieter man grabbed the opportunity.

"You two are married?" he asked with a shocked face.

"No," she said. "But who knows what exists somewhere in the future."

"Right!" said the man. The two men glanced in each other's eyes and giggled afterward.

During their conversation, another customer entered the restaurant. Sarah, who had been in the kitchen, saw the customer come in. At the entrance, the customer glanced around for a spot to sit. Sarah realized the customer didn't know where to sit as the greeter was not at the entrance at the time.

She opened the kitchen door and began looking around, passing her eyes from one end to the other in search of a waiter. When she couldn't see a free one, she went over with the intention of seating the customer herself.

Prior to reaching the customer, she glanced to the left. She saw her two girlfriends with some gentlemen she didn't recognize. At the time, Chuol's head bent over his scrumptious meal.

With the gentle nature of an unmarried woman, politely voiced her appeal. At once, one of the girls backed up where the new customer was standing and the other one went to the kitchen.

Meanwhile, Sarah returned to the kitchen door and lingered there as the new customer got served. Before she went fully back inside the kitchen, though, she, looked back at the gentlemen at the table. And that was when Chuol lifted up his head.

The two recognized each other right away. And with what appeared to be fear, Sarah dashed back into the kitchen as quickly as possible.

Some time passed. The girl who was with the men from the start returned for the purpose of collecting the plates. She turned here and there, trying to clean the crumbs that had fallen onto the table. And in front of Chuol, he asked her again, "Who did you say cooked the food?"

"The lady who was standing at the kitchen door a while ago," she said. "Sarah."

"Very impressive!"

"Her husband must be very proud of her cooking skills," said Chuol.

"Well, perhaps he will be," she said and rushed the plates to the kitchen.

Then the other girl came back. "Would you like a dessert?" she asked with tip of her pen ready to jot down their order. At once, the three men glanced at each other and upon perusing the menu, they each got something different to taste.

Outside the restaurant, the night was changing the colour of the day. And the three married men saw nothing abnormal about it. While nurturing their desires of meeting the possibilities of the night, they delayed swallowing each spoonful of dessert, chewing it slowly as though they were just learning how to eat.

The end of the shifts arrived. And to his great luck, Chuol came to have the chance to shake hands with not just a person named Sarah, but the Sarah he indeed was once deeply emotionally involved with.

"Sarah, I never thought I would see you again," admitted Chuol.

"Neither did I," added Sarah. "How is everything?" she asked Chuol..

"Everything is fine," Chuol replied after hesitating a bit.

And so this was the beginning of their reunion. And of course nothing happened immediately. The girl had a few questions that needed to be answered, but more then any other time in his life, Chuol was eager to supply them.

The man returned home with one mission. And that was to sharpen the tip of his tongue so the next time he met the girl, he would put an end to any concerns she may have. On the next day, though, Chuol's anticipated meeting was pushed to the end of the day due to the election. The one who was expected to lose, lost. He didn't see this coming. But despite his dedicated servitude to his fellow citizens, he was not considered a full citizen. In this place, it was not about what you do; it was about where you come from..

There were two main reasons for his downfall. The first was that he was the son of a man who was not from this clan men and he had been raised by a woman. The second was that his mother had been married more than twice. But the biggest of the two problems was that he fell short, biologically. However, no one could refute his outstanding record of service. But how could a society accept one's service without accepting the one who provided it?

Some people told him about what they thought might have been the problem, frankly. "A man who has been raised solely by a woman, what could he possibly do?"

It was because of his mother.

"Your mother spent her life running from one man to another— who are you? You are the son of someone no one respects."

The people used his mother against him because having two husbands was an automatic sign of prostitution. And no man would like this kind of association for himself. Better that people think at some point in time your mother was a thief than once upon a time she loved to sleep with men. It was the worst association to have.

No. This, he did not see coming. But, here, it takes being meticulously perfect to earn the citizens' respect and trust. After his loss, he went over to an elderly man and whispered in his ear, "How does something this small in meaning automatically disqualify a man like me?"

"Simply for having come into the world through her, I guess," said the elderly man.

"And may I add," he continued, "during your campaign, many people disagreed with you since your focus on what needed to be changed focused on this new ideology you seem to be carrying around. This didn't sit well with many, especially the elders. There was this argument you made about how girls get traded to the Murle after having been impregnated by their boyfriends, or their fathers just decide to sell them so they can increase the number of cows they own. I'm with you on that one. But here is how they are seeing it. One way to punish a sinful act is to give the person the opposite taste of what she chose to do and keep her nearby where the imagined smell of the taste could still break her nose. Or, you could pay for an airplane ticket and gladly deliver her to Bipor to your enemy, and in return collect ten or twenty cows, which he will then recollect from you with a battle in the windy season or anytime on their way home. You are right, we need to change this.

"With the recent peace deal with the Murle, though, many will see what you are standing for differently," he said. "Besides having an abundance of what others seem to be in need of, cows, the Murle know how to turn things around for themselves. This year has been one of the toughest years for them. The wetlands are a barrier. Their most fruitful lands have betrayed them, leading them to come to this side of the land for the sake of their own lives and those of their livestock. Life has become tough for both the people and the animals. And that is when they have always turned to seeking peace agreements with this

Nueri. They always get away with this, using the very weaknesses they know about us against us."

Starting from the beginning of the season, just after Christmas, the Murle came. They knew it would just take a small effort on their part and—boom!—doors were opened for them. And to sustain the continuation of this access from now until who knows when it could rain in Bipor, some of them made little moves. Like when the chief in charge from the Murle side gave his daughter to the chief in charge in this area so he would keep giving his undeniable support to the Murle. Or when some became Presbyterians, knowing the church would be effectively moved by them accepting Christ. The two didn't have to give a female to maintain this deal and the church didn't have to buy into this seasonal attendance because in many indirect ways, some just came to their grandparents.

Here, green has been the theme of the season. The lowlands, the valleys, all are green and full of what keeps these animals alive. The Murle, as the result of the signed deal, kept pouring onto the land in even greater numbers. But this gentleman was not just having a moment of desire for leadership. No, he knows what these people need to govern themselves. He wanted the leadership to change domestic issues and for other reasons, such as putting an end to this peace deal. He knew when the Murle want to return to their land, they usually pee on whatever deal has allowed them access to this land so they can return to their normal behaviours.

His loss says nothing about him, but perhaps where it's defined and how it's defined is not in the Nuer language but in the Nuer way of seeing the word 'enemy.' So far, there is only one person who is identified as the enemy. A woman who had the courage to say, 'I'm a human, too.' One thing this gentleman knew above the rest was that if strength is a man, therefore a child must be born of that strength. Then there is no doubt the Murle have been enriched and supplemented by Nuer's strength, if not with their exact physical qualities then certainly with half of what makes them Nuer. A Nuer, a courageous human being, fears nothing, regardless of its nature. That there may be some of this courageous nature on the frontlines with the Murlen has been seen many times throughout history. But there is nothing more pivotal in the history of the Nuer fighting the Murle than the attack that took place two years ago.

The time came when the Murle again had come to terms with their peace-loving neighbour, this Nueri. But things inevitably turned bitter. It happened when the cattle were coming back from the wetlands where they landed as the dry season moved people for the sake of their survival. Nothing was known prior to the attack. There had been no speculation of any kind, the Murle just said good-bye after enjoying the outpouring of hospitality. It turned out some had been hiding themselves in bushes waiting for the first group to go home.

The return of the animals has a ways to go. According to the sub-clans within the territory, each sub-clan takes responsibility for returning its cattle to its place.. The Murle knew this way before this moment. In the bushes, they divided themselves into groups and the plan was to attack each sub-clan so they would have no time to help each other. Shortly after the first sub-clan hit the road, Murle attacked it. Then they attacked the second sub-clan, and like a provoked storm of unforgiving heart, the attacks hit most of them almost at once. About five sub-clans were hit at the same time. Three hundred people shortly thereafter left the earth from the Nuer side, but that death toll rose even higher, making it four hundred and seventy the next day. In the first attack, Mr. Tut Gai was among the people the bullets hit first. His attacker was a younger man whom he tried to bargain with at first. It turned out that as he pleaded for his life in the Nuer language, the young man replied to him in Nuer, as well.

"'My son, I'm an old man, don't kill me. I just finished the marriage of my last wife . . . and she doesn't have a child yet,' he pleaded.

"'Forgive you? Why so? You have not done anything wrong to me. Except maybe to reject what I practise as a Murlen man. And that is there is no point of leaving these animals for you, even if it causes me my death,' said the young man. He finished the old man with his first bullet but shot him four more times anyway to show he had no mercy whatsoever. The attacks continued the whole morning and half of the afternoon. The Murle left a few brothers on the frontlines, as well, but the animals they took with them outnumbered the left-behind brothers. That day they left with more than a thousand cows in number. There was some speculation that some Nueri could possibly have been fighting other Nueri on the frontlines. It usually takes two or three hours when it's just the Nueri versus pure Murlen. And that death toll? Well, it came as a surprise.

"You see, even if it would make others ask why you are selling your own daughter to your enemy, it's far better than keeping her knowing she has questioned the source of your pride. And no doubt about it, some girls will leave at the end of their stay."

The young, failed candidate sharply moved his head as if he had seen something bad. "So now you know why you couldn't have been named their commissioner."

"I now know, yeah," said the failed candidate.

Chuol along with his fellow tradesmen congratulated their candidate and celebrated his victory. Their supporting team of women drank with joy, despite his scary behaviour. And after that, everyone went home happy.

"What happened?" Sarah asked Chuol that evening. And by asking the question "What happened?" she meant why he hadn't chosen her and married her first.

This is a piece that most women of this culture see as a reasonable complaint. For there is a certain pride or sense of dominance that comes with being the first chosen and married by a man. It is very important to be a man's first wife.

"I was not ready to get married at the time. But I do respect what my father says," Chuol said, proving that there was an outside influence at the time of his decision. "I don't like that woman. I never liked her. She never was my type. And up to this point, the road we've walked has been so bumpy," said Chuol.

Sarah looked convinced after having listened to the man's heart, forgetting that sometimes it is in their gender that they can soothe your troubled soul.

Then it was Sarah's turn to tell her side. "Well, it's a long story," she began. In the process of telling her side, she stopped unexpectedly. She started walking around, avoiding the muddy, emotional areas which seemed to hurt the most.

"What happened to me is, I was married. And . . . " And then she stopped. But what she meant to narrate was that after this lover of hers had made his interest in her adversary clear, she found comfort in another man's arms.

Then this happened. Here, as far as cultural definition, it's not so much that one can just enjoy the state of being human. But rather, one lives by its underlying reason. And so one cannot redefine the state of marriage as opposite to the notion underlying its origin.

The hungry-for-marriage man poured out the needed cows and back to his home he went with a wife. The three-to-six-month period that usually reveals any growing being passed two years of childless marriage. Sarah sadly questioned her ability while the man was expecting an explanation.

Within the second year, the man unleashed his disappointment over what he claimed to be empty commitment and moved on by marrying a seemingly childbearing woman. However, he refused to let Sarah go. Sarah's brothers became ripe, ground peppers upon hearing the man's refusal. Because there is only one exception to this matter: A woman's womb refuses a child, you let her go.

"No," the man said. "She is still my wife."

After hearing himself claiming that, however, he went back to the field and only came back with another childbearing lady. Sarah became the maid to his good women. All the heavy, all the stressful, and all hardest jobs landed in her hands. She took care of these women's children. She would even be asked to spend nights with one of his wives' children whenever the mother went to try for another one. She had nothing to her name; she didn't have a child to claim any part of him. Every time he gave his wives their share, he gave Sarah whatever was left over and he would say, "You can't compare yourself to them. They have got kids to feed." And that would make absolute sense to Sarah since all the children really were him to feed.

Of course, this constant, ongoing behaviour was not a refusal of the childless wife, according to the man. The truth is, in this culture, where a woman stands in a family line is determined by the children she has borne for the family. At the start of the third year of their marriage, the brothers didn't act too friendly to him. They took their little sister away with no respect for the man's claimed loving ownership of her. He agreed, after her family forced him to accept, and counted his cows back into his hand. And that was when she was released.

The grounds for an official divorce here are when a man himself refuses a woman or when an external force demands him to let her go. Otherwise he can simply say, 'She is still my wife,' and she will forever carry the burden of never divorcing, yet never feeling truly married. And his words will be recognized by the society over hers.

Luckily, Sarah still had brothers, and up to this point, she had been free, devoting herself to the family business and nothing else. Now, seeing this opportunity, Chuol was amused at the possibility of unlocking this rusted womb of this young woman.

After three consecutive months of nonstop talking, Sarah finally gave in. But Chuol kept one thing in mind. It is commonly viewed that a man declaring a relationship with a woman who had previously been in a childless marriage paid no penny until she proved she worked. Therefore, Chuol hid from the eyes of his friends and his father.

Today marks the second day Sarah spends with her new family. When the Power separates the strength of the night with that of the day and night loses its ability, Chuol, with gladness, sends the amazing news over to his parents.

And the elderly couple doesn't give it a day. They walk in the same day to see what the man brought in this time.

Sarah meets her in-laws' approval immediately. She is all the in-laws could have asked for in a wife. Her smile, the tone of her voice, and the beautiful, musical way she arranges the flow of her thoughts charm them. Her natural ability to say the right things wins over the in-laws in just in one day.

Mr. Malual, feeling overjoyed with what his son has brought home, waits no longer to speak to the girl's parents. He calls on the parents and a week later, the two sides sit down. With respect to the tradition, Mr. Malual apologizes first and foremost for keeping the girl for a week.

The apology is followed by the offering of the cows, having been aware that Sarah currently carries a child. Among the offered cows are two bulls.

Soon, Sarah's parents get over their feigned disappointment. They, per cultural practice, ask for their daughter back so she can give birth while with them. Mr. Malual's family gladly gives their wife back to her parents for the duration of her pregnancy.

During Sarah's absence, the distance between Chuol and Nyayang grows even greater. Since Nyayang's return, Chuol never wants to do anything with her anymore.

"You still mad at her? What about your children? You don't want your children?" Mr. Malual talks to his son after feeling compelled, following the completion of Sarah's marriage.

"I told you I don't want this woman. Take her if you want and give her a husband," Chuol says to his father.

"Fool! You are a fool," repeats the father. "Tell me, when her children and Sarah's children go out, will the world know them by which one comes from which mother or by the family name?" Mr. Malual loses it and reminds his son the reason men get married.

Chuol remains quiet, realizing the knowledge of what real men want is still with his father. "Tell me." Mr. Malual slaps Chuol at the back. Chuol looks him in the eye. "Why are you limiting yourself?" asks his father. "Even if you divorce her today, to get back all our cows would be hard." He throws that at his son, too, as one of the things he needs to think about first.

"I don't care about cows. I could compare them with the cows just taken by the Murle," Chuol says.

"Man, you need to listen to me," Mr. Malual says.

Some days pass. After the honest discussion between the son and his father, Chuol looks back and realizes there is a partial truth in what the elderly man has said. He then considers sharing a night with his abandoned wife.

Like she knew that was going to be it, Nyayang catches something for herself. When she realizes it, though, her soul becomes disturbed, having no understanding of what kind of jelly bean she has caught this time.

As little as four months later, news reaches Chuol about Sarah, who has, with willingness, borne him a boy. Chuol, hearing the news, refuses to dance with his closest friends alone. He goes on to invite birds and reptiles and beyond to celebrate the reassurance of his manhood. Mr. Malual and his wife come to town the night before. There is a conversation around how the child will be named. The two men talk about it and a meaningful name is found.

Nyayang cleans up after her father-in-law the next day. "We are getting late, maan Nyamuch, please hurry up," says Mr. Malual.

"We are coming," she says. Nyayang has bedsheets on her arm and Nyamuch has to go to the neighbour's house. A white plastic bag that is among the bedsheets falls off Nyayang's arm. It must have been Grandpa's. Nyamuch grabs it as she waits to be taken to the neighbour's house. Nyayang proceeds to store the sheets. Nyamuch opens the plastic bag. She pulls out a black toy truck. She throws the plastic bag on the ground and begins to look at the toy truck with excitement.

"Nyamuch, come let me take you," her mother calls her while standing at the gate already. Nyamuch runs toward her mother. And before she reaches the gate, she kneels on the ground and slides the toy truck on the ground.

"TOOK TOOK TOOK TOOK!" She makes sounds pretending the truck is making the sounds. It looks like it excites her. Her mother looks back and sees her dragging something.

"WHAT IS THAT, NYAMUCH? PLEASE PUT IT BACK, IT'S NOT YOURS," says her mother. Nyamuch still makes the sounds. She exits the compound and when she gets up, she turns to her mother who demands that she return the toy where she found it. "Put it back now," she says.

"It's mine," Nyamuch argues.

"It's Grandpa's, give it back to him."

"No, it's mine. I want to play with it. Look at it," Nyamuch says and places the toy back on the ground. "TOOK TOOK TOOK TOOK! Look, I can make different sounds too. Vroom, Vroom, Vroo —"

"Oh, get up already!" says the mother.

"Are you two are still around?" A voice emerges from the compound.

"Come, come, I have to go." Nyayang pulls Nyamuch by the arm and leads her to the neighbour's home as she appears to be obsessed with studying the toy and not walking. She holds on to it really tight. Her mother leaves her on her own to go into the neighbour's compound. And right before she reaches the gate, she lands on the ground and this time, she pretends the toy is flying.

"Poof, poof, pooooof!" She says before her mother yells at her.

"Get in!"

The whole family is there to welcome the new man in the family. On this first visit, Nyayang, the main organizer, wipes the sweat from her forehead. She prepares a huge quantity of food and serves wine, for the family cannot step on the in-laws' soil with empty hands. Before they leave the new in-laws, the child's name is pronounced. His name shall be Tut. This name is an acknowledgement of the two bulls which Chuol included during the submission of his cows. Tut. Everybody agrees.

Then the visitations begin. After every two or three days, the growing man is either brought to them, or the family goes out to see him. Meanwhile, Nyayang is very loose. The following month, she gives birth to the best of her ability. This surprises no one and so the far-away family members do not bother to visit the new person.

Prior to Nyayang's delivery, Chuol started building a room beside his room for his soon-to-return-home wife. Nyayang, in this project, was Chuol's primary helper.

A few things remain undone due to Nyayang's delivery. But the day on which Sarah is returning is fast approaching. Chuol refuses to let his dear wife walks into the unfinished room. Instead, he orders Nyayang to sand-paint the room. Nyayang tightens her loose belly and paints it all, and then the good wife walks in to enjoy it.

This time, according to tradition, Sarah walks into the family officially. Chuol calls the two before him one evening and removes the ring that designates Nyayang as the first wife from Nyayang's neck and puts Sarah in charge of everything. Nyayang, is cut off from all responsibility, including making meals for visitors, and if she is ever in need of anything, she must not make the mistake of approaching her husband, but approach Sarah, instead, and together, the two will make a decision thereafter.

Soon, Sarah gets pregnant again. When it becomes too heavy for her, her husband loosens the original orders and makes new ones. He stops Sarah from doing cooking and other heavy stuff. Nyayang comes back into the picture, but she is still not allowed to bring food before her husband, so Sarah does this still. Sarah gives her husband another baby boy. Chuol is extremely happy, as he is reaching his goal. But it appears to be, the happier he gets on one end, the tighter he knots the rope on the other end.

"Wuri, don't limit yourself," says Mr. Malual occasionally when he comes to visit his grandchildren.

"Why bother when all she knows how to birth are females!" Chuol replies.

"And what is wrong with that? Don't your sons need cows to marry when they grow up? "Yes, they do." Says Chuol. "Then this is not as bad as it seems," says Mr. Malual.

Every time there seems to be an agreement between Chuol and his father, Sarah becomes aware of it, and in her magical, musical way of talking, she talks their husband out of even considering having more children with Nyayang.

"If Sarah, is not here, bring the food yourself," says Chuol to Nyayang one afternoon when Sarah has paid a visit to her family with her children. Right after the food hits the table, Sarah enters the compound. She becomes angry, not that her duty has been taken, but the forgiveness of one thing loosens up a whole lot of other things.

"Don't ever try to do that again," Sarah says to Nyayang."

"I never would have done it if he himself did not ask me to do so," Nyayang defends herself.

"It doesn't matter. Now stop taking food or water to the man's table. I'm here. I will do it from now on." Sarah then goes to their husband and says, "I'm now stronger than ever. I'm resuming to my duties." She says this while leaving out her underlying reason for saying it. She speaks as though she really just got over the pain of childbirth. Nyayang falls off the duty list immediately and goes back to being Sarah's side helper. She is water bringer, wood collector and dish washer. Her children eat after Sarah serves her children first. But Sarah's biggest accomplishment among all is that when she sends her somewhere, she complains afterward about her so their husband realizes Nyayang is not home.

For one, he so knows Nyayang does not help her; for a second, he so now thinks she may be after another man. There is usually no reason for a woman to be frequently leaving the house other than having an affair. And though she may no longer be worth sleeping with, the thought of his wife finding someone else crushes the very heart of Chuol's manhood.

Sarah knows the kinds of thoughts he will surround himself with once he suspects her of this deed. Sarah has a mission. And her ways of reaching it are working. Chuol finds himself having his original thoughts again, leaving his father's wise words behind. His way of speaking to Nyayang goes back to being angry.

Life continues and Nyayang strives to face each day's challenge as she keeps imagining what it would be like for the children if she ever ran away.

During these well-spent times, the good wife notes where her rival and their husband stand. On multiple occasions, Sarah follows the feet of her husband, treating Nyayang the same way he treats her. Occasionally, she will find something to argue about with Nyayang. And Sarah will express her opinion of her, asking some vague questions. Confusing questions like, 'Who are you?' Then she will wait for a reaction. Nyayang seems to take none of this to heart, knowing clearly the odds are against her.

Usually a determined bully doesn't relax until she fully delivers on her mission. And in this case, the unwillingness to react exhibited by Nyayang ends up escalating the anger her rival thrives on.

One afternoon, it happens that the two gifts of Sarah womb and the two disappointments of Nyayang's womb play together. Earlier, Nyayang had given her youngest daughter the toy truck that was once Nyamuch's. In the children's station, the truck toy is now in Nyamuch's little sister's hand.

Then their small brother cries, wanting to play with the toy as well. "Give it to him," demands the elder brother. "She is not a boy. She should not have it," he insists.

"It's my toy and I give it to my sister," says Nyamuch.

"But your sister is not a boy. Why should she play with a boy toy?" the brother fights back.

In a bit, the noise becomes apparent, and Sarah goes to see what is happening with the children. She looks at them suspiciously and spots the problem. "Give it to him!" She pulls the toy out of the little girl's hand while verbalizing that she cannot play with it. But Nyamuch argues, saying "No" and hurries to pull back the toy. "Cars are not for women," says Sarah.

"No, this is my car." Nyamuch keeps pulling the toy.

Then Sarah reacts violently. She slaps Nyamuch on the face. Nyamuch's mother sees it from a distance. She walks over to Sarah with her eyes narrowed. She pulls her hand back and gives her a slap.

And Sarah, having been waiting for this kind of reaction for a long time, punches Nyayang right in the head. Instantly, the two go at each other.

In that moment, the neighbour approaches the scene and separates the two. However, Sarah sees no reason to stop. She goes on to reveal some of the dirtiest secrets between Nyayang and what she calls a husband.

"Who are you?" she asks her again. "Tell me, if it wasn't for Chuol's parents, would you have still graze in this family? And she thinks, she is so good! Why do his parents have to talk to him so your barren womb can be pushed to its limit? Will you—will you ever have child with him? Tell me, will you?" she says, and deep down inside her, she can't wait to burst out with her goal. The good wife just goes on and on, washing her clean heart out.

Nyayang, with no proof to refute on the other end, just keeps jumping up and down, for they are both still being held back. While still in the midst of this chaos, the husband arrives. He calls on everyone to leave the compound. Some leave, others stick around. Then he strongly condemns Nyayang's response when he suggests it was all her fault. Sarah leaves the scene, where Nyayang wrestles with the fault that is not her own. But denying usually doesn't go well with Chuol. So, hard slaps on the head reach Nyayang soon. Sarah enters her room. She leaves the door open halfway, so now she can see how her man does it on her behalf. Nyamuch and her sister help only by crying on their mother's behalf. Sarah calls them into her room as soon as she realizes they are making noise over nothing. As soon as they enter, she grabs them by the ears and that magically reduces the noise.

"I don't care, Nyayang, you go where you want to. You have made my home a home to thunder. "Go! Chuol asks her to leave his house after brutally beating her in front of everybody. Sarah keeps watching. She can almost determine when the two's quarreling will end.

"That's okay. I will leave your house," she says. "Nyamuch, come." She calls her children to leave with her.

"No, no, no! You don't get to take my children with you! No. You, yourself, leave without anything, just like the way you came."

Nyayang looks at him. She looks at the room where the children are. Finally, she says, "Okay, I will leave." She exits the compound. She goes to the second-closest neighbour. Her friend sees her. She comes and finds Nyayang has been served a glass of water by the mother of the house. The mother of the house goes back to her things. The two friends sit opposite to each other as they listen to each other's versions of what is wrong with their worlds.

"How are you doing?" Nyayang asks.

The friend bows her head down and when she brings it back up, her face has tears flowing down..

"I mean, I'm okay," she says finally, while tapping the tears off with her cloth.

"What is going on this time?"

"Nothing new. Just accusations after accusations. And now my mind cannot take it anymore! I'm falling apart! It is not easy seeing him treating other women as if they have slaughtered the biggest elephant in the land for him. I don't know where I belong. I really don't," she says. She appears frustrated. She comes tenth. She is a mother to many of the man's children. Mostly males. An abundant blessing that made the Boke unhappy. Despite the many children, she has come up short and has failed to meet the man's standards of perfection. She is very careless when it comes to how she dresses. In this business, men demand to be entertained in multiple ways. Children keep you married, but if you want to live in close range with him, you have to be physically perfect.

"Whenever it should be my time with him, she messes it up. She doesn't like me. Sometimes I just want to leave. After all, I was only given to him. It's not like he has anything to come after if I leave," she says.

Nyayang looks at her and says, "I know and I wish I could advise you to leave. But unfortunately, I cannot. It is not our place to advise ourselves to leave our homes because it never was our mothers'. But if I can say anything, it would be that, perhaps, why things are the way they are."

"If not in the entire world, at least here, women have been systematically placed in many distinctive boxes but, for our purpose, let us say three distinctive ones. The first box is the loved wife. This is the woman you and I know doesn't do much, yet for all the reasons we don't know, she is loved, respected and therefore in charge of his affairs.

"The second box is home to the undesired wife. It could be her looks, or her inability to satisfy her man—however he defines his test. And with that, she becomes loose. And with all that looseness, she is often on top of the water's surface, floating, so that even one with tilted push, she is gone." She says this while experimenting with the cap of water in front of her.

"The third box is any woman who, while not loved by her husband, is still his wife, as well as any women he may have had an affair with outside of marriage. This is the wife who often hears about her husband's well-being from the loved wife if she is in the picture, or she is standing on the outside, awaiting the day when the undesired wife will drift off with the water's stream. You are a woman and with that, you are not of the designer's. You see, a designer's craft costs more because of the durable feeling attached to its originality. The other stuff is only a copy of the real thing, which is why their glamorousness wears off the moment they are worn. Or perhaps humanity has just decided to advertise one kind over the other."

Her friend looks concerned.

"I know it does not make sense, but just recall one of the famous verses in Genesis and you will see where the twist comes from.

"Here is what you need to know about the boxes, though. The existence of each box is inspired by the existence of the other box. And here is where it was all made possible. Women have come to terms with the fact that they are timed, determined and therefore expire. With these three items in mind, the fight that was originally man's with woman becomes woman-to-woman, because there is only about this much time before all the glitter of something unreal withers.

"They made us think this way. Even the loved wife cannot think beyond the four sides of the box. All she can do is hate as much as she can, or watch herself fall off the ladder. Now you may wonder what does the third box do, knowing she has no clear relationship with the husband? If you are familiar with the notion that says 'once this, no longer that,' you may well know this. She is the wife without clear position who has nothing to do with society, and that is where she is keeping her gaze.

"A female is only a girl once. And how on earth does the third box linger in this world? The key to keeping all three boxes is through fluctuation. You see, no man loves more than one woman a time. Even if two women can be equal in their abilities, he often finds fractions that distinguish one from the other and thereafter leans to the one with more of these that appeal to his current preferences or desires.

"With that, man's love fluctuates. A man may love a woman for a lifetime, but it takes a day to change to a new road. And that is what keeps us on the frontline, ready to serve when we are called. Plus, where else would we really go?

"Now I understand what you meant when you said 'I don't know where I belong.' I don't know where you belong either. But having talked about these boxes, where do you really think you belong?"

"Definitely the third box," says Nyayang's friend. The two sit in silence for a moment.

"This woman you are sharing this man with has gripped him by the collar. Knowing her, she will use it. What she is doing specifically to you is an act of reduction. To make sure no woman ever reaches the position she is in, she deals with those of you who have the potential to ever be liked by this man. She births less than you; you are her top target," says Nyayang.

"For me, I think I know which box I belong to, but let me go in and find out for sure from him," she says and they both leave the neighbour's house.

CHAPTER ELEVEN

Chuol, having thought through what the best solution would be, sends Nyayang and her two girls to his parents. And in a nonverbal motion, she withdraws herself along with her offspring and arrives where the couple believes she will have a chance to grow again.

And so, she arrives with one mission: to win her in-laws' hearts. She makes it her focus to bring back a happiness that never existed in their presence. But in this environment of survival, no matter what one's intentions are, opposition is common.

With a crying child and a meal, to prepare she has to reach the in-laws at a specific time, Nyayang is targeted to experience yet another set of hurdles. And though she tries doing things as expected, she finds things shifting around. But who has to be blamed? That is the nature of things in this environment. Because here, the beauty of your work comes first prior to its acceptance.

Doing nothing, yet seeming ever more preoccupied, the in-laws show no interest in helping. They seem more obsessed with those males in downtown. While preparing the meals, Nyayang puts her child away, at a distance, so it takes her longer to reach her mother again. However, with her big heart trying to reach the depth of her in in-laws' hearts, she keeps strategizing how to complete her multiple tasks. The more she tries, the more she miserably fails in the eyes of the in-laws.

On the day of her return, there were some agreements between Chuol and his parents. These include that she is timed whenever she leaves for a neighbour's house, or when picking up water from the river. Nyayang must follow the rules or a report will be filed and brought to downtown to be placed in the hands of her master. Her promise to follow the rules wiggles a little sometimes. Sometimes she finds herself outside of the compound getting herself into the very sorts of predicaments she has been warned to avoid. But how can she not be expected to leave the house when she is the servant in this family? Servants bring water from the river so that those who have used their animals can enjoy this gift of exchange. But some of the services outside the compound do come with unintentionally meeting or seeing other women. Even seeing women that somehow Nyayang has come to hold grudges against. To be the woman a man prefers to spend time with is a strength women take pride in. It is believed that there is something about her that makes her special. It is true that even though all the wives are tied to him through marriage, he is expected to treat each one differently.

Nyayang returns to her in-laws' home. The women laugh about it but only out of her sight. She knows about it, though. She wishes though that she was the only one that people laughed about for a fault that is not her own. She got into a physical fight about this blaming of innocent people one time as she defended another unlucky mother whose daughter was raped by somebody who lives in the same house as Nyayang. The rapist did what he could never be held accountable for and at the same time shared his experience with his friends. For months, the poor girl avoided being around her agemates who had heard about her misfortune. The young local men called her many different names. The mother figured something had happened and dug in further. It took her a while to find out what exactly happened. She was a single mother who survived each day by fixing her gaze on the one and only daughter she had for she was blind.

This kind of bad news didn't come easily to her. The daughter who notified her about the incident was dealing with the shame and embarrassment. Somehow, the other women had not yet heard about it. The mother worried that once it got into their hands, she would have to forget about anyone marrying her child. Rape is the kind of doing whose details the outside gets to shape accordingly. Somehow, it is always the female victim who gets blamed, somehow it is always her fault, men do not rape strong women. It is a scar that will always signal her diminished worth.

A new man arrived in the area. He appeared educated and he wanted a wife. He wanted this woman's daughter, but by then some women already knew about what happened to the girl. Women have power when it comes to recommendation. When a man wants to marry, he first asks the local women about his potential wife. And whatever answer he gets is to be believed and taken seriously. He heard about the rape, too, as a result. The man wanted a wife who would reflect his educational level. An educated man is one who understands the meaning of life. Therefore, his demand for the purest daughter of the land was justified. The girl's name came up as an insult in the conversations of some of these women after the man left. And that was when Nyayang lost it.

The mother of the girl pleaded with Nyayang to leave things alone. "I don't want anyone else to get involved in this. Plus, once you go and ask them about it, more people will hear about it and I don't want that," she said to her. Nyayang understood how she felt, but she felt so much animosity toward these women. There were three women she could not stand in particular. These were the young lady's ex-husband's wife and the two wives she was sharing her murderer with. She went to one of the women and demanded she admit it was one of their group who had informed the man about what happened to the girl.

"We heard it. Everybody heard about it. How is that you know it was one of us, huh?"

"It was one of you because that is what you do. Like, when will your eyes believe what they see? How will you ever be satisfied with someone else's suffering, whose pain is felt outside of you?" she said angrily and slapped the woman right inside her own compound. The other women came over and they both started fighting with Nyayang. There were other people who heard the noise and came to watch. The three women were divided, but they wouldn't stop throwing punches at each other.

"Who knows, she may have been the one who asked for it!" a woman who was standing on the sidelines said to the other people she was watching along with. Nyayang turned around and saw that this had come from her mother-in-law, the rapist's step-mother.

"What did you just say?" Nyayang asked and walked toward her, forgetting that this was the woman she, too, called "mother." She stopped, baring in mind that whatever reaction she showed would confirm that she was not a respectful woman.

"Why are you nagging people about something that's not your business? Just mind your own business!" said her mother-in-law. Nyayang looked disgusted. But this was her mother. And Nyayang knew many ways this woman could make her miserable.

Right after she finished fighting, the husband of two of the women thought Nyayang had gone too far. He struck Nyayang right there in front of her mother-in-law, the other three women and everybody else who was watching. Soon enough, other men learned about what happened really to the girl, too. This was what the mother had worried about. The more and more people who learned about it, the faster word would be spread. When he finished beating her, he pushed Nyayang out of his compound. Nyayang returned to her house. Mr. Malual, being old, couldn't do a good job of disciplining her. He called the one who knew how. Chuol arrived as though he had wings of air and showed Nyayang the way one more time.

Week after week, the blame switched sides. One time the man admitted he did it; another time, he said the girl asked for it. And to make the matter worse for the girl's family, he said he did it because she had wanted him to. When the mother wanted to come forward about it after all, the community came back and said, "He says she asked for it. How are you going to sue someone whose services were asked for?" The mother lost. And in the week that followed, she lost big. It was that time of day when the sun set. The daughter prepared her mother's meal and asked her to eat.

"No, I want to have a word with you. What happened to you has already happened. There is no magical eraser to take it away from the minds of the ones who heard it. If you would have had a brother, this individual would have feared the inherent consequences of his actions, but you don't. It is unfortunate it had to happen to you, but this is by far not the end of you. The person you are is different from what happened to you," said her mother.

"Mama, why wasn't I enough for the man who wanted to marry me, but I was before this happened?"

"It is okay. He is just looking for someone pure. It is okay that person is not you. Let him look for the perfect one—someone who will deem you to be perfect is on his way."

"You mean one of the old men?" she asked.

Her mother hesitated. "Someone your age will come along, but we need to be patient."

"I doubt it! Anyone who hears my story and my age won't want me. What are the chances, Mama?" Her mother kept quiet. "Your food. Eat please, Mama." She brought it closer to her mother.

"Where is it?"

"Here." She placed it between her hands. The girl entered their room and her mother continued eating outside in the compound.

"I'm done, come and take the bowl," she said but there was no answer. The next sound she heard was the sound of her daughter crossing the line between Heaven and Earth. "Waah!"

She got up and unstably rushed to the room. She missed the entrance. She fell on the ground and got up swiftly. The neighbours heard her crying.

"What happened?" they asked and entered the room. There were no words after they entered. She was done. She had killed herself. The whole neighbourhood arrived in the compound. Some women held down the mother, who was trying to kill herself as well. The elders who came proceeded into the room. The body was covered. They heard the sounds of the women outside. The mother stopped breathing. She died in the hands of the people holding back her hands. She was gone. They covered her body.

"Now, everybody, leave." The elders asked the people to leave. They buried the bodies that evening.

"Now what?" Nyayang asks herself after the death of the family members she fought for. While mourning the loss, she learns something very close to her heart. The co-wife of her downtown neighbour friend finally showed her husband's wife what was coming to her. Nyayang's friend knew this would happen but not how, exactly, and not when she would get the courage to do it. It could have been anything, but boiled oil had always been a great possibility in her mind. It had a great chance of killing the enemy or it would at least guarantee a scar. She poured all the oil she had heated up over her enemy's face. "This could mean she is going to lost her sight," the doctor said after realizing there was nothing that could be done about her deformed face. That up to now she is still alive, though, is not good news to her far-away friend, Nyayang.

Every day becomes just another yesterday, thinks Nyayang as she mentally jots down the occurrence. More than any other time in her marriage, Nyayang learns that anytime she cries calls for insulting her mother's name—petty, dirty, insulting talk which her mother-in-law initiates to disqualify her mother for not having taught her daughter properly.

Sometimes she experiences weariness, but she reminds herself that she must carry on for the sake of her two little ones.

As usual, the mother puts her child to bed for an early sleep, on a cold, breezy evening. She then returns to her evening duties and she puts the water on the fire for her father-in-law. The first pot boiled, she puts on another potful of water, this time for the mother-in-law.

She walks the first pot of boiled water over to the bathroom. Inside, she realizes the soap is missing. She rushes into her room. As she walks back, one of her children opens her eyes. The mother passes by and, not far away from the child, she says, "Father, your water is ready." The little girl at once hears the voice of her mother. The child quietly gets up and begins walking to where the voice was coming from. She goes on unstably.

She gets closer to where she believes her mother should be. Suddenly, however, she steps on a small wooden stick on the ground. This leads her to stumble and suddenly roll over to where the fire is. She knocks the fire pan askew, which unbalances it and pours some hot water over her leg. Immediately, the little girl sends out her voice. Nyayang, upon hearing her, numbly runs over. Helplessly, she embraces her hurt child.

As she stands with the child over her shoulder, the mother-in-law and father-in-law stop some metres away. "How could she not get burned when there is nobody taking good care of her!" her mother-in-law says. Nyayang swallows it but gives her a look of disbelief.

"Oh, there you are getting annoyed again because I'm telling the truth," says the mother-in-law. Nyayang, hearing her the second time, turns her back and walks away.

Nyayang stays up all night for two painful different reasons. She wishes that only there were a way pain could be transferred from child to mother. But she is even more fearful of how the situation will be narrated to her only master.

The morning emerges. And like it disturbed her soul last night, the news reaches Chuol, who is up on his feet immediately. He arrives and demands to know what led the child to be beside the firepan. And his parents, being the voice of his unloved wife, believe a lack of cleanliness in the compound has richly contributed to this incident.

People from around come to visit the child. And throughout the day, the visitation continues, holding Chuol back from delivering on what he really came to do. The evening waits no more. A heavy fight erupts between the man and his wife. With no one to hold back his hand anymore, Chuol finishes out his colourless heart. When he has done as he wants, he leaves the body in the room and immediately leaves for his house. However, on the following day, he returns. He asks Nyayang to leave his parents' home.

For fear that arguing with him may result in another brutal battle, she holds both hands of her children and leaves. "Why are you here?" asks her father.

"The child got burned and I was told I could have prevented it," says Nyayang.

"Yeah, and you couldn't have prevented it because obviously you don't have the same capability other mothers have."

"You are loud and clear about your stance, Father," she says.

Before she can further clarify her statement, her father asks, "And what is that supposed to mean?"

"You seem to support Chuol and defend him whenever something wrong is going on. That's what that means," she says and starts crying afterward. "I know, in your heart, everything that has happened was my fault in one way or another. But if I can speak for myself, especially in this case, there was no way I could have prevented the burning from happening.

"Father, there is just no way I could invoke the rain to fall over the sown seed and pose the sun to smile over them at the same time. No, one thing had to happen first. I know if there is anything you could care less about it is the fact that there is an abnormality in this union between me and my husband," continues Nyayang. "You can always tell me to go back and being the obedient daughter I am, I will always go back. But that will never mean I will fill the eyes of my husband."

"What makes you think like that?" says her father quickly.

Nyayang straightens her gaze and says, "I didn't choose to say this. I'm forced by the evidence. Look, when you were getting married again, you informed your wife prior. But not here. That is not a glimmer of what happened. And now the presence of his new wife has become a threat to us since he has given her all the authority. And the least Chuol can do is to shift me from place to place, yet you sure don't have an eye for it."

"Stop! Stop, enough!" screeches her father. "All of that, the things that happened between you and him, have nothing to do with the fact he married another wife.

"Your husband is a man and he doesn't have to seek your approval. If he feels he wants to do something, he is entitled to make his own decision whenever he wants. Now, don't ever compare me with him.

"You make me ashamed. I don't know how to talk among men anymore. Every girl stays with her husband. Only you come back. And it's about nothing. I give you only three days and I'm only allowing this much time because of the child." He walks away from his daughter irritably.

Back at his parents' house, after Chuol sends Nyayang away, he now sits down with his parents and declares what he plans on doing.

"This time, I want your hands out of this," Chuol tells his father.

"My son, I just want you to have a legacy. And you can't have that world of your own without people. Any people, both perfect and imperfect," says his father. "But now that you have a definition of your own, it's up to you."

With the help of his father, Chuol meets the chief in charge of the law the next day. At the meeting, the when is put in place and the chief places the matter in his own hands.

"Mama, all I want is for my father to see where the problem is," Nyayang cries on the third day when she is about to leave.

"And so do I. But what can I do when I will never be a man!" The mother wraps her arm around her daughter's shoulder. And immediately tears begin rolling down from both of them.

"Hello!" a voice suddenly greets them from the gate.

"Go and see who it is," says her mother. Nyayang goes to the gate.

"Mali," says a middle-aged man.

"Mali," says Nyayang.

"Can I have a word with Mr. Jock?" asks the man.

"No, he is not at home at the moment."

Mr. Jock has been gone since the start of the day. In a house not too far away from his, there was an unreasonable argument between the owner of that house and a man whose outlook on life brings confusion to the real men of this area. It began when the brothers of Mama Nyalock realized their sister was impregnated. The poor girl was beat up and when the brothers finished, they asked her to go and find the father of the child.

However, prior to that, this happened between the lovers. "I don't want you," the boyfriend said. He went on in detail saying that he was not the only person involved. After the brothers bitterly pushed her out, she went away and wandered about with no specific direction to go. She came back home a few hours later—and the brothers did the same thing. While they were beating her up, she confessed to them there was nowhere she could go. The man refused her, she said.

There was one thing left to do: the case was taken before the law. The boyfriend insisted on the same thing. The girl's family became very bitter and they took their anger out on her. One of the brothers lost his patience. He slapped his sister and followed it by saying, "Why did you let him impregnate you?"

During the hearing, this controversial man was absent. In fact, he had not been seen by anyone lately. Part of the reason for this was that he was not needed for things that were typically handled by men. They called him fool or something of a "women's man." In situations like these, he would have said this, his famous aphorism: "Why would you impregnate a girl you didn't want to be your wife" as opposed to what the brother said.

The family dug more into what the boyfriend was claiming and when he had exhausted all his other options, he walked the truth forward. He said he simply didn't think the girl was his type. However, he made one thing crystal clear. He said, "I'm the father and so I want my child when he is born."

The girl's family didn't like his end speech, because they knew this was not a joke. It was legitimate and legal and an everyday response for a girl to be refused. And still, a man is more than right to sip from tuna soup and throw its poisonous body away.

The girl returned home, and a man of her father's age came forward with an offer of marriage. The opportunity was too good to be ignored. Another month went by and the couple were pronounced married and began their life together.

Two years later, the husband thought of a brilliant idea. At this time of his life, he was no longer the energetic young man he used to be physically and productively. So he passed on his new wife to his first son, with one caveat. And that was, he was still in charge.

However, when a man steps in to produce children, ownership and supervision are inherently not too far behind. The old husband wanted to know where she was going, why she was going there and when she was coming home. Also, the new husband, as well, had his own needs since he had stepped in to produce the children for his father.

The fool man had been watching closely the life of the new wife, for his house was close by. In the area, there was a football field. Around the field were young bushes that added beauty to the overall look of the field. The fool man came to the field at sunrise and he began cutting the branches off the bushes. He immediately bulked them in groups and burned them. The branches refused to burn; instead, they formed clouds of smoke.

People become concerned about what he was doing. And because he was a man, he was approached by other men. "What are you doing?" asked the first man on the scene, who happened to be Mama Nyalock's father. He declined to answer. Instead, he knelt down and dug a couple of holes in the ground. He took some seeds out of his pocket and sowed them in each hole. Other men heard the voices of the first man. And among them was Mr. Jock. About four men surrounded him and immediately demanded answers for his act

He said in response, "Look at the ground." The men looked. He said, "There are two stories I'm going to tell you. One morning, a full family of rabbits come to a newly sown farm. The father, being the strong one, began to dig out the growing seeds. Once he dug one out, he threw it to the children. But once the children had a seed, they bit it in half and scattered the pieces around and waited for the father to throw another one. The owner's wife saw them and wanted to chase them away. However, the husband said, 'Let them eat. They won't finish this big farm.' So they continued doing the same until they left on their own.

"Five years passed by. The same rabbit family returned to the same farm in the same season. The parents, however, were now old. And so this time the children dug up the growing maize for them. And this time, while they were uprooting the maize, they would cut the stem of the plant in half before throwing it to the parents. And the elderly parents would wrestle with the plant, and when they couldn't really piece it up, they would throw it back to the children."

"Nonsense!" said Mama Nyalock's father. "You made us stand before you to listen to this nonsense you call stories? Has it ever occurred to you that we are men? We are men, not fool like you." Mr. Jock and Mama Nyalock's father began to leave. Real men were tired of him. He had no speciality and yet he showed up at places where he was hated. This was where he had been the last time anyone had seen him. But the biggest war with this man erupted when he said something and it turned out to be true. Even though he did not come out and say, "I tell you so," it really bothered real men.

Mr. Jock had had a few of these dealings with him. He and this man had a moment a few years ago in a court hearing. It was a dispute between a married couple. And this was a simple one. This couple were going on fifteen years without a child. Actually, she was going on fifteen years without a child with him. He had children with his other two wives. The cause of infertility was not clear, but could only be one thing: he had sucked her breasts the first day after they were married and several times after that. This was thought to interfere with fertility, according to the ears that lived in the past. After this confession, the girl was relieved. She was the only one at whose feet the whole infertility issue had rested, as it was obvious the man had no issues.

"You have to let her go. Maybe she will get pregnant with someone else," someone suggested, but the man refused it with silence. The second time this suggestion came again, it was from the girl's family. And even then, he refused. He claimed that he still loved his wife even without a child. It was then very difficult for the parents to buy back their daughter. But foolish people like this guy didn't care about what most men cared about whenever your daughter returned, which was the marketing part. Although the girl's family was weak and could not argue anymore, someone else took the chance.

He asked, "What is her share in this?" Her share was that she was married to this man. That was her share.

Someone responded to him, "If she were my daughter, she would have been released. Look, this is teaching the wrong lesson to these people you think are the humans. She is not your daughter, case closed. No, case not closed. You—" he said to the woman "—they only think about themselves, now you think about you, too." He then walked right out.

The woman took his words to heart and in the following year, she had her share of men on her arm. Men like Mr. Jock did not like these kinds of ways out for their daughters. They were often left in debt.

"We have to change this!" the fool man said as the two walked away.

"This? What is 'this'?" said one of the other men.

"Just leave him. Who is this guy? He is just a mentally ill person," the other man said and pulled his friend away.

The last guy left with laughter in his mouth, a mocking kind. "You should worry about dying alone, not this," he said as he walked away.

Something was odd about this man. But often, the confusion was blamed on something else. Those who were brought up in different places had difficulty conforming to the principles of what made a man a man. This man came back from somewhere and feebly took some wife who had once been married and who already had children and stubbornly fed people with the line that "he wanted to be with her." But how could he want her over these virgins? The men couldn't understand. The woman was a widow at the time of their meet-up and he knew about it and he ignored it until the law claimed the children on behalf of the deceased husband. The children the two had together plus those she came into the relationship with were claimed back, in addition to the woman herself. Indeed, he should have been worried now that he was walking back to an empty compound. But instead, he showed no surprise. He had by now gotten used to the fact that he was disrespected by others his age.

Like last spring when he watched himself mocked in public. He never got an official invitation to be part of any gathering. No, that's not how it worked here. You do not declare yourself one thing and expect others to call you something else. He was an enemy to manhood. Last spring he said this: "If you are going to talk about him anyway, better you bring the issue to his attention." He got no answers for this.

A former medical doctor had been trying to find his soul mate for years after his return just before the country split into South and North Sudan. In his earlier thirties, he worked in Malakal Hospital. And when the war began threatening more southerners, he began to see more wounded people from the place he grew up. A few years later, he thought he may have to address the wounded nearby. He relocated to the eastern part of Bieh state. He continued helping, working with the local hospital until one day he was bitten by a snake, leaving him paralyzed in his right foot. His career was put on hold and after he healed, his appetite was lost.

He married his first wife. They both stayed childless for the first two years. He married another woman. The three stayed unlucky for two more years and the first wife unleashed her head. Through the dirtiest way known to women, the only way she could get out, she committed adultery. He asked only for his cows back. He remained with the second wife and quickly added another one. He married his third wife. By then, the second wife had been staying with him for four years, bearing no children. In the fifth year, she ran away, but first made sure she was carrying someone else's child for society to possibly allow her to escape.

There had been some speculation suggesting he may be medically shortened. But this was just a rumour regarding why the third wife had been carrying an empty womb for three years now. He noticed the behaviour in the eyes of the community. He became emotionally unavailable and physically threatening to her. She became pregnant following the footsteps of the strayed wives and after the realization, she thought a bold declaration may not be the safer option for her. She wisely informed him that she had now accepted to be pregnant after mistakenly making it known to the biological father of the unborn child and had an agreement that the two may call it a journey. The news was made available to the haters who had thought otherwise. Now, there was only one thing left for him to do. After having received his cows back from his second wife's parents, he doubled his chances and wedded two women at the same time.

The child was born with an immediate confusion over his appearance. Three years after was a great time to begin a conflict over who could have possibly produced this male child. But the little man's big ears reduced the agony to one fellow brother in the community. The fellow was killed, as his education qualified him for the sub-clan's killings, just as the boy's second birthday drew near.

Some rumours were circulating about the wife. They arrived at the husband's attention and, for some reason, he became curious, not about the one that his child resembled the deceased person but the one about his wife's current pregnancy. "That is what people say," he heard. But what people? And what were they saying? That he wasn't the father. The husband gleamed this snippet from bits of conversations he overheard. And after that, no one really want to talk about it. The issue of male infertility was by far one of the most complicated and deadly ones in the culture. As a matter of fact, people often died when the public had access to this information. He knew about his condition and he didn't like it that another dude could be producing children for him.

He now knew what to do about the cause of his embarrassment. But before he could take action, this happened. The little man became sick to the point of nearly dying. At some point, the hospital became a second home for him and his mother. Nothing was found to be medically wrong with him so something with a cultural root was thought to be the cause. He had been hidden from his biological father, people believed. But between biological matters and those of commoditized market exchanges, you would be surprised what really mattered.

"What you are doing to this child is not good," some decent humans would say to the mother who just happened to be holding back two different secrets after her son made it all the way to a state of unconsciousness. "This child will suffer death. Tell the world who you got him from."

But the whole truth refused to come out. However, with small crumbs of it falling out of her mouth due to her fear, the gossipers related what they heard to the community and the dots were connected to form the likelihood of the whole truth. But it was someone else who finally wanted to set the record straight. The deceased man's younger brother. The secret biological father's final words shook the world of the husband when the community was stirred to again rethink this obvious error.

The deceased's younger brother lay it out plainly for everyone at the hearing. "As the end of his last breath neared, he held my hand in both of his. 'Please bring home my boy,' he said. I asked who he was talking about and that was when he told me about his affair with this woman and that this child belonged to him."

Now the two secrets were exposed; the wife's double life was revealed. And for every other person who may have thought otherwise, the hearing made the truth known. The husband furiously got up and gave his wife the longest stare man has ever given in the history of man. "I am not the father?" he asked rhetorically, looking straight in the little boy's uncle's eyes. His anger was visibly clear now. He looked at his wife. He looked at the uncle again. He swiftly moved toward, leaving a bleeding mark on the forehead of the young man.

People came between the two. The chief in charge peacefully calmed the calamity. The husband stormed off, leaving the wife in suspense of her next staying place, after having made the crowd hear, "Come to my house if you want to follow your husband."

"Even if the child is your brother's, we will still follow the law as it applies here. He married this woman and therefore this child is his," said the ruling chief to the rest of the crowd after the husband stormed off.

The hearing ended with the wife going with her family, since things would get uglier if she chose to go home with the situation still fresh on the husband's mind. That he was infertile became the word on every street and in every place where men gathered. And what was bothering him the most was that he knew everybody was talking. And then a clever plan presented itself in his mind. He called his wife and the child back home, claiming he had gotten over his disappointment. The family returned. And the talk on the street? Oh, that one was recreationally rewinding itself.

"If it's that wrong that his wife was impregnated by some other man, how is it not wrong that he is now getting away with a seed which never sprouted out from him?" the fool guy asked a crowd of men.

"Because children are what causes us these prices we pay. He is his, regardless." He got himself answered this time.

"Then if you are going to talk about him, anyway, it's better you bring the issue to his attention." He threw that one out again after being irritated about what couldn't be termed "a straight blame." It wasn't even on the surface. If you just passed by, you wouldn't know or grab it. But no, they were definitely talking about him. One word here, some laughter there. It was all contained in their inner judgments.

"But shouldn't this act of deception, misleading and manipulation be put to an end? I mean, who did we think we had done the favour for here? The girls, when we let the goat in through the front gate and into the growing plants? Or him, after only half-testing his freedom, asked him to hurriedly find his way through the thorn fence?" The not-so-manly guy said this after the community learned of the unprecedented event.

The husband gunned down his wife with her unborn child, the little boy and lastly himself. "Man, if only we understood and saw what it is we do to them, we would be ashamed of ourselves." He threw that one out again. And for good reason, it uproariously ignited some unpleasant feelings in one of the other men present. A man people called "Guan-cuani" (the twins' father). He got each of both genders. He had other children before the twins and after the twins. But twins were so controlling! The fool and this man didn't like each other in general.

One thing which stood perfectly clear in the mind of this small-minded man was what this father did to his twins in their teens years. Math was a tough lesson for the boy twin. The girl, on the other hand, was very good at math. But a girl with a mind, what was God thinking? No, He couldn't have just placed the wrong mind in the wrong body and allowed that to be born intentionally. Such a betrayal!

Every time the girl solved her math problems and obediently helped her brother, this father imagined himself in some sort of alternate world where he would arrive at the scene where the mistake was made. And in his physical form in his mind, he would carefully remove the nails that held both the heads and the bodies in places, unzip the heads and exchange their brains. And that was how he would undo the mistake if he ever were at the scene of the day of their creation. Though he was not able to do that, he did the next best thing. He found a man for her. She didn't like the man, so she got herself impregnated by her boyfriend, who had just the right amount of intelligence. Her father said no. He gave her to the man to take home. She ran away with the boyfriend. He tricked her into coming back and, exactly as he wanted, he gave her back to the man. This time, though, her mental fortitude was gone. And she stayed with the man her father wanted.

The fool heard about the story and with his unsafe mouth, he found himself preaching to people that this was not good. "Because we are supposed to marry them, it's such a pain for them to stay with us in a thorny predicament. This is where we run into difficulties." He attempted to demonstrate this point. "When they finally come into our lives, we quickly jump into swallowing them so the room for the next one is surrendered. And here is the trouble. When you find one who has somewhat escaped the mental damage from her parents, they naturally refuse to go down your tummy, don't they? They stop right here." He gestured with his hand and pointed at his esophagus. "Right here," he said again. He went around the village saying so.

"Clearly, you love women. I don't know why, but you do. Tell us, what part do you mostly disagree with? That we shouldn't practise polygamy or that we should think they are just like us?" Guan-cuani asked him one time.

"Yeah, that too," he said.

"Hahaha, he must be mad! He doesn't like polygamy!" Another man burst into laughter.

"But if we take care of the notion that they are just like us first, that will take care of other errors we keep on making," he said.

Every time the fool man spoke like that, Guan-cuani felt his approach to life was being questioned. "You think you know more than us? Why do you think He made you first and not second? Why do you think He called you the head and not the tail? Why do you think He created you a man and not a woman? Why do you think she was made out of you not out of dust? Why do we marry them not them marry us?" He got really busy proving he was right and that his actions were justified. The volume of his voice shot up.

Another man said this, "You may have to just let it go altogether. I find talking to him very exhausting." He said about the fool man.

"None of the things you listed has anything to do with why we behave the way we behave," the fool said. "I'm not a good reader of His words, however. I don't think He meant to say 'Go and divide the women among yourselves.' He said, 'Go and fill the earth.' I'm thinking their existence is supposed to be parallel and equal with ours. And don't cover my head with that whole rib thing if that is your main source of answers," he said, visible frustration on his face. This face got him in more trouble.

"Get out of here, you are not worthy of this men's gathering!" said Guan-cuani.

Others were saying things in support of Guan-cuani also. And by saying nothing more, he got thrown out.

Every time he stood up and said this is wrong or that is wrong, though no one wanted to hear it, his thinking about whether he was a true believer and why his actions were commonly viewed as some type of conspiracy got mixed up in his spirit. He was now watching the real men departing from him and into their own troubled worlds. They refused to listen to anything he said. And all he could do now was leave the field.

"Okay, then this is a letter for him. Would you give it to him when he returns?"

"Sure." Nyayang holds the letter. "But who will I say has brought the later for him?" asks Nyayang.

The man by that point has turned around. He turns to her and says, "Oh, yeah. Tell him it's from the chief." The man proceeds and Nyayang walks back inside.

"What is it?" asks her mother as Nyayang gets closer.

"A letter."

"A letter? For who?"

"For Baba." The two females stare at the enclosed letter.

Five minutes later, Baba walks in. "You still here?" he asks Nyayang the moment he walks in.

"What is in your hand?" he asks as he becomes aware of the letter in Nyayang's hand.

"A letter for you." She hands it to him. He opens it. He starts reading what is inside. He stops and suddenly shows a surprised face.

"What does it say?" asks his wife. He refuses to say. He walks into his dwelling and continues reading on the way.

From what he has read so far, he sees it's Mr. Malual's family calling. In the letter, he has been given a week to appear before the law.

Upon finishing the letter, Mr. Jock feels less energized to leave his dwelling. As the day changes to a darker colour, he comes out and tells his wife what was in the letter. "Nyayang's in-laws are calling me," he says in a low voice.

"Calling about what?" asks his wife. "Calling about what?" she repeats when he doesn't answer right away.

"How would I know?" he replies harshly. He starts walking around trying to believe in something he doubts.

Then there is a weird silence that falls over the three of them suddenly. Some minutes pass and there is no longer a need to discuss Nyayang's leaving. The atmosphere now changes to what lies in the thoughts of the old man that they don't see.

CHAPTER TWELVE

The day arrives. The two families are seated opposite each other and around them are people running from relatives to everyone in general. Among the crowd are women who make up the number at the back of the crown. Everybody is hungry for this case to begin. But the chief is still busy with another "Release my cows, I'm done with your daughter" court hearing.

It has been three hours since they have been pinned down by this case and the husband is losing it. She committed adultery right after they got married. "Because we know who did this, we are just laying charges against him once he appears before this court," says the chief. He explains the simple procedure against those sleeping with other people's wives, hoping for the usual conclusion.

"No, she and I are done. How could I sleep with a woman who is apparently every man's wife?" the husband responds. He was done with her the moment he realized it, and all he wanted were his cows back. Prior to this, he and his family had tried to talk to his in-laws about the cows' return, but they said, "We don't have all of them together. The Murle have taken a few of them from the relatives to whom most of them were distributed to. What we will do is, you will have to wait for her to get married and whatever comes out of that will be given to you."

Of course, the husband and his family were furious about this response. They said her family and everyone who had taken a cow had to bring it back. After three hours of unproductive talking, the chief cuts it loose and seemingly agrees with the girl's family. He says, "You will be given the full number of your cows when she gets married. However for now, the father will give you whatever he has, and everything else, you will get after his daughter gets a husband." He wraps it up and leaves quickly for Chuol's and his in-laws' case.

"Mr. Jock, I do believe you know why your family is here," the chief begins.

"I didn't exactly know the meaning of this, but now sitting opposite to my child's in-laws, I believe I know," says Mr. Jock.

"There are a number of things which have happened between your daughter and her husband. And the most disturbing claim we heard from her in-laws is that they believe you and your wife have dived your hands deeply in these constant, most embarrassing behaviours your daughter has exhibited in her marriage, as they put it."

"Uh, from the start of the marriage, the couple has had a rough time coming to a collective agreement. But what usually generates the disagreement has up until now been unknown to us," Mr. Jock says when he is given a chance.

"Mr. Jock, you haven't answered my question," insists the chief. "Why do the in-laws suspect your hand in regard to the problems the couple has been having?"

"Well, I'm not refusing to give an answer to the question. But I don't see a clear justification demonstrating the piece my family plays in the matter," Mr. Jock tries to clarify.

"Mr. Chuol, would you tell us why you believe your in-laws have constructed the problem you have with your wife?"

"Thank you, Chief," says Chuol after he clears his throat. He adjusts himself before moving on. "Just like everyone here knows, when you marry your wife, she is no longer under her parents' supervision.

"My wife and I started fighting from the moment she was welcomed into the family. My wife chose not to listen to me as a husband. And so we have been on the run every since.

"Now, why I believe my in-laws have had a hand in the problem? Look!" he says and begins roaming the crowd with his eyes. "You beat your wife, she runs back to her parents. The next day, she comes back and she is still the same person who fled yesterday. And here I am, trying to understand what it is her parents tell her whenever they have the chance to tell her how a woman should be. Here are some of the things that have caused me to have no desire left for this woman." He raises his voice. The crowd goes even quieter.

"Nyayang is stubborn. Unlike any other woman, she raises her head higher to be exactly with man's head." He gestures how high Nyayang's head is with his hand as he continues. While he is still talking, the crowd begins to rumble. Some men take some big steps toward Nyayang to eye her more closely.

"She is a lazy woman. Which does not comply with and rather interferes with the lifestyle I have. I'm a young businessman with people to come home with. And when it's my time to shine, I'm held back. You see right here, this particular problem has put many constraints on how well I can socialize with my age mates. And yet, I'm only asked to take it.

"She is quarrelsome. This issue really gets in the way of how my own parents converse with her," Chuol continues. "Nyayang has her own means of interpreting things. You don't tell her this, she argues with you. You don't tell her that, she argues with you.

"You see, many times with my wife, she has let herself have the permission to access the key that unlocks the anger gate rather than being the woman she is supposed to be."

"Okay, that is enough," interrupts the chief.

"No. I still have something to say," Chuol argues. The chief offers him another chance.

"Although I can put up with all those things I have already mentioned because it's the unfortunate curse we men have to live with nowadays regardless of our dowries, there is one thing I cannot live with," he says.

"Nyayang is not a woman who stands on one man. No." He shakes his head. "She has an eye that runs from one man to another and I will not take that!" He then sits back in his seat.

Now, having listened to the young man, Mr. Jock feels even smaller. Nyayang, being negatively exposed, can't stop her tears from flowing. Her mother, well, she does what she knows best—she holds on to her child's shoulders, hoping to give her the strength to accept the inherent fate of being a female.

The crowd noise is now picking up a little. Some have started running ahead of the game and declare which side they are for.

"So, what are you doing? Why don't you marry yourself a faithful wife?" One man's voice is higher than the rest.

Another man says, "No, no. Divorce her! Adultery is the kind of sin you must divorce your wife for. It's there in the Bible."

"Quiet everybody," the chief summons the people. "Mr. Chuol, I'm going to ask you about one thing among all the other nonsense I have heard. And I'm calling it nonsense because based on my own experience, when a man is faced by an issue like this, divorce is the last resort. There are many ways that you could have resolved this." He looks straight into Chuol's eyes. "But here, if I may ask you. Do you believe your wife committed adultery?"

"Yes, I do," says Chuol quickly.

"Okay. And to whom would we hold this grudge against? Do you know who is responsible?"

"No, I don't know exactly. But I know many times my wife has done it. These times include her leaving me with one of the children and spending the day away without notifying me of her whereabouts. Other times, she would slip out as though she is picking up water and then spend the whole day away.

"And on one of these occasions, it happened the man actually came and stood nose to nose with me. The man escorted her to the entry of my compound. When I decided to see what was going on, the two disappeared in the cloud before I could confront them," Chuol continues. He now cannot stop proving that he is right.

Mr. Jock, on the opposite side of the circle, recalls the event vividly. And Chuol's responses don't seem to provide him any comfort now.

"Come to think of it." Chuol still can't stop himself. "This is a married woman." He points at Nyayang on the opposite side. "And if you are the man in this scenario, how would you feel?" he now yields. at the crowd.

"Not so good!" says the chief. "But Mr. Chuol, if I have heard you correctly, you didn't catch your wife's husband, correct?"

"No, I did," says Chuol.

"No," denies the chief. "You saw a man. That doesn't prove anything."

"I caught the man, Chief. This is the proof," Chuol goes on non-stop.

"Mr. Chuol, Mr. Chuol, wait," says the chief. "I understand your frustration. However, according to the guidelines we treat these situations by, I am afraid you have to tell us the name of your wife's husband and possibly where he lives so we can bring him before the law. Otherwise, I don't know how we are going to proceed with this issue." The Chief wants to press the mandatory charges against the man in question but without him, his knowledge is being put on hold.

"Okay, I would like to dismiss everybody. Come back to this station next week for the appearance of this man. And possibly the continuation of this issue," announces the chief.

Nearby, there are other court hearings going on. The court hearings, as usual, are designated as A, B, or C. The "B" hearing marks the third attempt at a verdict, yet there is no progress to put an end to the fight between the parties. It has to do with a woman who was forced into a marriage she didn't consent to. In the midst of the marriage process, she ran away with her old boyfriend but was soon returned to the other man. In spite of the fact that she and her boyfriend claimed to be in love, the parents were making her marry this man she expressed deep loathing for. In despair and in hopelessness, she pushed through the first two years of marriage, and she bore him a son. Sometime in that period, her abhorrence of her current situation got to the point that she secretly got engaged to her old boyfriend for the second time. She was never faithful to the old man, even during the making of their first child. He knew about it. But the balance this time was on his desire to have a family. And with little wisdom of what could happen in the future, she and her boyfriend called it a journey, leaving her son behind.

Right after their disappearance, her parents reached out to the left-behind husband. They asked him whether he would like to take back his cows. But he was very sure the wife was still his. He immediately went to the field. He found a girl who reciprocated his feelings. The two got engaged, but an unseen family issue from the girl's side put the process on hold. Up until then, the girl he had gotten engaged to had been raised by her mother's brother. Her father denied her at birth because he lacked an attraction toward the mother. When the fiancé learned about this, he postponed the upcoming ceremony. He further expressed that he would not go on with the plan until he found out what the girl's biological father's side of the story was.

"He doesn't want anything to do with this girl," the mother-in-law said. But that statement was immediately proved to be wrong. The father didn't want to do anything with her because there was no reason for him to. Unlike if the child was a boy, there is not much usefulness for a female child, except in a moment like this, when a man offers to give the family something to take her. The biological father heard about the engagement, and he came forward and claimed his position. However, between the biological provider and the nurturer, there is no balance. The girl sided with her nurturer, but it was very risky. People told her if she wanted to have a husband, she may have to consider knowing who she really came from and make peace with him, or it would be hard for her to find a man who would take her from one of her mother's brother's hands. With each side of the girl's family warring over some senseless issue, the fiancé saw something he quickly called dysfunction and withdrew himself.

But it was not over for the old man. He went back to the field again and found himself another beautiful girl. Unlike the previous girl, this girl showed some dislike for the old man. But it was not her decision; she had to accept him. She bore him a first child but intentionally made a horrible mistake with the second child. Someone else was responsible for her second pregnancy. The child was born clean and healthy but his mother had to bury him a year later when her husband ended up shaking him to death out of hate.

"You deal with it. Eat him or bury him. It is up to you. We, your family, have washed our hands of this. We will never come to your defence." The family sided with the husband, leaving the daughter to find a place to bury her lifeless child. She went home and to compensate for her error, she was asked to cook for her husband upon her return and, whether she liked it or not, she had to go to bed with him on the same day. He did it this way to show her who makes rules. He then updated people on his reasonable claim and said he couldn't accept the fact that he now had to raise some child who was never his biologically.

"Let them multiply," the husband would say ambiguously about his disappearing wife, an aphorism that every man understood. At first, there was no one knowing the couple's whereabouts. But then that changed and people were sure they were staying somewhere in Khartoum. Thirteen years later, the girl returned home with her boyfriend and their little army—four girls. And that was when the husband called her parents and brought her and her boyfriend before the law. His reason for calling them was not necessarily to take back his wife but the children were his, despite his biological absence.

At the first trial, the husband won and went back to his house with his trophies, the girls. But that was just the beginning. The biological father had a big problem with the basis for the decision—that because she was somebody else's wife at the time of their departure, there was no recognition of her being his wife. And because of the first child being the old man's, every child after that was inherently considered his. This problem was mostly fuelled by the woman's son, who the people believed was man enough to bring back his siblings and his mother. And from the start, he had been the voice of his father, who had placed his faith both in him and the animals.

However, every argument for why the right decision was made only caused the boyfriend to become more upset. There was definitely something else that no one was addressing. What was the real problem? The difference between the two men? Well, one bought her while the other one came up with the children. And since both the wife and the cows were considered property, it would be a great loss for the husband to walk back empty-handed without the fruit of his cows. The decision was made, but they returned, for the third time now. And at the end, there was only one thing left for the mother to do, which was to follow her children.

And what of the "C" hearing? Well, that one was already in its final stages. This hearing, though, involved blood. It involved three people: one woman and two men. One of the two men had a relationship with the female. The other man was his cousin. During the two's relationship, the two had an encounter in a room in which more than four other people were present. Their indiscretion was later discovered by others in the room and those who became aware of it had something to say, not merely about them but about the man's cousin, also.

In this culture, it always comes down to blood. But in what way? What really kills? The blood in hearing or the blood in seeing? The cousin soon became sick afterward, and this was believed to be because the cousin was in the room during the encounter. It often brings people joy to know that someone closely connected to them by blood had convinced some girl to have relations with them. But you must not be there, or the blood connection will have dire consequences.

The connection between the cousin's illness and his presence at the encounter of his cousin and the woman was realized fairly soon after the incident. A plant by the name of Jel was quickly cut, fresh from the garden, and chopped into pieces. It was placed in water and the two cousins drank the concoction. And that should have put an end to the whole cultural curse had the families not learned some more emerging details from the sick cousin. The sickness actually didn't leave him after the drinking of the plant juice and according to everybody around he was very sick. His body was reduced to a skeletal frame; he was a living corpse. He confessed that he himself had a moment with his cousin's presumed wife-to-be. In a case like this, the less contact the person has, the less dangerous the consequence. But when two blood-related men shared a female, it could easily lead to high-fiving Death's palm if not properly handled. And that was what the families did this morning.

Early in the day, a bull was vertically slain to prevent this natural death. The experts had the two cousins on each side of the bull, along with his family. Each team pulled its body away from the other, as the animal's soul was sent to heaven. After that, it was pure joy: the eye of life was seen in the dying fellow. And as to the third person in this story, well, if she shared her mistake with other girls to warn them about the consequences, that would be very educational. And the child with the two possible fathers would live to find another father if ever one could be found.

The two families at the court hearing designated "A" leave the court and each goes on their separate way while filled with differing emotions.

At the same time, the families from the other court hearings also leave their appointed rooms.

Reaching home, Chuol's mother can't collect her thoughts properly. "You worry so much," says Mr. Malual.

"Yes. Because we have no name. What are we going to present before the law next week?" she says annoyingly.

"Why do you care, Mother," says Chuol. "Is Nyayang his wife or my wife?" he asks and leaves for his home downtown. He returns hurriedly and enters an empty compound. Sarah is out with the children. In fact, the entire neighbourhood has been stirred to go gawk at some behaviour not seen before in the neighbourhood. The Boke of Gatwech's family is under the influence of some unknown attacker. It all began this morning. It is not clear how it all got started—she just burst into excessive talking and has been wandering, and now, whatever has overtaken her has turned up its intensity, leading her to refuse even to keep her clothing on. Chuol walks out of the compound and goes to the gate overlooking the mob made up mostly of women encircling the naked woman. He is disturbed, mostly by the noise coming from the woman. She has taken off all that covers the skin and some women are trying to put some of it back on her and it is a challenge. While still standing at the gate, two bodyguards sent by her husband arrive.

"Wait outside," someone from the inside of the compound says to the bodyguards. The women manage to wrap a blanket around her body. Chuol decides to stay at the gate of his compound even after they take her to the local hospital.

When Sarah returns with the children, she asks, "How did it go?"

"Nothing was decided," he responds. Sarah turns around uneasily and walks away.

The new court date arrives. Everybody gathers around the two fighting families again. And unlike last week, today the chief has a different approach in mind to initiate the discussion.

First, he gives the opportunity to the crowd to speak. He wants to see the community's perspective on the issue. A few people speak. And even as some wrestle with the awkwardness of the situation, it appears divorce is all that Nyayang deserves.

"People, this is not new," says a middle-aged man among the crowd. "We all have been there, and if only the truth could be exposed as it should, it's indeed better having no wife than having a prostitute and calling it a wife.

"As a man, you waste your dowries and, for goodness sake, all you learn is you are sharing her with another man?" the same man continues.

"No, no," interrupts another middle-aged man. "I object to your stance. I know how it feels to be among other men when you suspect your wife of adultery," the man tells Chuol. "However, I don't believe divorce is the necessitated solution to your specific matter."

"Why? Why not?" shouts Chuol.

"Listen. Chuol, listen." The man calms him down. "Do you have another wife or she is the only one?" Chuol nods his head that yes, he does. "Okay," continues the man, "so, this is the mother of two of your children. You divorce her today, you take your children. And you are sure this is the step you want to take?"

"Yeah, and what do I lose? I take my children right away—they are 'Gaat Hoke' (children for my cows)," says Chuol, disturbed by the man's response.

The man looks at him. Chuol looks back. But everyone else is quiet. "Mr. Malual, I suggest you leave her in your midst so she can raise her children," the man speaks to the father now.

"Which means I'm still the husband?"

"Yes, you are," says the man irritably.

"Okay. Let's stop there for now," says the chief. "Before I give the other party a chance to speak, I would like to know this.

"Mr. Chuol, do we have our person in our midst?"

"No. We don't. We haven't located this man. But that shouldn't slow down this process."

"Hmm. Mr. Chuol, I'm afraid it will. If divorce is all you want, I suggest we must wait until we know where this person resides. And until then, I'm not going any further than this," concludes the chief.

"Mr. Jock, do you have anything to add?" he asks.

"No. I believe our best time to say anything will be when we have this person we are looking for," he says.

"Good!" says the chief. Again, the two families go their separate ways.

At Nyayang's parents' home, the silence that has fallen over them begins to dissolve. Mr. Jock is thinking clearly again. "Now that things have returned to normal between you and Chuol, it's time for you to go back," he says.

"Is it not too soon? Why don't you let her stay for a bit so that Chuol can also take some time to think about his actions," suggests her mother.

"I believe you are saying the opposite. By keeping her here, it will only prove to them that we partook in the problem," says her father.

"No, Jock," objects her mother. "If you don't stand up for your child, her in-laws will keep treating her as though they picked her up under a tree.

"You need to speak to her in-laws like a man. You need to stand up like a father. What will it take for you to say it is wrong of them to treat your child poorly?" The mother raises her voice at her unwilling husband.

"But if you just keep sending her back whenever she has run to you for safety, these in-laws will have no respect for either you or your daughter. Besides, the man has another wife," she adds.

As the wife takes the place of her husband, Mr. Jock stoically looks her in the eye.

She reads the message imparted by the given look. Nonetheless, this persistent mother who frets about nothing anymore except for that which concerns her child, refuses to be intimidated.

"You are not sending her back without telling Chuol what a father says," she goes on while moving closer to the angered man.

Mr. Jock faces his wife with his frowning face and says, "I'm not going to have a word with him. You are going to, since you have become the man of this family. Go. Talk to your child's husband." The husband becomes serious. "Now, it's up to you. Divorce her or not. Up to you," he says and walks away.

He walks away and immediately exits the compound in a hurry. "Where is he going?" Nyayang asks her mother.

"Where else would he go? His feet always race to places where someone has been wronged, and he likes knowing that he can witness such incidents over and over again. Such a cold world," says the mother. She and her daughter watch him till he disappears.

Mr. Jock has been invited to be part of a discussion held about a marriage which finished about two and half months ago. The discussion is taking place at the girl's parents' home. Nyayang's mother is suddenly haunted by a disturbing memory. And through her God-given intuition, she can envision in detail everything that happened prior to this moment.

"Such a cold world," she says the phrase with her eyes closed and tears flood out.

The elders sit down with the in-laws but there is an immediate worry that falls on these elderly men. Every passing moment it seems as though someone could just walk in and inform them that the girl whom they are spending their valuable time discussing is no longer in their reach. Each elder speaks with extra caution so that he may go back and unsay it. And why wouldn't they worry? The poor girl has spoken.

"I don't like this person," she has said many times to the man who raised her. But could the absence of her biological father be the violator of her rights?

The years leading up to the emerging decade were unbearable for the two Nuer sub-tribes. Then in 2001, things were at their best-worst.

The two sub-tribes would intermarry in the morning and when evening fell, they would fight the natural side of darkness till it sent a few souls to the cemetery. Lives were easily lost. A couple got killed on the month of their sixth anniversary. The two had borne two beautiful daughters for their little family. But this senseless off-and-on war robbed these two fragile daughters of their parents.

The grandmother from the mother's side stepped up to raise the children, a position she was quickly denied. The father's older brother shunned the grandmother, claiming that it was his responsibility to carry on the family.

The girls, who quickly grew into adulthood, soon became desired by many men. Men came for their hands in marriage, especially the older girl's. The number of cows requested by the father in charge had become somewhat of a barrier for some of the potential husbands. In fact, it became an auction of "who has the most cows takes the girl" for this father. And it could have taken them into the next decade if it wasn't for the next contender, a man with physical impairments.

At a very young age, he had both his right hand and leg lamed. The cause was believed to be polio. He advanced himself with the help of his family through the father in charge. The two families talked behind the girl's back. When she became aware of their plan, though, she voiced her big fat no. Her sister supported her, considering their future. But a "no" in this valley of the parentless? Her opinion was not needed. The father's son was now presiding over the field of marriage with his bare hands. But why would this be the case?

"You are marrying him," said the father in charge. The marriage quickly took place. Her voice shrunk as she got closer to the man's hands. And as her world all of a sudden went south, she began hating life. She began each sunrise with powerless thoughts. She hoped and wished she would meet her end sooner than later. But death in this marrying land is in some ways the groom's best man.

In the absence of her voice, the marriage reached its conclusion. She was given to the man without her consensual agreement. And per tradition, the couple were given a room somewhere on the property. The husband would come home and learn his wife ran away an hour prior to his arrival. Sometimes the family would disperse to look for her, and when they finally found her, she would be brought in and locked in her room with her husband.

However, things didn't always end as the family wished. The next morning would come and the husband would come out of the room with disappointment on his face since the wife had fought hard and freed herself during the night.

The husband, fed up, brought the issue before his father-in-law after a month of unreasonable struggle, and he pretended he was done and wanted his cows back. A pretend quit, knowing what would be done on his behalf.

"I hear you. And you are not going to take back your cows," said the father-in-law. "My suggestion," he said, "is instead of coming tonight, come back tomorrow night." He dismissed his son-in-law.

"How could you have deceived your family like this? You have misled me to the point of taking someone else's cows and now you are not keeping your word?" the father called out to his daughter.

"No, no, I have not misled anybody. I said I didn't want to be married to this man. But you forcefully placed me in his hands anyway," she said.

"What did you just say?" asked the male brother in the house. He then followed the question with a punch and immediately grabbed her by the throat. The girl's younger sister jumped onto the brother's back.

"You sold her because our parents are dead!" said the younger sister. The father in charge quickly took her off his son's back. And cornered her somewhere with a few slaps.

The brother finished his job nicely; he tied up the bride and placed her in her appointed room. He came back and warned the others that no one should open the door for her until the next day.

There was an imminent struggle the moment the next day arrived. Over the course of the day, the girl was kept at a close watch until the most anticipated event: the husband arrived.

Things fired up the moment the husband walked in the room. She knew she could go head to head with him and instantly have him on the ground, or let the man proceed as planned. But mistakenly, she tried exiting the room, which the entire family became aware of instantly.

"You open that door and you will see what I do!" a voice outside the door said. The room went quiet for a moment. She then fought back, aiming higher to exceed the doorstep, except her unrepaired arm collapsed and failed her immediately.

"Knock, knock." She heard a knock at the door. "You let him leave this room and I will kill you before you see the new day." It was the brother speaking at the door. He sat there for few seconds; he looked furious and ready to hold his sister's head for the man if that was what it would take. He kept some threatening words near his mouth for the moment he needed to say them. He departed afterward.

The new day came and the brother was sure he didn't want to kill her anymore. Now the father in charge sits down with the elders, demanding the remaining cows. His wife passes by the group of elders and the husband stops speaking. The men in the group stop talking too. But she passes without realizing what she just did. He brings his attention back to the men and apologizes on behalf of the wife. No one responds. It is not customary that a woman would just pass by an area where men are gathered. And as for their current conversation? He reassures them that their words won't go to waste. You see, it's a form of self-love in itself, hating the self which made it a self.

"It breaks my heart that even in your own home, you are devalued," she points at the soil. She now puts her hands on her head. *What did I do wrong?* she thinks to herself. Inside the room, the mother and her daughter go quiet for about four minutes.

"We are leaving." Nyayang finally opens her mouth.

"Where are you going?" asks her mother worriedly with more tears on the verge of falling.

"Mom, this problem is never going to end," says Nyayang tiredly.

"Without anyone talking to Chuol? That will not happen! No, not this time around," says the mother. "Someone has to talk to Chuol before you go back and carry on your slavery to his irresponsible parents." After she says this, the two go quiet again.

"By the way, what do you expect Dad to talk to Chuol about?" asks Nyayang suddenly.

"All I want is for him to say to Chuol, 'Hey, this girl is my daughter. I wasn't bartering for her with your cows when you were marrying her,'" says her mother. "At least then Chuol will know your father has your back and that he can give back his golden life-saving cows if he doesn't do something about his pathetic, childish, manhood ideology," she says.

"Unfortunately, the most your father can do is to walk away from what is supposed to be his responsibility," continues the mother. "What is wrong with this creature called man!" She turns her frustrated face toward the door.

"Well, we both know Dad isn't going to speak to Chuol, so let's just drop it," says Nyayang.

"Drop what? I'm talking to him," declares her mother.

"Talking to who?" Nyayang asks her mum.

"I'm talking to Chuol!" she says.

"Wait, wait, wait. Do you have any idea what that would indicate?" asks Nyayang.

"What would it indicate? That I control the man and I have become a man? Well, let whoever thinks I claim to be a man by warning an abusive husband go ahead and think that. I don't care about the outcome," she adds.

The two go quiet again.

"If men think they are gods, then they should show prove that they are through their actions, not just their craving for irrelevant titles," her mother continues. She then turns away her face from the door.

"Mum, this dream you have is not going to happen." Nyayang comes and holds her mother's hands. "Like you and I know, I will never be comfortable seeing my children being enslaved on one end of the city while I'm on the other end."

"I know, I know. Nyayang, I've lived this life. And it breaks my heart seeing you going through the same thing. But when I decided to live this life, I thought if I suffered, maybe you wouldn't suffer like me."

"But why do you suffer so when this whole thing was made possible by you?" Nyayang says as if she didn't know better by now.

The mother starts crying. "But I never thought about the second life," says her mother with tears in her eyes. Mr. Jock walks in quickly. He stares at the two emotional females and goes to his room.

Nyayang starts crying, too. She releases her hands and rushes outside. She starts putting all her belongings into a bag. "We are leaving," she calls out to her mother. Nyayang leaves, leaving her parents each on the other side of the river.

In no less than two hours, Nyayang reaches her in-laws' home where she just misses a meeting held specifically in regards to what will be done.

CHAPTER THIRTEEN

In the meeting, Mr. Malual solved the problem between his son and his daughter-in-law. In the circle were some of his older sons. He voiced in his opening speech, "If only things had gone our way, we wouldn't be holding this discussion today. But unfortunately, they haven't.

"Chuol, your mother and I thought we should talk to you while your brothers are here. We understand and respect your stance on this issue. However, since the divorce, all we had hoped for has been lost, so we thought it's about time we faced reality."

"Nyayang is still our wife," continued the father. "We are not forcing you to treat her as if she is still your wife or saying that she has to go back downtown, even. No. Nyayang is no longer *your* wife. But we all know we have to do another marriage for your late brother. But now that things have gone this far south between you, we think that perhaps we will just flip Nyayang over to your brother instead. And when it comes time that she should have another child, we want you to come here," he said.

"Then what is the difference? What is the difference? Huh?" Chuol shouted.

"The difference is, she is Khor's now, not yours. All we ask of you is that when it comes to that time," repeated the father, "I want you to come."

"Let Gatwech produce children for Khor." Chuol pointed at Gatwech. Everybody became silent all at once. Even Chuol himself rethought what he had just said. Gatwech was his stepmother's son.

He could not produce children for Khor or the natural ownership of the property would shift to the other mother whose son produced the children. They felt like that. Chuol knew this. But his biggest problem was not even the shift in ownership. He just wanted nothing to do with Nyayang anymore. "We will find someone else for Khor. Not Nyayang," he added at last.

"Chuol, listen," said his mother. "Remember she is no longer your wife now. She is Khor's now. All the responsibility is on us. Except this one thing."

Chuol got up. "Chuol, Chuol get down." Gatwech brought him down.

"You produce Khor's children," Chuol said to Gatwech harshly.

"You don't listen to our parents? Tell us, what are you going to do about this situation?" Gatwech asked.

"Leave her be and when she gets tired, she will leave on her own," Chuol said.

"And that is your solution?"

"Yes, that will be the solution," he said.

"Okay, okay. That is enough," The father interfered as the conversation became fully between the brothers. "Let's discuss this in another time," he said with the hope that Chuol would think about this solution. The moment his father ended the discussion, Chuol left for downtown. And Mr. Malual followed after him.

When Nyayang arrives home, she asks, "Where did Baba go?"

"He went downtown. Please bathe this child," her mother-in-law replies and hands her the baby.

"Is he coming back tonight?"

"How would I know?" her mother-in-law says, irritated as always. But quickly after that, Mr. Malual returns home.

"How did it go?" his wife asks.

"It was beautiful! The man loves his wife. He covers her from head to toe," he says.

"Who is the lucky girl?" Nyayang asks.

"I believe you know her. She is one of our closest neighbour's daughters."

"Oh, I do," she says. She goes around the house, concentrating on what she is doing. Once she knows which girl it was, there is no need for her to hear any more. She can still hear her father-in-law praising both of the families for hosting a successful bride-price discussion. It probably ended well today, but that was not how it started. At least not from what Nyayang can remember.

The groom, who was a native of Nuer but an Ethiopian resident, had just returned for one purpose. He came to find a wife for himself, as he believed the further a girl lived from the city, the more faithful they tended to be. He caught one almost upon his arrival. She was all he wanted physically: light skin, hair that flowed from her head to her toes, and a mouth that spoke two beautiful languages—Arabic and Nuer. She brought him to her acting father, her father's brother, for her father was gone before her family made it back from North Sudan.

Halfway through the marriage, the man learned something that was rather a deal-breaker for him. He was asked one day if he knew anything about a little girl who was often seen with his fiancée. He said he knew her and that she was his fiancée's little sister. "She is not, she is her daughter," he was told. "Daughter!" He was shocked and there was just no way this journey all the way from a foreign land could come to an end with a half-empty package. No! He stormed over to her that evening. He stood up to her and told her in no uncertain terms that there would be no marriage. She was very embarrassed to talk about it, but she did confirm the child was hers.

"It was my mother's idea," she explained. "When my boyfriend rejected both me and the child, my mother said she was going to raise her as her own, that way I would have a chance to be married again," she said. The groom withdrew himself immediately. He thanked the secret revealer for rescuing him from what was not going to be a reputable marriage for him. The person asked him to keep his thanks to himself till the end, for there was a perfect woman this person knew of for him. It turned out, the mastermind behind the chaos was the commissioner's first wife. She wanted her daughter to be married instead, which was her last resort for getting the attention of her husband after she was miserably demoted from the top of the ladder by his seventh wife.

"How many cows did he pay?" Nyayang asks her father-in-law at last.

"Oh, many! He was asking to marry the commissioner's daughter, he had to pay," he says. Nyayang nods her head from a distance and moves on with her duties.

On the day Nyayang returns to the compound, she dives straight back into her everyday responsibilities. Except, this time, whether it's about good or bad things, the conversation between her and her in-laws is in its dying phase.

Her tasks take up all her time in the house. Twenty years ago, the late, last wife of Mr. Malual's household gave birth to her firstborn, Rebecca, who has now become a mother herself. According to what is said about girls in this lovely living place, they don't swing by age fifteen without being reserved or taken. However, that was not the case for this young lady. Due to her disability, buyers refused to give her the benefit of the doubt. Last year, Mr. Malual finally gave her up, free of charge, to a fellow he'd known for years. Rebecca is now at home with a new baby, who she constantly needs Nyayang's help with.

"The food takes so long, you never do anything sooner than needed, what kind of wife are you? YOU TOOK IT ALL FOR NOTHING IN RETURN!" says Gatwech to Nyayang, allowing his angry voice to lead him. It's true that dinner is taking a bit longer than usual today. And for the big man in the house, the issue needed to be addressed one way or another.

"I had to help Rebeca with the child," Nyayang explains as though no one else was around to witness that moment a minute ago when even Gatwech had to free himself from the compound due to the vomiting and frequent abnormal evacuation the child was going through. He was there when it all happened and up he went elsewhere so those who were designed to care for sick children could deal with these unmannered illnesses. And just as she is designed to nurse the sick, so is she designed to serve men on time.

"You give me another stupid explanation, you will see what I do," he threatens. Nyayang tunes him out. This could go anywhere. But he is just one piece of the problem. He storms out of the compound again just as the food is about to be served.

"When it's this late, I don't feel like eating," says the other piece of the problem. He pushes the food off the table in front of him. It's not the first time Mr. Malual has refused to eat. He does it all the time. He is now a man of particular age and his manly outlook on life has become more unforgiving. At five p.m., he takes his meal, no later than that. She comes and picks up the food. Then Gatwech enters the compound. He looks around. The compound is very quiet. Everybody is silent. It seems as if everyone has found something to be mournful about. Nyayang returns inside the room, returns the child to her lap.

"MAAN-NYAMUCH, MAAN-NYAMUCH!!" Nyayang hears something. Somebody is calling her name. She places the child back in the bed. At the door, she hears a waving sound behind her. She glances back quickly. The child starts vomiting again. She goes back to the child but Gatwech had seen her coming a moment ago. He makes the usual, premature judgement: "I'm male and I am being disrespected." He goes closer but a child and an illness are in the room, so he shelters outside the room. "Come out this very moment," he demands of Nyayang.

She comes out. He punches her in the face, leaving all her front teeth bowed backward. One of them goes further and gets moved out of place, and that's the last time Nyayang has all her front teeth parallel.

"Leave her, Gatwech. Leave her. Let her do her things," Mr. Malual says.

"Nyayang thinks I don't see what she is doing," Gatwech mumbles to himself. "SHE HAS GONE TOO FAR! My father has to sleep in hands even though you have been covered head to toe? Go, leave! Leave this house. I never want to see you again. Go!" He keeps pointing his finger right at her eyes.

Nyayang re-enters the room. The front of her clothes are smeared with blood. She picks up the child again. She knows she can't make any reference to the pain she is experiencing. One tooth is gone, the rest have a look that will only increase Chuol's anger when he sees her.

Thankfully, he is not here now. He will hear about it a few days later. It's great now that the rest of the family members are seeing what he has been telling everybody, Chuol will think.

The following day, Mr. Malual receives some Murlen visitors. Forever accommodating, he invites ten gentlemen to come take accommodation at his residence.

Day and night, Nyayang fixes the eye of her soul on the hope that Chuol will eventually listen to the voice of reason and find a space for her in his stuffy heart so she can continue mothering her children.

With each sunrise, she sees an opportunity to prove to her in-laws that her presence is useful. But what she does not know is that life is not about what she can improve on, but whether she can endure it or not.

The business, the hope, the focus she strengthens her weak soul for each day, have somewhat kept her untouched by how fast time has really moved on. And the only thing that proves the faithfulness of time is when she is startled by another piece of good news coming from downtown.

It's been a year now and the boys' productive mother has given birth to her third son. The news is rushed to the grandparents' ears.

Nyayang, as well, sings with joy. "We have to visit Sarah. You have to prepare some food," her mother-in-law commands. Nyayang goes on doing all the things needed for the boys' mother. Mr. Malual, meanwhile, doesn't sleep all night. The good news has reached Mr. Malual at a time when something seems to be sweeping the males of his household to the grave. He seems extra tired lately. Death has been grazing over his growing plans. But what better way to put a bounce back in his step than to reward a man with another male? If it was a prayer that made it happen, then God must certainly have heard it. And if it was a man's strength that made it happen, then he is definitely gaining it back.

The next morning, the whole family goes downtown where they find Sarah family has come, as well. The compound is full of other people, mainly women. There is joyous laughter in the women's hearts. Chuol's in-laws visit with the new child in what used to be Nyayang's room. The women can be heard laughing in the other room, Sarah's room. Among the women is the closest neighbour's senior wife. She seems less talkative today. Things seem to have been tested between her and her master. She almost had the man to herself for life. But something went wrong.

It was after the final ceremony of her daughter's marriage that it happened. She was pregnant with another man's child all along. The man for whom her mother had broken another mother's heart said, "There will be no marriage." Now where she stands on the ladder is rather unstable. So she did what any powerful woman would do. She took care of the Boke once and for all. Because of her, their husband had to get rid of most of his wives. Even the ones that were given to him free of charge. Half of the children are now sharing mothers. Between then and now, she has been the lead wife, even though the relationship has some minor rust on its communication coating. But there is a great chance she is here to stay, nonetheless.

Getting there took some work from other people's dark spirit. She wasn't always at the top of the ladder, as her seniority lost out to beauty, but there was one great force that could override beauty that was right up her nose, and that was evil. She knew she only had to do one act of evil just as when beauty was threatened by fertility, and then she would be left alone. She made this her area of focus the moment her foreign mother-in-law showed a desire to only have her son marry a girl from her land of origin. She brought other people into the circle to fight her fight, and those who knew the way stayed with her throughout the journey.

It was a shame after the family learned the trusted daughter had given herself up to someone else other than her husband-to-be. Her father was extremely disappointed. Ashamed even. He ordered the girl and her mother to get out of his sight for some time. But that too was fixed between the two parents, even thought it momentarily resurfaced every now and then.

"A way to keep him is by giving him boys. He will never leave you, I tell you," one of the women says to the group.

Nyayang, in the corner, almost asks, "How do you do that?" but she is an outsider here. And she knows it just like they know it.

"Food, food is the other thing which keep him at your side. If you know his taste, then you are good. Serve his visitors with honour and hospitality. He will be proud God gave you to him," the same lady continues. Those, too, are things Nyayang knows how to do. But, oh, no, the list runs from the most effective to the least effective items. She fails the biggest one. And everything else is fairly meaningless.

Her mother-in-law joins the women for a quick chat. "Mandholi (mother of boys), how are you, my daughter? How is your body doing?"

"I'm doing just fine, Mom," Sarah replies. She smiles at her mother-in-law. The mother-in-law exits the room. The women go to the other room where the child is with Nyayang. Mr. Malual is still outside with his grandchildren, the twins.

"Mali man-wuni (Mother of men)!" he greets Sarah.

"Hi Baba," says Sarah. She and the women and Nyayang, behind them, enter the room.

Chuol has barely been around the new baby. Chuol is in the process of becoming a leader in the months to come. His plan to become commissioner and let go of being a businessman has come to fruition. He wants to have a strong relationship, not just with the citizens but with the seasonal visitors, as well. There have been many people in town he has been spending time with lately. Murlen people have come again in big numbers since the dry season began. Women, children and men, all. Famine has destroyed the land of the Murlen again. But there is nowhere else to go but to the nearest neighbour. They have been received well. Shortly after, children and women and some men returned home. But some men remain. They seem to be everywhere. And they seem to enjoy their new-found freedom.

Early today, Chuol met a few Murlen men. He found them while they were watching a man who tried to escape a prison building the day before being brutally beaten by two prison guards.

"Gatwech, Gatwech!" one of the guards cried out, in an effort to calm the man down. The prisoner appeared very young in age and very naïve in the world of imprisonment. He was unknowingly overreacting to a "no water" punishment by the guard who had been watching after him. The act of stupidity and his escape attempt the day prior prompted the guard to call for help and have him dealt with. He started crying the moment the stick landed on his body. His unmannered, crying voice lured the Murlen men, who were about everywhere now. They came and stood against the tall prison fence that encircled the building full of young Nuer men.

The prisoner was fighting back but the two guards threw him to the ground. There were other prisoners being guided out of the prison building. Behind the fence, they laughed while watching him get beaten. Chuol joined them shortly. He too watched him being thrown on the ground as he was walking alongside the fence. There were other prisoners coming from somewhere else at the same time. They were taken to an overgrown local park as part of their daily work duties. There was only one guard walking behind them with a loaded gun hanging at his side.

They first lined up at the gate before a guard opened it for them. They were all chained together with silver chains. They walked in with their stand-out orange uniforms. They quickly grouped around distant stations. The guards who opened the gate for them brought food and, without saying a word, they plunged into the bowls of food.

Chuol approached the new people and quickly befriended them. "Know anyone around here?" he asked them in Nuer. One man shook his head. They had their guns slung over their shoulders. "Come with me. I will buy you water." The Murlen men followed him. He led them directly to the marketplace.

Chuol arrives shortly after his family. He comes with some men he suddenly call friends from Murle. But when he sees his father, he starts laughing. He slaps the back of one of the Murlen men he has come with. He pushes him playfully and says, "Go to your identical you, Malual Jr."

The twins laugh along with their uncle. "Guandong, Guandong, look at yourself!"

Mr. Malual looks at the Murlen man. "He looks just like you!" says Chuol. The Murlen man looks like Mr. Malual, indeed: his height, his teeth, his overall appearance. The resemblance is undeniably uncanny!

"I know! Isn't God so loving that He makes everybody like the other so all shall claim no differences but know they have been made by the same hand?" Mr. Malual says while he comes to stand side by side with the Murlen man to compare heights. There is a sudden joy in him. The men hardly speak Nuer. But uncoincidentally, Malual Jr. speaks some broken Nuer. He says his name in Nuer. The family laughs at his accent. His little knowledge of the language alarms no one; Murlen speak broken Nuer all the time. He says his name is Lok (refused).

"That is a Nuer name. How come?" says Mr. Malual. The man can't properly explain why. Chuol and his nephews, the twins, leave the old man and the Murlen men while laughing at his hilarious question.

Chuol and the twins enter the room. Both sides of parents greet him joyfully as they stumble over themselves on his arrival. And Nyayang, having no side to lean on, rambles in between.

Nyayang continues to struggle in the very same room she gave birth to her children but which is now where Sarah and the baby are. She comes in and before she can take one breath, she is called out to do something else, like an orphan child in a delusional rich family.

"Don't you want me to show it to you, Nyada?" says Sarah to Nyayang in the other room. Chuol sees the two are arguing. He comes in and demands that Nyayang leave the room.

"Come, come with me," he says. When Nyayang comes out, Chuol steps back and stands at the gate of the compound. "Come on," he says again. Nyayang walks toward him. Sarah comes out of the room. She stops and stares at both of them at the gate.

"I will show you," she mumbles to Nyayang in her rather low voice.

Nyayang reaches the gate and Chuol steps outside of the compound. "Come on," he says. His voice is picking up a little angrily now. She comes out. He grabs the handle of the gate's door and closes the gate from the outside. He says, "Who told you to come today?"

Nyayang says nothing. Chuol pushes her by the head. Both Nyayang and Chuol disappear out of the neighbour's view quickly. He leads her farther. And as they walk, he keeps pushing her forward. Out of everybody's sight, he asks her, "Where are you gonna go now?" And in that moment, he begins to rain down on her like a pounding rain.

Chuol pushes, Chuol kicks, Chuol throws her to the thorny, cracked, muddy ground, and when he fully understands that she is, by no doubt, a dead body, he pulls her dress upward. He pulls her Yat low, and with the tips of his fingers he removes it completely. And before he does what he wants to do, he swings his arm and throws the Yat far away while saying, "On what grounds would you once again be in this family?" He throws the garment quickly, the way a person throws something that smells awful. He comes and violently places his hand inside her private part. When Chuol is done, he dries his hand with her clothes that are hanging over her face now. He dries his hand with her clothes the way he would use a hand towel. He leaps over her completely dead body and goes back to his family.

"Where is she?" Mr. Malual asks his son when he comes back inside the compound.

"Oh, she went home," he says. "Giving people a headache for nothing," he mumbles as he walks toward him.

The women with Sarah hear him, and like they know he may have not just sent her home without a few slaps, they wear crooked smiles. There is something attractive about a man who fights his wife's enemy. Soon enough, the men enter the man's room, and it begins to rain.

There, in the bushes, life miraculously starts coming back to Nyayang's body. She feels some sensation in her toes and then the rest of her body. The rain keeps pouring on the land. It begins to darken the area. She pulls herself up and sits. In her mind, she remembers how they were coming but she does not know what happened after that. She gets up and, naturally, her dress bounces back down her body. Suddenly, she feels lighter from her waist down. She pulls her dress away and glances down at her body. She finds the Yat is missing. She starts searching for it. She sees some scattered pieces of the ripped Yat. Indeed, Chuol did not leave it at the power of his words; he physically tore it into pieces. The stains on her dress have been washed away now. She walks to her children in her hollow, soaked dress. She reaches home. She takes her dress off and changes into a dry Yat and a new dress.

The following morning, she informs her mother-in-law that she wants to visit her parents. "No, you can't leave, the children aren't feeling well," says her mother-in-law.

"I can leave them if that is okay," says Nyayang.

But instead of saying yes, her mother-in-law says, "When are you coming back?" to which Nyayang says, "Tomorrow morning."

"I cannot let you go. You need to discuss this with your father-in-law," her mother-in-law advises Nyayang.

"Father, it's been a year now and I haven't seen my parents. I need to visit them," explains Nyayang.

"And you plan on coming back when?" asks her father-in-law.

"Tomorrow morning, God willing," she says.

"I want you to be here by ten a.m. tomorrow," he says.

Nyayang immediately puts her offspring in front of her and leaves for her parents' home. Not long after, there is an outcry all over the area. The Murle have finally got a hold of what they have long wanted: they got a hold of the animals. A man rushes to Mr. Malual and says, "A considerable number of cows have been taken."

Before she reaches her parents' house, there is an ugly argument between Mr. Jock and his wife. It all derives from a brutal discussion which the two had yesterday.

It's been a year now and her parents are fully aware that Nyayang spends all of it at her in-laws' home.

"What if Chuol is up to something again, will you still say nothing?" Nyayang's mother confronted her reluctant husband. And in answer to the question, he said, "I will talk to Chuol when I want, not when you tell me to." So his wife decided to give it a day.

Today she has come back to finish what the two started. "I told you, I'm not going to talk to him. I'm not going to talk about another man's business." Mr. Jock claims a different reason today. "Chuol is doing what he is doing perhaps to teach his wife a lesson."

"A lesson? For what mistake? What mistake did she make that you believe qualifies Nyayang for this lesson?" his wife asks.

"Oh, I know what you mean," she says then. "She is not strong enough to give the man a male child, which has always been our problem, right? Right?" she says again while bending down to look in the man's eye.

"You say another word, I'll kill you," he declares.

"Come on, do you think I care anymore? Tell me, is that not the mistake Nyayang has been making?" she continues.

Mr. Jock loses it. He slaps her on the head. The slap turns her head in the opposite direction as a result. No one can tell him to stop now. Nyayang's little sister had finally been given to her husband. She turns around again and says, "In all these years, you have never stopped hitting me. But I tell you what, I will not let you finish me." She stares at him. "Not here." She draws a line between her and him with her finger.

But the more she says, the more her heartless husband keeps coming at her. "Kill me. Go ahead. Go ahead, do it!" she cries.

"You two can stop now, if you are fighting because of me." Nyayang's voice startles them.

"Nyayang!" her mother calls her name in shock. She runs to her and embraces the children with her loving arms. The father sees them. He turns around and walks away.

Meanwhile back in Mr. Malual's kingdom, the day is gradually coming to a close. A man rushed over to him around noon today and related to him that a good number of his cows had been abducted along with those of other folks, as well. Everybody knew right away who took them: it was the Murlen man. At the same time, the names of some individuals who had been gunned down started to come in. People he knows were mentioned. Another man told him the attack had spread and downtown was under lockdown. He now gazes in the direction of the road leading to downtown. He suddenly needs to walk there. But suddenly, in the distance, he spots a woman running toward him. It is Sarah. She throws herself on the ground before reaching her father-in-law. Mr. Malual runs toward her. There are other people at the same time approaching her, as well. She has a piece of cloth tied around her belly. She appears very tired and as if she has been crying.

"He is dead, right?" Mr. Malual says.

She lifts up her head and shakes it. "My children. My children are taken!" she says, seemingly forcing herself to say it.

"The children," he says while in shock. He slowly walks back to the compound. His wife comes out of the compound. She notices something no one has yet noticed. Sarah has been wounded.

Some people pick her up to her knees. On her way up, she says, "The twins are wounded."

Mr. Malual hears her and in that instant, he freezes, as a memory comes to his mind. He knows the Murlen are responsible. He remembers the young Murlen man who introduced himself as Lok, a Nuer name which means "refused." But that was the extent of what Lok said when they were all together. After the twins and their uncle joined the others in the room, the young Murlen man told Mr. Malual how he got his name. He was not very fluent but every Nuer word he managed to say, he immediately credited to his mum. Biologically he was Nuer, he said. In Mr. Malual's mind, there were a lot of girls being sent to the Murle for different reasons every year.

He asks Sarah, "How?" but Sarah has been made weak by the wound. While speaking in shock, the commissioner's beloved wife appears. She has most of her children with her. He gazes at her as she is running toward her father-in-law's compound. The Shilluk mother-in-law comes out, too, and unlike last time, she starts crying and mumbling in her native language. Mr. Malual decides to find out what happened for himself.

Sarah gets brought into the compound and she suddenly stops breathing. Her mother-in-law calls her husband, who is a distance away already, but he now starts walking faster.

"Chuol!" he starts calling. No one is home at Chuol's home but Lok's body is at the gate where Chuol no doubt managed to gun him down shortly after he took the precious lives of his nephews, the twins.

"Chuol is at the hospital now. One of the twins still has life in him. The other is gone," a neighbour says to the elderly man. He runs to the hospital. When he arrives, he falls on his knees. Chuol steps aside. Mr. Malual goes over and holds the boy's head up. He can still speak. Mr. Malual brings his eyes closer.

"You are not going to die, Maah." His tears drip onto the surviving twin's face.

The twin closes his eyes. He opens them again. He stares at his grandfather and says, "Mah. Mama."

"Your mother is not here," says the grandfather.

"Why? She doesn't know I'm dying?" he says.

"I will send somebody to call her," the grandfather says.

Chuol is staring at both of them. He tries to be present but only in physical form. His mind and his spirit are still chasing the Murlen man who now has his three boys. He hears the approaching sound of someone crying. Before they see who has come, the twin says, "Mah. Mah." He thinks his mother has managed to come.

"That's not your mother," says the grandfather.

"Why, why Guandong? Why am I dying and she doesn't want to come?" He slowly brings his head down. "I want my mother," he says and that is the last phrase he manages to say. It is Chuol's mother who is crying.

"Mah! Sarah!" Chuol says. He tries to run over to see her but he freezes when he sees that doctors now are running around her, a look of hopelessness in their eyes. Chuol blows up like a woman.

"No, don't!" says his father. Mr. Malual picks up the twin's lifeless head now. He stares at him for few seconds. And he remembers something he is not willing to share with his son, who is torn between seeing the lifeless body of his nephew and his wife, whose body, now, is also empty of life.

The evening arrives on what seems like the other side of the world. And when the little ones have gone to bed, Nyayang brings her mother before her father.

"Baba, from the time I have known you as my father, I never had any doubt that if there was anything in this world causing me discomfort, you would be the one to ignore it. I do not have to come here each and every day and talk about things you don't see. And perhaps this is all my fault. Because every time when things go wrong, I mistakenly think if I could just come and present my concerns before you, you would listen. But as wrongfully as I interpret what I really am, I wrongfully choose to come to you when I'm just wrongfully choosing what looks wrong to me. Here," she says.

"What is it?" Mr. Jock asks.

"Look at it. You will recognize it." Nyayang hands a small plastic bag to her father. He extends his hand and holds it while looking at his daughter. He opens the bag. It is her Yat. He goes on unfolding it, as it is hard to identify the kind of clothing it is at first. It is so covered in dust and mud that he does not recognize what it is.

"It is the licence, Baba. I know you can hardly believe the size or the shape, or even its colour, when the person it licences finally says, 'I'm done!'"

"Did you just take your Yat off?" Mr. Jock asks while extending the hand he holds it in, as if he is going to throw it away.

Instead of looking at Nyayang, he looks directly at his wife who instantly loses her mind and screams, "NYAYANG, YOU KNOW YOU CANNOT DO THAT!" She grabs the Yat from Mr. Jock's hand and frantically throws it back at Nyayang. It lands right on her face. She lets it fall off her face then she follows it with her eyes. It lifelessly falls to the ground. She looks at both of her parents.

"What happened to you?" her mother asks as she comes down from her shock at last.

Nyayang looks at her mother. "You did your part. You did your part, Mama. But, though it falls as a feather, it has been given the will to decide what label there is." She looks at her mother and says again, "It is stronger than both of us." She looks at her father and says, "I'm going back, and I hope we will never again discuss these pointless, empty concerns I tend to come here for every now and again."

"What do you mean?" Her mother looks very disturbed.

"Mother, I'm not here to cause another uproar between the two of you. And I don't need you to question me about anything," she says while touching her mother's shoulder gently.

Upon finishing her speech, she leaves and walks into her room.

Her parents remain stunned. They watch her going into the room. "Waah, Nyayang!" Her mother stands up. "I'm done," she says. She wants to say what she thinks Nyayang is doing but the words do not come out.

Nyayang goes into her room and immediately closes the door. Her mother comes after her and stands at the door. "Nyayang come out, talk to me," she says. Nyayang refuses. After some time, her mother walks back to her room, but she doesn't close her eyes. She lies down, looking at the ceiling.

Around twelve a.m., her mother gets up and walks back to the room where Nyayang is sleeping. She finds the door still locked. Nyayang is aware her mother is standing at the door.

Finally, her mother goes back to her room and closes her door. That is when Nyayang opens her door. She comes out. The big star is shining a lot brighter than usual. The compound is very still. She looks around. There is no sound. She feels stronger, so sure and confident in the meaning of being nothing. She exits the compound. She starts walking toward the big, beautiful tree between her father's and mother's room. She stands under the tree. Immediately, her mother senses something. She thinks she hears something outside and she waits to hear it again. But she does not hear anything. The compound is very still.

Under the tree, Nyayang looks up and sees the branches as a perfect metaphor for how hard it is for girls to reach anywhere. She directs her focus on the branch that is closest to the ground. She sees the rope that boys used to play with as children long ago. It is only her now. Whatever she wants to do is possible. The only presence is all that bright light coming down from heaven. And up until now, the owner has not said anything.

She tightens the rope around the branch.

A few seconds after she finishes, her mother comes out of her room. She runs to Nyayang's room again. And this time, she acknowledges the door is open. She rushes outside the compound and begins calling out Nyayang's name. She runs to all the dark shaded corners. And, suddenly, under the light of the full moon, she sees the feet of her dear child hanging under the beautiful tree.

She dashes to the tree with all that she can give to the power of moving, only to find the fruit of her womb leaving the world while her body sways from the beautiful tree.

"NYAYANG!" she cries. "Oh God, I'm finished."

ACKNOWLEDGEMENTS

It was easy for me to think about what I wanted to write, but it was definitely challenging to see the reality come to life, as sometimes my fear tends to shift gears over my vision. For those who stood with me, thank you.

I want to say thank you to William Agamah, a man I came to know unexpectedly, for what has become an amazing friendship. We became friends instantly, and when I asked you to read my first draft, you whole-heartedly accepted to read it from start to finish. Thank you for your careful insights and unwavering wisdom. Thank you for all your feedback and suggestions. Thank you for taking a mentorship role at a time when I needed it the most.

A huge thank-you goes to John Wiyual Chuang for reading the first draft. Your knowledge of the terminology of the Nuer culture has helped me make some important corrections. To you, we are just family, but you are closer than that. You are a mentor to me. Thank you for your wisdom and guidance.

Thank you to my best friend, Nhial Gany Wol. From when writing this book was just a glimmer in my mind to now, you have been a believer in its existence. There were moments I doubted if I could do it, and you would unapologetically take my place and stand in front of me for me. For that and so much more, thank you!

I want to say thank you to my brother, Johnson Reach Biel. Without even knowing it, you have been providing me with the correction of names and places throughout this process. I guess I should take this moment to apologize. Sorry, I have been writing a book.

A special thank you goes to Lara, my editor whose creativity has turned what was an incomplete work to this final, beautiful piece. Thank you Lara.

Last but not least, I want to say thank you to my beautiful daughters, Chudier and Joyce. I don't know how you knew this, but you always believed I could do it, as both of you would come and tap my shoulder and say, "You can do it, Mom," and wave goodbye so I would have time to do it. You are my inspiration when all doors are closed.

ABOUT THE AUTHOR

Tabitha Biel Luak is a mother and a second-year psychology student. She was born and raised in South Sudan, Africa. At the age of fourteen, her marriage, which later became a thirteen-year prison cell, was arranged between her and a man she never laid eyes on until four years later. In 2011 she moved to Canada to be with him, and she left him a year later for her safety. Tabitha uses music and writing as ways to make peace with the nearby past.